The

Devil's Fool

By

Rachel McClellan

The Devil's Fool
A novel by Rachel McClellan
www.RachelMcClellan.com

Cover design by Rebecca Hamilton
Printed in the United States of America

Other books by Rachel McClellan:
Fractured Light (book one)
Fractured Soul (book two)
Fractured Truth (book three)
Confessions of a Cereal Mother
Unleashed
Simon Says (a horror short story)

When the darkness comes, keep an eye on the light—whatever that is for you—no matter how far away it seems." –Jan Berry

1

I always knew my father was a monster, but watching him torture someone other than me made me ill.

A girl dangled before him, her pale hands clinging to the rope around her neck while her naked toes struggled to touch ground. I leaned over, high on my perch of a Scotts pine tree, and drew in the crisp night air. Normally the smell of our home's dense woodlands—a rich earthiness laced with the aroma of an approaching storm—would've soothed my nerves, but nothing could calm the growing turmoil in my gut. The scene below wouldn't allow it.

The towering full moon shined into the forest's wide clearing, spotlighting four figures as if they were actors in a play. My father stood at the center, pacing near the young girl, stage left. I'd seen her once from the window of our home. She was the daughter of our closest neighbor, almost a mile away. We resembled each other with our honey-blonde hair, though she may have been a year younger. Sixteen, maybe.

Her mother, Madelyn, kneeled to the right, hands clasped together and tears pouring from her eyes. She was wearing only her nightgown.

And finally, there was my own mother—a mere spectator in this production. She sat on a blanket spread out on the grass; her long black gown gathered up, exposing her thin legs all the way to her thighs. Even the chill in the air didn't seem to faze her. The only thing holding her attention was a jasmine plant resting in her lap, which she repeatedly plucked leaves from and tucked into a leather pouch.

"Please, stop." The girl coughed, her hands tugging on the rope.

"You're begging the wrong person," my father said, his gaze focusing on Madelyn. "You have your mother to blame for this."

The rope tightened, and the girl's legs kicked harder. Strangling her wasn't enough for him; he had her feet only a blade of grass away from the ground, as though her false hope was some sort of sick tease.

As the pain in my stomach worsened, I doubled over. My balance slipped, and I almost lost my precarious seat on the thick limb. But then I vomited, sending my dinner onto the branches below. I worried I might've been heard, but a growing wind smothered my sounds. I wiped my mouth with the back of my hand and inhaled deeply; cold air rushed into my lungs, and for the moment, the pain in my stomach subsided.

The girl tried to speak again, but the noose tightened further, silencing her. For a moment, it sounded as though she'd been trying to say "Mama".

"Please, Erik," Madelyn said, her arms outstretched. "I will take back my words. I'll tell everyone I was drunk, that I mistook what I saw. Please!"

Madelyn had been speaking like this for some time, trying to convince my father that those in his affluent circle of New York's upper class would easily discount her accusations, but my father only watched the girl, using only the power of his gaze to tighten and release the rope. The noose itself was just as disturbing to look upon as the dangling girl–it hung from the air as if tied to an invisible tree limb.

"Please," Madelyn begged again. "You're not devil worshipers. I see that now. You're more like Gods." She gasped at this revelation and forced a smile. "Yes, Gods!"

This got my father's attention. His gaze bore into her, and she cowered. "You *people*," he said. "How is it you can still believe in the power of God, but not in the power of anyone or anything else? It wasn't so long ago that world believed in witches. Why should now be any different?" He leaned close to her face. "But you believe now, don't you?"

She nodded quickly.

"You thought we were devil worshipers. Why? Because you saw something that frightened you?" He straightened. "*We* worship *no one*, understand?"

She nodded again but cried out when the noose constricted even tighter, her daughter's arms falling limp. "No, please! No one believed me! They thought I was crazy!"

"Damage to our reputation has been done. You made them question us."

Though I was hidden well behind the pine branches, I saw the girl's eyes bulge from the pressure around her neck. A blood vessel must've have popped, because the whites of her eyes now shined red.

"No! Please," Madelyn said. Tears spilled onto her bare trembling shoulders. "Take me. Let her go!"

His head held high, my father tugged on the sleeves of his tuxedo, lengthening them around his wrists. By the way he was dressed, he had probably just returned from another fundraising event for the next mayor of New York City. Elections were in one month. It monopolized a large part of my parents' time.

"I can't do that," he said. "A lesson needs to be taught. I need to make sure you never say another word again."

"Then take me! Kill me!" Her sobs drowned her words.

My heart ached for Madelyn. I wished desperately I wasn't so terrified of my parents. Maybe if I was stronger, I would—

"I can't kill you," my father said. "Not after accusing us of such ugly things. It would appear suspicious. But a suicidal daughter of a deranged mother—well, now, that only proves our case."

In what I can only imagine was an act of desperation, Madelyn sniffed and wiped the tears from her face. "But, Sir, if you kill her, then what will stop me from telling the whole world what you've done?"

It was at this moment my mother finally decided to speak. Keeping her eyes fixed on the jasmine, she said, "You have two boys at home, correct?"

3

Madelyn's head jerked toward the cool voice. "You stay away—"

"Erik, dear," my mother said, rising up like a ghost from its grave. "I'm bored. Are we about finished?"

He inhaled deeply, nostrils wide. "These things take time, *dear*."

My mother returned his venomous glare. "Actually, they don't." With a flick of her wrist, the rope tightened and cut into the girl's flesh. Her body convulsed for several seconds until blood pulsed from the wound, covering her in a blanket of red.

I cried out, but quickly covered my mouth; my terror was masked by Madelyn's relentless screaming.

They killed her. They actually did it.

And in that moment, when the forest swallowed a young girl's soul, hatred for my parents seared my heart.

I remained hidden while my mother returned home and my father oversaw the pitiful efforts of Madelyn calling the police to tell them that she had found her daughter dead in the woods. A suicide hanging. When my father finally passed below me, I held my breath. I didn't want to inhale any part of his evil wake. This terrible power was what corrupted everything around him, and I wanted no part of it.

I waited until I could no longer see him before I moved. Under my breath, I whispered a command. The great branch of the tree lowered, taking me with it. When it bent as far as it could, I leapt to the ground. For most people, the fall would've injured them, but when I said, "Extendam," the ground stretched and lowered, softening my impact. Once the earth returned to its natural state, I walked away.

This would be the last time I would ever use magic, I vowed. My parents had been trying to get me to use it for as long as I could remember, but now I knew why I had kept my abilities a secret. Deep down, I must've known how my powers would change me—turn me into heartless monsters like them.

But not now.

Not ever.

I would rather die than be like them. From that day forward, I was no longer a witch.

2

A splash of cold water hit me in the face. The shock of it forced me awake, and I gasped for air.

"You shouldn't sleep in, Eve," said Jane, my tutor and sometimes an unwilling maid. She held an empty glass in her hand.

I moaned and pulled the covers over my head, already wishing the day away. Tonight, Erik and Sable, my father and mother (though I'd never call them that again after what I'd witnessed in the forest several weeks ago), were hosting an early All Hallows Eve ball to try and raise more money for their political favorites. It was also my eighteenth birthday, but like my other birthdays, it would go unnoticed.

"Why are you here so early?" I asked from beneath the covers.

It was a Saturday, and Jane only showed up on weekdays to tutor me. I wish I went to an actual college, having obtained my high school diploma almost a year ago, but my parents said that was only for good kids who did what their parents wanted. And since I wouldn't use magic, I was never able to attend any type of public school.

"As if I had a choice," she said. "Your parents wanted me here early to help you get ready, so get up so I can get out of this hell."

"Sorry," I mumbled and sat up. I was painfully aware of how much she and everyone else who worked for my parents hated the employment, but either the pay was too good to pass up, or they were too afraid to quit. Jane had been working for us for almost ten years. She was almost old enough to retire. "I can dress myself."

"Not according to your mother." She jerked the covers from my lap. "Hurry. You don't want to make her angry."

I swung my legs over the edge of the bed, cringing when my bare feet touched the marbled floor. "Is she ever anything else?"

"Yes—terrifying." Jane fumbled through my closet, her wide

backside knocking several of my schoolbooks off a chair. She handed me a black slip. "Put this on. Your mother is coming."

"Why?"

Jane's pudgy fingers wiped sweat from her forehead. Her brown hair was pulled into a bun; parts of it were already falling loose. "She wants to make sure you look your best. Now hurry!"

She took a deep breath and fled the room.

This worried me. Sable never cared how I looked before. Something different was going to happen tonight, and with my parents, different was never good.

I removed my gown and pulled on the slip. Goosebumps broke across my skin, but I don't think it was because I was cold. I moved to my vanity and combed my hair. After the restless night I'd had, thanks to another nightmare, it would take time to untangle my long tresses.

Just as I set the brush down, Sable burst through the door, bringing with her a gust of icy air and two women I'd never seen before. Her face, framed by gold hair curlers, was the same color as her white satin robe, making me think of a blizzard. Instinctively, I pulled my arms against my chest.

"You slept in." She said the words as if I'd committed a treasonous act.

I glanced at my alarm clock. A little after eight. I kept my voice calm. "Did you want me up sooner?"

"I want you to use your brain. Can you do that?"

"I'll try."

Sable's thin upper lip twitched; her left eye mimicked the movement. I might have considered her beautiful if it wasn't for the hateful expression permanently plastered to her face.

Sable closed the distance between us. She smelled like jasmine and my father's cigars. I'd learned early in life that those smells brought pain. Inwardly, I trembled, but I willed my stomach not to churn.

"This is a rat's nest," she said, grabbing a fist full of my hair and snapping my head back. "If tonight wasn't so important, I'd have it shaved." She let go of my hair and inhaled deeply. "This is going to take a lot longer than I thought."

The next two hours were a whirlwind of demands and insults. The two women Sable had brought with her were hired to help me look my best. I'm sure Sable had paid a high price to find the very best stylists around. The dress she chose for me was a backless, blood-red evening gown she'd purchased from some designer I'd never heard of. This was not like Sable at all, who could care less how I dressed. It was Erik who purchased all of my clothing for the times they wanted to parade me in public, which wasn't often.

After I dressed, Sable instructed one of the girls to sweep my hair up into a tight French twist, leaving no strand out of place. The poor girl, who couldn't help but check the time on her phone every few minutes, had to redo the style four times before Sable appeared satisfied.

"Can we do anything about her green eyes? I prefer blue," she said, her lip twitching again.

The girl frowned. "Do you want her to wear contacts?"

"You're useless," Sable snapped, but she continued to stare at my eyes as if conjuring a spell.

I remained silent throughout the entire ordeal. I'd learned long ago that it was easier to endure than to open my mouth, even if I was trying to help. Sable looked me over one final time and left with a flick of her wrist and an unsatisfied grunt. The two women followed after her.

The moment the door closed, I replaced the dress with jeans and a t-shirt and planned my escape. I had to get outside and take a break from the contention that poisoned every person in the house. I would never make it through the night otherwise.

It wasn't difficult to sneak away, my head down. It also helped that I hid my face by carrying a tall vase of flowers as if I was part of the event staff.

The moment I opened the back door, I bolted toward the edge of the nearby forest and didn't stop until safely behind a thick oak tree.

I glanced back at the home. It was an ugly site. It wasn't really a home but more of a gaudy mansion made of brick and stone. It was several stories above ground and several below, though only a select few knew of its depths. My room was in the east wing, opposite my parents. What I wouldn't give to live in a suburban area, surrounded by normal people. Come home from school, play video games or watch TV. I wasn't allowed to do any of those things. Occasionally, Erik allowed me to use his laptop for schoolwork, and when Jane wasn't watching, I would visit different webpages, hungry to learn all I could about the outside world.

From inside, the hired orchestra played a hauntingly beautiful tune. Erik put on many events like this throughout the year. Anyone of importance, human or fiend, received an invitation. These events were the only times the two species willingly crossed paths. Of course, many of the humans had no idea who or what was sitting beside them. Demons, vampires, and other creatures were required to appear human-like. The whole event was a ruse to gain power over others. And my parents were the puppet masters, using their magical abilities to manipulate those who could further their political agenda in the human world and gain more clout in the supernatural one.

A few hours later, the first guest arrived. I shouldn't delay getting ready any longer. When my parents began letting me attend these events a few years ago, I thought I would enjoy them since I was rarely allowed to socialize with others. But I never did. They all wore masks. I couldn't trust any of them—not even the humans.

Pushing myself up, I straightened my shoulders and prepared for the worst. It would all be over soon.

Back inside my room, I slid into the red evening gown just as Jane opened the bedroom door, panting heavily. "Your parents need you."

"I'll be right there," I said, but she had already closed the door.

I finished forcing my arm through a strap of the tight gown and sighed wearily. I didn't recognize the reflection staring back at me in the mirror. Black eyeliner framed my eyes like the edge of storm clouds, and my darkened eyebrows and reddened lips only added to the illusion. The two stylists had commented on my beauty, but to me, I looked like my mother. Not something I wanted.

Quietly and carefully, I walked downstairs, hoping to go unnoticed, and passed by the entrance to the ballroom that smelled of freshly baked pastries and wild roses. I didn't have to look in to know its design. I was all too familiar with my parents' outlandish décor of diamond-laced curtains, gold satin linens, and crystal chandeliers the Queen of England would envy.

I endured the evening by staying outside on the veranda as much as possible. The cool night air felt good against my bare arms and was a welcome distraction from the boisterous noises echoing from the brightly lit party.

"You stupid girl," a voice said behind me.

I turned around. The black silhouette of my mother stood in the doorway of the ballroom. If it hadn't been for her voice, I might have mistaken her for an unmasked demon.

"Get in here," she said. "I want you to meet someone special."

"Not tonight. Please." It was a dumb thing to say. I knew it the second the words left my mouth. Maybe my mother was right.

"It wasn't a question."

Reluctantly, I stepped forward. Sable took hold of my arm and dragged me through the room, weaving in and out of the guests. I tried to see where she was guiding me, but dancing couples blocked my view. When she nudged aside two women in the middle of a conversation, I finally saw whom I was to meet.

I yanked my arm free and froze. Though he looked human, I knew better. A murky blackness clung to him like thick tar.

This was no man.
This was a vampire.

3

Every fiber of my body screamed to run. There was an energy, dark and ancient, that filled the area around him. Despite my instincts, I found it difficult to look away. His commanding presence sucked me in as if an invisible cord were pulling me toward him. I resisted, and a sharp pain stabbed in my lower spine.

Sable whirled around and dug her nails into my wrist and jerked me forward. "Don't you dare insult him."

Erik, who was shaking hands with the vampire, turned. His slicked-back blond hair looked as greasy as his tanned complexion. "Eve, darling, this is Boaz. Boaz, meet my only daughter, Eve."

The light seemed to flee the room as Boaz's eyes met mine. He was strangely captivating with black hair, high cheekbones, and a distinct jaw line. My heart fluttered, and I grew faint. If it weren't for Sable's hand on my elbow, I would've staggered back. But it wasn't his appearance that made me weak. My mind tried to capture what it was, but his stare became too intense, forcing me to look away.

Erik said something under his breath and then chuckled.

"She may be, but I'll have to find out for myself," Boaz said.

Erik smirked, and Sable laughed obnoxiously. I was disgusted with all three of them.

"It was nice to meet you, *Sir*." It took all the strength I had, but I managed to yank my arm away, turn, and walk off, my heart racing. Out of the corner of my eye, I saw Sable begin to follow, but Boaz grabbed her wrist and held her in place.

I walked calmly, yet briskly, toward the stairs leading to the second floor. I nodded and smiled politely to several people who said "hello," but I refused to stop.

As I stepped upon the first stair, cold fingers touched my back.

I gasped and whirled around. To my amazement, no one was there. I slowly continued upward but again felt the touch of a hand caress the skin of my naked back. The icy coolness of it stole my breath. I spun back around, peering into the crowd.

I scanned the many faces, some of which appeared human, but I wasn't fooled. My eyes settled on the only one who stood out—not because he was different, but because he was their leader. They circled him like starving dogs anxious to devour whatever scrap of attention he might toss them. But Boaz paid little heed—his focus was entirely on me. His eyes bore into mine like those of a predatory animal. I could practically hear him snarling from across the room.

Frightened, I turned back to continue up the stairs, this time using the handrail for support. The invisible caresses continued until I was out of his view.

Safely hidden on the second floor, I leaned against a white pillar, my breaths coming in short gasps. My toes tingled, and a familiar, dark feeling crept up my body—magic. *Relax.* I couldn't let myself feel it, not here, not now, not ever.

A ways away, I spotted the narrow staircase leading to the kitchen. I descended the steps quickly and darted through the hot, steamy room, ignoring the staff's curious looks. I paused at the entrance to the ballroom. It would take twenty steps to reach the glass doors that opened to the veranda. *I can make it.*

I closed my eyes, took a deep breath, and counted to three. *Go!* My eyes snapped open, and I bolted.

Fifteen steps left.

Ten steps.

Three.

I reached to push the door open but froze when I heard my name. The beguiling voice of the devil himself. I turned around slowly.

"Yes?" I asked Boaz, desperately trying to sound curt.

"Will you give me the pleasure of dancing with you?" He

extended his hand.

"I don't feel well."

"One dance, love."

Before I could refuse, he took hold of my arm and pulled me onto the dance floor. When we reached the center of the room, he spun me to him and wrapped his arm around my waist, pressing me to his chest.

"Try to have fun," he said. "This is a party after all."

I avoided his eyes, instead staring beyond to envious faces. The song ended and another began: a bitter harmony of plucked violins and sobbing French horns. It was a torturous melody—one that should be played for the dead, not the living. Boaz's lip twitched into a subtle smile, as if he knew what I was thinking.

I did my best to act indifferent, but if I came across as cold, Boaz gave no indication. He held me close as if we were lovers, and I couldn't help but blush. Every touch, every sway of his body, overwhelmed me—whether from revulsion or pleasure, I couldn't be sure.

Finally, he pulled away and asked, "Why are you afraid?"

I swallowed hard. "I'm not."

"You're a horrible liar. Look at me."

I turned to him. My body weakened, and he tightened his grip.

"Why are you frightened?" he asked again.

I bit the inside of my cheek. "There's something about you. I don't know—"

"What do you feel?"

I tried to articulate my emotions. "I feel as if I'm spinning and can't keep my balance."

"The power. Intoxicating, isn't it?" Boaz danced flawlessly, every step obeying his silent command like the tides obey the moon. Other dancing couples retreated from his path as if he were royalty. I didn't know his real age, but by the way he spoke and carried himself,

I'd guess centuries. Maybe he had been royalty at one point in time.

"Do you always get this much attention?" I asked.

"They know to respect power when they see it."

"Arrogant much?"

He moved his head back and looked at me, dark eyes wide. "It's not me, love. It's us."

"There is no *us*."

Boaz smiled. "Your parents are watching."

I glanced behind him. Sure enough, Erik and Sable stared in our direction. Sable especially looked excited, her nose scrunched up, hands rubbing together as if anticipating a winning lottery number.

"Why do you think they look so eager?" Boaz asked. He spun me out and brought me back into his arms.

"Because you are their type, and they'd like nothing more than to see me with you."

"And what would you like, Eve?"

His question surprised me. No one had ever asked me that. "I want to be free to do as I please."

The smile on his face spread.

"Is something funny?" I asked.

"How would you like to play a little joke on your parents? Teach them a lesson for spying?"

"Like what?"

"Slap me," he ordered.

"What?"

"Slap me as hard as you can and walk away. Your parents will be furious, and you may pay for it later, but I promise their expressions will be well worth it—and you might actually enjoy it."

I didn't have to think twice. I stepped away and let my hand fly. It struck his face hard, stinging my palm.

I glanced over at my parents who looked as though I'd struck them rather than Boaz. Their eyebrows were pulled tightly together, and their mouths turned down. Lines I never knew existed appeared in sync with bulging veins on their necks. It was a comical scene, for they were still trying to keep up the appearance of having a wonderful time. Their poor faces looked as if they were having twin seizures.

I grinned and walked away. That felt much better than I'd expected. I headed straight to the veranda and stepped into the night, strangely elated. That was the first time I'd done exactly what I wanted without fearing the consequences.

"Very good," Boaz said.

I jumped. He was resting in a chair as if he'd been there all night. There was no trace of a handprint on his face. Next to him, a massive black wolf stared with one blue eye and one white.

"How did you—" I looked back toward the ballroom. There was no way he could've beaten me here.

"Don't be naïve, love. You know what I am."

My gaze lowered to the strangely still wolf. Without a sound, he bared his sharp canine teeth. "And who's this friendly beast?"

The wolf growled.

Boaz ran his fingers through its thick, bristly fur. "This is Hunwald."

"Interesting name. Where did you get it?"

"I didn't *get* it anywhere. He chose it."

"All right," I said, not understanding. "How long have you had him?"

"He's had *me* since I was a child," he corrected again.

"What do you mean?"

Boaz leaned forward. The movement was too quick, too smooth, reminding me again how inhuman he really was. Instinctively, I stepped back.

"My mother was a vicious woman. The kind of woman who should never have had a child, but apparently Fate thought it amusing, and she bore me. Though in the end, I'm not sure who the joke was really on." He smiled to himself. "My mother used to carry a big stick everywhere she went. She called it *Thorne*, and every time she said its name, she would laugh atrociously, as though it was the funniest thing she'd ever heard. Her saying *Thorne* meant only one thing—that I was to receive a severe beating for failing to fulfill one of her absurd expectations. It was in the middle of one of these beatings that Hunwald found us in the woods. He tore my mother to shreds right in front of me." He turned to Hunwald and ruffled the fur on his face between his hands. "Didn't you? You good boy!"

"That's terrible," I said.

Boaz's head snapped up. "Don't tell me you haven't ever wished your parents dead."

"I couldn't, wouldn't—"

"Give it time."

I stepped toward the ballroom. "I should go inside—"

Boaz appeared in front of me, blocking the door. Air caught in my chest. He took hold of my wrist and, with his thumb, rubbed the flesh beneath my palm, exactly where my pulse beat.

"Stay for just a moment longer," he said, his tone commanding.

My head spun. The circular motion of his thumb on the sensitive part of my wrist made me lightheaded as if I'd had too much to drink.

"I want to wish you a happy birthday," he purred.

It took me a moment to process his words. "How did you know?"

"How could I forget?"

I tried to communicate that I didn't understand, but I couldn't clear the growing fog from my mind.

While continuing to stroke the underside of my wrist, he said, "Your dress is extraordinary."

He lifted my hand to his slightly parted mouth and pressed his lips to my flesh. I felt the gentle pressure of his tongue wet my skin. I slowly shook my head.

Finally I broke free of his spell and stepped away, my arms falling limp at my side. I looked down at my dress, suddenly realizing why Sable had chosen it. "This dress was meant for you."

He laughs. "I hope not. I don't think it would fit."

"Sable," I stutter, hating that he's flustering me. "She chose it because she knew you would like it."

"Mmm. She does have impeccable taste."

"You can have it if you like."

"Only if I can have what's inside, as well."

In response to my growing anger, the power within me stirred to life for the second time that night, but I resisted its pull.

"Let me make this perfectly clear," I said, pointing my finger at his chest. "You will never have any part of me."

"But, my love, I already have," he said, licking his lips.

My bravery exhausted, I darted around him and returned to the ballroom, leaving him and the wolf to the darkness where they belonged.

4

I returned to my bedroom for the remainder of the party. I knew it would upset my parents, but by their earlier expressions, they couldn't get much angrier. Alone, I waited for my punishment, my heartbeat growing louder by the minute.

Several hours later, the party died down, until all I heard were the servants cleaning up after the guests. I didn't get ready for bed. My night was not over. Not yet.

It wasn't long before Erik and Sable's heavy footsteps slapped against the marbled floor. The steps reminded me of a hammer and a pickax. I slowly stood from my bed, swaying slightly, prepared for what was to come.

Erik pushed open my door. He was still dressed in a black tux that looked too tight for his solid frame. Behind a row of perfectly shaped teeth, his tongue clicked repeatedly. Next to him, Sable, who must've sensed his impatience, said, "Eve, dear, if you would just use your abilities, we could stop these *training* exercises."

I pulled on my slippers, knowing I would be leaving soon. "I've told you both a thousand times: I can't use magic."

Erik clicked his tongue again. "Nonsense! You're pretending, but don't worry, we will break you. I'm trying something new tonight."

I wrapped a thick robe around my nightgown. It was cold where I was going. "Whatever you say, Erik."

Sable moved to my red dress, hanging from the top of the bedpost, and inspected it. "Did you get anything on it?"

"No."

She glanced back at me. "Are you sure? You're not very graceful when you eat."

"I didn't eat."

"Good." Sable removed the dress and draped it over her arm.

"Let's get this over with," Erik snapped.

Sable's long fingers caressed the satin material. "You go ahead. I'll be there in a minute."

Erik scowled but didn't argue. "Don't take long," he said and walked out of the room with me in his shadow.

I knew exactly where we were going. I could've made the trip with my eyes closed. Our footsteps echoed as we made our way down a narrow, circular stairway to the very bottom level, hidden far below the mansion. The only way to get there was through a secret door in Erik's office. The smell of alcohol drifted behind Erik, turning my stomach inside out. I quickly covered my mouth to stop from gagging. The smell was always a precursor to pain.

Erik removed a key from his pocket and pushed it into the keyhole of a thick metal door. The creaking and groaning of the hinges furthered my nausea. I remained where I was, my heart pounding.

"Get in here," Erik said from within the room. I heard him open a drawer.

Knees weak and shaking, I stepped into my father's "training" room. The smell of jasmine hit me, forcing me to stumble back into a wall. The plants hung everywhere; some draped from the ceiling while others had been arranged in specific patterns in the corners of the room. I had a sudden urge to smash them all, but my body wouldn't move.

Long white counters lined the walls; inside their drawers held all the tools Erik thought necessary to force my compliance. On the surface of the counters, cages contained different animals, from spiders to rats—Erik kept them as pets and treated them each with great care. And finally, in the center of the room, rested a single, immoveable metal chair with black straps bolted to its underside.

After Erik had carefully inspected each cage for proper food and water, he said, "In the chair."

My nails dug into the wall behind me. "Please, father—"

"Do it."

By the time I reached the cold chair, my legs were shaking so badly that I had no choice but to collapse into it, sweat breaking on my brow. *Stay calm.*

Erik ran his fingers across the different animal cages on top of the counter. "I don't understand why you make this so difficult. This would all end if you'd only accept your birthright."

I closed my eyes and breathed deeply. "I told you. I'm not like you. I have no magical abilities." I'd said this so many times I almost believed it.

"I've heard that before," he muttered. He lifted a basket-like cage and peered in between the tight weave. I couldn't see what was inside. "It is utterly impossible for a child born to the Segurs and Whitmores not to have powers. You are deliberately holding back."

"Why would I do that?"

Erik's head snapped up as if he'd been shocked. "Quit wasting my time!" His slicked-back hair left its place and fell to his forehead. "I am not a fool. You have power—I can feel it."

"No I don't," I whispered, wishing desperately it was true. But even now, with fear about to crack through my feigned calm, I felt magic's ancient power as strong as the overpowering smell of jasmine. Only my vow kept me from using it.

"Have I missed anything?" Sable's voice asked behind me. She crossed the room to her usual place in the corner and sat on a stool surrounded by jasmine. She'd changed into a silky green, short-sleeved housecoat. Tucked beneath her arm was a watering can.

"We were just beginning," Erik said, smoothing back his hair. He walked over to me and set the cage down before proceeding to fasten the straps around my chest and legs. In my ear, he whispered, "For your protection."

Sable poured water into the nearby plants and touched their leaves tenderly. "I trust this won't take long? I have a meeting in the morning."

Erik glared. "It will take as long as it needs to."

"Very well." She sighed as she plucked off wilted leaves from a plant hanging above her. "Just make sure Eve is punished for her behavior tonight."

Erik knelt in front of me and removed my slippers. "Don't worry, darling. I was going to do that first."

I tried not to let my mind wander with what new torture he may have devised. He lifted the cage and peered inside its tight slits again, the corner of his mouth rising. I shivered.

"You embarrassed us, Eve," he said as he opened the top of the cage. Whatever was inside bumped the whicker walls, almost knocking it from Erik's hands.

"What are you going to do?" I didn't mean to whimper.

"Teach you to respect us once and for all."

Water poured from Sable's can.

I closed my eyes and prepared for the inevitable. As if sensing my thoughts, Erik took hold of my foot and guided it into the trap. Something bit me hard, and I yelped.

"This rat hasn't eaten for days. Hope your foot has enough flesh on it—"

My screams drowned out the rest of his words. The hungry rat was tearing into my skin with teeth and claws. I tried to kick at it, but that only made it madder, and it clamped onto my pinky toe with sharp teeth.

To escape the pain, I did what I've always done: left reality and traveled to Eden—a secret haven I'd created when I was just a child. It was a refuge hidden deep within my subconscious that I used to protect myself from Erik and Sable's constant abuse.

I'd first heard of Eden when I was only six from an elderly woman who'd marveled when I revealed my name.

I was standing outside a jewelry shop in Manhattan waiting for my father, when a woman with thick eyelashes and a gentle smile approached me. "What's your name, little one?"

I'd been taught not to speak to others, but the woman's eyes felt like a canopy, sheltering me from the world. In a small voice, I answered, "Eve."

"What a beautiful name," the old woman said, her gnarled hands gripping a cane. "You must be really special."

"Why?"

"Because Eve was the mother of all living. She was beautiful, kind, and full of love. It's a great honor to be named after her."

"Where is Eve?" I asked, hoping I could visit her.

"She lived in a wonderful place called Eden where there was no pain or sorrow. But that was a long time ago. Eden is gone, along with Eve. But I can see in those rare emerald eyes of yours, that you will be just as great as our Mother Eve."

It was at this moment when Erik, who seemed to appear out of nowhere, shoved the old woman backward. She stumbled and tripped over the curb and fell into the street.

"Keep your idiotic stories to yourself," Erik said.

He pulled me away from the crumpled woman lying in the street. Before she disappeared from my view, I glanced over my shoulder one last time. She was struggling to stand, but our eyes met, and she smiled.

Out of nowhere, a bus rounded the corner, going faster than it should. I screamed a warning, but it was too late. The bus ran over her as if she wasn't there. I turned to bury my head into my father, but stopped when I noticed he was chanting under his breath, a deadly spell.

That was the first time I created Eden, and I had returned many times since. As long as I had Eden, I was out of their reach.

I arrived there now, just as the full moon reached its peak in the night sky. Its silver light brought the dark world to life, illuminating trees and flowers that blanketed the ground. The air smelled of salt and pine, and in the distance, waves hushed against the shore. I moved into a groove of trees, anxious to see the ocean.

I didn't get very far. Somewhere inside my subconscious, a man was yelling. Something crashed, metal against metal. I didn't listen too closely for fear that returning to the real world would bring excruciating pain again. I reached the edge of the woods, but the man's angered voice persisted until my curiosity overrode the fear of torture.

I closed my eyes and willed myself back to reality, but as soon as my mind connected with my body, the pain was greater than I'd anticipated. I cried out and fought against the straps around my chest.

"What have you done?" the same male voice said.

I forced my eyes open. In front of me kneeled Boaz.

5

Boaz gazed at my bloodied feet, his eyebrows pressed together. Erik stood against the wall, the cage in his hand. Sable was gone.

Breathing shallowly, I glanced down at my right foot. It would've been unrecognizable if it hadn't been for my first and second toes, which were mostly intact. The rest of my flesh had been shredded, exposing bone in some places. I gripped the sides of the chair and threw my head back, stifling another scream. Boaz released the straps around my legs and chest. He seemed to be at a loss for words as he stared deeply into my eyes, his cool hand smoothing back my sweat-drenched hair.

He turned to Erik. "You tell Sable to fix this tonight!"

"But Boaz, you must understand—we were only trying to teach her a lesson."

"Can you stand?" he asked me.

Though the pain was severe, I ignored it. The last thing I wanted was help from a vampire. I pushed against the armrests, lifting my body to a standing position.

"Breathe," he whispered in my ear while he steadied me with his hands.

I exhaled the breath I didn't realize I'd been holding.

"Can you walk?" he asked.

His hands remained on my hips. The coolness of his fingertips ignited the skin beneath my nightgown's thin material. Nodding, I continued upwards—each step felt as though I was stepping on nails. Boaz stayed by my side, guiding me out the door and up the steps.

"I can carry you, if you would like," he said.

"No, but thank you." I stopped. "Why did you come back?"

"I never left. I was exploring the grounds and the local wildlife."

"This late?"

He raised his eyebrow, and I looked away, embarrassed.

"I'm glad I didn't leave," he said.

I forced my body up another step. "But how did you find us? Only a few people know of these lower levels."

"I heard your screams. Are you sure I can't carry you?"

"No. I'm fine. In fact, you can leave now. I appreciate your help, but I'll be fine." I didn't want him to think I was vulnerable, an easy victim.

"Good. I need to talk with Erik." He grasped my arm, and his fingers caressed my skin. Strangely, the pain in my foot dissipated. "I hope I will see you again."

My gaze traveled up to his bicep peeking out from his black short-sleeved shirt. A red and black snake tattoo twisted around the large muscle. I met his gaze. "Not likely, but again, thank you for your help."

As quickly as possible, I moved away, the pain returning the second his touch left me. I continued up the stairs, but when I didn't hear his footsteps going back down, I glanced behind me. Boaz was gone, as if he'd evaporated.

When I reached the top of the stairs, Sable met me with a bowl of wet jasmine. "These are for you. Wrap them around your knee and your *owie* will be better by morning."

"It's my foot," I clarified, but she was already walking in the opposite direction.

Once inside my bedroom, I collapsed into bed, gritting my teeth. I couldn't ignore my parents' abuse any longer. Not because it was much worse than anything else I'd endured, but because today was different; I was eighteen. I always knew when this day came, I would move out. I had no idea where to or how I'd make a living, but I needed to figure it out and soon.

Several minutes later, I withdrew a long jasmine vine from the basin and wrapped it around my foot. I wasn't sure how I was supposed to do this, as Sable hadn't given any instructions, but it seemed the most likely way. I did the same with a few more vines and then pulled a long sock over the wet plants. Within a few minutes my foot was numb.

I didn't sleep at all that night. I couldn't stop thinking of my future, and, to my dismay, Boaz. I couldn't understand the electrifying sensation that overcame me whenever he was near. It haunted me for hours, and I didn't know if I was angrier with him or myself for thinking about him.

Because I couldn't sleep, I rose early and wandered the grounds surrounding the mansion. As Sable had promised, the flesh and skin on my foot had healed. Thy sky was gray, and a light mist lingered in the trees.

Several cars were still parked in the driveway. It was only a matter of time before Erik kicked them out. He never could tolerate the presence of others for very long, including the company of his wife. I wondered every day why they bothered to marry, but more importantly, why they bothered to have a child. Together they were powerful enough. Why did they need me, and why were they so desperate for me to use my abilities?

I liked to think normal parents would've been happy with the way I turned out. I always did what they asked, often times going above and beyond, even if I wouldn't give them the one thing they wanted most.

My powers only manifested when I felt fear, anger, or hatred, and I'd spent my entire life controlling these emotions, despite what Erik and Sable did to me. Boaz, however, had elicited those negative emotions in a single evening.

I moved quietly into the house, hoping to go unnoticed as usual, but today was not a usual day.

Sable called from the kitchen, "Eve, darling, come join us for breakfast." She was using her sweet voice, which meant she wanted something.

Erik and Sable stood together, shoulder to shoulder, next to the dining room table. Their eyes followed me until I sat at the only chair with a place setting in front of it. I picked up a spoon and took a bite of cold oatmeal.

"Aren't you going to say hello to your parents?" Sable asked.

"Is that what you want?" I never knew.

Erik's left eye twitched, and his upper lip receded. "You better not mess this up."

"Mess what up?"

"Your relationship with Boaz."

"I don't have a relationship with him nor will I."

"Yes, you will. He made his intentions very clear last night. You and he will be an excellent match."

"What is so special about Boaz?" I said, without thinking.

Sable slapped my face hard. "Never speak of him that way! We are alive because of his mercy."

I resisted the urge to roll my eyes. Sable could be very dramatic, but I noticed that Erik did not disagree. He simply looked away as if it were fact—one he was not pleased about, either.

I hated that I had been born into a supernatural family. We lived by rules that normal humans didn't. Where they were free to choose whom they married, those like me often had arranged marriages, which had nothing to do with love. It was all about elevating our position of power among our kind and the humans. We needed to be able to influence laws and policy for the day we made our kind known publicly, an event my parent's assured me was soon coming.

"Does it matter at all what I want?" I asked, my voice softer.

"Has it ever?" Sable countered.

Erik walked out of the room without looking back. He'd said what he'd wanted and would not waste another word. Sable looked as if she wanted to say more, but apparently thought better of it. She turned and rushed after Erik.

I sighed and pushed the bowl away. I would never have a relationship with Boaz. The thought sickened me. Besides, he was a vampire, and I was a human. It couldn't work even if I had wanted it to—not well anyway. So what were my parents thinking?

**

A week passed, as did the image of Boaz from my mind. My thoughts returned to my immanent plan for escape. I needed to earn just enough money for a bus ticket and food to the city. Once there, I could stay at a shelter until I secured a job. I'd found one the other day on the Internet while Jane was preoccupied speaking to one of her children on her phone. I wish I could ask for her help, but her allegiance was to my parents. Besides, I would never put her in that position, especially not after what they did to our neighbor's daughter.

It was late in the afternoon and a beautiful day for October. I had no intention of staying indoors. At least that's what I told myself, but the truth was, Erik and Sable were returning from a visit with Erik's parents, whom I'd never met, in Connecticut. I never understood why, but they always returned home angry at each other. Weeks, sometimes months, would go by before they would speak to each other again, which meant their attention was on me. Most of my abuse had been during these times.

I dressed in my riding gear and headed to the stables. Horse riding was the only activity they sometimes would allow, and since they weren't around for me to ask, I figured it was okay.

After saddling my gray mare, Storm, I rode into the forest. My parents owned hundreds of acres, all private with no trespassing signs. I only knew half of what went on in these woods; the other half I didn't want to know. My parents didn't just throw parties for humans but also for those in power among supernatural creatures. Those parties were always outside, deep inside the forest. I avoided them at all costs.

When I reached a small clearing besides a shallow creek, I

stopped Storm. During the cooler months, this was my favorite place. The wide gap in the canopy of trees let in just enough sunlight to warm the ground. I withdrew a heavy blanket and spread it over dead grass.

With a book in hand, I lay there and buried my feet beneath a fold in the blanket. I'd only read a few pages when a soft wind blew my hair away from my neck. It was surprisingly warm for the cooler temperature, and I closed my eyes, enjoying the warmth. Suddenly the air became more focused and the slight breeze changed to that of a soft caress down the nape of my neck. I sucked in air and let the gentle touch linger against my skin longer than I should have. Finally, I exhaled and opened my eyes.

It didn't take me long to find Boaz leaning against a tree on the other side of the brook, his arms folded to his chest. His black hair fell long to his shoulders. When a familiar flutter of confusion clouded my mind, I quickly averted my gaze.

"You shouldn't be out here alone," he said. Hunwald, the wolf, stood absolutely still by his side.

I kept my focus on the book, even though a part of me wanted to look up and see his face, to feel the power lurking behind the glossy surface of his eyes. "I'm perfectly fine alone, and if you don't mind, that's how I'd like to stay."

"What kind of gentleman would I be if I left a fair maiden alone in the big, bad woods?"

"I can assure you, you are no gentleman and therefore are not required to act like one." I continued to pretend to read, but after a minute under the pressure of his stare, I dropped the book and said more forcefully, "Please leave."

"I told you: I'm not leaving you alone."

I slapped the book down at my side. "What are you even doing here?"

"I heard you were in trouble."

"Trouble? What are you talking about?" I sat up, thinking hard.

Maybe my parents came home early and found me missing. They would definitely be upset if they knew I left without permission. A wave of nausea washed over me.

"You don't look so well," he said, stepping toward me.

"I have to go." I quickly gathered my belongings, praying my parents were still away.

"I should see you home," Boaz said.

I shook my head and lifted onto Storm's back, my thoughts torn between him and getting home. "I'll be fine."

With a nudge to her gut, Storm galloped away. My heartbeat matched the rapid rhythm of her hooves, bu-bum, bu-bum, over and over. Boaz appeared in my mind. Bu-bum, bu-bum. His caress sliding down my skin, his tongue against my wrist. Bu-bum, bu-bum.

I pulled the reins, bringing Storm to a slow walk. What was wrong with me? I looked over my shoulder, expecting to see Boaz, but I was alone. I shouldn't have these feelings, but I couldn't deny there was something that drew me to him. The air hummed in his presence, and it electrified my skin and vibrated my nerves. It was as though the magic inside me was reacting to him, as if he were metal and I a magnet.

Storm stopped abruptly, jolting me out of my thoughts. She stomped her feet and snorted.

I patted her broad neck. "What is it, girl?"

Without warning, she reared, making me lose my balance, and I tumbled to the ground. The bone in my arm snapped just before my head smacked against a rock and exploded in pain. Stunned, I reached for the back of my head with my good arm and felt something warm and wet. I moved my hand in front of my eyes and sucked in air—blood.

To my right, an unnatural movement caught my eye. Something shaped like a man with grayish white skin from head to foot stepped out from behind a tree. His chest was abnormally large on top of his skinny legs. Each bulging rib looked like it was about to burst from his leathered skin.   His patchy hair and wide eyes shined a brilliant white; only his lips were a dark gray. The creature hobbled awkwardly toward me, shifting in uneven spurts. There wasn't anything particularly frightening about his expressionless face, but his intentions clouded and darkened the air around him.

He meant to kill me.

6

I scooted backwards on the ground, away from the gray creature whose strides were extraordinary long. His upper lip flared into a snarl, revealing razor sharp teeth, and he snapped them like a rabid dog. My mind raced, trying to recall any kind of spell I might use against him, but my head was more full of pain than any useable thoughts.

He was almost upon me when out of nowhere a dark blur slammed into the monster, flipping his grayish body into the air. As the beast fell down, I recognized my savior: Boaz. He caught the creature in his arms and snapped its back upon his thigh. He rolled the limp figure from his leg, and before the body hit the ground, Boaz was by my side.

"Are you all right?" he asked. His eyebrows pulled tightly together, shadowing the dark tunnels that stared at me.

Words were even harder to access than my thoughts.

"What is it, Eve?"

I wanted to say that I was fine, but my eyes fluttered close. I forced them open again and attempted to sit up. I had to get home. I had to get away from Boaz.

"Let me help you," Boaz said. He reached around my shoulders, but stopped suddenly. He must have seen or smelled the blood—I couldn't be sure which. Very gently, he turned my head to the side and smoothed the hair away to examine the wound.

His face contorted and twisted into rage, but he said nothing. Instead, he stood up and returned to the lifeless body he had killed. With one hard kick, he sent it flying into the top of a tree. The branches groaned under the weight until they snapped, and the monster fell. On its way back to the ground, branches tore at its leathery skin, exposing a black substance that oozed like tar from the

35

wounds.

The last thing I remembered before losing consciousness was Boaz picking me up and cradling me to his chest.

***

I opened my eyes, blinking several times. I was back in my bedroom. The red sheer curtains around my canopy bed were drawn except for a small gap at the corner where the curtains met. I couldn't tell whether it was night or day; someone had drawn the blinds on my windows.

I was about to call out, hoping Jane might be around, but quickly shut my mouth when I heard Boaz's voice: "This isn't the way. You hurt her."

He spoke low, but the sharp tone of his voice was as if he were yelling. He stood not far away, his dark silhouette looming over Erik's.

"Sable has already taken care of it," Erik said. "For now."

"You better be right." Boaz crossed the room to my dresser and picked up something small from its top.

"She's useless to us, Boaz," Erik said. "You know that. My father gave us permission."

Boaz dropped whatever he was looking at, and faster than I could blink, was across the room gripping Erik by the throat. "You won't touch her without *my* permission, do you understand?"

He didn't answer, but I assumed Erik must've agreed, because Boaz said, "Good. And I expect Sable to obey as well."

He let go of Erik, who stumbled back.

"Now leave us," Boaz said.

After Erik closed the door, Boaz moved to the side of my bed and pulled back the sheer curtains. I quickly shut my eyes and resisted an urge to swallow.

"You can't fool me, love. I heard your heartbeat quicken moments ago." He took my hand and gently caressed it.

The swallow I'd been trying to hold back came now. The loud

gulp seemed to echo throughout the room. I didn't dare open my eyes for fear of losing myself to him. At first hearing him speak, I'd felt the twisting of my stomach and a sharp pain in my heart. But what did it mean? He was the opposite of everything I believed in, yet the depth of his eyes, his velvet voice, and the way his touch ignited my skin, made me forget the evil that lay beneath his perfect exterior.

His fingers grazed the side of my cheek. "If you don't open your eyes," he breathed, suddenly inches from my face, "then I will be forced to kiss you."

I wavered only for a moment, wondering what it would be like to feel his lips against mine, but the reasoning part of my mind finally broke through the haze. I opened my eyes.

Boaz leaned back, a slight frown on his face before his mouth curved into a smile. "Another time."

I turned away to hide the burning heat in my cheeks. In the corner of the room, I locked eyes with Hunwald. "Does he go everywhere with you?"

"Absolutely. Hunwald and I are inseparable."

At the sound of his name, Hunwald stood and walked over to Boaz, but he kept his eyes fixed on me.

"I don't think he likes me."

"Hunwald doesn't like anyone."

"That's comforting. Does he have to be in here?"

Boaz looked at me and then at Hunwald. He pursed his lips together as if deciding. Finally he said, "He can wait outside."

Hunwald's bushy head jerked in Boaz's direction as if he understood. Boaz motioned toward the door, but Hunwald stared stubbornly back. Boaz motioned again with a little more force. This time, the wolf turned and left the room, but not without casting me a dangerous look.

"Friendly dog," I said.

"He's not a dog, and I don't have him because he's friendly."

I sighed and attempted to sit up, but a tight wrap on my arm made it difficult. They must've put it on me while I was unconscious. "Is this really necessary?"

"Your arm was broken. Of course it's necessary."

"But there's hardly any pain," I said, moving my arm around.

"You have your mother to thank for that. She can do the most amazing things with jasmine."

I grimaced.

"You don't like jasmine?" Boaz asked.

"I can't stand it."

"Is it because your mother loves it, or is there another reason?"

"What does it matter?" I reached up to tear the bandage off of my head, but instead, I froze. My eyes flashed to Boaz.

"What is it?" he asked.

"Is it difficult for you to be around blood?"

He smiled. "Not at all. I've been around long enough that my craving for blood is similar to what you might feel toward chocolate."

"Appetizing," I said and tried not to grimace as I unraveled the bandage. It didn't feel near as good as my arm. "How old are you anyway?"

"Old enough to know when a person isn't safe in their own home. That Diablo almost killed you."

"Diablo?" I wasn't familiar with the name.

"A Diablo is a demon who has taken over a human body. Their unnatural presence slowly kills the human's body, making them appear like a corpse. They are merciless and determined. If one's been sent to kill you, more will follow."

"I don't understand. Why would they want to kill me?"

Boaz leaned back in his chair. "I have two theories. The first is someone among our kind has sent the Diablos to kill you. You're less of a threat if you're dead."

This surprised me. "How am I a threat to anyone?"

"You're the daughter of the most powerful witches to ever exist."

"But I'm nothing like my parents." I shuddered. The thought of demons after me was frightening enough, but being compared to my parents was even more terrifying.

"You're right. You are nothing like them—you're much greater."

I shook my head to dismiss what was, in my mind, an empty compliment. "And your second theory?"

Boaz averted his eyes. "Your parents. I think they sent them."

I shook my head slowly. "They wouldn't."

"Perhaps, but I must find out for sure." He stood. "I should let you rest."

"Not yet," I said, wanting him to explain further. Granted, my parents were horrible, but kill me?

"Close your eyes and sleep, love. I need to speak with your father, and then I will return."

Boaz left, and the room felt overwhelmingly empty without him. After several minutes, I threw back the covers and stood. My head pounded but hardly enough to keep me in bed. I smoothed my long black nightgown and walked to the dresser to see what Boaz had been looking at.

Several items sprawled across the dark wood surface: a grotesque-looking porcelain doll, a ceramic gargoyle, and a music box that played a song that was neither happy nor pleasant. None of them represented beauty and love. They were all constant reminders of my parents attempt to turn my heart as black as theirs.

I scanned the remaining items. Only one was out of place: an unframed photograph of me taken months ago, just outside our home. Jane had captured it with her cell phone and had given it to me as a gift. It was the only picture I had of myself.

After slipping the photo into my top drawer, I walked to the window and opened the blinds with my good arm. It was later in the day than I thought. The sun clung stubbornly to the horizon, but night would soon have its way.

I rested my forehead against the cool glass. Darkness had already reached the edge of the forest. Out of the corner of my eye, I noticed a familiar movement. My heart skipped a beat. Several was more like it.

Two more of the white creatures—Diablos, as Boaz had called them—were moving in and out of the trees. They wandered randomly, their bodies jerking in uneven spurts. They seemed to be waiting for something—or someone. As if sensing my thoughts, their heads jerked in my direction, eyes entirely white.

A chill erupted on my skin. I stepped away from the window and right into Boaz. His arms came around me, and I sucked in air. With my back to him, he whispered in my ear, "They will not harm you. As long as I am near, no one will ever hurt you again."

I caved, letting him hold me longer than I should have, but to be held like that was nothing I'd ever experienced before. It was almost impossible to resist.

But I had to try.

I turned around and said with as much strength as I could muster, "I can take care of myself."

"Like you did this morning?" Boaz brushed past me to the window and closed the blinds. "Learn to use magic, and then you will be able to take care of yourself."

I huffed and sat down at my vanity to search the drawers. "I want nothing to do with those evil powers."

"They're not evil. They're a necessity. Your abilities will save your life one day."

I finally found what I was looking for: a long, sharp envelope opener. While I thought about Boaz's words, I shoved the silver knife under the material on my arm and jerked upward. It tore in two and fell to the ground. Other than my arm being red from the cast, it was completely unscathed.

"Let's say then," I began, "that I am able to do magic. How will I know I won't lose myself in the process? I've seen how magic changes people, and it's never for the better."

"Nothing is black or white, love. Life is full of gray. You'll change whatever way necessary to fit your environment, and right now, you need to grow up and get over these foolish ideas of love and purity." He reached for a book on my bookshelf, one that happened to be hidden behind one of my parent's approved books, and tossed it onto the bed. "You are wasting your time and talent, and it's disgusting."

I stood abruptly, knocking back the chair I was just sitting in. "How dare you! You don't know what I've had to endure living with those—" I struggled to find the right words. "—those *people* who have the nerve to call themselves parents."

Boaz grinned, his eyes dancing. "Then stop enduring! Maybe then we can start having some fun!"

"Get out," I said.

"You'll have to do better than that."

"I said, get out!" I pointed to the door, which flew open at my silent command and slammed into the wall behind it, leaving a gaping hole. I shrank back, terrified. In that small moment, when I had allowed myself to hate, the room had turned cold, and the light darkened. Even the floral smell had turned bitter.

Boaz laughed. "Didn't that feel wonderful?" He walked to the door and inspected it. "Amazing! You didn't even have to try. I knew you had it in you."

"Please leave," I said, barely above a whisper.

Boaz's expression darkened. "If that is what you want. I'll check on you tomorrow."

He tried to shut the door on his way out, but it closed crooked; the top hinge was broken.

I dropped into bed, appalled by what I'd done. What if Boaz told my parents? I rolled over and covered my head with a pillow. Boaz had caused this. He'd made me feel hate, the one emotion my parents had tried to teach me since birth, and he'd managed to do it after meeting me only a few times.

Even now, the remains of hate's power tingled inside me, coursing through my blood like hot lava, darkening my thoughts. If I'd been born normal, would the feeling of hate still have been as strong? The emotion overwhelmed me, filling me to the point where it physically hurt and the only way to relieve the pain was to expel it through magic.

I needed to stay away from Boaz.

All night, I tossed and turned, my mind tortured with dreams of death and destruction. Boaz was there—the black conductor leading the symphony of carnage. I couldn't escape him even as I slept.

"Eve," I heard his voice say. The symphony played louder.

"Eve, wake up!"

His image left my dreams and appeared before my open eyes. Unsure of my surroundings, I recoiled in fear. I rubbed my eyes, but when I opened them again, Boaz was still there, looking more devilish than ever. His disheveled hair was pulled back into a loose ponytail; several strands fell into his face as if he'd been running only moments before.

"What are you doing back?" I asked, sitting up. It was barely eight in the morning.

"I never left."

I furrowed my brow at him.

"I was going to, but a problem arose. I've been trying to decide how best to deal with it."

"What sort of problem?"

"The Diablos," he answered. He crossed the room to the window and parted the blinds to peer out.

"They're still out there?" I threw back the covers and left the warmth of the bed.

"Yes, and they've multiplied exponentially. It's only a matter of hours before they come into the house."

"Why?"

He turned around so suddenly I stumbled back. "They're coming for *you*."

"Erik and Sable—"

"Are the ones who summoned them," he finished. "I have confirmed it. They excused the staff and left hours ago. I'm all you have left."

"I don't believe you. They wouldn't kill me, not after all they've put me through." But even as I said the words, I didn't believe them. So what if they exhausted countless hours trying to get me to use magic? I never gave them what they wanted. This made me think of something else, something Erik had said many times. "Besides, if they wanted me dead, they'd do it themselves."

His left eyebrow rose. "And give anyone the opportunity to question them? When your body is discovered torn and mangled tomorrow morning, no one will suspect your parents. They will be far away from here, attending some charity event."

And there it was: a dirty, ugly truth.

Boaz looked back out the window. "I argued with them well into the night, but they've washed their hands of you, said you were a waste to their kind, an embarrassment. Even Erik's father, your grandfather, agreed. They all want you dead."

My legs weakened, and I slouched onto my bed. I'd never met my grandfather. Why would someone I didn't even know want me dead?

He stepped in front of me. "You need to come with me. It's your only chance to survive."

"Where would we go?"

"Just pack a few things and get dressed. Be ready in five minutes," he said and left the room.

I sat there, stunned. This can't be happening.

For a full minute I didn't move, but after the shock, a new thought revealed itself like a shiny new gift. I didn't have to stay here anymore. I didn't have to see my parents ever again. *I was free.*

This discovery spurred me to action, and I packed quickly, my mind processing different scenarios. I could leave with Boaz and possibly talk him into giving me some money. Maybe he would even drop me off at the bus stop. And if he wouldn't do any of those things, maybe he would let me work for him doing … what, exactly? I knew nothing about him.

I pulled on my favorite jeans. I could figure it out later. At least I never had to see my parents again. And I would be alive, thanks to Boaz. But why was he helping me? I would have to be extra careful around him.

I was just pulling a sweater over my head when I heard: "You are a work of art."

I jumped and turned around. Boaz sat in the corner on a small chair, hidden within the shadows. Somehow, he had snuck back into the room, and my face reddened, wondering how much he had seen.

Swallowing hard, I said, "I'm ready."

"Good. The Diablo's are growing in numbers even as we speak."

"How do you know?"

"I can sense it, and so can you."

I shook my head. "But I can't sense anything,"

Boaz appeared behind me, as fluid as water from a tap.

"Close your eyes, love," he breathed into my ear. The breath from his lips warmed the skin on my neck, making me feel lightheaded. One arm wrapped around my waist, pulling me into him, and the other moved slowly to the side of my neck where his fingers rubbed up to my earlobe and back down to my collar bone. "Focus on the Diablo who tried to take your life. Picture what a vile creature he was, and how he deserved to die."

A murky fog clouded my rational mind, and I obeyed. I thought back to the Diablo in the woods as it had approached me with malice on his face. I remembered how Boaz had slammed into him, killing him within seconds. I was glad he was dead. He deserved it.

I inhaled deeply, letting hate for the Diablo fill my being. The smell in the room changed to that of rotten flesh, but I didn't waiver. I pushed my consciousness to the forest beyond and searched for the rotting creatures. Not far away, I found them moving sporadically in jagged, circular motions. There was no order to their movements, yet their graceless march slowly moved closer to the house. There must've been fifty or more.

I let out my breath and opened my eyes. The room was darker than I remembered, and the colors were dull, as if I'd entered a whole new world.

"There are so many of them," I whispered, grimacing from my new surroundings.

Boaz removed his hand from my collarbone. "I knew you would see them."

"Why is the room so dark?" I asked.

"It's the reflection of true power. Get used to it."

"I don't like it."

Boaz spun me around. "Right now I don't care what you like. I need you to be strong to get out of here. You're going to have to fight." He took my hand and pulled me from the room.

Fight? I'd never fought anything before—not physically, anyway. Boaz's pace was so fast I barely managed to keep my footing. "But aren't you strong enough?"

"Not like you." He continued to pull me down the long steps to the foyer. My wrist ached from his tight grip.

"Please stop, Boaz. I don't want to do this!"

He didn't slow down. "Look outside, Eve. The sun's light will weaken me—not much, but enough that I can't fight them all alone.

At least help me to save *your* life."

I tried to resist his grip, but he was too strong. He jerked me through the front doors and flinched when the light from the morning sun touched his skin. He lowered his head and continued to drag me toward a black car parked in the circular driveway.

Boaz opened the passenger door. "Get in."

I hesitated a moment before I slid into the passenger seat. I wanted to leave this place more than anything, but I was terrified to fight those creatures. The only way I could do it was if I used magic.

Boaz rounded the car and jumped in the driver's seat.

"I can't do this, Boaz."

"Do what?" he said, bringing the car to life.

"Use magic. I won't do it." I didn't want to smell that horrible smell again or watch the world go dark, even though by now it had mostly returned to normal.

"You'd rather they kill you? Kill *us*?"

I glanced around frantically. "Can't we go another way, by horse maybe? We could go around them."

Boaz clenched his teeth. "It doesn't matter where we go. They will find you. You must fight them now. They must see your power."

Tears sprung to my eyes. My chest tightened, and my breathing went sharp. "I can't do it!"

Without warning, Boaz grabbed me behind the neck and pulled me toward him. His lips crushed mine, and his tongue forced open my mouth. An uncontrollable rage swelled inside me until all I could do was force the power outward. The windows of the car shattered into a thousand pieces.

Boaz released me. "There. That's more like it."

Then he stepped on the accelerator, propelling the car forward.

7

I gripped the side of the door, knuckles white, and struggled to breathe. The world had darkened again, and a bitter, rotten smell stung the inside of my nose. A dark magical power, more than I could contain, bled from me as an invisible force, turning the trees black the moment my gaze touched them. I closed my eyes and took a few deep breaths, trying to go back to an emotionless state. Some of the anger left but not much.

Air blew in from the glassless window, whipping the hair around my face. I opened my eyes. Boaz was looking straight ahead with grim determination, yet he was smiling as if he knew something I didn't.

Boaz careened the next corner, the back wheels of the car skidding out of control. He quickly turned the steering wheel the opposite direction, forcing the car back on the road.

"They're up ahead," I said, sensing the presence of many Diablos.

"I will try to get through them, but if they attack us, you must fight to kill."

My stomach sunk to a place it wasn't meant to be, and it was all I could do to keep from vomiting. "I can't kill."

"This is to save your life! These demons will not take pity on you. Kill or be killed."

Fear replaced my anger, and I half-considered jumping from the speeding car to run away, all the while knowing I would only make it so far before the Diablos caught up to me.

"Hold on!" Boaz said.

Up ahead, the Diablos blocked the road. Most of them

appeared corpse-like, but a few still looked human. They had hair, patchy as it was, and a touch of bronze to their skin. For the first time, they all stood eerily still with backs hunched over, hands clenched tight.

Boaz pressed on the accelerator, attempting to push through their blockade. The first few we hit bounced off the car with a sickening thud, but then we crashed into one that didn't budge. The back end of the car reared off the ground, throwing my head forward. Before I could react, Boaz was out the door, fighting the nearest Diablos. I fumbled with the door, my fingers searching for the lock. My only thought was to keep them out, and me safely inside.

To my left, Boaz attempted to lure the monsters into the shade, but they seemed to deliberately keep him in the open, beneath the glare of the sun.

I should help him. After all, he had helped save me.

Dark magic was still inside me, humming just beneath the surface of my skin, and I was pretty sure it was powerful enough to make a significant dent in the Diablo's numbers, at least enough for us to get away. But I was afraid if I used my magic, I wouldn't be able to stop. I'd seen firsthand how addictive it could be, my parents a perfect example.

Metal grinded behind me. I swiveled in my seat in time to see an emaciated Diablo tearing the metal frame off the back of the vehicle. The moment the back end was gone, he climbed inside, the joints of his elbows bending unnaturally.

This time, I desperately tried to unlock the door, but my hands were slippery with perspiration. I was breathing fast and hard—at least I think it was me. Just before the long, jagged-nailed fingers of the Diablo clamped down on the back of my head, I burst free from the car, gasping for air. I barely managed to get upright before I was surrounded by several of the gray demons, their long and thin arms stretched toward me.

"Kill them!" Boaz shouted.

I shook my head, tears stinging my eyes, and backed against the car. This couldn't be happening!

One of the Diablos lunged for me, and I raised my arm in defense. My fear, laced with anger, was so great that the power inside me broke free and struck the Diablo. It flew back several feet as if shocked with electricity. I stared at my hands, surprised and frightened by my own strength.

Just then, my head was jerked back and smashed into the top of the door. The Diablo who had crawled inside the car had taken hold of my hair through the broken window. Off balance, I fell to the ground.

"Eve," Boaz yelled. "Get up!"

Before I could, a child-sized Diablo scurried toward me and crawled up my legs. I struggled hard and tried to kick it off, but it was as if the demon had suction cups. Screaming, I swatted at it, but it continued upward until it reached my chest, where it decided to sit and watch me with wide eyes almost as if it didn't know what to do next.

"Kill it," Boaz shouted. He was at the front of the car, trying to make his way toward me, but there were too many Diablos blocking his path. He took hold of a tall one's arm and tossed him into several others, knocking them down.

From behind me, a heavy-set Diablo with scraggly black hair crept toward my head. I tried to dodge him, but the child-monster was still sitting on my chest and was immoveable. I hit at it and screamed until a cold finger belonging to scraggly-head was shoved down my throat, making me gag. It was more than I could take.

Power, dark and cruel, surged to my eyes, and the moment I met the gaze of the Diablo, whose finger I currently held between my teeth, it's body withered into itself until all that remained was a pile of snake-like skin. I turned my attention to the demon on my chest. With the same venomous look, I shocked it off me.

I scrambled to my feet, greeted by a new, darker world, only to be surrounded again. I glanced at Boaz in time to witness him snapping the necks of two of them. His momentum spurred me on. With a flick of my wrist, I removed the head of the fattest one in the group. It dropped to the ground like a fallen coconut. I quickly did the same to many of the others. Whatever way I imagined their death, my magic made it happen.

The remaining Diablos hesitated before coming near me again. Their bodies twitched and jerked, and they looked to one another as if waiting for a command.

But I didn't wait.

Anger and fear, mixed with adrenaline, forced me onward until I could no longer control myself. One after another, I crushed their bodies, turning them to ash and smoke and filling the air with smells of ammonia and mold. Or maybe it was my dark magic that was causing the horrid smell.

I would've killed more, but I froze when a chill raced up my spine. I had felt this sensation many times before under the accusing eyes of Erik and Sable. I spun around, searching for them in the woods. Boaz, who had managed to destroy the Diablos around him, stood erect, watching me keenly. I wanted to cast him an angry look but wanted to find Erik and Sable more.

Where are they?

Everything felt wrong about what just happened. Boaz. My parents. But most of all, me. Never in my life had I used such power. If my body wasn't still humming with magic, I would've collapsed to the ground, disgusted by what I had just done.

Unable to locate my parents, I returned to the car without saying a word to Boaz. I needed time to think. The few remaining Diablos slowly moved back into the forest, no longer interested in me.

Boaz slid into the driver's seat and wrapped his hands around the leather steering wheel. "You did well."

"Can we just go?" The last thing I wanted was to talk about what had just happened. As it was, I was having a hard enough time calming down. My entire body stung as if a thousand needles pricked my skin, and I was afraid one wrong word would send me out of control again. Boaz seemed to sense my predicament and kept his mouth shut.

We drove for several hours through upper New York's rural country. At one point, I thought we may have crossed over into Vermont, but I'd seen no signs to confirm my suspicions.

The clouds above had grown thick until a light snowfall burst from their seams. Cold air blew through the broken windows, freezing my skin, but I refused to complain. Boaz must have seen the goose bumps on my arms, because he reached behind his seat and grabbed a jacket. When I wouldn't accept it, he dropped it into my lap without a word.

By the time we reached our destination, which ended in the White Mountains in northern New Hampshire, I'd managed to rid myself of a lot of the anger. Mostly confusion and doubt remained.

Boaz's home wasn't as large as the one I'd come from but was still huge and set far away from any neighbors, a common thing in the supernatural world. The outside was all gray stone with tall wooden beams in the front, matching two massive cedar front doors. Hunwald was perched out front looking more like a statue than a wolf.

I took a step toward it and then stopped.

What am I doing?

This wasn't my plan. When Boaz's hand touched the small of my back, I jumped.

"Your new home awaits," he said.

"This isn't my home."

"Would you like me to take you back then?"

"Of course not."

"Then where will you go?"

I looked past his shoulder. I had no one else to turn to. No money. No friends.

"Stay with me for a few days," he said. "Give yourself some time to rest and to come up with a plan. Then I'll take you wherever you want to go. It's your choice."

I inhaled a big breath. A few days should be plenty. In fact, it was more time than I should spend with Boaz who seemed to share my parent's obsessiveness for power.

"Why were my parents in the forest?" I asked suddenly.

His expression went still. "What do you mean?"

"Earlier in the woods, with the Diablos. They were there watching us."

"That's impossible, love. They left hours before we did."

"First of all, stop calling me *love*. Second, they were there. I felt them."

"*Eve*," he emphasized. "A lot was happening. I'm sure you confused it with something else."

"I don't think so," I said, but I frowned.

A lot had happened, and fast, too. Maybe something else had been in the forest with us. Another witch, perhaps? All I knew for sure was that I still felt horrible with hate only a thought away. It had left patches of darkness in my mind like the hot embers of an extinguished fire.

"You've had a terrible ordeal," Boaz said, crossing the threshold into his home. "Let's get you something to eat and a place to rest."

I hesitated briefly before following. Only a couple of days. It would all be over before I knew it.

8

Boaz opened the doors into a grand foyer that was as wide as it was tall. I stepped inside, and when a gust of cool air rushed by me, I rubbed my arms with my hands.

"Wait here," Boaz said before disappearing behind a door to his left. I didn't have a chance to stop him.

The inside of the home was a sharp contrast from the décor of my parent's. It was more rustic and … cruel. It was the first word that popped into my head, but I couldn't pinpoint why. It's not as though the oil paintings of various night landscapes hanging on the walls screamed 'I-want-to-hurt-you'; in fact, they were quite beautiful on their own, but combined with the rest of the home's decorations, including a silver spiked chandelier just above my head, I didn't feel safe.

In less than a minute, Boaz returned followed by a thin woman with graying hair. Her black dress made her complexion appear paler than she really was. When my eyes met hers, she quickly looked down and did not look at me again.

"Eve, this is Mariel. She will be your personal servant while you are here and will get you whatever you need, whenever you want it."

Mariel nodded vigorously.

"No, really," I said. "I can take care of myself." Poor Mariel looked as if one more task might make her collapse.

"I wasn't asking."

Before I could argue, Boaz was across the wooden-floored foyer with his hand on another doorknob. "I will return soon. Mariel, feed her whatever she desires."

She jerked at the sound of her name, and then Boaz was gone.

I waited for her to say something, but she continued to stare at the ground. Her right hand was shaking. "Don't worry about dinner. I'm really not hungry. Could you just show me to my room, please?"

"Boaz said to feed you," she murmured.

"I know what he said, but I'm not hungry. It's been a long day, and I just want to lie down." My tone was sharper than I intended, probably a side-affect from using magic.

Mariel wrung her hands together and bit her lip.

I placed my hand on her shoulder but removed it when she flinched. "It will be all right. I will tell Boaz I didn't need you. Really, don't worry. But I would love your help tomorrow, if that's all right with you?"

For the first time, she looked at me, her gray eyes vibrating within her sockets. I tried not to stare, but the constant shifting of her beady eyes was something I had never seen before.

Mariel nodded slightly. "Right this way."

I waited a second before following after her. Maybe she was overworked. Having servants wasn't common, but for families high up in the supernatural world, it was expected. And many times, as I had seen with my parents, those servants weren't always treated the best. If this was the case with Mariel, then I needed to get out of here as soon as possible. I didn't want to substitute one bad for another.

Upstairs, more paintings of night landscapes hung on the walls. Some were cities lit up by the moon, others were forests painted in the night sky, and a few were black and white photographs. There weren't any day scenes and not a single one was of a person. This unsettled me, but I still wasn't sure why.

Mariel stopped in front of a wooden door at the end of the hall. She hesitated before opening it, revealing a room slightly smaller than mine at home, but decorated much nicer. The one item I focused on the most was a built-in bookshelf that took up most of one wall. It must've held hundreds of books.

I turned to comment on how nice this was to Mariel, but she

had already slipped out the door. I sighed and surprised myself by wishing Boaz was here. At least he was someone to talk to. I flopped to the bed, groaning and tightening my jaw. He had made me use magic, more than I ever had before. *It was to save your life*, I reminded myself. Was that so bad?

Turning my head on the pillow, I noticed a door on the other side of the bookcase. Because of the bookcase's immense size, it would've been hidden from me as I walked into the room, but from the bed's angle, I couldn't miss it. I stood up to investigate.

Inside was a closet, more like a room with how big it was, filled with some of the nicest clothing I'd ever seen. I walked among them, my fingers trailing their soft fabrics. At the back of the room, an open doorway led to a marbled bathroom. In the center, four black columns surrounded a massive tub.

I walked over and turned it on; water shot out of a gold, snake-shaped faucet. While the tub filled, I returned to the closet to admire a row of designer dresses. I couldn't help but wonder who they were for. Boaz probably had one, if not several girlfriends, and most likely the dresses were for them. I grimaced, thinking of the kind of women Boaz associated with. They were probably women just like my mother—cold and calculated.

A red dress with a line of diamonds around the waist caught my eye. I bravely pulled it off the rod and held it against my body. It looked like it would just barely fit. The material felt like silk but much softer, almost like cashmere. I smiled and returned it. After my bath, I would try it on—just for a minute.

The warm water, the clothing, and a room full of books were a welcome distraction from the fact my parents had tried to kill me. But I had survived, and now I was free from their wrath. I sunk farther into the bathtub until my head was covered by water. Soon I would be starting a new life all on my own. I surfaced and smoothed back my wet hair with a smile on my face.

I could've stayed in the tub all night if it hadn't been for the red dress, which lured me out prematurely. I dried off completely, including my hair, before I slipped it over my head. Its soft material was like warm breath all over my skin. I twirled into the bedroom and stopped in front of a mirror, gasping in surprise. I looked regal and confident, two things I'd never felt before.

Is this what freedom felt like?

A knock at the door had me frantically glancing around, trying to decide if I had time to change. "One minute!"

I snatched the bathrobe from off the bed and was about to pull it on when the door opened. Boaz stepped into the room. He had showered and changed his clothes into dark pants and a gray V-necked sweater.

I pressed the robe against me, trying to hide the red gown. "I said give me a minute."

"My mistake, I thought you said 'Come in'."

"Sure you did." I took a tentative step back.

His eyes narrowed. "What are you hiding?"

Busted. I sighed and dropped the bathrobe. "I'm sorry, but I just wanted to try it on. It's so beautiful."

Boaz eyes widened, and his eyebrows lifted. "It's not the dress that's beautiful. It's you. The dress only compliments what you already have."

"Regardless," I said, turning toward the bathroom. "It's not mine. I shouldn't have tried it on."

Boaz frowned. "Of course it's yours. All of this is: the room, the clothing, and most importantly …" He took my hand before I could stop him and pulled me toward a dresser. "These are yours."

Boaz pulled open the first drawer. Lying on black velvet were all kinds of jeweled necklaces. Diamonds, rubies, emeralds, and sapphires twinkled in the light.

I shook my head. "I don't understand."

Boaz closed the drawer and opened another one. It was filled with gold and silver rings, all of which were adorned with the same exotic jewels. "These belong to you. I bought them to show my devotion."

Boaz moved to open a third drawer, but I stopped him. "I don't want all of this, Boaz. It's too much."

He laced his fingers through mine. "It's not enough. You deserve more."

"I'm sorry, but I can't accept them." I let go of his hand and stepped away.

The corners of his mouth turned up, and he said, "Then earn it."

"What?"

"Let me teach you to use your powers."

My shoulders sagged. I'd let my guard down. Boaz was just like my parents and wouldn't quit until magic was a part of me. "I know how, but I don't want to. Don't you understand?"

"But this is what I want in return for all that I give you. I want to help you become the greatest witch the world has ever seen."

"Why does it matter?"

"Because I can't stand to see your potential wasted. You're like a thoroughbred stallion that's never ran a race. I must know what you're capable of."

"I'm not a dog trying to learn a trick." I moved to the bed and sat down, exhausted. It hurt to even think.

"Learn from me, Eve. I beg you."

I shook my head. "I'm sorry, I can't. Anything but that."

"Now it's my turn to ask—why?"

"I don't like the way it makes me feel or what it does to the world around me. Everything goes dark."

Boaz knelt in front of me on one knee. "Did you ever consider that the world might naturally *be* dark?"

"Then why don't I see darkness now, when I'm not using magic?"

He pursed his lips and then said, "How about if I help you to control magic so you can do small things like controlling fire, moving objects, and growing flowers? You would like that, wouldn't you?"

"Don't patronize me."

"I'm not, love. Just learn a few things that will protect you and others if need be. It won't change the world around you, I promise. Besides, you've already used your abilities, so what does it matter?"

Crap. He was right. Or maybe I was just tired. "I don't know."

"We'll start out slow. If you feel it's too much, then we'll stop."

It sounded harmless enough. Before vowing not to use magic, I would sometimes use it. It still had the same bad side effects, but I managed to keep it under control then. Why couldn't I do it again, especially with the help of someone? Someone who wouldn't force me to use it.

"Fine, but you must promise to stop when I say."

"Deal." Boaz held out his hand for me to shake.

I moved to accept it, but stopped. Something inside whispered that I was making a pact with the devil. I searched his eyes, but they revealed nothing.

He sensed my reluctance. "I *promise*, love, everything will be fine."

I reached out, but when my fingers touched his open palm, dark images flashed through my mind like a lightning storm. They were of torn bodies, decayed flesh—shocking violent visions beyond anything I could ever imagine. Recoiling in fear, I tore my hand away and scrambled back to the bed, no longer caring about hurting the dress.

"What is it?" Boaz's eyebrows raised in what looked like genuine concern.

He took a step toward me, but his movements only made me

scurry farther away until my back hit the thick headboard.

"Eve, please. Tell me what's wrong."

I couldn't answer as I was holding my breath, hoping it would keep me from screaming.

"I'm afraid I've been inconsiderate," he said. "You've had a rough day, and here I am pestering you. I apologize if it seemed like I was rushing you to use magic. We'll take it at your pace, all right?"

I nodded weakly, finally taking in some air. The graphic images slowly faded. Looking at Boaz now, at his kind expression, I wondered if all the recent events had finally taken their toll. I relaxed and forced a smile. "You don't need to apologize. It's just been a long day."

Boaz moved to be near me at the front of the bed. He reached out and smoothed my tussled hair away from my face. This time when he touched me, I saw nothing.

"Get some rest and sleep in if you would like. In my home, you can do as you please," he said.

"Why are you being so kind?"

Boaz stopped caressing my hair and let his hand drop to my bare shoulder. His fingers gently traced the length of my arm. His eyes met mine, and they burned with an intensity that made me stop breathing again. He didn't answer. He didn't need to. His eyes said it all, yet I struggled to understand.

My lips parted, and my body tingled. I breathed in air that suddenly felt electric. An indescribable pleasure coursed through my body. Boaz's eyes glazed over as he, too, seemed to be experiencing the same exhilarating high.

He inhaled deeply. "Do you feel the power between us? Isn't it amazing?"

I could feel it. My whole body felt light, almost as if any moment I would float away. Without warning, Boaz let go of my hand; the connection dropped. I tried to hide my frustration, but Boaz grinned.

"That's just a taste of what you are going to experience with me, love."

He turned and left the room.

9

The next day, I didn't sleep in as Boaz had suggested. I was too excited to explore the home and the grounds beyond. It felt strange to be in a place where I had no restrictions. I dressed quickly in the simplest clothes I could find from the dresser drawers: a pair of jeans and a black silky shirt.

I left the bedroom and headed down the long hallway toward the stairs, stopping to peek at every room along the way. They were all similar to mine: ornate wooden furniture, richly colored walls, crown molding, and chandeliers except for one room at the end of the hallway. It was a library filled with books. I slipped in and scanned the shelves, reading the titles.

"Would you care for some breakfast?"

I jumped. Mariel stood in the doorway looking as worn out as she had the night before.

"You startled me, Mariel."

"I apologize." She bowed her head.

"It's all right. I would love some breakfast. Can I help you in the kitchen?"

Mariel's head snapped up at my suggestion. "No Miss, that wouldn't be proper. I will prepare whatever you like."

"All right then. I will have eggs and toast, if that wouldn't be too much of a burden."

"Not at all," she said and turned to leave.

"Mariel, is Boaz here?" I tried to sound casual, but even I could hear the anticipation in my voice.

"He will appear when he's ready, Miss," Mariel said, her voice hard and back still turned to me.

Ooookay, I mouthed as I continued out of the room. Our short conversation reminded me I didn't want to be in this world with all of its formalities and rules. I wanted to be normal. No special abilities, no wealth, no expectations. With Boaz, that could never happen.

I shook my head and returned to the books, stopping only when I found one titled "Tender is the Night". I removed it from the shelf and headed downstairs to find the dining room. The downstairs was even larger than the upstairs and took me going through several rooms, including discovering a locked door, before I finally found Mariel.

"Mariel, what's behind the locked door in the west wing?" I asked when I entered the dining room off of the kitchen.

Mariel placed eggs and toast in front of me. "That is the master's area. We are forbidden to go there."

Master? Odd title, even for our kind. I took a bite. "Who cleans it then?"

Mariel shrugged and left the room.

I ate by myself. Other than Mariel, I'd come across two other servants who were cleaning rooms downstairs. Neither of the younger girls had spoken to me even after I had said hello. To anyone else, this might've been upsetting, but I was used to it.

When I finished eating, I headed straight for the back door, but took one step outside and then turned back to retrieve a coat. Dark-edged clouds had congregated as if to discuss their desire to snow.

With my long wool coat wrapped tightly around me, I roamed the gardens, taking in the smell of roses that stubbornly clung to the air. A light mist blanketed the ground; it seemed to be halting nature's natural death process. Plants were still green and flowers in bloom. I regretted leaving my hair down as the wind whipped it back and forth, and I constantly had to wipe the blowing strands away from my face. But when I reached the edge of the forest, the wind died down, and my hair returned to its rightful place.

The forest, not far from the home, had also been meticulously maintained. There were no fallen branches or overgrown bushes, allowing me to move in and out of the trees with ease, but after a short time, the temperature dropped even further, forcing me to turn back. I was about to cross to the paved path leading to the house when I noticed Boaz riding on a huge black stallion with Hunwald trailing behind. My heart quickened.

Boaz attempted to stop the horse directly in front of me, but with little success. The animal stomped and snorted as if it had never been ridden before. Boaz was struggling to keep it still.

"Come with me. I want to show you something," he said.

"Good morning to you, too."

Boaz grinned and pulled on the reins, forcing the horse to face me. The black stallion reared up. "A little help here?"

I laughed. "What do you expect me to do?"

"Surely your parents taught you a calming spell of some kind. It should be an easy task for you to perform on an animal." The horse reared up again, nearly throwing him off.

I did remember Sable saying something about how to calm an angry animal—or had it been a person? Regardless, I didn't want to start using magic so soon.

"Please, love. I'm dying here," Boaz said while the horse repeatedly turned its head to nip at his thigh.

Boaz looked so helpless I just couldn't say no. One little spell wouldn't hurt, right?

"Very well, but I'm doing it for the horse's sake," I said. "He looks extremely uncomfortable."

"*He* looks uncomfortable?"

My smile widened, and I closed my eyes. After a deep breath, I tried to think of something I hated as that was the only way I knew to call upon my abilities. Immediately, an image of a black widow spider appeared. Erik had once used the spiders on me when I was twelve. I'd remained as still as possible while they climbed up my legs, but one of them still bit me. Erik finally removed them when I'd passed out from the poison, making me incapable of using magic even if I'd wanted to. That's when my hatred for spiders had first begun. I used that hate now to do as Boaz asked.

Like always, the negative emotion made using my abilities possible. My feet tingled as if they were asleep and, slowly, I let the energy crawl up my legs, careful to keep it under control. I approached the excited horse and placed my hand upon its neck. In my mind, over the image of crawling black spiders, I pictured an open pasture full of white daisies. At the far end of the field, a herd of wild horses ran free. *Peace*, I thought, and transferred the calming image to the horse. Beneath my hand, the bulging neck muscles of the stallion relaxed. The horse stomped a few times before it finally lowered its head. Its eyes glazed over, and it stilled.

Once again, the use of magic gave me an incredible feeling of power. It made me lightheaded but in an enjoyable way. I almost didn't want to let go of the hate that allowed the power to remain, but the horrible smell it produced forced me to push away the images of the black widows. I didn't think I would ever get used to the smell.

"Thank you, love, much better," Boaz said. "Now that I don't have a horse trying to kill me, I can be more polite. Have you enjoyed your morning?"

"It's been wonderful. You have an amazing home and grounds to match. I could spend days exploring."

"I'm glad you find it satisfactory. If you didn't, I would have to change it all."

I laughed. "You would do that for me?"

"In a heartbeat."

When I realized he was serious, I said, "Boaz, this is all fabulous"—I gestured around with my hand—"and so much like a beautiful fairytale, but I must confess, it's not what I want."

"And what do you want?"

I glanced past him. In the distance, the morning sun crested the tops of the trees, bathing them in a warm glow. "To be free from our world. To live among the humans as one of them." I paused. "And I want answers. I have so many questions about myself, my parents, and even you."

"I will answer what I can. But first, come with me. I want to show you something." He offered his hand.

I glanced at his open palm, wondering if the creased lines could tell me something about his past.

"Don't you trust me?" he asked.

I met his gaze high up on the horse. "No, I don't."

"If I wanted to hurt you, than I wouldn't have saved you. Now please, let's go before it begins to snow."

He had a point. Despite my conflicting feelings toward him, he had been nothing but kind to me. I lifted my hand. Boaz took hold of it and effortlessly lifted me onto the back of the horse. I wrapped my arms around his solid torso and hung on tightly. A growing buzzing sensation vibrated my skin in a pleasurable way, much to my dismay. I wondered if Boaz felt it, too, but wasn't about to ask.

Alternating between a fast gallop and a slow walk, we rode the horse for what seemed like a long time over rough terrain through the dark forest. The area was hilly here, and in some spots the horse struggled to maintain its footing on the rocky path. Boaz only stopped when we approached a fast-moving river.

"This place is amazing," I said, slipping off the stallion. Enormous, moss-covered boulders held the river in its place, and in between their deep crevices, colorful flowers grew. The sharp contrast of greens against reds, yellows, and blues was breathtaking. I walked around in awe, careful to avoid the slippery moss.

"I thought you would like it," Boaz said. "I imagined this place to be right out of one of your books."

"Oh no, it's so much better. How do the flowers stay in bloom with such cold weather?"

"It's the mystery of the river."

"It's beautiful."

I moved up the river toward the roaring of a waterfall. The clouds above had dissipated, deciding against snowfall. Their lack of commitment gave the sunlight a chance to dance upon the waters. It was almost hypnotizing the way the light fractured and twinkled, sparking like lit matches.

"Are you coming?" I asked Boaz over my shoulder, unable to contain my excitement.

"I wouldn't miss it for the world." He smiled warmly and climbed after me. He didn't struggle along the boulders as I did. It was as if his feet only skimmed their slippery surface.

When I slipped, Boaz caught me. "Careful, love."

He took my hand and guided me the rest of the way. Once again, my skin tingled at his touch. The sensation spread to the rest of my body, and my smile grew.

After several minutes of walking upriver, we finally reached the waterfall. It must've been at least thirty feet high, and its mist filled the air, dampening my face.

"Do you mind getting wet?" Boaz shouted over the loud downpour.

I glanced down at the swirling, turbulent water below us. "You can't possibly mean—"

"Follow me," he said and half-carried me toward the side of the waterfall.

As we drew closer, I noticed the rock face disappear behind the falls. Boaz walked into the opening, dipping under a spray of water. I stumbled behind him and yelped when the cold water poured onto my head. With my free hand, I smoothed my wet hair away from my face.

Boaz said nothing but continued to pull me forward into what looked like a never-ending cave. The roaring of the water grew more distant the farther we walked. He stopped only when it became too dark to navigate.

"Would you mind providing some light?" he asked. "I forgot how dark it was in here."

I raised an eyebrow. "And how would you suggest I do that?"

"Use your imagination."

"No more magic. I need a break."

"You'll be fine. Using your abilities is like using a muscle: the more you use it, the stronger you become."

"I said no."

"I'm only asking you to use a little—just enough to see in front of us."

"I already helped you out once today, remember?"

"I remember." He cupped my hand with both of his. The power between us jumped, and I sucked in air. "You've been so good to me. If you really don't want to, then I'll understand."

He moved to take his hand away, but I gripped it tight, unable to let go of the high. "I'll do it, but only because you asked nicely." With my free hand, I felt the damp walls around us.

"What are you doing?" Boaz asked.

"We're surrounded by rock."

"Nothing gets by you," he said with a hint of playfulness in his voice.

"What do you have on you?"

Boaz squeezed my hand. "Mmm, I like this game. I'm wearing a rugged brown coat, tight fitting riding pants, and snake-skin boots. Your turn. What are you wearing?"

I stifled a laugh. "Be serious. Do you have anything small I can use, something with glass?"

He let go of my hand and patted his clothing until he found something in his right jacket pocket. "I have a pocket watch. Will it work?"

I took it in my hand and rubbed it. "I think so."

I closed my eyes and began the process all over again, using my animosity for the black widows again. The smell was just as bad, but I ignored it and focused on lighting up the face of the watch. It took only a moment before a brilliant light burst forth, filling the area around us.

"Excellent," he said.

I glanced around. The cavern we stood in was smaller than I expected. Other than a gaping hole in the floor just to my right, the place was bare.

"Is this it?" I asked, slightly let down.

Boaz looked insulted. "I would never waste your time on this. Hold on."

He wrapped his arms around me tightly and, before I could protest, he jumped down the dark hole.

10

I cried out, but my scream was cut short when we landed on a hard surface. "Where are we?"

"It's the only way to get there," he said.

I followed his gaze. Up ahead, light poured into the cave, filling a narrow crevice. I walked toward it, occasionally having to turn my body sideways to fit through the tight gap between the rock walls. I stepped out of the cave and into the light.

At first, I couldn't tell where I was as the sun was directly above me, but when my eyes adjusted, I discovered we were surrounded by rock again, almost as if we were in a wide lava tube, but with the top open. Grass covered the floor, and the same brilliant flowers that were by the river grew in colorful patches. Occasionally, the wall jutted out, giving enough room for more flowers and grass to grow.

"How far down are we?" I wondered aloud.

Boaz took no more than ten steps to the other side to sit in a small sliver of shade. "At least twenty meters," he said and removed his jacket. A tattoo of a snake curled around his forearm.

"How did you find this place?" I asked.

"I accidentally fell in."

"You fell? How did you survive?"

Boaz looked at me, raising one eyebrow.

"Right. Vampire. Sorry. It's easy to forget when I'm with you. Why is that?"

"I want you to think of me as a man."

"But I want to know the real you."

He leaned against the rock wall and lowered into a sitting position. "What exactly would you like to know?"

I sat down opposite of him, remaining in the light. "First,

where do you get your blood?"

"I take it from willing participants."

"Willing?"

"Willing enough. What else?"

I hesitated briefly, wondering if I should press the issue but thought better of it. No matter how Boaz explained it, I would never understand how someone could willingly give blood to a vampire. Instead, I asked another question. "How often do you eat?"

"As often as I'd like, but I could go months without eating if necessary."

"When do you sleep?"

"For the most part, my body no longer requires sleep. It did in the beginning, but for the last several hundred years, I've been able to go without it. Anything else?"

"Yes." I chose my next words carefully. "What do you want with me?"

Boaz tilted his head. "Isn't it obvious?"

"Enlighten me."

"We belong together."

This was not the response I'd been expecting, and I grimaced. I thought only my parents wanted us paired together, and Boaz merely wanted to use me for … what? A temporary girlfriend? Clearly I hadn't thought through his motives, but I would never have expected anything long term.

"Tell me you don't feel it, love," he said. "We were meant for each other. The power between us will not be denied."

"I don't deny there's something between us, but that doesn't make it right."

"I'm not talking about right and wrong," Boaz said coolly. "I'm talking about power."

"Well, I'm talking about right and wrong. And it's wrong."

"Because I am a vampire?"

"Partly, but mostly because you're evil."

He scoffed. "Evil is an opinion. Have I done anything to make you think I'm this way?"

"You kissed me without permission."

"Out of necessity to save *your* life. What else makes us wrong together?"

"Well, there's the fact that you are a vampire, and I am human," I said, not really answering his question.

"That can be fixed."

"For you or for me?"

"For you, of course."

"I have no desire to become a vampire."

"Yet," he added.

"Ever."

Boaz smiled. "How about you just agree to let me show you the world and all it has to offer you. Your parents neglected this great teaching, and maybe if you understand how the world really works, you might come to appreciate the power between us."

"And what would all this involve?" I asked, unable to deny him just yet. He had piqued my curiosity.

"It would involve adventures, traveling to other countries, socializing with humans of all cultures, and learning to do things you never thought possible."

I held back a smile. I had never traveled anywhere in my whole life, had never done anything but attend political parties held at our home. All the pictures I'd seen on television and on the Internet. All the *people*. It would be years, if not decades, before I could afford to do this on my own.

"For how long?" I asked.

"For as long as you want."

I inhaled deeply. "What if I only want to be gone for a week?"

"Then we will have as much fun as possible during that time, and then I will take you to wherever you want to go. I'll even loan you money for your first apartment. Or I can get you a job through one of my many connections. Whatever you want."

"I don't want a relationship with you," I said. "Friendship only."

His lips tightened and then relaxed. "Like I said, whatever you want. Do we have an agreement?"

"Fine, but only because I have nothing better to do." I grinned.

"I'm glad I can cure your boredom."

"We all have our place in life."

***

The following morning I was wakened by a new servant with short brown hair and lively brown eyes. Her features were small and delicate with a turned-up nose. She looked maybe sixteen-years-old.

"Good morning, Miss," she said. "My name is Lisa, and I'll be attending to you from now on."

"Please, call me Eve. Where did Mariel go?" I slid out of bed and pulled on my robe.

"Master felt she'd be better suited serving him elsewhere."

That word again! "Why do you all call him 'Master'? Isn't that a little old fashioned?"

Lisa giggled. "I think so, but it's what he wants."

"Can you not do it around me? It's weird and kind of creepy." I made a mental note to give Boaz a hard time for it later. Even among those in the supernatural world, it was a strange thing to say.

"I would love that," Lisa said, breathing a sigh of relief. She entered my dressing room and turned on the tub.

I followed after her and asked, "How long have you worked for him?"

"Only a few days. My mom thought it would be good for our family. What dress would you like to wear today?" Lisa strolled among the many dresses in open admiration.

"It doesn't matter. You can pick. Why would it be good for

your family?"

She removed a light purple floral dress with spaghetti straps. "Because my family is Fae, and Boaz is as close as you get to royalty around here. My parents think if I show on my resume that I worked for him, I'll have a better chance at getting into Dartmouth."

I smiled, remembering how I had once wanted to go there. All supernatural creatures aimed for Dartmouth College where they could meet others of their kind. The elite school, located in a small town of a remote part of New Hampshire, was the perfect place to go unnoticed and still get a reputable education.

"But they will flip when they find out you're here, too," Lisa continued. "You're family's like the Kardashians of the underworld."

I glanced away embarrassed. If only she knew the truth. There was nothing grand or wonderful about being a Segur.

"Can I ask you a personal question?" Lisa asked.

"Of course."

"Are you engaged to Boaz?"

Heat flooded my face. I didn't think how our arrangement might appear to others. "I'm only here as his guest. My parents want to k—I mean, our house is going through a major renovation," I finished lamely. No one wants to admit that their parents literally want them dead. It's jacked up.

"Oh," she said and reached her hand into the water to check the temperature. "But he is handsome, isn't he?"

"Very."

Lisa stood up. "Master, I mean Boaz, wanted me to inform you to be ready to leave in a few hours. He's taking you to a movie."

"Really? I've never been." I removed my robe and stepped into the deep tub.

Lisa's mouth fell open. "You're joking, right?"

I shook my head. "My parents were very strict."

"Wow. And I thought my parents were bad." Lisa disappeared

into the bedroom but came back moments later. "I'll have breakfast for you when you're ready."

"I can take care of breakfast. I really don't need a servant, Lisa."

"I know, but Boaz insists, and something in his eyes makes me obey." She paused. "Does he ever frighten you?"

"Yes," I admitted. "He frightens me a lot."

***

"What an awesome experience!" I said as we left the theater. The sky had turned dark and the air cold while we were inside. I really did love the movie. It was an epic adventure that covered a voyage to the South Seas. The hero was perfect in every way, from the words he spoke to the way he stood up for injustice. It was as if I'd been watching another world come to life where goodness always prevailed.

"I'm glad you enjoyed it," Boaz said. He guided me through the crowds of people and back toward his car, his hand gripping mine.

I stayed close to him as there were a lot of people exiting the theater at the same time, and it made me nervous. These were the most humans I'd been around in one place. Other than Boaz and me, the only other supernatural creature I had sensed in the theater was a werewolf. We had given each other a knowing look, but said nothing to each other. "I feel stupid saying this, but did you know that was my first movie?"

When the crowd thinned out, Boaz pulled me forward to walk beside him. "I never realized how isolated Erik and Sable kept you. It's a shame how much of life you've missed."

Thinking about this made me both sad and angry. And it all came down to our family's stupid magic. "Do you know why they wanted me to use magic so badly?" I asked suddenly.

Boaz stopped moving, his eyebrows rising. "They never told you?"

I shook my head.

"It's not my place to say, but I think you have a right to know."

Boaz stepped close to me, secretively. "Your ancestors have helped shape the world's largest countries into the powerhouses they are now. In fact, have you heard of Ann Boleyn?"

"Wasn't she one of the wives of King Henry the 8th?"

"Yes. She's also your grandmother many centuries ago. She almost attained absolute power in England, but the German side of your family, the Segurs, secretly put a stop to her before she had the chance to rid England of its King. Your two families have been fighting like that for a very long time, that is, until they decided to breed you. Your birth was a peace treaty between two powerful and very magical families who have been enemies for centuries. They knew combining the genetics from both sides would produce the world's most powerful witch: one who would rise to power to shape the world as they saw fit."

"But I don't care about politics or policy, and I sure as hell don't want to rule anyone. The whole idea is absurd."

I pulled my coat tighter around me to block the cold. Boaz took off his own jacket to drape over my shoulders. My gaze lingered on his snake tattoo just below his short-sleeved shirt. The red ink seemed brighter somehow.

"You still don't get it, love," he said and started walking again. "The potential of your power will put you in whatever position you want to be in."

"Then I choose no position." I looped my arm through his. "Why haven't I ever met my grandparents?"

Boaz shrugged. "Your parents probably wanted to wait until you were ready. The Segurs especially are rather blunt and are often described as cruel."

I couldn't imagine anyone worse than my parents. Hopefully I would never have to meet anyone from the Segur family.

When we reached the car, Boaz reached inside his pocket.

"Oh no," he moaned.

"What is it?"

"My keys. I seem to have misplaced them." He continued to search his pockets.

I glanced inside the car. "They're in the ignition."

Boaz scowled. "I swear when I'm around you, I can't remember a thing. Would you mind opening the door for me?"

"With magic?"

His dark eyes widened. "Oh, right. I'm sorry. I didn't mean to ask you so soon."

I stepped to the car door, seriously considering it. It would be such a simple thing to do. Above me, a heavy darkness had swallowed the night sky; even the stars and moon had been devoured.

"Really, Eve, I mean it. I can just break the window, even though I did just have them replaced thanks to you." He grinned and then lifted his arm to smash the glass, but before he could, I popped open the door with just a thought. I was surprised at how easily the power had come to me; even the awful smell wasn't as bad as I remembered.

"Thank you, but it wasn't necessary," he said.

"It's the least I can do. This was the first time in my life I've actually had some real, normal fun."

Boaz winked before opening my door. "We're just getting started."

11

A few weeks later, over breakfast, Boaz said, "I've invited friends over tonight."

"Really?" I took a sip of milk. I'd barely touched the eggs.

"People I think you will like," he continued. "They are witches like you."

"That will be nice, I think." I scooted the food around on my plate. Even though I knew Boaz didn't eat normal food, it still seemed rude to eat in front of him.

"You've seemed bored the last few days, so I thought you might like some company other than myself."

My eyes widened. "Hardly bored. I've had a great time! I still can't believe some of the things we've done."

And it was true. Boaz had spent most of his time with me, showing me all of the things I'd missed growing up. Like going to the beach. It was night when we went, but I still enjoyed it. We also spent a few days in Rhode Island where we toured several of the mansions in Newport. He'd stayed at a few of them back in the day. It was fun to learn of the different time periods, especially from someone who had actually been there. But the most fun I had was a few days ago when he took me skydiving. I'd never felt more alive.

I didn't mean to stay as long as I had. Every morning I woke with the intention of telling Boaz it was time for me to leave, but then he would surprise me with some new adventure that I couldn't pass up. Maybe it would've been easier to do had I felt any pressure from him, but he continued to be a perfect gentleman. Maybe even *too* good. There was a growing attraction to him I couldn't deny. And it wasn't just physical. It was a feeling of invincibility. That's the only word I could use to describe it.

"I'm glad you like it here," Boaz said. "As horrible as your parents may have been, I was worried you might miss home."

I laughed out loud. "There is nothing I miss about home. And thank you for the break from magic. It's been nice to live as if I'm normal."

"Of course," he said. "All in due time."

***

That night, before his friends arrived, Boaz surprised me with a candlelight dinner on the back patio. The whole area was lit by dozens of candles grouped together on the sides, and some hung in little baskets from the lattice roof. At the center of the dining table, a gas fire pit provided just enough warmth to keep autumn's cool sting at bay. Mozart played from speakers in the corner.

"I hope you like it," Boaz said and handed me a full bouquet of blood-red roses.

Eyes wide and eyebrows lifted, I said, "No one's ever done anything like this for me before."

"I should hope not." He walked to the table and slid out my chair.

"It really is beautiful." I sat in front of a decorated plate brandishing a thick filet mignon, fettuccini Alfredo, and a steamed artichoke with a side of melted garlic butter. As delicious as it looked, I remained still, even after Boaz sat opposite me.

"Is something wrong?" he asked, and I swore anger tinged his voice.

Over his shoulder, my gaze locked with the yellow eyes of Boaz's wolf, Hunwald, who was sitting at the edge of the forest, watching us closely. I glanced away quickly. "No, not at all. It's just—I feel funny eating in front of you."

He tsked me. "Eat. All this was done for your enjoyment."

"But it's hardly necessary."

"But it is. And you should expect it. Don't settle for anything less."

I nodded, but I didn't really understand. I cut the steak and took a quick bite while he watched me intensely.

"Must you do that?" I asked.

"Do what?"

"Watch me while I eat?

He licked his lips. "It's amazing the way your mouth moves."

"And some think it's amazing the way dogs mate, but it doesn't mean you should stare."

Boaz leaned back in his chair. "You surprise me sometimes."

"Not as much as you surprise me." I took another bite.

Boaz's gaze lifted past my shoulder and to the darkness behind me. "We may need to leave soon."

I lowered my fork. "Why?"

"I don't like staying in one place too long. When you've lived as long as I have, you tend to gain enemies."

"Where would you go?" I asked. I nervously tapped my fork against the porcelain plate. This might be the time I split ways with Boaz. This thought created a pain in my gut, and I wasn't sure if it was because I was dreading living on my own or leaving Boaz.

"*We* could go to London, perhaps."

I swallowed hard at his emphasize of the word 'we'. "I didn't know you had another home."

"I have several. It's a necessity." He placed his hand over mine to stop the clanking of the fork.

"Why?"

"You never know when you might need to escape."

I swallowed the lump in my throat. "Do you escape often?"

"Not anymore."

"What changed?"

"You."

My gaze lowered to my lap, and my cheeks burned hot.

And then he said, as if he'd rehearsed it a thousand times, "Why should one escape when they've found true love?"

"That's not it," I blurted. I wasn't sure how I knew this, but I knew he didn't love me, at least not in the way most men love a woman.

"Of course it is."

"No. It's not."

Anger flashed in his eyes but only briefly. "I guess I'll have to *make* you believe me." He stood up. "May I have this dance?"

My heart raced. Why was it always a rollercoaster of emotions with him? I hated him, I loved him. A sigh escaped my lips. I wouldn't reject him.

I removed the napkin from my lap and accepted his cold hand. He pulled me to his chest and wrapped his arm tightly around my waist.

As if on command, the music changed—a dark and exotic tune. Violins hummed to the beat of a bass drum, and the low notes pumped my body as if it were a heartbeat. I felt the vibrations in every part of me, and it ignited my skin with an intense heat. Boaz spun me around, dancing to the throbbing rhythm, round and round, faster and faster.

The candles flickered and burned low, taking light with them. A heavy mist seemed to rise from the ground, almost as if a thousand ghosts. They crowded and swirled around our legs, parting for us only when we danced through.

My eyes never left Boaz's, even when our feet barely lifted off the marble floor. We continued to spin in a whirlwind of darkness and power that seemed to grow stronger the more I stared into his now entirely black eyes. He opened his mouth to give room for growing fangs, and his eyes rolled back. My own body seemed to be experiencing the same climactic sensation, and I moaned in excitement.

The force between us reached an epic high and took on a life of its own. Below us, snakes appeared. They slid and twisted in and out of each other, hissing and spitting almost in time to the music. I should've been scared, but I wasn't. Boaz flashed me a wicked smile.

It was the smile that stopped me.

This is wrong, I told myself, even though I couldn't understand why. I closed my eyes and tried to fight against the dark magic. Finally, I dropped my arms and stepped away. The illusion instantly disappeared, and all was as it was before.

Boaz's black eyes bulged from his sockets, and his upper lip sneered. Frightened, I stepped back and glanced behind me toward the closed glass doors, but when I looked back at Boaz, there was no hint of malice on his face.

Touching his head as if it ached, he said, "That was strange."

"What?"

He collapsed into his chair, breathing heavily. "I've never experienced magic like that before."

I shook my head in disbelief. "You're saying I did that?"

"It sure wasn't me. I'm not that powerful."

"It couldn't have been just me," I whispered.

A loud chime echoed above us.

"My friends are here," Boaz said, and he left me alone outside to go greet them.

The air was cold, but I didn't move closer to the table where I could get warm. There's no way I could've produced something so dark and disgusting with my magic. My parents did those sorts of things, not me. *I was not like them.* I said this over and over in my mind.

Muffled voices echoed from within the house, but as they drew closer, they became clearer.

"If William would learn what a gas pedal was for, we might've arrived only half an hour late instead of a whole hour." The voice was shrill with a hint of playfulness.

I turned around to peer through the glass doors. Coming toward me was a petite woman in a low-cut, tight green dress. She looked a little older than myself. Next to her was a tall, mousy-looking man in a dark blue, tailored suit. The sides of his brown hair held patches of gray. They were both smiling and chatting with Boaz as if they were all close friends. I quickly turned away and took several deep breaths.

The door opened, and Boaz said, "I'd like you both to meet Eve Segur, although she hardly needs an introduction."

I turned around and forced a smile. I hated that everyone knew who I was, yet I knew no one.

"Eve, this is William Mioni and Liane Basset. William lives in Italy, but he is visiting the states for a few months, and Liane's from New York City."

"It's nice to meet you both," I said.

William approached me and placed a light kiss on each cheek. "The pleasure is all mine," he said and stepped back. His short, slicked-back hair looked wet—so much so that I wouldn't have been surprised to see water drip onto his shoulders. His blue eyes lay hidden beneath bushy eyebrows, and his nose looked too large for his narrow face.

"Boaz has told us all about you," Liane said, her eyes flashing to Boaz, just before she embraced me in a quick hug. Her brown hair was shaped into a stylish bob that cradled her delicate facial features. Her unnaturally wide eyes matched the color of her dress—they were her most striking feature.

"Did we interrupt something?" Liane asked, glancing around the candlelit patio.

Boaz turned to me, as though expecting me to answer.

"Not at all," I said. "We were just finishing up."

Liane's gaze lowered to the table. "You say you're finished?"

"Apparently we are," Boaz said.

"Boaz," Liane said, "be a dear and bring in two more chairs. This is much too beautiful not to enjoy, and I see you're being wasteful." She sat down in my chair and eyed the food greedily.

William chuckled. "Really, Liane, you're such a scavenger."

"Waste not, want not," she said, and then plucked the leaf of a cooked artichoke and scraped the meat from it with her teeth.

I liked her instantly.

"So tell me, Eve, what do you like to do?" Liane asked as she drank from my cup.

I joined her at the table and sat on a chair brought in by a servant. Boaz sat next to me. "I love the outdoors. There's something mysterious and beautiful about nature."

"I couldn't agree more," William said.

Liane wrinkled her nose. "Nature is dirty and smelly. Have you smelled New York City lately?"

William coughed. "New York City is hardly nature. Have you ever walked into a forest or climbed a mountain?"

"Now why would I want to do that?" Liane asked. "What else do you like, Eve?"

"I enjoy reading."

Liane took a bite of pasta, the white sauce dripping onto the top of her breast. William rolled his eyes, but Liane wasn't embarrassed in the least. She dabbed at the sauce with a napkin. "Do you like to go to dancing? I know some great clubs in the city."

I shifted in my seat uncomfortably. "I've never been."

"That must change immediately." Liane leaned back in her chair, her lips slightly turned up. "So how was it living with the great Segurs?"

"Torture."

Liane laughed. "Isn't it always? My parents won't let me move until I marry, and as far as I'm concerned, that's not going to happen."

"So you're going to live with your parents forever?" William asked.

"Of course not. *Parents* can't live forever." An uncomfortable silence followed her grin.

Suddenly, Liane jumped as if she'd been shocked. She turned to me. "I just remembered! Did you know we are distant cousins?"

"Really?"

"Our great, great grandmothers were sisters. They were scandalous, mischievous women. In fact, they were once kicked out of an entire city because of their pranks."

William snorted. "A relative of yours causing trouble? I can't believe it."

"I've always wanted a sister," Liane said, ignoring William. "Maybe we could be like our grandmothers and have all kinds of fun."

"I've always wanted a sister, too," I said. *Had I been born to a different family*, I wanted to add. No one else needed to suffer my parents' abuse.

"Then it's settled. We are sisters, you and I." Liane took my hands in hers. "William, could you say a few ceremonious words, binding us as sisters forever?"

"You can't be serious," he said.

"Of course I am. Just a few words. Go on, now."

William glanced over at Boaz for help, but Boaz just smiled and shrugged. William sighed and lifted his arms into the air. "Oh great mother of ... sisterhood. Bind these two women as sisters for all eternity!"

My hand suddenly tingled. I looked down surprised. When I looked up, my eyes met Liane's. She, too, seemed surprised.

"It's done," she said.

"Want to be brothers?" William asked Boaz.

"No."

"Let's play a game." Liane looked to each one of us.

"If it involves a monkey, I'm out." William said, crossing his arms.

I laughed. "Why would a game involve a monkey?"

"Ask Liane."

I turned to Liane, waiting for an explanation, but received none.

Liane said, "Fine, no monkeys. Let's play—Dare the Demon."

"What's that?" I asked, trying not to swallow.

"It's simple really," William told me. "We dare each other to do stupid things. You see, we are the demons."

"Oh."

"It will be fun, don't worry," Liane said. "Who wants to go first?"

"I will," said William. He looked around the room until his eyes settled on Liane. "Since this game was your idea, I dare you first."

"Go right ahead," she said through a mouthful of more food.

"I dare you ..." He tapped his finger on the table and eyed Liane thoughtfully. " ... to take us to your most favorite secret place."

"Now William, I thought you liked innocent games," she teased.

William blushed. "That's not what I meant, and you know it."

"Of course not," she said and laughed. "As if you could ever mean anything like that. Fine. You want to see my secret place?" She closed her eyes and took a deep breath.

I waited anxiously. I was in awe of Liane and her straightforwardness. Her uncouth behavior from the way I was raised was refreshing. I wished I could be just like her.

Without warning, all the candles blew out, plunging us into darkness. Both William and I gasped at the same time. Boaz didn't make a sound, but his cool hand slid across mine. His thumb caressed my palm, sending chills through my whole body. Inwardly, I moaned. I was beginning to enjoy his touch way too much.

Just beyond the patio, high in the sky, a dim light appeared and continued to grow as the walls of the home disappeared behind us. A thick fog rolled in, blanketing the ground that was no longer concrete but now appeared as dirt. Rising from within the fog, differently shaped stones took their places in rows all over what used to be Boaz's back lawn.

"Amazing," William whispered. "It's a graveyard."

He was right—it was amazing. The light in the sky had formed a full silver moon, and all around us were what looked like endless headstones, mausoleums, and statues.

Liane opened her eyes and stood up suddenly. She tapped me on the shoulder. "You're it!" She turned and scurried away.

William stood up quickly, too; his chair tipped over as he ran in the opposite direction of Liane. I looked over at Boaz who was pulling his hand away from mine.

"Apparently, you're it," he said, and he walked away from me into the maze of statues and graves, gray fog billowing up behind him.

I grinned. I'd never played games like this before, but I was more than ready to start. I called out, "I'll have you all know that I am the queen of sneakiness!"

A giggle erupted to my left. I headed in the direction of the laughter, quietly stepping around old headstones and angel-like statues. Out of the corner of my eye, a shadow crossed where I had just walked. Someone was following me.

I continued forward, but when I passed a tall cross-shaped headstone, I stepped behind it and hid. Liane walked right by me unaware of my presence. I reached out and touched her back. "You're it!"

Liane screamed and jumped. "Oh, you little witch!"

When I ran away, she tried to follow me, but I lost her in the fog. I ducked behind a stone mausoleum, smiling big and trying hard not to laugh. Sliding with my back against the wall, I inched forward to peer around the corner. Liane's shadow was on the other side, walking up and down the rows of headstones.

"I can hear your heavy breathing, William," she called.

I was about to cross over behind a statue when arms wrapped around me and pulled me through the open iron doors of the mausoleum. Instinctively, I opened my mouth to scream, but a familiar hand closed over my mouth. Boaz's partially shadowed face smiled at me in the dark.

"Are you having fun?" he whispered.

"Surprisingly, yes. How is she doing this?"

"Magic."

"It's incredible."

"Not really, love. Look around, I mean really look, and you will see this is just a simple illusion."

I reached out to touch a stone coffin lying inside the mausoleum. It felt solid. I pushed harder until the coffin dissipated along with the entire illusion. The lit candles returned, as did our table, which lay a short distance away. Not far on the lawn, William was hunched over in a ball; Liane was almost to him.

"Do you see it?" Boaz breathed near my neck, sending a wave of chills down my body.

"I do, but it doesn't make what she did any less remarkable."

"It's simple magic, just a trick of the mind. You would be able to do so much more with your power."

I sighed, not knowing how to respond. After a few seconds, I said, "I prefer to see the graveyard."

"Then see it."

I closed my eyes, counted to three, and opened them again. We were back in the cramped mausoleum, facing each other. I suddenly became very aware of Boaz's hand on my waist, the slight pressure where his palms pressed. He looked down at my lips and then into my eyes. His own lips parted, and he stepped forward, closing the gap between us. His fingers caressed my cheek, and before I realized what I was doing, I pushed up on my tiptoes and pressed my mouth to his. His lips were soft as they moved against mine, slowly at first, but when my tongue touched his bottom lip, his grip tightened and he pulled my body against his eagerly.

"I've got you," Liane's voice echoed across the way. I heard scuffling, then a loud grunt as if someone had fallen over.

I pulled away from Boaz and looked down, too embarrassed and frightened to see his reaction. The illusion around us had permanently disappeared. Liane and William strolled back to the table.

"You can be such a baby," Liane said.

William dropped into a chair. "I don't like graveyards. They're for the dead, not the living."

"I think they're beautiful," Liane said. "I'll just remember not to invite you next time I go."

I returned to the table. Boaz walked behind me, his gaze somehow warming the bare skin on my back.

"Who would like to dare a demon next?" Liane asked, looking at each of us.

"I would," I said, surprising them all.

"And what Demon would you be daring?" William asked.

I turned to Boaz. "You. Since the day I met you and Hunwald—" I glanced over at Hunwald, who was still sitting at the edge of the forest. "—I've always wanted to know who would win in a race. I dare you to race Hunwald around your property, three laps, following the line of trees over there." I pointed in the distance.

Liane laughed. "I love supernatural races!"

Boaz gave a low whistle. When the wolf jogged over, he said, "What do you say, Hunwald? You think you can beat me in a race?"

Hunwald cocked his head.

Boaz stood up. "I accept your dare."

Liane walked to the edge of the patio, where concrete met grass. "Here is the starting and finish line. You must each pass it three times. The first one to do so wins." She frowned at Hunwald. "Does your dog understand?"

Hunwald growled.

"He's a wolf, not a dog," Boaz told her. "And yes, he understands perfectly."

"This ought to be interesting," William said from behind me.

Boaz and Hunwald both stepped up to the line. They looked at each other, and I swore I saw Hunwald smile.

"On your mark," I said. "Get set, go!"

Hunwald and Boaz took off together, trailing the edge of the forest. We could just barely see them, two shadows that looked more like they were out on a nightly run instead of being in the middle of a race.

Liane frowned as they both ran past us on their first lap. "You run like bunch of old ladies," she called after them.

Boaz looked down at Hunwald, grinned, and then was off. He raced near the line of trees faster than I'd ever seen anyone run, but when he reached his home, he jumped onto the stone exterior and scurried along it like a spider. Hunwald had also picked up speed and was right below him, his powerful hind legs propelling him forward. In a matter of seconds, the two became a blur as they raced around the final lap.

Liane burst out laughing, William snorted, and I just stared in awe. When they both finished the final lap, they stopped abruptly at the edge of the concrete. There was no slowing down or screeching of feet. They simply stopped moving.

"Who won?" Boaz asked, not out of breath in the least. Hunwald, however, let his tongue hang from his mouth and panted heavily.

"Honestly, I'm not sure," I said.

Liane clapped. "Perfect! A kiss for both winners." She bent down and tried to hug Hunwald, but he backed away with a growl.

"Your loss mutt," Liane muttered and straightened. "I guess only Boaz receives a prize."

She placed her hand upon Boaz's chest seductively. As she leaned in to kiss him, Boaz's eyes flashed to mine. Deep down, I wished he wouldn't kiss her back, but I couldn't bring myself to stop them. Instead, I simply watched as Liane closed her eyes and lifted her mouth to his.

Just as their lips were about to touch, Boaz put his hand up, stopping her. "I must politely decline as well."

I secretly let out a sigh of relief.

Liane glanced back at me with a smile and winked.

"Whose turn is it now?" William asked. He was back sitting at the table, straightening the table. The rest of us joined him.

"I'll go next," Liane said. "Eve, you're the demon I dare."

12

My stomach dropped as if I'd just been asked to speak in front of a crowd of people with no preparation. "I'm not—"

"Choose someone else," Boaz said. "Eve's not feeling well tonight."

I looked at Boaz, surprised. I couldn't figure him out. Sometimes he was incredibly thoughtful and other times he was ... something else entirely. I studied his face. His porcelain skin was void of any wrinkles, making it difficult to read his expression, but his eyes. They were filled with so much intensity that I couldn't look away. Maybe it wasn't him but me. Maybe I'd been too hard on him. He'd been so kind to me these last few weeks. And I couldn't forget that he saved my life and took me away from a world that I hated.

"I think Eve looks fine," William said.

"I agree," Liane said. "You don't need to cover for her, Boaz. If she doesn't want to play then simply say so."

"I am just fine," I said, still staring at Boaz, his gaze boring into mine. "And I will play. What are you daring me to do?"

Boaz raised his eyebrows and smiled. I could only imagine how pleased he was with me.

"How about this?" Liane said. "Since it's your first time, you may do whatever you'd like. But it has to amaze us."

"Deal." I closed my eyes and took a deep breath. Under the table, Boaz reached for my hand. I gripped it tightly and concentrated hard, focusing on the power that always lay on the fringes of my mind as if waiting for me like some long, lost friend. I invited it in.

Surprisingly, I didn't have to feel hate to conjure the magic like all the other times. Instead, it was pride that invoked the power within me, for I knew in that moment I was more powerful than anyone on the patio. I could feel it inside me as sure as I could see the silver light of the moon, hanging above us, barely a crescent. With this thought, I had a sudden urge to laugh as I prepared to show them my strength.

The candles blew out when I summoned a cold wind. It swirled all around us, lifting my hair off my warm neck. It felt amazingly good, and I squeezed Boaz's hand; a burning heat passed between us. This time the effects of using magic didn't bother me at all. Even the normally pungent smell wasn't as bad. It reminded me of burnt toast.

I kept my eyes closed and imagined the floor all around us sinking. I saw it in mind, how the earth would open, where the concrete would have to break, and the depths to which I would take it. My destruction became a reality.

I didn't move a muscle, not even to open my eyes when the ground shook making the china on the table clank together. Liane gasped and William swore, but I ignored it all and continued to focus on my desire to impress them, which only strengthened my magic.

In place of the stamped concrete, which was sinking quickly, I summoned water from the earth. It bubbled upwards at an alarming rate from every crack and crevice, filling the spaces. The burning intensity of my power seared my chest, but it was a pleasurable feeling, one that spread throughout my body.

I opened my eyes and took a deep breath when the water became level with the only piece of concrete left—the same space we sat on.

"It's an illusion of water, right?" William asked.

"I don't think so." Boaz let go of my hand and stood up. "Do you smell it?"

They inhaled deeply. I smiled, already knowing the truth.

"I think he's right," Liane said. "It smells like the sea."

William leaned back on his chair. "All part of the illusion."

"There's only one way to find out." Liane kicked his chair backwards.

William's arms flung out as he tried to catch himself. A high-pitched girly scream tore from his lungs when he plunged into the murky water. He surfaced a moment later and doggy paddled in front of us, gasping for air.

"I can't believe it's real," Liane whispered. She bent over and skimmed her fingers across the wet surface.

"A little help here?" William asked, breathing heavy.

Boaz reached out and easily pulled him up.

"I don't know how you did this, but you must teach me," Liane said, grabbing my hands.

I shrugged, as though it was no big deal. "I just think about it, and it happens."

Liane stared at me, mouth open. "It really is true what people say about you."

"What do they say?"

"That you will be an unstoppable witch and will transform this world. You're amazing! I've never seen anything like it."

I blushed, but inwardly grinned.

"Well, I've had enough for one night," William said. "Can you please get rid of this water so we can go home?"

Liane slapped him in the shoulder. "You're such a bore sometimes, do you know that?"

"Yes. Now let's go."

This time I didn't close my eyes. I simply looked at the water and willed it away. A wave of energy passed over me as the magical power left my body. I kept my gaze on the water, making it recede just as fast as it had come. A moment later, after the earth shook, the dirt and concrete moved back into position, fixing itself where needed. Only a few minutes had passed, and the patio looked unscathed, no cracks, not even a drop of water left behind as evidence of my power. Except for William, of course. His clothes were dripping wet, and he was drying his hair with a cloth napkin.

Liane hugged me suddenly. "We've had such a wonderful time. Let's do it again soon." In my ear, she whispered, "He loves you."

I looked at her, surprised. Liane nodded her head as if to say, "It's true."

"Do you have a towel I can take with me?" William asked Boaz.

"Of course." Boaz opened the glass doors. "Come inside."

I followed everyone into the house, my body pulsing with magic's power. I wanted to suggest that we all go do something, dancing maybe, or even hiking. I didn't care that it was night. I *needed* a release.

"Are you sure you guys have to go?" I asked. "Maybe we could play a game? Or go—"

"Sorry, sweetie," Liane said, her eyes flashing to Boaz's. "But we can't. We'll get together soon, though. I promise."

William patted himself with a towel he'd retrieved from the foyer's bathroom. "Next time alert me in advance to any plans of swimming? This suit was expensive."

"I'll pay to have it dry cleaned," Boaz said.

William glared at Liane. "Liane will pay."

She laughed as though that was the most ridiculous thing she'd ever heard and walked out the front door. "See you soon!"

William followed her out, mumbling to himself.

After waving goodbye and closing the door, Boaz turned to me, his body inches from mine. "You didn't have to use magic tonight."

I swallowed. "I know."

"Then why did you?"

"It was fun."

"It was, wasn't it?" He grinned, something alight in his eyes.

I nodded.

His gaze dropped to my lips for the briefest of moments, but enough to make the magic swell within me again, taking my breath away.

"I have somewhere I need to be," he said. "Do you mind if I call it a night too?"

"Of course not," I stuttered, feeling suddenly stupid. Maybe the kiss we'd shared earlier had only been amazing to me. I faked a yawn. "I was going to go to bed anyways."

"Very well then," he said and disappeared behind the door I wasn't allowed behind.

"No, it's not very well," I whispered as I turned to go up the stairs. My whole body was tingling and yet numb at the same time. I glanced down at my feet. They were still there and moving, yet I felt like I was floating.

I spun a few steps before I danced into my bedroom and closed the door behind me, trapping me in a dark room. I reached for the light, but then stopped. My arm lowered to my side. Breathing in deeply, I focused on the darkness, the way it crawled over my skin and the way it breathed on my skin, whispering seducing words I couldn't understand but could feel.

I opened my eyes as realization dawned on me.

Darkness felt good.

13

That night, I lay awake, unable to sleep. Magic's power still pulsed through my body, and it ached for a release, but I fought the urge. I rolled over and faced the window. It must've been at least two in the morning by the way the moon's light crowded into my room.

I thought of the evening I'd shared with Boaz, wishing I could fully enjoy this fairy-tale that was beautiful, yet dark. Like the fair maidens in the stories, I, too, had been whisked away to a far off, mystical place. But whisked off to where? The fairytales spoke of far off places as being full of light, with colorful flowers, talking animals and mystical creatures.

There were beautiful flowers, and Hunwald was strange enough that he probably could talk, and Boaz, he couldn't be more mystical. But my fairytale lacked the light and the constant beauty that should exist, too. Maybe that's why they're called fairytales—because something as beautiful as all that just wasn't possible.

I moved out of bed and welcomed the moonlight by opening the window. The cool wind rushed in and raced around the room, catching and twisting my long gown in its wake. I wrapped my arms around me and closed my eyes. I could still see the faint glow of the moonlight behind my eyelids.

I stayed like this for some time, my front bathed in moonlight, my back immersed in darkness. I only opened my eyes when the faint sound of hooves galloping nearby drew my attention to the window. Not far off, a rider dressed all in black dismounted a horse and walked toward me. My heart skipped a beat.

The rider stopped just below my window and looked up. Boaz's eyes met mine, and I sucked in air when my magic seemed to shock my entire body. I giggled inwardly. This is what I wanted, to feel *this* every second of every day. My desire for dark magic's power snuffed out any thoughts I once had for light and purity. The desire to be different, to be *good*, was now gone. I simply didn't care anymore.

I stepped up to the tall window and looked down briefly before I jumped. I used my powers to cushion the thirty-foot fall, and then walked toward Boaz, my chin up and arms at my side. I didn't care that I wore a revealing black nightgown.

Without saying a word, Boaz held up a dark cloak. I stepped into it. The weight of it seemed to suck the moon's light away from me.

Boaz lifted the hood over my head and stared back and forth into my eyes, as if searching for something. "Come with me?"

I nodded and accepted his outstretched hand without hesitation.

We walked across the cold earth; the heavy mist parted for us as if on command. Boaz's black horse was waiting for us at the edge of the forest like a loyal soldier. He stood erect, eyes forward.

Boaz leapt onto the horse's back and pulled me up easily. My hands slid across his abdomen and locked tightly. Boaz didn't have to kick the horse to get it go forward; it seemed to move on his own as if sensing Boaz's thoughts, even knowing what direction to turn. Boaz gripped the horn with one hand, and his other hand he pressed into mine. A strength, intense and powerful, expanded around us, making my muscles tighten and then release. Every last one of them. I moaned from both pleasure and pain.

I threw my head back when an indescribable feeling of invisibility overwhelmed my entire being. It grew inside me like a noxious weed, snuffing out any gentleness, kindness, good thoughts. I let go of Boaz's waist and stretched out my arms into the night, feeling that at any moment I might be thrown from the horse. I began to chuckle and then laugh. It escaped from deep inside me, from somewhere dark and cold. Boaz didn't join in my laughter, but I knew from our connection that he was as intoxicated as I was.

Boaz continued to ride the horse hard and fast through the

forest, maneuvering the large animal as if it were an extension of him. We rode faster than I thought possible, and I wondered if there was something supernatural about the horse, too, like Hunwald.

While the horse continued to race forward, Boaz, in a move faster than I could see, twisted and turned until he was riding the horse backwards, my legs suddenly wrapped around his waist. He took hold of my shoulders and stared into my eyes, his expression serious. I thought he was going to kiss me, but without warning, he leapt into the air, taking me with him. We seemed to float for a moment before we landed on the ground with me in his arms. I exhaled. The running horse disappeared around a bend and into the darkness.

"Where are we?" I asked. The overgrown woods were thick with vegetation and a thin layer of frost covered the ground.

"Quiet." He placed a finger to my lips. "Follow me." He crept through the woods like a panther, stealthy and agile. I tried to move as gracefully as he, but it was impossible. Thankfully, Boaz said nothing about my noisy footsteps.

"Over here." He motioned to a tall and still leafy bush.

I glanced down to mind my footing, but when I looked up, Boaz was gone. I walked to the shrub. "Boaz?"

A hand shot out from beneath the branches and jerked my ankle. I threw out my arms to catch myself from falling, but came up empty handed. Just as I was about to smack my head against the ground, I was yanked underneath the bush. Boaz caught my head in his hand before it made contract with the earth, his face only inches from mine.

"Oh!" I cried. "We're under a bush."

"It's the only safe place for you to be for what I'm about to show you."

"There's not much room under here, is there?" Turning over was a slow process. Branches poked at me, and the wet ground soaked through my cloak.

"It will be worth it, just wait," Boaz said as if sensing my frustration.

Finally, I maneuvered myself onto my stomach and whispered, "Do vampires usually hide under bushes?"

"No. This is a first." He peered into the darkness, scanning the forest. "He's coming. Any second now."

"I don't see anything," I hissed, craning my neck in each direction.

"You'll smell him before you see him."

Even before the words left his mouth, the pungent smell of decay and feces filled my nostrils. I moved my hand to cover my nose and mouth. The smell grew stronger and a rumbling destroyed the peace of the forest. Something rotten was moving toward us.

I spotted a shadow in the distance, sauntering between two trees. It was enormous. "What is it?"

Boaz didn't answer.

The beast moved closer, grunting as it swatted a large paw against a fallen tree. It shoved its enormous head into a log, splitting it in two. And then I knew.

"A grizzly bear?" It was at least a head taller than me, with shoulders just as wide. "But how? I thought only black bears lived around here."

"How he got here doesn't matter. He goes where he pleases."

The bear rose tall and clawed its massive paws into a tree. Moonlight shined on its back through the cracks of the forest canopy. The tips of its fur were blond, almost silver looking, and for just a moment, I thought it shimmered.

"Look at him, Eve," Boaz said. "Watch how he moves with strength and power, while creatures around him cower in fear. The bear doesn't waste time thinking about others. He cares only for his desires and will stop at nothing to get what he wants. He who can show his might holds the greatest power."

I held my breath, while his words sunk in. The bear dropped to all fours. I was beginning to understand what Boaz had been trying to teach me all along.

"You wanted me to see this," I said aloud, not as a question, but more of a statement.

"Yes. The bear is the king of the forest, invincible."

I turned my head to him. "Not invincible. We could kill it."

A smile played at the corners of his mouth. "We could, couldn't we?"

"Yes. But we won't. He is like us." Before I knew what I was doing, I wriggled free from beneath the bush.

"Eve!" he called in a hushed tone. I heard him scramble after me, but he stayed back. I didn't doubt that he was as anxious as I was to see what the bear would do.

When my footsteps cracked a twig, the grizzly lifted its head and growled low. I closed the distance between us until we were maybe forty feet apart. The bear sniffed the air and snorted in my direction. We watched each other then, a silent assessment of one's capabilities.

I reached out my hand. The motion caused the bear to charge. It stopped only a dozen feet in front of me, lifted onto its hind legs, and let out a monstrous roar that shook me to the core. As if waking from a dream, I quickly realized my dangerous predicament. My body froze, and I stopped breathing, afraid any movement might make him attack.

Boaz's voice appeared in my mind. "Do something! Use your powers!"

"Get out of my head." I pushed the thought back to Boaz and closed my mind. If there hadn't been a bear standing over me with fangs bared, saliva dripping from razor sharp teeth, I might've been surprised that Boaz and I could suddenly communicate telepathically, but under the stressful situation, I could think of nothing else.

The bear crashed down on all four legs. It bounced its upper body up and down, threatening me, but I didn't budge. Adrenaline coursed through my blood, and although I was frightened, I wanted to see what the bear would do next. I wouldn't use magic just yet, even though it was racing through my blood as if searching for a release.

Off to my left, another growl filled the night. This throaty snarl was not as loud as the grizzly's, but was just as menacing. *Hunwald.*

Hunwald moved carefully toward the bear whose attention had now turned to the wolf. Hunwald circled behind the bear, turning it away from me. He continued to growl, and when the grizzly charged him, he darted away but quickly turned back to harass the bear again, nipping at its legs. He continued to this process several times, until the bear was no longer near me. I admit I was disappointed.

Boaz appeared at my side. "Why did you push it so far?"

"I was curious."

"Curious to see how long it would take for a bear to rip your head off?"

I set my jaw, knowing I would've been just fine. After realizing the strength of my power earlier, I knew I didn't have to worry about anyone or anything ever hurting me again.

"I can't afford for you to be careless, Eve."

"What's that supposed to mean?"

His face softened, and he pulled me close. "I couldn't bear it if anything were to happen to you."

I searched his eyes. "You are a mystery, Boaz. One day, I might see the real you."

"You already have, love."

I tilted my head. "I don't think so."

14

Time passed quickly, and I anticipated every day like a child on Christmas Eve. I couldn't get enough of my new life. Boaz showered me with gifts and opened doors to all kinds of new and exciting experiences. He took me to the opera, plays, parties, and political events. If anything of importance was happening, regardless of where, Boaz and I were present.

We traveled all of Europe. I enjoyed learning the many cultures and seeing how the landscape changed, but I especially liked Ireland and its lush green mountains and impressive coastlines. I could've stayed there for weeks, but Boaz was inexplicably anxious to leave.

In addition to traveling, Boaz introduced me to many important people. I was amazed to learn how many of them knew me simply because of my parents. My family name gave me instant respect, especially from other witches.

I grew to love the attention, so much so, that I used my last name as if it were my first. I would say, "I'm Ms. Segur, the daughter of Erik and Sable Segur."

I loved to watch their eyes grow big and listen to the sound of their loud gulp.

Speaking of my parents, I saw them once from a distance at a political convention party. I didn't know if they saw me back, nor did I care. Boaz never spoke of them, and neither did I. They didn't exist in my new world.

What surprised me the most of my newfound life was discovering how many supernaturals held important positions in the governments of almost every country. They used their abilities to pass laws and change their countries into what they desired. The "dependents" (the word I'd given to naive humans) were easily manipulated, making it easy for our kind to take over. After seeing what others like me could do, how they could change the rules people lived by, I, too, was anxious to get into politics.

Every day I used magic a little more than the day before until, before I knew it, I used magic for almost everything. I'd catch myself using it for dumb things, like starting the bath water or combing my hair. At first, it scared me, and I vowed to cut back, but the alluring power proved too great.

The world, once full of light and joy, became dark and loathsome. I no longer took pleasure in simple things like nature or books. For me to experience even short-lived joy, I had to have more: more parties, more jewels, more experiences, and they had to be greater than before, or anger would swell within me and only strong magic could release it.

Boaz was the only thing in my life that brought satisfaction. He was the giver of everything I needed. Our relationship was a violent, passionate one, consumed by one another. But it wasn't just his body I craved—it was the power within him I fed upon. Soon, I came to depend upon him like a flea on a rat, and the dependency quickly turned into what I thought was love, until one day I couldn't imagine my life without him.

***

It was a cold winter evening. We had just returned from New York City, where Boaz had taken me to his most favorite place, the Metropolitan Opera House. I hoped I would enjoy the play, but instead found it dull and lifeless. Even the music left me feeling empty.

Afterwards, we met up with Liane and William again for a late dinner at an upscale restaurant. We were the only supernaturals in the whole restaurant surrounded by clueless humans. If they had any idea of our power, they'd run away in fear. I smiled, liking this thought very much.

"Let's play a game," Liane said after finishing up her lobster tail.

William shook his head. "Not another one of your games."

"You're such a bore, William," she said. "What about you guys?"

I turned to Boaz. He was leaning back in his chair, looking past me as if deep in thought. Lately, he would do that: sit right next to me, yet be a million miles away. It was really starting to annoy me.

"Boaz?" I asked.

His gaze slowly met mine. "Hmmm?"

"We're playing a game. Do you want to play?"

"Not if it involves magic. I don't stand a chance of winning against you three."

"Then you can watch," Liane said. "The rules are simple. All you have to do is prank someone, and it's got to be funny. Nothing as lame as making someone sneeze or something." She looked pointedly at William.

William chuckled, a smile brightening his normally serious expression. "I can handle this. I'll even go first." He looked around the room, his gaze settling at the corner of the room. "See that man over there? The one in the black suit jacket?"

"The cute one with dark hair?" Liane asked.

"I guess," he said. "Watch what he's about to do."

A few seconds later, the man raised his glass of wine and threw it into the face of the woman sitting across from him. The man's eyes widened in horror while the woman shrieked.

I burst into laughter along with Liane. The corner of Boaz's mouth turned up slightly.

"My turn," I said just as the woman with the wine stained dress hurried by me. The man she was with was right behind her, apologizing profusely. I settled my gaze on an approaching waiter whose arm was up holding a full tray of food. Mentally, I pushed a paralyzing thought to the man. Literally. The man no longer believed he could walk. He fell face forward, food from the tray falling across the floor. Part of his cheek landed in a puddle of marinara sauce. I released my mental hold upon his mind, but it still took several seconds for the waiter to gather himself up.

Boaz chuckled at this one, making my heart swell.

"I can do better," Liane said. "Be prepared to crown me queen."

She glanced about the room. I wasn't sure what she was going to do until a large woman sitting three tables over from us rose from her seat unexpectedly. I giggled when she attempted to climb onto the table, knocking over her glass and breaking her plate. The woman she was with attempted to stop her, but the large woman continued upward, awkwardly bending and moving until she was standing shakily upon the table. Two waiters rushed over, asking repeatedly for her to get down.

"It's okay," William said, but he was smiling.

"I'm not finished," Liane replied. She kept her focus on the terrified woman whose eyes were darting about at all the people staring at her. A moment later, the overweight lady took off her light sweater jacket and proceeded to unbutton the top of her blouse.

"Oh no, Liane," William said. "Please don't."

"You are so evil!" I said and tried hard to hide my laughter.

Then the unexpected happened. The table collapsed and the woman fell hard to the floor.

"Time to go," Boaz said. He was up and pulling me with him before I had a chance to set down the glass in my hand. William and Liane followed us out, arm in arm, and laughing hard.

I sipped from my stolen glass, and then lowered it to ask Boaz, "Having a good time?"

"Of course." He smiled. It looked genuine, so I leaned into him and inhaled deeply.

I was glad he wasn't bothered by me and my friend's abilities. Boaz couldn't use magic like we could, being a vampire and all. He knew a few things, but nothing impressive, not real magic. But he made up for this shortcoming in other ways. He was extremely strong, fast as lightning, and I swore he could disappear and reappear at will, but he had yet to admit to it.

"I'm so proud of you, love," he said and wrapped his arm around me.

"For what?"

"For becoming you."

I tiptoed and kissed his mouth briefly. "Thanks to you."

"Hold up, Eve!" Liane called.

I turned around.

"This is where we part," she said, smiling mischievously. "William and I are going back to the hotel. I'll call you soon."

I said goodbye and watched them walk away, thinking how great it was to have good friends. I'd never been able to say that before. And all of this—my friends, my fun, my travels was all because of Boaz.

He squeezed my hand. "Let's go."

I was about to turn back when a tall man beneath a lamppost caught my eye. He wore a long dark coat with a black derby hat. He stared at me beneath thick eyebrows, and his thin lips were as straight as piano wire. Hands stuffed in pocket, he held still while people shuffled by him completely unaware of his powerful presence—the power of which I could feel even though he was standing across the street.

I tugged on Boaz, stopping him from going any further. "Who's that man?"

"Where?"

I pointed across the street. Boaz's hand tightened around mine. "He shouldn't be here. It's too soon."

"Who is he?"

"Your grandfather. Wait here."

My grandfather? I squinted to get a closer look. That was him? He didn't look frightening, but a dark, electric force seemed to pressurize the air around him, similar to what one might feel before a storm's arrival. I shook my head, still unbelieving that the man who had elicited months of silence and hate between my parents was only a stone's throw away.

Boaz was saying something to him while pointing his finger toward me. My grandfather repeatedly shook his head.

I took a deep breath. Time to go see what this was all about. I moved to step across the street, but was interrupted.

"You are to stay with us," said two feminine voices from behind me.

I turned around, surprised that someone had spoken to me like that, and came face to face with identical twins. Their blonde, almost white hair was cut short, framing their pointy chins. They had large noses to match, but nothing was as unnerving as their eyes. Their irises were narrow slits swimming in luminescent sea-green eyes—the exact same color as my own.

"Who are you two?" I asked.

"We are your cousins," they said in unison.

"I'm Helen," the one on the left said.

"And I'm Harriet."

I glanced back at Boaz. "How are we related?"

"Our mother is your father's sister," Harriet answered.

This sparked my interest. "I didn't know my father had a sister."

The twins looked at each other and then back at me. "She is much stronger than your father."

"Awesome," I said and snickered. As if I cared. I hadn't thought about my parents for weeks. "You know, it's great that I have cousins, but I'm sort of busy right now. Let's do this another time."

I turned to leave but found a force blocking my path. Startled, I pressed my palms against the invisible wall. *Magic.*

I swiveled around. Both girls were smiling, their noses pointed downwards, dipping into their wide grins.

"Going somewhere?" Helen asked.

"Trying to get away from us?" Harriet added.

"Um, you guys are creepy. I need to go talk to Boaz."

At the mention of his name, a far off look filled the twin's eyes, and air escaped their lungs in a long drawn-out sigh. The invisible wall weakened, and I quickly moved to take a step forward, but both girls reached at the same time and took hold of my arms.

"You are not to speak to Boaz," Helen said.

"Ever," Harriet added.

"Let go of me, freaks!" I said, struggling against their surprisingly strong grip. I tried pushing them away by using magic, but somehow they managed to block my attack. This frustrated me even more. No one had ever stopped me from using my abilities before.

"You can't use magic against us."

"We're too strong for you."

My gaze went to Boaz. His back was to me as he was still talking to my grandfather. The girls spun me around, away from him.

"What do you want?" I asked.

"To prove to Boaz that we are more powerful than you."

"To get what is rightfully ours."

"You can't be serious." One look at each of their faces told me that they were very serious. "Boaz is a grown man. He can choose whom he wants to be with."

"Boaz will choose who is most powerful," Helen said.

"And it's not you," Harriet added.

"That's ridiculous. Boaz will choose whom he loves."

Both girls laughed; the sounds were ugly and cold, sharing pig-like grunts between the both of them. Without warning, their laughter stopped as they eyed our grandfather. I turned around in time to see him nodding at the girls.

"Time to go, cousin," they said.

"Go? I'm not going anywhere."

They tugged on my arms.

"Boaz!" I called.

Boaz turned around slowly, his expression blank.

"Boaz, help me!"

Still, he did nothing.

One of the twins opened the rear door of a nearby vehicle, while the other one shoved me in, making me fall onto my back. *Why wasn't Boaz doing anything?* Without my legs being visibly touched, they were pushed in and the car door slammed shut, banging my knee. I whirled around and put my hand against the back window. "Boaz!"

He stood next to my grandfather, arms at his sides. The street lamp above cast an eerie light upon him, stretching his shadow beyond what I thought it should be. He stared at me, unblinking, his face no different from a stone statue.

As the car drove off, I startled when it appeared that his shadow detached from his body and followed after me. I must've imagined it, for when I looked back again, only the darkness of the night remained.

15

We were the only people on the road and had been for miles. A forest on each side of us pressed up against the pavement, never giving me a clear view of what lay beyond.

"Where are we going?" I asked.

Neither twin answered.

I sighed. "Come on, girls. We're family. Can't we at least be nice to each other?"

Still they didn't speak.

"Fine," I mumbled. I slumped against the cold leather seat and stared out the window. Occasionally, the vehicle's headlights would flash against a green sign. Soon I realized we were headed to Vermont, to my grandfather's home.

Was that really so hard to say?

I tried to endure the silence by thinking of Boaz. At first, I was angry he hadn't tried to save me, but surely he had a good reason. He'd never let me down before, so why would he start now?

In front of me, the back of the twin's white-haired heads hadn't moved for the last two hours. It really annoyed me, their oddness, almost as if they weren't mentally all there. It was like they each shared half of a brain between them. Despite the silence, I laughed.

Helen and Harriet turned around simultaneously and glared.

I nodded toward the road. "Watch where you're going. I want to make it alive so I can figure out what this is all about. Someone's going to pay."

They turned back around, wordlessly.

Because I hated to be ignored, I decided to goad them, having a pretty good idea what would make them talk.

"You're mother's hardly powerful," I said. "Did you know my

father once crushed a giant tree with a single blast of air? All that remained was a circular wood disk, one inch thick. It was one of the most remarkable things I ever saw."

Helen gripped the steering wheel, but still, neither responded.

I tried again. "Then another time he completely changed his appearance for over three hours while he sat in on a meeting with the governor of New York. The entire time he thought my father was a high-up European diplomat and divulged some very valuable information. It was impressive, for sure."

The hair on both girls' heads ruffled while the temperature in the car seemed to rise. They were close to breaking.

"Most importantly," I continued, "my father married my mother, the most powerful female witch of her time—that is, until they gave birth to me."

Slamming on the brakes, Helen swerved the car to the side of the road and stopped. The twins turned around.

"You are not powerful," they said, each of their half brains working together.

I let my eyes burn bright, power coursing through me like a live wire. "How do you know?"

"Our mother said," Helen said.

"Our grandfather said," Harriet echoed.

"They lied," I snapped back. I clapped my hands together suddenly, and with a simple command from my mind, the windows shattered and blew into the night in tiny shards as small as snowflakes. Then, as if time had stopped, the shards of glass suspended in mid-air, floated for a few seconds, and then returned to the car doors, forming windows once again.

"This is our father's car," Helen said.

"We must not hurt it."

"I will tear this car apart piece by piece, unless you tell me what's going on," I said.

"It is for grandfather to say."

"We are forbidden to speak to you."

I gasped, appalled by their child-like behavior. "How old are you two?"

"Twenty-two," they said together.

So they weren't much older than me. "Then how is it you can't do what you want?"

"We are good daughters," Helen said.

"Better than you," Harriet added.

"So you keep saying. And because you *think* you are better than me, you want Boaz."

The far-off dreamy look returned to their faces.

"If you're so much better than me, why aren't you two with him now?" I asked.

"We haven't proven ourselves yet."

"It isn't the right time."

"And who do you have to prove yourself to?" I asked.

"Grandfather."

I leaned forward. "Then do it. What does this have to do with me?"

"Grandfather will tell you," Helen said. She faced forward and pulled the car onto the road.

"Yes, grandfather will tell you," repeated Harriet. She joined her sister.

Silence returned. I could've pressed the issue, but realized that these two were about as brainless as the humans who allowed themselves to be taken advantage of. They were followers. I closed my eyes and leaned my head against the seat. I focused my anger, which still surged through me. I had a feeling I was going to need all the hate I could muster.

Eventually, a light sleep came, but when the car slowed, I forced my eyelids open. It was still dark. In front of the car, an enormous iron gate opened up. We drove down a long lane until we approached a mansion twice the size of Boaz's. It looked like a castle right out of the Stone Ages, towers and all.

Lampposts lit up a circular driveway, and at its center, two red lights shined up from the ground, lighting two statues of lions fighting each other. I couldn't take my eyes off of it, even after the car stopped. There was power in those two lions, frozen in combat.

"You must get out now, cousin," Helen said.

"Don't try to run," Harriet said.

"Why would I run? Someone will be held responsible for the treatment I've received tonight."

They ignored me and exited the car. I followed behind them up stone steps and in through double wooden doors. I couldn't see much of the inside of the home as all the lights were off, but I could hear our steps echo against stone floors, which told me the entryway must've been enormous.

The twins approached a cupboard along the wall and removed two candles. While holding them, the wicks ignited at the same time.

"Follow us," Helen said.

"Not far," added Harriet.

The twins pushed open a door that led us through a narrow hallway. The light from the candles made shadows twist and turn unnaturally upon the dark paneled walls. Was it a trick of the light or something magical causing the illusion in an attempt to frighten me? I yawned loudly.

At the end of the hall, one of the twins opened a door. I still couldn't tell them apart unless they were standing next to each other. Helen always stood on the right and Harriet on the left.

"This is your room," Helen said.

"It's well-guarded tonight, so it's useless to try and escape," Harriet said.

I stepped into the room and then turned to insult them, but the door had already closed and locked from the outside. I pounded on it with my fists twice, before I stopped. *Get a hold of yourself. You must stay in control.*

I took a deep breath and looked around. The bedroom was bare except for a table and chair in the corner and a nightstand with a lamp on its top next to a single bed. The room had the same wood paneling as in the hallway. There were no pictures or decorations anywhere.

After waiting a few minutes, I tried to open the door by using magic, but as soon as I touched the doorknob, a jolt of electricity shocked my body, sending me to the ground. Angered, I jumped up and rushed the window opposite the door, but again was shocked. The room had been fortified with magic. No wonder there weren't any decorations. The simpler the room, the better guarding spells worked.

The twins were right—I wasn't getting out.

I peered out the window, frustrated. The dark sky glowed as the morning sun began to burn the night away. Surrounding the mansion, a pine forest and jagged mountains jutted sharply from the ground, trapping me as if in a cage. I leaned my forehead against the cool glass. On every exhale, my breath fogged the cold windowpane and then disappeared. What I wouldn't give to be back with Boaz.

Just then, a shadow moved into my view from the left side of the house. It slid across the lawn, a dark mist, until it disappeared into the forest. A ghost perhaps? I'd encountered others while playing with the dead, a game Liane and William had taught me. Ghosts did nothing but tease my curiosity.

A few hours later, after lying in bed, my eyes snapped open to the creak of the bedroom door opening. I quickly sat up. A woman wearing a silk red robe entered the room in a grand gesture, her gown swaying back and forth. She looked eerily similar to me—long blond hair, almond-shaped face, small straight nose, but instead of green eyes, the woman's were an artic blue. They reminded me of Hunwalds. In her hand, she carried a champagne glass filled with a red liquid.

"It's a little early for a drink isn't it?" I asked.

"Not early enough." The woman took a sip as she stared at me coolly. "So you are my brother's daughter."

I stared back, mirroring the woman's venom. "And you must be my father's sister. Funny. I never knew he had a sister."

Her eyebrows rose. "And I never knew he had a witch for a daughter. We assumed you were *average*."

I moved to the edge of the bed. The slit in my dress opened, exposing my naked long legs, which I crossed. "Hardly. Average is what my twin escorts were last night."

The woman's lips tightened, as did the grip on her glass. She opened her mouth as if to argue, but after a deep breath, she said, "We could insult each other all day, and as much fun as that sounds, I have a headache. I'd rather we get this conversation over with as civilly as possible so I can go back to bed."

"You are my aunt, yet I don't even know your name. You have kidnapped me to who knows where, and you expect me to be civil?"

"Very well. If you want me to be formal, then my name is Anne Swithin. I am your brother's older sister, and we live in northern Vermont. Your grandfather's name is Erik Segur the second. His wife's name was Gertrude. She died ten years ago. Now can we have a civil conversation?"

"Why am I here?"

She strolled toward the window. Her long robe stirred the dust in the room, spinning and twirling it in the morning light spilling in from the window. "There is a matter of an inheritance that needs to be resolved."

"An inheritance? What does this have to do with me?"

Anne turned to me. "Absolutely nothing until this year. You were supposed to have been a dud, a boring human with no abilities. At least that's what Erik told us, but according to Boaz, you are quite the little witch."

"Boaz?"

Anne smiled as if she were keeping a great secret. She took a long sip before saying, "Personally, I think my brother knew all along of your talent and waited until the last minute to let our father know." She paused briefly. "His little way of getting back at me."

"My father tried to kill me for believing I was *average*."

Her gaze met mine. "Of course he did. Segurs don't waste time on useless humans. I'm surprised you lived as long as you did."

If I could've used magic in that small room, I would've shown her who was the useless one.

"How long do I have to stay here?" I asked.

"Until dear old daddy decides who is more powerful: my twin daughters or you. All his fortune will then be given to the winner's parents and eventually passed on to their children. Personally, I think it's a waste of time. My girls are more powerful than I could ever have dreamed."

I stood up. "I don't care about any stupid inheritance. Keep it. I want nothing to do with the Segur fortune."

Anne shook her head. "You are such a disappointing child."

I laughed, harder than I expected. "You think I care? Erik was a horrible parent who should never have had a child."

It was Anne's turn to laugh. "This is not about raising children. It's about raising power. And whoever has the most will get the money." She tipped the glass to her lips and swallowed the last of the wine. "I need another drink." She moved toward the door.

"When can I leave this room?"

Anne stopped and looked around as if seeing it for the first time. "Anytime you'd like."

"I can go outside?"

Anne shrugged. "Be my guest. You'll be stopped when you've gone too far." She exited the room, leaving the door open behind her.

I took a step toward it hesitantly. Could I really just leave?

When Anne didn't return, I peered out the door and down the hallway. Voices echoed in the distance. I moved quietly, pressing myself against the wall to avoid squeaky floorboards.

Up ahead, the hall opened into a living area. I stuck my head out. The room was massive with high ceilings. Old-looking wooden beams crossed overhead, and more dark wood trimmed the rest of the room. On the far wall, a huge fireplace was encased in stone, from the floor all the way to the ceiling. Sitting areas were scattered throughout the room, positioned just right for entertaining.

The twins were sitting in the middle of the floor. They sat in the same position opposite each other: crossed legs, elbows on knees, books in hand. They were reading aloud, their voices in perfect unison with each other. By their words, it was some kind of history book.

The foyer we'd come through last night was just past them, but the only way to get there was to go into the open.

So be it. Anne said I could go outside.

"Hello, cousins," I said, moving into the room.

They stopped reading at the exact same moment and looked up at me with blank expressions.

"Don't stop reading on my account. Please, go on. It sounded like a best-seller."

Neither of them said a word. They simply stared as if they'd never seen me before.

I waved my hand. "Hello? Remember me?"

Simultaneously, they returned to their book and began to read again.

"I guess not," I mumbled. I walked toward the exit and, after realizing no one was going to stop me, opened the front door and walked out.

Of course, I should have known it wouldn't be that easy.

16

I walked, half-ran, from the house, afraid to turn around for fear of being stopped. The ground was cold and wet, winter stubbornly hanging on. Luckily, I still had my coat with me. I wrapped it tighter around my chest and kept moving until I reached the shade of the trees.

Once hidden, I let out a breath and smiled. *Freedom.* Now all I had to do was find the road we came in on last night. I hurried, making my way through the forest, but it was difficult with the high heels I was wearing. When did nature become so annoying?

I took a few more steps forward, when all of a sudden, I smashed into something, but there was nothing visible in front of me. Just sort of a pressure, similar to when the twins had created an invisible barrier. With arms outstretched, I touched the see-through wall that blocked my escape. For some time I followed the length of the barrier—it circled through the woods, the house at its center. Now I understood what Anne had meant when she said I would be stopped.

Frustrated, I placed my hands against the invisible wall. My palm hummed from the force of the electric current it contained. It felt strong, but not strong enough. Given enough concentration and time, I could break it.

I closed my eyes and let the familiar dark magic take over. Light dimmed, and the colors in the forest dulled. The smell of the magic filled my nose, but it was no longer repugnant. In fact, I preferred it to any other smell. Why hadn't I used magic growing up? *It was amazing!*

With my hands upon the wall, magic warming my palms, I became aware of a sudden stillness in the forest. Birds no longer chirped, animals no longer scurried, and the wind ceased to blow. I continued to concentrate despite my growing unease. I wasn't alone, and whatever was in the woods with me wasn't human.

119

When the pressure in the air changed, I dropped my hands and turned around. I peered into the trees, squinting, but saw nothing. I waited a moment longer before I returned to the task at hand, but stopped again when something moved out of the corner of my eye.

Floating directly to my left was the black fog I'd seen the night before. It was my height but wide, the length of two of my arms. The mist never kept one shape as it was constantly shifting and moving. But I didn't care about its strange form; it was the dark power emanating from it that fascinated me.

The fog moved toward me, and I felt the shapeless shadow's power grow proportionately stronger the nearer it drew. The thick smoke parted then and circled round me, rising in stature. Ever so slowly, as if not to frighten me, it crept up my body until it had entirely consumed me. I inhaled deeply, enjoying what felt like warm wine going down my throat. It was intoxicating, powerful and … familiar.

"Boaz," I whispered.

Immediately, the black fog retreated and crossed the invisible barrier to the other side. I couldn't help but smile as the smoke took shape into the man I craved. Boaz stood across from me, grinning back.

"How are you doing, love?" he asked.

"Better now that you're here." I smoothed back my tangled hair. "So you can turn into smoke."

"Only when I need to, but if I cross this barrier as myself, those inside the house will be alerted." He looked me up and down and frowned. "You haven't changed your clothes. Are they not taking care of you?"

I laughed. "Is that what you're worried about? I could care less about my clothes. I just want to get out of here."

"Eve, listen to me. You must treat this place as if you are their queen. Do not allow them to treat you any less. Do you understand?"

"Last time I checked, I'm their prisoner. I highly doubt they're going to give me what I want."

"Demand it. You must not appear weak in any way."

"Are you going to help me get out of here or what?"

He glanced away. "I'm sorry, but I can't. You must stay."

"But I want to leave. I'll *demand* it."

"Anything but that," he said. "I'm sorry."

"I refuse to stay here a second longer, and if you won't help me, then I'll do it myself." I raised my hands to do just that.

"Stop! Don't you want to prove to your family, to your parents, that you are more powerful than all of them?"

"I don't care about proving myself. I know what I'm capable of, so what does it matter what they think?"

"Trust me, it matters. Do this for me, Eve." He leaned forward, almost on his tiptoes, as if any moment he might reach across the invisible wall and shake me. "Show them what you can do and don't hold back. They must witness your power."

His passion surprised me. "It means that much to you?"

"It's all I ask."

I lowered my head and sighed. "Fine. I'll do it, but on one condition. When I get out of here, will you tell me why this was all so important?"

"Deal."

"Do you want to know what will be the hardest part of all this?" I asked.

"Tolerating those twin horses?"

I laughed. "That will be difficult, but not as hard as being away from you. What am I going to do for fun?"

"I'm not going anywhere."

"And what exactly am I supposed to do with an intangible ball of smoke?"

"Sorry, love. It's the best I could do under the circumstances. I'll come visit you whenever I can."

"I guess it will have to do." I glanced back through the trees and toward my grandfather's home. "How long do you—"

I turned to Boaz, but he was gone.

***

I waited a little longer before I returned. The twins were sitting outside on the steps, looking much younger than their actual age. They wore identical pink floral dresses and held a sucker in their right hand. Both heads turned as I approached.

"Grandfather's been waiting," Helen said.

"For hours," added Harriet.

"Poor grandfather." I walked past them and through the front door. I headed straight for my room despite hearing my name being called. Inside, I searched the closet but only found a couple of plain dresses. If I was going to be here for a while, there was no way they were going to treat me like my parents had. I was done with that life.

Taking Boaz's advice, I stormed into the living room. My grandfather, sitting in a high-back Queen Anne chair, watched me curiously. Anne stood next to him with another drink in her hand. She still had on the same robe from earlier.

Anne swayed slightly. "We've been waiting for you."

"I need clothes."

"You have some," Anne said, clearly upset she was being ignored.

"I'm not wearing those rags in that hole you expect me to stay in. If I'm going to be here for a while, then I want my own clothes. And speaking of my room, I demand a new one."

My grandfather remained expressionless, but Anne's eyes grew wide and her nostrils flared as she sucked in air. "You will have no such thing!"

My grandfather raised his hand, silencing Anne. "Another room is not necessary. You will not be here long enough to warrant that, but you may have better attire. Anne, fetch her a new and much nicer dress."

Anne looked down at him her mouth open and eyes narrow

slits; her drink spilled over its glass edge. "But father—"

"Do it. Now leave us before you pass out drunk."

Her ivory face turned a deep scarlet but she obeyed.

"Sit down, Eve," he said after Anne left.

"I prefer to stand."

"I said sit," he repeated. A chair from across the room magically slid behind me, knocking against my legs. Startled, I sat down.

He spoke, a loud deep voice: "I appreciate your boldness, but do not forget who you are speaking to. I will not be trifled with."

I clenched my fists and tried hard to keep my voice even. "You take me, unwillingly, from all that I know and then demand my respect?"

"I expect no less from anyone else. Why do you think you should be any different?" He reached inside a drawer and pulled out a pipe.

"I respect those who have earned it."

His stare turned deadly. At the same time, my throat constricted as if I were being choked. I coughed a few times, trying to get air into my lungs.

"Then let me earn it," my grandfather said in a calm voice. He lit his pipe and inhaled deeply. He watched as I struggled to remove the invisible grip from around my neck. Stars burst into my mind in sprays of blues and purples.

"Do you respect me now?" he asked.

I was barely conscience enough to nod my head. The grip from my neck relaxed, and I sucked in as much air as my lungs could handle.

"I'm sure Anne told you why we brought you here," he began.

I nodded again, weakly.

"I need an heir. You were never an option before, but I've been informed otherwise, thanks to Boaz."

"Boaz has nothing to do with this."

"You keep telling yourself that," he said, puffing a wide ring of smoke.

In the corner of the room, a shadow shifted. Boaz or a trick of the light? I continued to stare, but nothing moved again.

"I have staged a simple test for my granddaughters," he said. "Whoever wins, their family will inherit all that I have."

"And when the test is over?"

"You will be free to leave." Smoke spilled from his mouth.

"When do we begin?"

"Tonight."

Good. The sooner the better. Just sitting near the old man unnerved me. No wonder my parents were always at odds after visiting him. It was like being near a hungry tiger with amazing self-control—you could see the aggression in his eyes, but he remained as still as a boulder. I left my grandfather to his pipe and thoughts and found Anne standing just outside of my room with a full glass of wine.

"What did he say?" she asked and wiped at her mouth with the back of her hand.

I walked past her into the room. "He said the twins are going to lose, and I'm going to win."

17

After showering, I returned to my room to find a stylish red dress lying on the bed. It had a blood-red sash around its waist and was made from the same silky material as my other dresses. I quickly pulled it on, feeling somewhat better.

A knock at my door startled me. I said nothing, but moved to the window seat, warm sunlight spilling in through the glass, and sat down to wait for whomever it was to simply come in. They did just that. Helen walked in first followed by Harriet.

"Do you two do everything together?" I asked.

"Two is better than one," Helen said.

"Much better," agreed Harriet. They stood next to each other, shoulders touching.

"Do you two date much?" I asked.

Simultaneously, a smile spread across their faces.

"We have had our fun," Helen said.

"Boaz was wonderful," said Harriet.

I raised my eyebrows. "Really? And what exactly did you do with Boaz?"

They looked at each other conspiratorially. Helen giggled. "Only the birds know."

"And the worms." Harriet giggled harder.

Realizing this was not a conversation I wanted to have, I asked, "Did you two like growing up here?"

"We didn't grow up here."

"Our home was in Burlington."

"Why did you move here?" I asked.

"There was a fire."

"It destroyed everything."

"What caused it?"

Both of them flinched as if someone had just shoved lemons into their mouths.

"Magic," they said together.

"Whose magic?"

"It was an accident," Helen said.

"We were learning," added Harriet.

I stood up, surprised by their confession. "Was anyone hurt?"

Swallowing hard, they said, "Father. He died."

"That's horrible. How old were you?"

"We were young."

"Ten."

"Did you like your father?" I asked. If my father had died, I wouldn't have cared, and I hoped it was the same for the twins.

It took them a moment to answer. "We loved father."

"He was different. Not like them."

I knew exactly *whom* they were talking about. "I'm sorry. That must have been hard."

They said nothing, but I noticed their pupils were moving back and forth, just barely, the same way a pendulum clock swings.

"Listen, cousins," I said, feeling suddenly sympathetic toward them. "This whole inheritance thing is silly, don't you agree?"

"No," they said in unison.

"Are you saying you want to fight?"

"We do what we are told," Helen said.

"We do not have a choice," added Harriet.

I snorted. "Of course you have a choice."

"You do not know grandfather."

"We must obey him."

"You don't have to. All three of us can run away. I can get us out of here, I promise. And once we're free, Boaz will move us somewhere safe."

Their eyebrows drew together, confused. "Boaz will not help."

"This is what he wants."

"What do you mean?" I asked.

Without warning, the lamp on the nightstand crashed to the floor, breaking into several pieces. All three of us turned to it in surprise.

"I wonder how that happened?" I asked.

"We will get the maid to clean it up," said Helen.

"Right away," added Harriet.

They turned to leave.

"Wait!" I cried, but they were already out the door.

I stooped low and picked up a large shard of the broken lamp, frustrated by its suspicious timing. After inspecting it, I walked around the room, searching all the shadows, convinced I'd find Boaz hiding among them. It had to have been him.

When the maid showed up, I gave up and left the room. I wanted to find the twins to finish our earlier conversation and hopefully convince them not to participate in our grandfather's idiotic competition.

Passing by a bedroom window, a red-bricked building some distance from the house caught my eye. It was at least two stories high with no windows. I wondered how it was possible that I hadn't seen it from the woods earlier that morning.

A shadow crossed over behind the building. Maybe it was one of the twins. I escaped out a back door and followed a worn path to the strange building that looked a lot like a factory. When I was within sight of the only door, it opened as if it had been expecting me. Hesitantly, I stepped over the threshold. The door closed behind me, and several lights turned on automatically.

"Hello?" I asked.

Silence.

The room was incredibly long with high ceilings. In the middle was a narrow banquet table that looked as if it could seat at least a hundred people. All along the sides of the walls were hand-carved curio cabinets filled with beautiful, antique-looking china. I would've considered the room quite grand if it would not have been for all the weapons and what looked like torture devices hanging above the shelves. I recognized some of them from my father's collection. The room turned suddenly cold, and visible breath puffed from my mouth.

"You should not be in here," a voice from above said.

I glanced up to a balcony jutting out into the massive room. Two ornate chairs rested upon them as if they were made for a king and queen. In one of them, Anne sat clenching a bottle of wine. She had finally changed her clothing into a tight blue dress.

"What is this room?" I asked. I searched for a way up there but found no stairs.

"It depends on the time of year."

"And what would it be this time of year?" I asked.

"It's our training room. When I was younger, I learned to use magic in something similar."

I moved about the room, examining the different kinds of china and weapons. Many of them were etched in gold and silver and several had jewels adorning their fronts. There seemed to be no difference from the china they ate off and the weapons they killed with. "It's interesting, to say the least."

"It's repulsive," Anne spat.

I looked up, surprised.

"Just look at it all. This room is filled with beautiful and expensive *things*, giving the illusion that greatness happens here. But great things require windows so the world might know of them, but there are no windows. Only dark secrets that remain forever hidden." She took a drink from the bottle; some of it trickled down her chin and onto her dress.

I remained still. Staring. Wondering.

After swallowing, Anne tilted her head and squinted her left eye.

"You look like her."

"Like who?"

"Eve."

"That's because I am Eve," I said. The alcohol was clearly getting to her.

"No, you're not. You are an imposter. My brother should never have given you that name."

"If I'm an imposter, then who is the real Eve?"

"Our younger sister," Anne said, looking away as if remembering another time. "She was so different from the rest of us."

I was named after my aunt? I'd always wondered why my parents had given me a name that seemed to go against all they believed in. "Where is she?"

"Eve died when I was sixteen. She was fourteen."

"What was she like?"

Anne chuckled. "Stubborn, brave. She defied our father constantly, refusing to do what he asked despite the torture he put her through. She had this remarkable ability to tune it all out. It was as if she were somewhere else."

My mouth dropped open. I couldn't believe it! It sounded as if my aunt had the same ability as me.

Anne continued, "My father was embarrassed by her. He thought she was a regular human, but little did he know that she was more powerful than both Erik and I combined."

"How do you know?"

"I saw her once. In the woods. She thought she was alone, but Erik and I spied on her. We watched as she somehow managed to reroute a whole section of a stream, creating her own personal swimming pool. When we told our father she could use magic, he vowed to make her use it in front of him. He tried everything, torturing her mercilessly. But she just laid there with a calm expression on her face as if she were sitting on a beach somewhere and not enduring a hot stake through her palm." Anne sipped from the bottle again. "She had that same expression on her face when his torture finally killed her. After she died, he walked away, not glancing back once. He hasn't mentioned her since."

"He killed her?"

"Does that surprise you? His son raised you. Didn't Erik try to kill you, too?"

I didn't answer.

Anne crossed her legs and slumped farther into the chair. "The Segurs have always been about money and power. You can't be in our family if you feel differently."

I spoke, my voice low. "The twins said your husband was killed in an accident."

"There are no such things as accidents in our world."

"But the twins were too young! They couldn't have killed their own father."

Anne chuckled. "Of course not, but imagine the guilt they'd feel for *thinking* they had. Whatever humanity they had was destroyed the moment they believed they killed him. They stopped caring about anything else and finally became moldable."

"All for money and power," I whispered.

"Is there anything else?" She moved the bottle in a circular motion, watching the last of the liquid slosh around. "The twins will beat you tonight."

"How can you be sure?"

"There is still hope in you, small as it may be. It makes you weak."

I smirked. "I might surprise you."

"It doesn't matter. Win or lose, you will be destroyed tonight."

18

I sat alone in my room, staring out the window. The last of the sunlight was chased back by the darkness covering the night sky. I craned my neck, searching for the moon, but there was none. It, too, had abandoned me.

I slumped against the wall. I hadn't been nervous about tonight until my conversation with Anne. An ominous feeling had grown steadily ever since, and I was unable to shake it. I needed Boaz.

Quietly, I unlocked the window and pulled it open. "Boaz!" I whispered into the night. The wind carried my small voice to the woods beyond. Within moments, a black mist glided across the lawn toward me. I stepped away from the window when the darkness poured over the windowsill and into my room.

"I can't do this, Boaz."

His darkness swirled at my legs, rising higher. The coolness of his presence ignited every part of my body, and then it turned electric, shocking new life into me. I'd never felt this much power from him before, and it overwhelmed me.

"Do not be afraid," Boaz's voice said in my mind. His icy touch brushed against my neck, sending chills down my spine. "They are weaker than you."

My body lifted when his mist engulfed me, trapping me inside a wispy cocoon. Every part of him pressed into my skin, shaping and molding, creating something dark and beautiful. I breathed him in, enjoying the intoxicating power as he moved inside me.

"You will destroy them," he said one last time, but I barely registered his words.

In the distance, a bell rang out, shattering the climactic moment. Boaz lowered me to the ground.

"Go!" his voice commanded.

In a daze, I obeyed.

***

"Welcome, Eve," my grandfather said from the balcony in the training room. His hands rested on each armrest of his king-like throne. He wore a three-piece suit as if he were attending the theater, a play that would never make it to Broadway.

Anne was sitting next to him. She gave me a questioning look, and I wondered if somehow she could sense the new power within me.

Across the room, on the other side of the long dining table, Helen and Harriet sat statue-like upon two chairs. Hanging above them on the wall was a silver shield that had not been there before. A circular piece at its center was missing.

"Have a seat," Anne said, motioning to a lone chair, opposite the twins. Above it was another identical shield with the center piece also missing.

I moved to the chair and sat down. "Musical chairs? Isn't this a little first grade?"

No one said a word, so I exhaled loudly. Did they all have to be so damned serious? I didn't think it was written anywhere that one couldn't have both power and a sense of humor.

Just then, my grandfather raised his right arm. At the same time, a spinning silver disk rose from the balcony with a quiet hum. It was no bigger than my fist and had razor sharp edges. When it reached the center of the room, my grandfather lowered his arm, and the disk dropped to the middle of the long table. Painted on its top was the Segur family crest.

He spoke: "The first one to get the crest to their opponents shield wins. There are no rules. Begin."

"Wait!" I cried when the room was plunged into darkness. I'd hoped for at least a countdown or something!

I heard the metal disk scrape the table as it lifted into the air.

Act quickly! I "opened" my eyes, the darkness only an illusion created by the twins. The disk was flying directly toward the shield above me. I whispered, "Subsisto", and the disk stopped, floating a couple of feet away. I took hold of it, and, with as much strength as I could muster, flipped it back toward them. Their eyes followed the disk's movement until they managed to stop its progression. We both mentally pushed on it from opposite directions, suspending it in midair.

To distract them, I created an illusion of my own. It took just a thought to make the ceiling seem like it was moving. The sound was deafening as it creaked and groaned. Pieces of it appeared to fall to the floor.

Harriet flinched briefly, giving me the upper hand. The disk flew in their direction, but she quickly recovered and rejoined Helen's steady gaze upon the disk, stopping it just above their heads.

A loud pop made me jump. The ceiling lights exploded one by one; glass fell like a sudden burst of rain. Razor sharp shards of glass stung my skin.

This was not an illusion.

Unable to see the disk any longer, I faltered. I heard it whizzing toward me. I quickly created a barrier, like the one in the forest, to stop the disks flight, but when it hit my invisible wall, the twins immediately began to burrow past it.

I concentrated hard upon sustaining the barrier, while also trying to figure out what to do next. The memory of the pocket watch in the cave came to mind. It took a lot of mental effort, but I managed to light up several of the china plates throughout the room. The light was just enough for me to see the hovering disk not far from me.

For several minutes, no one moved. We each mentally pushed upon the disk, trying to gain ground over each other. I focused on my breathing, the disk, and the twins. My feet tingled. The feeling spread throughout my body, the magic expanding, growing until I thought my skin might literally stretch. In that moment, I felt more powerful than I ever had before.

Just then, a ceramic dish from one of the curios exploded. It, along with other dishes, flew from their shelves and toward me, an army of broken china. I easily dodged the jagged pieces, my focus still on the disk, but somehow a shard escaped my notice and hit me in the side of the head, cutting deep into my scalp. My grip on the disk slipped, and the small sphere spun again as it whirled toward my shield.

Despite the searing pain in my head, I sprung from my seat, leaping to an unnatural height, and took hold of the disk. It sliced open the skin on my palm, but I didn't hesitate. Instead, I tossed it right back at the twins using both mental and physical strength. They easily stopped its motion within a few feet of them, surprising me. I fell to the ground amidst broken china and glass, hurting myself even more.

Anne laughed from the balcony. I clenched my jaw tight and puffed air through my flaring nostrils. Magic once again swelled in response to my growing anger; just in time, too. I used a portion of it to knock the wine glass from Anne's hand. She jumped and cursed when it shattered on the floor.

I battled the twins well into the night to the point of exhaustion. Even they sat hunched over, breathing deeply, but neither they, nor I, gave up. We had each tried everything we could think of to distract each other until finally we reached a standstill.

There were only a few illuminated plates left on the shelves, lighting what no longer looked like a room but more of a war zone. Broken glass and china littered the floor, and the long table had been smashed into unrecognizable pieces. Even the chairs had been destroyed except for one, but it had been firmly embedded into the wall hours ago.

Both twins were pale, and Harriet had a bloody nose. I sat on the floor with my back against the wall, trying to keep my eyes focused on the disk, afraid that if I looked away even for a split second, I'd lose my mental grip. I kept expecting our grandfather to say something like,

"Let's take a short break" or "We will continue this tomorrow," but he remained silent, as did my aunt. For all I knew, my grandfather was asleep, and Anne passed out from too much wine.

A cool breeze brushed over my legs, startling me. The cold pressure in the air, which had darkened significantly, crowded the space around me. I sucked in too quickly and nearly froze my lungs.

"Finish this," a deep voice whispered.

My heart pumped faster. *Boaz?*

"Now!"

My shoulders slumped forward. *But I'm so tired. Help me.*

"You are the great Eve Segur," he hissed. "Push harder!"

But there are two of them!

"There are two of them," he repeated, his voice thoughtful.

I shook my head slowly. "I don't understand."

"There are no rules."

I thought hard, trying to grasp what he wanted.

"End this!" he shouted inside my mind, making me jump.

And then his words made sense.

I *could* end this. Right now.

Before I could think twice, I used the last of my mental strength to take hold of the wooden curio cabinet behind the twins. There were nails driven into its back, holding it fast to the wall. At first, they groaned and resisted my pull, but their rebellion couldn't last. I jerked it one last time. The curio moaned and creaked as it fell forward. It suddenly looked much bigger and heavier than I originally thought. When it collapsed on top of the girls, dust and debris billowed into the air. A single scream was all that escaped.

I stared at it, the image before me like an abstract painting. The disk dropped to the floor nearby, making me jump.

"Eve …" Boaz's voice said, his voice stern.

My gaze lowered to the silver disk. Without opposition, I lifted it with minimal concentration and directed it across the room and into the shield where it fit perfectly.

From the balcony, a slow clap began, and the room lit up, the lights magically fixed. My grandfather stood there, his hands slapping together. Anne was next to him, but she wasn't celebrating. She was staring at the overturned curio, her mouth open and her face pale. Wine from a tipped-over bottle poured from the balcony.

I slowly followed Anne's gaze to the toppled-over hutch; a dark pool of blood stretched out beneath it. A sharp breath caught in my chest, and my knees weakened.

What have I done?

I stumbled forward, pushing my way through the broken debris and shattered glass, while my grandfather spoke.

"You have won, Eve. All that I have will be transferred to your parents' account, and in time the fortune will become yours. Like generations past, you will use this money to further our political power in both our world and the humans."

I reached the curio cabinet and tried to lift it but was too weak. "Help me!"

My grandfather and Anne had somehow moved off of the balcony and stood not far from me. Anne's color had returned, her expression unreadable.

"It is done. You are free to go," my grandfather said. He turned around and walked toward the door. Anne followed him.

"Anne!" I cried. "These are your daughters. Help me!"

"I'll send a maid," she called over her shoulder as she stepped outside into the night. The door closed behind her.

I yelled in frustration and tried again to lift the heavy shelving, even trying to use magic, but either I had nothing left or my emotions were somehow blocking it. I glanced all around the room. "Boaz!"

The door opened, and he strolled in with open arms and a huge smile. "You did it! I knew you would."

"Get over here and help me. Now!" I again tried to lift,

grunting and groaning.

Boaz came next to me, but stepped back to avoid the red puddle I was standing in.

I took hold of his arm and jerked him forward. "Lift this. *Please.* The twins are beneath it."

His expression twisted into horror. "You did this?"

I blinked. A few times. Words struggled to come out of my mouth. "You told me to."

"I would never tell you to kill someone." Boaz bent down and easily tossed the curio aside.

I turned the first twin over. I think it was Helen. Half of her head was caked in blood, but I couldn't tell if it was hers or not. She moaned and her eyes fluttered open, exposing a glossy blue surface.

"Helen?"

She stared through me.

"Helen?" I asked a little louder. "Are you all right?"

I waited a few seconds then patted her cheek. No response. At least she was breathing.

"Help Harriet," I said to Boaz. I reached under Helen and pulled her body away from the broken glass and to the corner where I propped her against the wall. "Helen? Can you hear me?"

"She's dead," Boaz said.

My heart skipped a beat, and I straightened. "What did you say?"

"This one's dead," he repeated. "You must've killed her."

My mouth dropped open, and I shook my head. I forced my gaze down at Harriet's body. Her arm was twisted awkwardly behind her back, and her knee was bent the wrong way. But it was the broken shard of a china plate protruding from her eye that I would remember the most.

"Can you help her?" I asked Boaz. "Turn her or something?"

"It's too late."

I stumbled backwards into the wall and slid to the floor. "I didn't mean to. It was an accident. I only wanted to—"

"Win?" Boaz finished for me. He walked back to me, and knelt down, taking my head in his hands gently. "You did what was necessary."

"But I didn't have to do that."

"Look at me. She is gone and there is nothing you can do to fix it. Let's go home and get you taken care of. *You* are all that matters." Boaz helped me to my feet.

I leaned into him, my breaths coming in short gasps. "We should do something. An ambulance. The police."

"No," Boaz said. "Your grandfather will take care of it. This is no longer our concern." Boaz guided me toward the front door, his hand warm against the small of my back.

I dug my feet into the floor, but I was too weak to stop my momentum. "This feels wrong, Boaz. We can't just leave!"

"It isn't right or wrong. It just is."

Before Boaz helped me out the door, I glanced back at Helen who still sat motionless in the corner. I mouthed the words "I'm sorry" but Helen didn't see. She was somewhere else, somewhere dark and lonely.

As we walked toward the house, two servants scurried past us. I could only imagine their reaction when they saw the carnage, but then again, maybe they were used to seeing death while living with the Segurs. In my mind, I saw Harriet again, lying face down in a pool of blood. I stopped moving. "I should go back. I should help Helen."

"There is nothing you can do for her. Without Harriet, she is dead, too."

I leaned into Boaz. "What have I done?"

"Only what you were meant to do." He pulled me forward until we reached his car that was parked a short distance down the lane.

I didn't speak the entire ride back to Boaz's, nor did I speak for several days after. I couldn't even sleep or eat. Over and over, I replayed the events in my mind. Every move, every word. Boaz hadn't told me to kill the twins. I had done it all on my own. This nightmare played out every hour of every day until I refused to come out of my room.

I was a murderer.

Boaz sat next to my bed daily, saying nothing, but on the seventh day, when the moon's light filled the window, he finally spoke: "What you did was horrible. You destroyed the body of one and the mind of another. There is nothing more evil than taking a life. But for someone like you, that is to be expected. You are more powerful. This gives you the ability to do whatever you want. Remember the bear? People like us do not have to live by the same rules as others. You must learn to think differently. What you did is considered murder in the human world, but among ours, you simply did what was necessary. In fact, you will be admired for it."

I blinked, moonlight disappearing and then reappearing. "Why was it so important to you?"

"Excuse me?"

"You promised to tell me why I should fight the twins."

Boaz leaned back into his chair and squared his shoulders. "Because I wanted to see if you could. Only the strongest will be at my side."

Afraid his answer would be that simple, I closed my eyes, tucked my hands beneath my chin, and curled up even further into the quilted bed.

Boaz leaned over and found my mouth. He kissed it gently. "You need to get over this."

"I don't think I can."

"Let me help you. Take my power. It will make you stronger."

"Is that possible?"

"Between us? Yes. Take it from me, and let it overcome your guilt." His lips brushed over mine again. "Concentrate."

My gaze met his. A power, dark and alluring, swirled in his pupils until his eyes were entirely black. My heart leapt in anticipation. It was right there: a cure for my pain. Boaz's energy, his dark presence, was always stronger than mine. Deep down, I always knew that, but it wasn't until now that I was willing to admit it. And now I wanted it for myself.

I gripped his arms tight, willing his darkness from him, but I didn't just take it—I ripped it from his entire being. His chest tightened as if he'd been squeezed, and he gasped for air. This was the first time I'd ever seen him in pain, but I didn't stop. His dark energy raced through my body, flooding me with new life. I took as much as I could, having to suck in air to catch my breath. My eyelids closed, and my body swayed as if were on a boat, moving with the waves of the sea. Gently. Lightly. Floating across the waters of a forgiving sea, not as a deserted castaway, but as a God. Nothing could touch me now.

"That's enough," Boaz said, his voice pained.

"Just a minute. Let me enjoy this. You feel so good inside me." I giggled and wrapped my arms around him, pulling him close.

He nuzzled my neck and relaxed into me. "Finally we can move on with our lives. There is much to do."

19

I changed. All that I once hated, I now embraced. I no longer felt remorse or compassion toward anyone or anything. And I only hung around those who could make me stronger—like Boaz.

It was on a stormy night, the kind where really bad things happen, that I decided to change my life forever. Boaz seemed to sense the change, too, and all through dinner, he kept glancing at me, as if waiting for me to confess the reason behind my seductive perma-grin.

I let him wait.

We left the restaurant, huddled beneath an umbrella, and crossed the street to his car. On the way home, I said what I thought I would never say. "Boaz?"

"Yes, love?" His eyes stayed focused on the road ahead.

"I have been having the time of my life with you, and I don't want it to ever end. I want to be with you forever. I'm ready."

Boaz slammed on the breaks and steered the car to the shoulder of the road. A cloud of dust billowed behind us. "Are you absolutely sure?"

"I am, but only if you want it, too."

"I have waited so long to hear you say those words. I want you by my side forever."

He kissed my eyelids and then my cheek. His lips caressed my face until they found my mouth. He kissed me deeply, and his arms wrapped around me, forcing my body closer. Then, in a movement I barely felt, he lifted me effortlessly on top of him so my legs straddled his waist. His lips continued to stroke my face and finally trailed down to my neck.

This is it! I closed my eyes and waited to enjoy Boaz quench his thirst for the blood he craved, while also satisfying my own desire for ultimate power.

But my pleasure was short lived.

Boaz pushed me away. "I want to give you a surprise first."

"I don't want a surprise. I just want you." I took my turn of kissing his face, but he stopped me again.

"I have to leave town for a while. In the next few hours, in fact."

"Now? What for?"

"To work on the surprise."

"I don't want a surprise."

"But I want to give it," he said with more force.

"How long will you be gone?"

"Maybe a week."

I leaned back into the steering wheel and pouted. "A week? No good. I'll go crazy."

"You'll survive. I promise it will be worth it." He moved to lift me off his lap, but I clung to him.

"Not yet," I said and slipped my hand under his shirt.

He raised an eyebrow, a smile threatening to break. "By all means, love. I am yours to command."

***

Boaz left as promised. It was strange to have him gone. It was the first time we'd been separated in months. The first day, I was bored out of my mind, TV unable to keep my attention. And I didn't even bother trying to read. The most entertainment I found was using my magic to play tricks on the servants, but even that dulled with no one around to laugh with me.

I needed to go somewhere. *Do* something. The power within me was swelling and needed to be released. A solution came when the phone rang at two in the morning. It was Liane inviting me on a spur of the moment trip to New York City.

"William will meet us there, and we'll cause all sorts of trouble for New Yorkers. It will be great. We'll be just like our great grandmothers."

I couldn't say "yes" fast enough.

The next day at noon, Liane picked me up. I enjoyed her company almost as much as Boaz's. She was spontaneous and fun and wasn't afraid of anything. Her lack of fear had gotten us into trouble more times than I could count, but the adventure was always worth it.

"Don't you think it's time you cut your hair?" Liane asked, eyeing me sideways as she maneuvered her car onto the road.

I flipped down the passenger vanity mirror. I had curled my long hair into big waves. It looked okay. "Is it really that bad?"

"It's just so goodie-goodie. You need a punk style or something that makes a statement. Something that says 'watch out, here I come!'" Liane snapped her head to the driver's side window. "Did you see that?"

I glanced around. "What?"

"Up ahead. A man just passed me."

"Oh no," I moaned. Liane hated to be passed.

She stepped on the accelerator until she was even with the car that had passed her. "Watch this." She rolled down her window and said something under her breath. The tire on the man's vehicle popped, sending his car out of control. I looked back just in time to see the car hit a truck, spin around a few times, and finally crash into a guard rail.

I laughed. "That was horrible!"

That one potentially deadly prank set the tone for the remainder of the trip. Together, with William, we constantly tried to one-up each other in our viciousness toward others. At one point, we had the police chasing us through the streets, but a five-car pileup blocked the pursuit, thanks to William.

I no longer saw the faces of the victims we tortured. I reveled in the power I had over others and used it merely for my own entertainment.

When I returned home, Boaz was waiting for me in the bedroom. I immediately threw my arms around him. "You're home early!"

"I can't stay. I only returned to get a few more supplies."

My eyes narrowed. "For my surprise?"

"For your surprise. Where have you been?"

"I went with Liane and William to the city. We had a killer time."

"I'm glad, but I would feel better if I was with you. It's still dangerous." He sat on a sofa across from the bed.

"I don't think anyone's going to mess with me." I removed my coat and walked over to him and fell into his lap. "When are you leaving again?"

"In a few hours. I'm very close to fulfilling your dream. Soon, love. We will be together and unstoppable."

He tilted my chin and kissed me deeply. Gripping me tightly, he lifted my body and carried me to the bed. The air thickened and the electric current between us grew as it often did when we were so close. I stared into Boaz's eyes; a dark mist swirled in great swells as our combined power gave him a natural high. He smiled, but not at me, and I knew it. He was smiling at the power.

***

Boaz was gone the next morning, leaving no note saying when he would return. It bothered me that he was away from me so much. Working on a surprise? Unlikely. I thought about it all morning before choosing to ignore the uncomfortable scratching at the back of my mind. Boaz would never turn against me. I was way more powerful than him.

I decided to go somewhere, too. To the city for a few days. Relax. I knew several supernaturals there I could party with, or I could likely get Liane to come again. And if by chance Boaz came home and I wasn't there, then too bad. I wasn't going to wait around. Besides, the dark power inside me was already festering again. I was afraid if I didn't leave, I might hurt the mansion or those working inside it. Like Boaz, dark energy was incapable of holding still.

It was raining in New York; it dripped from the gray sky like a faucet that wouldn't shut off, making the city smell like a wet dog. I left the Cardigan Hotel, my umbrella tight in my hand, and headed toward 5th Avenue. That was where I would find the most people. Complete strangers that meant absolutely nothing to me. I would use my magic against them, giving me the release I desperately needed. Already my insides were beginning to hurt. The dark power within me could only be satisfied by pain and suffering—whether mine or another's, it didn't care. I preferred it be another.

A cold wind swept up an abandoned newspaper. It swirled at my feet before it was carried away into the night. I pulled my coat tighter around me and mouthed the word "Caldor". Invisible warmth blanketed my entire body.

I toured the city alone, walking from 5th Avenue to Central Park West. I'd never been alone like this, but I wasn't worried. It was everyone else that should be worried. Too bad no one warned them of my arrival.

I destroyed and hurt whoever and whatever I could without causing too much attention. People tripped, glass shattered, dogs bit. All freak "accidents". With every curse or incantation I uttered, dark magic left me, and I no longer felt like I was being stretched from the inside out.

As the hour grew late, I sat on a lone bench in Central Park to watch the full moon rise over the city. A few minutes later, a couple huddled together in quiet conversation walked by me. I was about to mentally shove the man into the woman, but something stopped me.

I rose from my seat and followed after them, frustrated by their obvious affection for each other. I was in love, too, but they looked different—they looked happy.

Why am I not happy?

The more I watched them, the angrier I became. They stopped

just before 5th Avenue to stare into each other's eyes. The tall man placed his hands on the woman's face, paused, and then kissed her tenderly. I could almost taste the revulsion in my mouth.

With one word and a flick of my wrist, I exploded the tire of an approaching delivery van. It swerved and veered off the road and into the park. The driver's eyes were wide as he gripped the steering wheel tightly, seemingly to try and gain control of the direction of his vehicle. But I wouldn't let him.

The van hit the kissing couple head on. The woman flew up and over the car, while the man went under it. They didn't scream. I didn't give them time.

For a few minutes, I watched as others attended to the man and woman. Everyone was so concerned. Even a teenage girl, surely a complete stranger to the couple, was crying.

Ridiculous.

The injured woman's leg moved, and she moaned. She would live. I wasn't convinced the man would, though. A person was sitting over him, pressing their palms into his chest.

Because I felt nothing, I left.

Back at my park bench, I had barely sat down when a voice asked, "What are you doing?"

Startled, I turned around. In a clump of trees behind me, the dark silhouette of a man stood tall.

"Excuse me?"

"You heard me," he said. His voice was deep and smooth.

"I was minding my own business, which you should do too."

"You're going to stop hurting people, starting *now*. Do you understand?" His figure shifted a fraction of an inch.

"Why don't you come over here so I can see you?" I dared him, wanting to know who or what would talk to me like this.

"You will stop," he said.

If he wouldn't come to me, then I would go to him. I stood up and rounded the bench. "Says who?"

"You will leave this city tonight."

I was almost to him, but his face remained hidden in the shadows. He stood erect, with legs spaced evenly apart and lined directly beneath a thick trunk. From where I first saw him, he appeared massive, but after moving closer, I realized his size was a trick of the light. He looked to be only slightly taller than Boaz.

He stepped from the shadows to meet me, and the light from the full moon shimmered in his incandescent blue eyes. I sucked in a breath. Not because I recognized him as a vampire immediately, but because of a sudden and foreign emotion that washed over me. It felt like joy, but I couldn't be sure.

Was it possible that I knew him?

The vampire had a square jaw line, a sharp crooked nose that looked like it had been broken a few times, full lips, and hooded, wolf-like eyes. It was his eyes that captivated me the most. They were filled with sorrow. What trauma could've filled him with so much pain that his eyes could do nothing else but bleed the strong emotion?

"I meant what I said. You will leave this city tonight," he said.

"Now why would I do that?"

"You're hurting innocent people."

"They were hardly innocent. Did you see what they were doing?"

The vampire's eyes looked in their direction. Lights from distant emergency vehicles turned the color of the trees red and blue.

"They looked happy," he said, his voice no louder than the quiet breeze ruffling my hair.

"It was disgusting."

His gaze turned on me sharply. "I want you gone."

"I have a better idea. What do you say you and I go have some fun tonight? You look like you could use some loosening up." I reached for his hand, but when my fingers brushed his, a jolt of what felt like light surged through my body. And, for a brief moment, I had a perfect vision of the innocent girl I used to be. I even heard my younger voice vowing never to become like *them*.

He stepped back. "I want nothing to do with your dark magic, Witch."

I ignored the strange, electric moment that only I seemed to notice. "You know nothing about me. I'm the most powerful witch in the country, probably in the world."

"Don't forget most humble."

"Don't insult me. You have no idea who I am."

In a calm, yet frightening voice, he said, "And if you knew who I was, you'd run away screaming."

I looked him up and down. "I can see who you are. You're a weak, confused, newbie vampire who—"

Before I could utter another word, his strong hand gripped my neck, and after moving himself and me at lightning speed, he smashed my back into a tree far away from the spot where we'd just been.

I pried at his fingers, trying desperately to get him to release his hold, but he was incredibly strong. I glanced at the limb above me and imagined it smashing down on his head. The limb snapped and fell, but he caught it with his free hand before it even came close to making contact. He was simply too fast.

With fangs barred, he growled, "This is your final warning. Leave now."

I quickly nodded, awash in an emotion I hadn't felt in a very long time. Fear. He released his grip, and I tumbled to the ground, sucking in air.

Once recovered, I straightened and smoothed my clothes. "I was about to leave anyway. This city is boring. No one knows how to have fun anymore."

He looked back toward the city whose lights could be seen above the tops of the trees.

148

"But before I go, could you answer one question?" I asked. He said nothing so I continued. "Why do you care about them?" I nodded my head toward the people in the city.

"They're innocent."

"But you're a vampire."

"What's your point?"

"You have incredible power. You're greater than they are."

"Power is a dangerous thing," he said. He turned and walked away.

Something stirred in my memory, as if I'd once thought the same thing.

"How is it dangerous?" I called after him.

"Be gone within the hour." He picked up speed.

"Wait!" I tried to catch up, but he had already disappeared.

I stared after him, at the empty space that felt so big. Tears stung my eyes, and I gulped in air. *What was wrong with me?* The faint imprint of the girl I used to be lurked near the edges of my mind, a ghost risen from the grave.

The thought repulsed me. I hated to think how weak I used to be before I met Boaz.

Boaz.

I returned home right away, hoping I would find Boaz there, but he was still gone. I curled up in bed, but I couldn't get my mind off the vampire I'd met. Over and over, his sorrow-filled gaze tortured me, and an unexplainable gnawing pinged in my gut. I felt pity for him, but it was more than that. It was as if the light from his touch still lingered inside me, and it made me question everything.

That night, when I finally fell asleep, I dreamed I was sitting with the vampire in a field of tall grass, the sun shining brightly. I thought it strange to see a vampire in full light, but he didn't seem bothered by it in the least. He was curled up on his side, head resting in my lap.

Looking down on him, compassion followed by peace overwhelmed me. The moment seemed to last forever, but the dream didn't. I woke to the howl of wind blowing outside. A winter storm was approaching. I rolled onto my back and stared at the high ceiling.

What had happened to me?

A flash of light filled my window, and I sat up. Boaz was home. I didn't have to look. I felt it.

Replacing my recent regrets, excitement and longing took over, and I rushed to greet him. Before I reached the bedroom door, he was already there, grinning mischievously. His arms came around me, hugging me tightly.

"What took you so long?" I asked.

"I finished your present." He pushed me away to look into my eyes, still the silly grin. Behind him, standing in the doorway, Hunwald, too, seemed to be grinning.

I laughed. "What have you done, Boaz?"

"I did it. I finally did it. I can't wait to try it on you."

"Try what?"

"Do you still want to be with me forever?"

I hesitated, but quickly shook it off. This was my life now. "There's nowhere else I'd rather be."

"Then that is what you shall have. I think I'll like you better now."

Before I could react, he kissed me hard. I barely had the chance to catch my breath, before I saw a flash of the snake on his upper arm followed by a syringe in his hand. Boaz plunged it into my back. The pain was immediate and dropped me to my knees.

"Boaz?" I reached behind me to try and get at the needle. A fire-hot sensation was spreading quickly throughout my body. "What did you do?"

"It will only hurt for a minute, love." He sat down in his usual red chair, petted Hunwald, and watched me expectantly.

I tried to speak again, but the pain became too great. It washed over me in great waves, rocking my entire frame. I gritted my teeth and clenched my fists as my body unwilling twisted into a tight ball. I tried to stop it with magic, but the pain was too excruciating, preventing me from thinking about anything else.

A horrific sound exploded in my ears as if I were suddenly stuck beneath the belly of a great roaring beast. The screaming filled my head, creating an unbearable pressure inside my skull. Pressure built in my eyeballs, and I was afraid at any moment my eyes might burst from their sockets, but instead, the blood found other outlets. It poured from my nose, ears, and out my mouth.

Finally the pressure proved too great, and I lost consciousness.

20

When I came to, I was lying in bed with a fresh nightgown and the covers tucked to my chin. The lights were off and the curtains drawn. I moved my limbs, expecting them to feel stiff, but they felt remarkably good, considering what I'd just been through. I only wished the inside of me felt as good as the outside. Something had gone horribly wrong.

I threw the covers back and jumped out of bed to turn on the lights. I had to find Boaz. I had to know what he'd done to me. I left the room and hurried down the stairs.

"Boaz?"

I called several times and searched every room. When I found no one, not even Lisa, my anxiety grew. The mansion had never been empty before.

I opened the front door to search outside, but stopped when I remembered Boaz's private study, a room I was still forbidden to enter. *Not anymore.* I turned around and walked toward the entrance. The door was locked but that didn't stop me. Using magic, I jerked it open.

The inside was not what I'd expected. Instead of a room, there was a long hallway. Its décor was completely different from the rest of the house. There were no pictures hanging on the walls, no elaborate decorations, and the temperature had to have been at least ten degrees cooler. There was very little light by the time I reached the end of the hall. Just enough to see a circular, stone staircase leading down into what looked like a black hole. I glanced back the way I came, trying to decide if I should go back to grab a flashlight or even an object with glass I could light up with magic.

Forget it. I refuse to waste any time.

"Boaz?" My voice echoed down the long flight of stairs.

When I didn't receive an answer, I began the long climb down, feeling my way as I went. The rock walls were wet with moisture, and the air smelled stale and a little like rusty pipes. When there were no more stairs, I slid my hands along the wall searching for a light switch. Eventually, I found one and flipped it on. Dull fluorescent, low-hanging lights flickered overhead, barely illuminating a long and narrow hall. Six doors were on each side, all with a single glass window. There was one last door at the end of the hall, black and as wide as the walkway.

I took a few hesitant steps forward to peer into the first room. It was empty except for one object: a girl with short uneven brown hair and pale skin that looked more grey next to the stark white walls. Her lips were the same dark purple color as her fingertips. She sat on the floor, leaning into the corner of the room. Her head was tilted up, staring at the ceiling with mouth open. Each of her hands rested on the floor next to her legs, palms turned up.

I watched for a moment, wondering how I felt about her. Most of me felt nothing, but a small part of me knew I should try to help her. I hadn't experienced this sort of caring, if that was even the right word, for a very long time.

The vampire in New York City.

He must have done something to me. Had this been yesterday, I might've walked right on by the girl to find Boaz, but this new feeling couldn't be ignored.

I opened the door and rushed in, hoping she wasn't dead. When I grabbed her by both shoulders, she slumped forward, her head dropping to her chest. I pushed her back up and checked for a pulse. It took me awhile to find one, but it was there.

"Are you all right?" I asked.

The girl didn't move, not even blink.

I squeezed her shoulders tight and yelled, "Wake up!"

Still nothing, other than the slow and steady rise of her chest as she breathed in and out. Very gently, I carefully laid her on the floor and smoothed back her hair. That's when I saw them: two red puncture wounds. I scurried away backwards, finally understanding.

No. Please, no.

All this time, Boaz had this girl trapped, slowly feeding off of her, slowly killing her, while I was upstairs having the time of my life. I glanced to the open door, remembering the other rooms. My throat filled with acid, and I turned to throw up but nothing came out.

I staggered out of the room and down the hallway. The remaining rooms contained more of the same: white enclosed areas filled only by empty human shells. The last room, however, imprisoned two girls sitting opposite of each other. I didn't recognize the one, but the other was Muriel, the maid I'd met when I'd first come to Boaz's home. She'd slit her wrists.

I stumbled into the black door at the end of the hallway and fell through to the other side, tears stinging my eyes.

"Eve?"

Boaz was standing in front of a fireplace, flipping through a book. He set it down and walked to me. Hunwald followed behind.

"How are you feeling?" he asked.

I looked back to the open door and into the dimly lit hallway. "The girls ..."

"What about them, love?"

"There's something wrong with them," was all I could say.

"Of course there is. They've been feeding a vampire. Come. Sit down. You look exhausted."

He took my hand and guided me to a wooden stool. He sat across from me in a plush recliner.

"Boaz, we have to help those girls," I said.

He frowned. "Help them? Why?"

"Because," I stammered, searching for something in me that would tell me why it was wrong, but it was as if my conscience was lost. "It's not right."

"When did you start caring about what was right?" he asked. When I didn't answer, he countered my logic. "Are you saying it's right for me to starve?"

"No."

"I'm a vampire. That's what I do. Don't be naïve."

"I just didn't realize—"

"Were you in your fairytale world again?"

My head jerked up. "What?"

"Never mind. How are you feeling?"

"What's wrong with you?"

He let out an exaggerated sigh. "Would you *please* just answer the question?"

"Why are you talking to me like this?"

"I've invested a lot of time and money into you," he said, "and I want to make sure it worked. Now answer the question. How are you feeling?"

I fought back more tears, but said, "I feel different, I guess. But what are you talking about, time and money?"

Boaz picked up a notebook from off of his desk. "What feels different?"

"Everything around me is sharper, more clear," I said, my voice full of frustration. But then it dawned on me, all his questions. "You made me a vampire, didn't you?"

Boaz scribbled on the lined paper, and then tapped a pencil on his head as if thinking.

"I'm a vampire now, right?" I asked again.

Boaz finally looked up. It took him all of three seconds before he burst out laughing. I'd never heard laughter like this from him before. It made me feel all kinds of wrong.

"Then what did you do to me?" I cried, tears spilling over.

Boaz's laughter subsided. "Well, if all my research proves to be right, then I have just made you an immortal."

"How is that different from you?"

"You won't have my strength or speed. Not even my blood lust. You will simply live forever, unless, of course, someone cuts off your head or you burn to death."

"How is that possible?"

"You wouldn't understand, but to put it in simple terms, I gave you the immortal part of vampirism and left out all the good stuff."

"But why? Why spend your *precious* time and money when you could've just made me a vampire?"

"And risk the chance of you becoming more powerful than me? I couldn't do that."

I reared back as if I'd been slapped. "I thought you loved me."

"I do. I love you like I love those girls out there."

"And how is that exactly?"

"They give me something I need."

"And what do I give you?"

He inhaled deeply. "Beautiful, untainted power. I've been playing this puppy love charade long enough. I'm so tired of it that if I have to do it for one more second, I'll slit my throat."

"I don't understand," I said, my voice small.

Boaz mimicked me in a shrill voice, "*I don't understand.*" He stood up and crossed the room, tugging on his hair. "I can't stand hearing you whine. You would think being with me all this time that you would've learned something. You are the stupidest, most naïve—"

"Boaz?"

"Shut up when I'm talking to you!" His arm swept books from off a shelf. I jumped when they crashed to the floor. "It's about power! It's always been about power. And unfortunately, I need someone to make mine unstoppable. Not just someone, mind you. I need you, Eve. You were bred for me. I was part of that treaty made over a hundred years ago. In fact, it was my idea. Whenever I came near either side of your family, I could feel my powers grow as it reached out to theirs. It was as if the dark energy between us needed each other. But it wasn't enough, and eventually the power would fade. That's when I came up with my brilliant plan. I knew if I could get the two families to breed me a life partner, then I would have enough power to make me invincible. There were some mistakes along the way, of course. Take the mental twins, for example, but ultimately I was right. I knew the moment I held your infant body in my arms that you would be the one. Pity you were such a disappointment. Your parents tried their best, but you were just too good for it all, weren't you?"

I stared at him, dumbfounded. A single tear traced down my cheek.

"Erik and Sable had their chance, but they failed. They begged me to take you. I didn't want to, but I couldn't waste any more time. And I knew I was the only one who could change you. Disgusting as it was, it was all so easy to play the knight in shining armor. You ate it up like a gluttonous pig. But it was unbearable for me. I've never felt so *dirty*."

The last of my tears fell. There was nothing left. I was numb. "It was all a set up. The diablos in the forest. They weren't real. My parents weren't trying to kill me."

Boaz clapped. "Ladies and Gentleman, she does have a brain!"

The hands in my lap looked small. Everything had been a lie.

"Don't be sad. You were created for me, yes, but I made you better, too. I mean, you didn't really think all of those magical stunts you pulled were all you, do you?" He waved his hand and chuckled. "Oh, who am I kidding? Of course you did! You're self-centered that way. That's one of the few things I liked about you."

"Not me? Not my power? But—"

"The water you conjured in Dare the Demon?" he cut in, raising his eyebrow. "I gave you my power. We did it together. I need you to be greater, but you're *nothing* without me. You should be thanking me."

Boaz raised his arms suddenly. At the exact same moment, my body jerked tight as if something had wrapped itself around my chest, and I gasped for air. Objects rose from the floor. Books, chairs, and papers lifted high and spun in a wide whirlwind throughout the room. My hair twisted and whipped across my face. I jumped when a stereo behind me turned on, blaring 'Ode to Joy'.

Boaz waved his arms back and forth, leading the debris in a dark symphony of destruction. His combed-back hair flipped forward, falling across his forehead. Without warning, he slammed his arms forward against the desk. Everything crashed to the floor, and the music shut off.

"You look surprised," he said. "You didn't realize I was this powerful, did you? Not using magic was the hardest part about playing the role of the *perfect* man. It was extremely difficult being around you and feeling your dark energy. It was always there, just waiting for you to give it to me."

"Then why? Why the elaborate scheming if you could've just taken it from me all along?"

Boaz straightened. "You have no idea how tiresome it can be to constantly force someone's powers from them. It's like trying to tame a lion. It can be done, but really, what kind of idiot does things the hard way when there are such easier methods? Besides, I like you, truly. It would be much more pleasurable for the both of us if you'd willingly work with me."

I barely heard his words. I was such a fool!

Boaz looked over the notebook again and scanned its entries. "There's still something I'm not sure about, though." He opened his palm. A dagger from across the room flew directly into it. He turned the knife over, eyeing it carefully. "I know you've been through a lot in the last several hours, but I must know if it worked. Please stand up."

"Why?"

"Just do it!" My body unwillingly jerked to an upright position.

I tried to fight it, but his magic was too strong, making me feel even more stupid.

"This will hurt a little, but if my calculations are correct, the pain won't last long." He raised his arm and tossed the dagger at my stomach. I cried out when the knife lodged itself deep into my gut. I stared down at the dagger, shaking from the pain until I finally collapsed to my knees.

Boaz walked over to me and knelt down. With one hand on my shoulder and the other on the dagger, he pulled it out slowly. I fell over and rolled onto my back. Blood pumped out of the open wound with each beat of my heart.

Boaz frowned. "That can't be good."

Death's darkness crept toward me, anxious to claim me for itself. I welcomed it. Death would be better than staring up at the devil who now stood over me with a quizzical expression upon his face. But my wish wasn't granted. The darkness receded into the shadows of the room, taking with it my pain.

Boaz hurried to the chair behind his desk and scribbled furtively in the notebook. "Oh, so it did work. Excellent!"

I slowly stood and inspected the bloody hole in my gown. The wound had entirely healed. "Tell me Boaz," I said. "What makes you think I won't leave you, now that I know your true motives?"

Boaz stopped writing and looked up. "Oh, there's nowhere for you to go now. You are one of us."

"I am *nothing* like you."

Boaz's gaze burned into mine. He stood up so quickly and with such force that his chair flew backwards, smashing into the bookcase behind him. He rounded his desk and grabbed me by the arm, physically dragging me in front of a tall mirror not far away.

"Look at you!" he said, holding me by my shoulders and giving me a shake. He grabbed my chin and forced me to face my reflection. "See how you've changed? You're so full of hate that it's changed even your physical appearance. You are cruel and ruthless. You use magic for your own personal gain, but most of all, you crave the power—just like me."

I stared at myself in the mirror, and for the first time in a long while, I *really* looked. I didn't recognize the woman before me. She had a hardness to her that only the worst kind of experiences could give. My hair, once a vibrant flaxen color, was now almost entirely black like the color of a raven's wing. The tight emerald green nightgown I wore was cut low, exposing the majority of my chest. I cowered.

Boaz shoved me back toward the mirror. "Don't shrink from it, love. Embrace it!"

I stumbled into the glass, suddenly frightened by the cruelty that stared back at me in those green eyes. They no longer reflected the chaste light I'd once guarded with my life. All innocence was gone. I reached forward to touch the reflection in hopes that when I did so, it would be an illusion like all of Boaz's other deceptions. But when I touched my face in the mirror, I touched evil. I felt the power of it and saw the same dark mist I frequently saw in Boaz's eyes rise in my own.

Behind me, Boaz laughed.

I fell to my knees and covered my face in shame. "How could you do this to me?"

Boaz stopped laughing. "You did this to yourself. You made the choice."

"You tricked me."

Boaz sat on the floor next to me, his back against the mirror. "Let me tell you a story. Maybe it will make you feel better."

When I didn't respond, he continued.

"There once was a young Indian boy who was gathering sticks for a fire. Across a river, he noticed a fallen tree where he could get plenty of wood. He was about to cross when a serpent stopped him.

"'Please, boy, carry me to the other side. There is no food to eat, and I will surely die if I cannot get across.'

"'But you are a snake,' the boy said, 'you will bite me and kill me with your poison if I pick you up!'

"'Nonsense, boy. I will not bite you if you help save my life. Now, please, pick me up and carry me to the other side.'

"The boy agreed and picked up the snake. When they reached the other side, the snake bit him.

"'Why did you do that? You said you wouldn't bite me,' the boy cried.

"The snake hissed back, 'You knew what I was when you picked me up." Boaz paused for dramatic effect. "You *knew* what I was, yet you still chose to let yourself be fooled because you so desperately craved love. You did this to yourself."

I lifted my head. "How was that supposed to make me feel better?"

Boaz shrugged. "I'm just saying you can't be angry with me. You were the stooge who let yourself be fooled."

"Leave me alone."

"This is my lair, remember? You leave if you want to be alone."

I stood up, too depressed to care anymore how he spoke to me.

"By the way, your parents will be here soon to see your marvelous transformation," he called after me. "Don't disappoint."

21

I had nowhere else to go but to my room. I could run away, but I wouldn't get very far, especially with Hunwald who could track anything. He frightened me as much as Boaz. I collapsed on top of my bed.

Escape was not an option, unless I used magic. A big part of me was begging for me to do just that. It could help me out of this mess …

Or could it?

Had Boaz really been helping all that time? Maybe I wasn't as powerful as I thought.

I rolled over on the crumpled blankets and thought about the injection Boaz had given me. I was immortal. I didn't know what that meant exactly or how it would affect my future, but it couldn't be good. Any creation of Boaz's should be destroyed.

Wouldn't death be better than to be like the black wolf that shadowed him day and night? Was my magic the only good thing about me? I had more to offer. Didn't I?

Several hours passed while I tried to decide between life and death. In the end, I decided to live and find a way to redeem myself of my past actions. It made me sick to think of how many people I had hurt, the lives I had damaged! No more magic for me, no matter how hard.

And with that seemingly small decision, the flame in my heart, already lit by the vampire I'd met in the city, grew, and I felt a sliver of peace.

The lights flipped on. Still wide-awake, I shielded my eyes from the glare, but when my parents walked through the door, I jumped to my feet and scooted backwards into the wall. Memories of the abuse they had inflicted upon me flooded my mind, and I thought I might drown in them. But then I took a deep breath, in and out, and cleared my head. I had to be strong for what was to come.

Sable crossed the room with a smile that made me think she'd just won a beauty contest. Her hair was pulled up into an elegant French twist, and an evening gown clung to her slight curves as if she were attending another one of her charity events. She threw her arms around me in a tight embrace—something she'd never done before.

"Eve, dear," she said, releasing me and staring me right in the eyes. "You look absolutely wonderful. Boaz told us all about your remarkable transformation. To think, he actually made you an immortal! I'm sure you can understand now why we were so hard on you growing up. We only wanted what was best for you, and now you have the best thing possible." She glanced back at Boaz, who was standing next to Erik in the doorway, and flashed another perfect smile.

Boaz nodded at me encouragingly. I wanted to give in, to be back in his arms, to feel the darkness that made me feel nothing. It would be so easy to do what they all wanted.

But it wouldn't be right.

Now, at last, that meant something.

"Well?" Sable said, looking at me expectantly.

"Sorry to disappoint, but I'm not who Boaz thinks I am," I said.

"What is she talking about?" Sable asked Boaz, her head cocked to the side.

"She's confused. Don't worry, it will pass." Boaz crossed the room and took my hand, but I jerked it away.

"This won't pass. I'm done with magic. I'm done with all of you."

Boaz chuckled. "You've already crossed the line. There's no going back."

"You're wrong."

Boaz slapped me with the back of his hand. Sable and I jumped at the same time. "Don't test me."

"What's going on, Boaz?" Erik asked behind him. "I thought you said she had changed."

"She has. She's just being stubborn, but I can change that. Leave us."

Before turning away, Sable shook her head sadly and followed Erik from the room.

As soon as the door closed, Boaz whirled on me. "I don't like hurting you, you must believe me."

"I will never believe another word you say."

"What's happened to you?" He eyed me up and down. "Where have you been?"

"I went to the city, alone."

"And what did you do … alone."

"I was my usual mean self. I used magic to hurt others."

"And?"

"And I met someone who reminded me of who I used to be."

Boaz grabbed my arm. "Who?"

"I don't know his name. He was a vampire, and he didn't hurt others. There was light inside him."

Boaz flinched, almost hissing.

"Do you know him?" I asked, startled by his reaction.

His expression darkened. "None of that matters now. We're wasting time. I need you, and you need—"

"No," I said. "I don't *need* you."

Boaz clenched his fists and breathed heavily through his nose, nostrils flaring. Without touching me this time, he sent me flying across the room and into the wood headboard. I cried out, but only for a moment as my body had already begun to heal.

"Don't think that just because you're an immortal I can't hurt you. I can spend hours breaking your bones, and after they've healed, I will break them again."

"It won't matter. I won't do what you want. I went years with my parents' abuse."

Boaz glided to the bed, his feet barely skimming the floor. "There are other ways to hurt you than just physically, love." He took hold of my ankles and jerked my legs toward him. He forced his weight upon on me.

More than anything else ever, I wanted to use magic right then to throw him from me, but that's exactly what he wanted me to do. I closed my eyes tight as he ripped open the front of my gown.

"What are you waiting for!" he screamed, spittle spraying from his mouth.

When I didn't give in, he stepped away and stormed from the room without Hunwald. The wolf remained, watching me with a satisfied expression upon his hairy face. I covered myself quickly and moved to jump out of the window. The impact of the fall would only hurt for a minute.

Hunwald jogged over and leapt upon the windowsill as if guarding it.

"Stupid dog," I muttered.

Hunwald growled.

Outside the open door, Erik argued with Boaz. "You said she changed. You've wasted our time!"

"I've wasted *your* time? I've wasted almost a year with that bitch."

"You're the one who so arrogantly insisted you could change her."

"Watch your tongue, Erik, or I'll rip it from your throat. I've made more progress than you made in her whole life."

Sable sighed. "This has been a waste for everyone involved. Let's kill her and start over. I know it will take more time, but really Boaz, don't you have plenty of that?"

Boaz scoffed. "You're too old to bear any more children. Besides which, I refuse to waste any *more* time. I want Eve!"

"Then what do you suggest we do?" Erik asked.

I heard silence for several moments, then, from Boaz, "Get the necklace."

"I told you it's not safe," Sable hissed.

"I'm willing to take that chance. Now get it and make it work or you will lose everything, the money, the power, but most of all your lives."

I couldn't hear anyone move.

"Get it, Sable," Erik finally said.

Sable's light footsteps moved down the hall. Boaz came back into the room and knelt by my side. When he tried to smooth back my hair, I flinched.

"I don't enjoy hurting you. And despite what you may think, I am quite fond of you, except for this side. The *poor me* part needs to be destroyed."

My shoulders slumped, and my gaze slowly lifted to meet his. "Is there any way you can just let me go?"

He laughed.

I tried again. "But there are so many others better suited for you. Helen?"

He stopped laughing. "*You* are suited for me. I will have no other!"

"Don't I have a say in this?"

"Of course you have a say! It's 'I will do whatever you want'. That's what you can say," he snapped.

I turned away from him.

"I'll give you one last chance, love. Give your whole self to me, the powerful part not the weak, 'I-feel-nothing' Eve. I want the part that loves darkness, loves to hurt others and takes pleasure in other's pain. That's the Eve I want by my side. Give me her, and I will not do what I am about to do."

The image of the vampire I'd met only yesterday came to my

mind. Had it only been a day?

"Power is a dangerous thing," I whispered.

Boaz snorted. "That's the most absurd thing I've ever heard."

I lowered my head, wishing I could be wherever the vampire with the sorrow filled eyes was.

"Last chance. Join me willingly."

I didn't answer, and I didn't care what he did to me anymore. There was nothing left.

"Very well. You will never be the same again."

He stood up and walked out of the room with Hunwald by his side. The door slammed behind him without being touched.

22

I remained alone in my room for days; no one even brought me food. At first, I was starving, but then I realized it was more from habit than true hunger. My body was only slightly weakened by the lack of food.

Since there were no distractions, I used the time to gather my strength mentally for what was to come. It was going to be bad; I knew that. But whatever it was, I couldn't use magic. The more I thought this—the more I said it out loud—the more my resolve strengthened. The spark inside me was growing, slowly snuffing out the darkness that had rooted itself inside me.

I stared out the window toward the full moon above. It was a clear night. Tiny pin-pricks of light dotted the black sky. When their footsteps approached outside my bedroom door, I focused on the strength of the stars. No matter how many times night came, they always managed to stay bright.

The door flew open. Boaz, Erik, and Sable all walked in at once. Erik and Boaz were both smiling—not joyfully, but triumphantly—but Sable's brow was creased, and she was wringing her hands.

Boaz set a wooden chest on my bed. Nobody looked at me except for Hunwald, who stood stiffly in the doorway.

"What is that?" I asked.

"Another present, love," Boaz said.

He opened the box and gently removed an old, intricately designed silver necklace. The short chain was made of many jagged strands of silver wound around each other tightly, similar to the thorned stem of a rose. At its base was a spider-like claw that clung to a glass orb. When Boaz raised it to the light, a thick red liquid sloshed inside, coating the sides with a layer of what could only be blood.

"I don't want any more of your presents," I said, backing up toward the window.

"I'm afraid you have no choice." Boaz turned to Sable. "And you're sure this is ready?"

"Like I told you before, the necklace wasn't made for this, but I think I have used its magic correctly. We won't know until you put it on her."

Erik let out an exaggerated sigh. "Let's get this over with. If this doesn't work we'll just kill her."

Boaz glanced at him sharply. "No one is to hurt her, do you understand? If this doesn't work, we'll find something else." He turned to face me. "Erik, hold her."

Erik moved behind me and pinned my arms to my chest. I didn't struggle—didn't see the point—but as the necklace moved closer and I was overcome by the suffocating feeling of absolute darkness, I thrashed wildly. It was an evil like nothing I'd ever felt before, the kind that exists only in a demon's nightmare. I tried to shake off Erik's grip, but I wasn't just fighting his strength. Sable was nearby, chanting under her breath.

With Boaz's free hand, he clenched my neck, and with the other, he twisted the necklace around me. He didn't have to latch it—it latched itself.

They all stepped away from me.

I held still, my hands outstretched as if I'd been doused with water. At first, nothing happened. But within moments, the darkest of dark energy was spreading throughout my body. My arm twisted and jerked, and then my leg shook uncontrollably. I collapsed to the ground in agonizing pain, but it wasn't physical. It was the pain of evil killing every part of humanity and decency inside me. I didn't think there was any left after all the horrible things I'd done, but evil searched me thoroughly and found parts of me, though they were few, that still had goodness in them.

After the dark energy had taken over my extremities, it turned inward toward my heart. It stabbed at it as if a hot poker, branding its mark upon my most vulnerable and precious organ. It burned with hell's fire, and I screamed. I didn't stop until evil's process was complete, leaving nothing left but pure, untainted rage.

I rose from the floor, power surging through me. Veins and arteries were visible just beneath my almost translucent skin; black blood pumped throughout my body. My hair had turned raven black, and it lifted in the air, swaying gently, despite their being no draft in the room.

Sable gasped, Erik grunted, and Boaz said, "Amazing."

"Look at her eyes," Sable whispered.

I couldn't imagine how they changed, but looking out from them, the world was covered in a red haze that accentuated the tiniest details. It gave the room an eerie quality I liked.

It wasn't just my vision that had been altered. Every one of my senses was magnified: I heard a deer breathing quietly in thicket far away, a bat's wings beating through the night air, and a tiny ant as it scurried to an underground destination. And even though all these events were occurring at the same moment, I had the ability to separate them, almost as if I were slowing time, if not stopping it.

I had become a God.

I curled my lips. "Mother. Father. I don't think I thanked you for coming out for my *transformation*."

"We w-w-wouldn't have missed it, Eve," Sable said and glanced at Erik hesitantly.

The sound of my former name felt as though she had pressed a cross to my forehead. "Don't call me that. Ever. Call me ..." I twisted my lips in thought. "Alarica. It means 'noble power'. Appropriate, don't you think?"

"How do you feel?" Boaz asked.

I moved my gaze to Boaz and slowly looked him up and down. I moaned and licked my lips. "I feel—omnipotent."

Boaz fed off my bliss. "It's incredible, isn't it? We are going to rule the world."

"We?"

"Of course, love. I fulfilled your dream. You and I together, doing whatever we want forever. With the power between us, we will be unstoppable."

"It wasn't my dream, *love*," I said. "It was Eve's."

Boaz's jaw clenched tight, but he controlled his anger. "No matter. You will realize that together we are more powerful."

I chuckled. "You really have no idea, do you?"

Boaz raised an eyebrow, Erik stood in a defensive position, and Sable backed up toward the door.

"I don't need you," I said.

Boaz took a threatening step toward me. "Let's not forgot that it was I who gave you this power. It can just as easily be taken away."

"Don't threaten me." With a thought, I sent him flying backwards into the wall. He smashed against it and fell to the ground in a crouching position.

When he looked up, he too had transformed himself into the true monster he was. His face was suddenly translucent. Black blood veins appeared behind his transparent skin. His blue eyes lit up like cold fire, and inside, his black pupils swelled from the darkness within them. They bulged outward as if the evil were trying to escape, but he shook his head once, and his pupils receded back to their original size.

Erik bolted for me. I grinned and stopped him with only a hand gesture. I then raised him to the ceiling and held him in midair. This new dark magic was so easy to control. I had only to think it, and my desires became a reality.

A stream of vulgar profanities spewed from Erik's lips.

"Rot in hell," I said and then flicked my wrist toward the window. He smashed through the glass and flew into the frigid air. His cries pierced the night until they were cut short by his body hitting the ground below. I scanned the room for Sable, but she had already fled.

Behind me, I sensed an object flying toward me at an incredible speed. I turned around and caught it a fraction of a second before it plunged into my stomach. I turned over Boaz's dagger in my hand. It was the same one that had pierced Eve earlier.

"I'm disappointed, Boaz. You turn me into what you desire, but now you want to destroy me?"

Still in a crouching position, with one hand on the ground, he growled, "Not destroy, but you need to be taught a lesson on who's boss here."

He rushed me and slammed into my body at full force. The weight of his body against mine threw us both into the wood headboard, splitting it in two.

I whispered a command, one in an ancient language—that of the first demons who roamed the earth before man. Boaz looked at me, surprised. In response to my magical command, the wooden frame bended and curled tight, trapping Boaz inside. I had already moved away and was standing on the other side of the room. I laughed at his predicament, but my laughter was cut short when Hunwald grabbed hold of the back of my calf. I cried out and jerked my leg away, throwing the wolf from me.

Meanwhile, Boaz had freed himself. "Very creative. You know more than I thought, but it doesn't change things. You will submit to me."

I smiled serenely, folding my hands in front on my lap. "You can't make me, and I'm not just saying that to be dramatic. There is absolutely nothing you can say to make me *ever* submit to you. But if you submit to me then maybe, just maybe, you might get out of here alive."

He let out a feral cry and rushed me again, but this time I was ready. I waved my arm and whispered the word "wall". Boaz crashed into an invisible barrier separating us. He stepped back, his eyes burrowing into mine. Something tickled my skin, as faint as a feather's wisp, and I smiled in understanding.

"You're trying to take my power, aren't you? Like you did to Eve. That's not going to happen." I paced back and forth, enjoying his frustration. "Before I destroy you, I want you to witness the destruction of the few things you might actually care about in this world."

Boaz wasn't listening as he was frantically searching for a way around the invisible barrier.

"Let's start with your feeder girls downstairs, shall we?"

His head snapped up. "What are you going to do?"

My eyes grew big, and I felt evil dance within them.

"Burn," I said.

An explosion downstairs rocked the house. Boaz cried out.

"And how about the immaculate gardens that you take such pride in?"

Boaz's eyes flickered to the window just in time to catch the woods bursting into flames.

"This isn't necessary," he shouted.

"Oh, but it is!" I shouted back. "You will be destroyed by the very evil you created. You stupid idiot! Did you really think true evil would share power?"

Frustrated, Boaz tossed a dresser across the room.

I closed my eyes briefly and opened them again. "I lost focus. Where was I? Ah, yes, destroying your 'creature comforts' of life. How about your precious opera house?"

Boaz stopped moving. "Impossible!"

"Is it?" I closed my eyes for just a moment before I snapped them back open and said, "Done. The Metropolitan Opera House is no more. Now for that Hell Hound of yours." I stared at Hunwald, who was barking furiously at me.

"Don't do it, Eve. Not Hunwald," he said.

"I'm not Eve," I cried. The wolf's fur ignited. Boaz was upon him in an instant with a blanket trying to snuff the flames.

"Awe, how touching," I said.

Boaz stood up very slowly. His chest heaved and, with both hands, he pushed against the invisible wall. I tried to fight back, but his rage proved too great. He broke through it with a ferocious veracity that sent a blast of air striking me square in the chest. I flew backwards out the same window my father had been thrown from only minutes before.

I hit the ground hard then, after taking a deep breath, I stood up and looked at the grand mansion one last time.

"Burn," I said, and I walked away.

Behind me, the very flames from Hell consumed their master and his home.

23

I returned to the only place I knew—my parent's home in upstate New York. Unfortunately, Erik and Sable were nowhere to be found. The torture I'd put them through would be my finest work yet. I had no doubts that Erik had survived the fall. Sable must have sensed what was coming and ran outside to either prevent it or fix his injuries. None of it mattered to me, though. As soon as I sensed them (most likely they were guarding their location with magic), I would destroy them like I did the Opera House.

It was a disappointment to still have Eve's memories, most of which were useless to me. There was the potential of many painful memories that I could have relished in, but whenever I tried to recall Eve's juicy abuse, they were cut short and replaced by a silly place she called Eden. This infuriated me because I only wanted to remember Eve's grotesque mistreatment.

It had been days, and I was incapable of sleep as the evil within me refused to hold still. It was restless and always searching for a way out, to destroy and mangle. I wish I could've released it all, but it would be stupid to destroy everything. What would be left? As a result, I released the evil in little spurts, destroying only what was necessary. I'd already burned the area around the home; I could still smell the smoke from outside. Only the mansion remained intact, but just barely. The only thing that saved it was focusing my dark magic on different areas of the country like I had with the Opera House. I'd picture it in my mind and then imagine its destruction. Buildings I'd visited, places I'd seen. Burned up in flames.

Containing the power required a lot of concentration, which gave me a constant headache. I forbade the servants from using all lights, allowing only the use of candles. This helped alleviate the pain somewhat as evil was not as restless within the dark. The first servant who balked at my request keeled over dead. The others obeyed out of fear just like they had with my parents. I knew the drill.

Every time I exploded something, I would have a few restful moments from the sharp pains in my head, but as days turned into weeks, the pressure grew, and I wondered how much more my body could take. If I could, I would have removed the necklace, but that was impossible. The evil inside me was far stronger than any will of my own.

All the recent fires and explosions baffled people. Because they couldn't come up with a logical explanation, they assumed it was terrorist attacks, and the country was on high alert. I laughed at them, at how the government tried to make the people feel safe. They would go to war if the attacks didn't stop—the President had said so earlier this morning. I hoped he wasn't bluffing. War would provide the perfect cover for my destruction.

Still without sleep, I paced the halls of the Segur estate at three in the morning with my hands clenched tight, nails digging into my palms. The pain was so intense that I couldn't think of anything else, not even a place to send the dark magic to.

The trapped energy screamed inside me, chanted and begged to be released. The skin on my arms vibrated strangely as if someone was holding a struck tuning fork to it. Then, to my horror, the skin began to stretch outward by the evil within. Physically, I could no longer control it. The left wing of the mansion exploded into flames, releasing some of the pressure.

It didn't take long for the old mansion to be consumed by the fire. The servants who had chosen to remain with me out of fear now fled. No attempt was made to save the home.

I walked out from within the fire; the flames did nothing but tease my skin. I drifted through the nearby blackened forest, no longer caring where I went. To prevent myself from feeling any more physical pain, I continued to expel the dark energy inside me, sending it whatever place I thought of first. Behind me, the morning sun touched the fading night sky and, if I could, I would've destroyed that, too.

"You've caused some major damage," a voice said.

Surprised I'd been caught off guard, I turned around. Not far stood the vampire Eve had met in New York City.

"I know you," I said.

It was his turn to be surprised. "I don't believe we've met."

He didn't recognize me, and I wondered if I even looked human anymore.

"What do you want?" I asked.

"To stop you."

"Is this a habit of yours? Stopping powerful women who just want to have some fun?"

"This may be fun for you, but innocent lives are being lost."

"You sound like a broken record."

His brow furrowed and his lips pursed together. Oh, come now, I couldn't be *that* hard to remember.

Levitating, I circled around him in a great loop, my bare toes dragging against the early morning frost. "How did you find me?"

He kept his eyes on me, his muscles tense. "Evil of your magnitude can be felt from any distance, if one is looking for it."

I liked him. He was brave when all others fled. I remembered how Eve had also been drawn to him, but for an entirely different reason, something to do with his eyes.

"Why do you seek out evil?" I asked.

"To stop it."

"Why would you do this, especially knowing my power? I could destroy you with just a thought."

"Then why haven't you?"

I titled my head. "You want to die?"

"I want to stop you. It is of no consequence to me if I die trying."

"You interest me, vampire."

He didn't respond, but his eyes flashed to my neck. "That's quite a necklace," he said. "Where did you get it?"

"It was a gift." My eyes narrowed. "Did you come for a friendly chat? I thought you wanted to stop me. Don't lose your focus."

He took my advice and bolted toward me at lightning speed. I let him attack, anxious to see what he was capable of. He struck me hard, and I flew backward to the ground. I thought he'd wait for my reaction, but he didn't stop. In an instant, he was upon me, fangs bared. His hands struggled to get at my neck or the necklace, I couldn't be sure which.

Finally, I'd had enough. I shoved him away hard, feeling his bones break beneath my palms. His limp body crashed into a dead, blackened tree that snapped in two. He collapsed to the ground, moaning and balled up with a grimace on his face.

"That was impressive," I said. "I thought you'd give a lady a chance to recover, but you couldn't get enough. I admire your passion."

The vampire hobbled first to his knees, then staggered to his feet, one hand clutching his side. His knees buckled, and his other hand reached out to steady himself against the broken tree trunk.

"I could use someone like you by my side," I said. "What do you say?"

"I'd love to," he said, breathing heavily. "But there's only one problem."

"What's that?"

"I *hate* witches." He rushed me again, but this time he jumped high into the air to flip over me. When he was directly above my head, I stopped his motion. He remained frozen in the air, feet up, his head dangling just inches from mine. He fought against my mental grip, but it was useless.

"Think about what I'm offering," I said. "I'm giving you life. I give this to no other."

He stopped thrashing and stared directly in my eyes. "Let me down."

I stepped out of the way and released him. He dropped to the ground, gracefully completing his flip. "Your plan tempts me. Maybe I will serve you."

"Just like that? You'd be my puppet boy?" I shook my head. "It's never this easy."

He shrugged. "I'm not a fool. You're clearly more powerful than me, and I've been with worse. It won't be that bad."

"That bad? You have *never* been with anyone like me."

Without warning, he lunged for me. I easily stepped out of the way. To me, his movements were slow, but in reality, he moved faster than I'd ever seen Boaz move. He reversed directions and ran at me again, scooping up a short branch in the process. I froze him within arm's reach.

"You're not learning!" I said. "You can't beat me. Why are men so dense?" I glanced at the tree branch in his hand. "And what exactly were you planning to do with that?" The veins in my face pulsed with anger. "No answer? Well, let me show you what I'll do with it."

Mentally, I took hold of the stick and turned it toward him, despite his resistance. The muscles in his face bulged from straining, and he grunted, spit running over his lips. He was strong but not strong enough. With a quick blast of mental energy, the branch stabbed through his gut and out his back, inches from his heart. He fell over, making a gurgling sound.

I casually approached him. "You are so beautiful, writhing in pain and agony. I could watch you for hours."

He struggled to speak.

I knelt beside him and stroked his head, but when my fingers went through his short black hair, I pulled it hard. "Don't ever trick me again."

And in that brief moment, while I was distracted, he reached up and tore the necklace from my neck.

24

Sunlight. Blinding, glaring sunlight. I squeezed my eyes tighter even though they were already closed.

I didn't want to wake up.

If I didn't wake up, then I wouldn't have to live. The thought of living right now was more frightening than anything I'd ever faced. Was that how it was with consequences? Could it be that living with them was more terrifying than committing the very act itself?

Despite the warm sunlight, a chill rocked my body. Alarica was gone. The evil that had existed within her no longer controlled my heart and mind, yet remnants of it remained like aftershocks of a massive earthquake. They were a constant reminder of all the damage I'd caused, all the innocent lives murdered by my alter ego's desire to destroy.

I tightened my fingers into the wet spring ground. The cool earth against my palm calmed my racing blood. The dirt brought life and death. I wasn't sure which sounded better at the moment. My reasoning ability was still muddled not only by Alarica's innate darkness, but also by my own. Because of my past actions, I'd lost the ability to choose right from wrong. I reasoned, however, that if I had the awareness to recognize my conscience had been lost, then maybe it was possible to get it back. I had taken a small step on that path before the necklace, but how would I do it now, after everything I'd done?

The vampire. The vampire who had destroyed Alarica. The vampire who had given me light. He would know. It was him who had told me that power was a dangerous thing. Maybe he could help me again.

Relaxing my fingers, I finally opened my eyes and sucked cool air into my lungs. I turned my head to the side. A glint of silver reflected the sunlight through the tall weeds. I squinted to get a better look. I jerked violently and scrambled away as quickly as possible until my back hit against a tree. I frantically looked around to make sure I was alone, and then returned my gaze to the necklace. *I must destroy it!*

I spotted a jagged stone poking out from the dirt and used my fingers to pry it free. I approached the necklace slowly as if it were alive. The blood inside the glass orb appeared frozen; ice crystals spread upon its surface like miniature spider webs.

Without hesitation, I lifted the rock and brought it down on the glass. I closed my eyes, expecting it to shatter, but instead the rock merely bounced off the orb. I peered out of one eye. The blood within the sphere was no longer solid—it was boiling. I reached for the orb, wanting to feel its surface for any signs of damage, but just as my finger was about to touch the clear exterior, the blood leapt at me, stopped only by the glass. I jumped and breathed heavily.

Before I could think twice, I raised the rock again and smashed it over and over until I could no longer lift my arm. Exhausted, the rock dropped from my hand. The necklace remained intact with not a single crack evident, but the boiling blood inside had turned black, and I had the eerie sensation that it was laughing at me.

Defeated, I stood.

Just over the tree line, a thin trail of smoke rose into the clear blue sky. I tore a thick branch from a nearby bush and placed it over the necklace, then I jogged toward the fleeting smoke, knowing I was close to my old home. After some distance, the trees thinned out, and where my parent's mansion once stood, only the walls of the east wing remained. I scanned the area looking for signs of life. If someone had come to inspect the source of the fire, they weren't here now.

I approached what was left of the home. Several fires burned low in different areas, and coals glowed bright. I carefully rounded the back to the remaining brick walls. There I found a few of my family's belongings that had not yet been destroyed. There was no sadness for the lost items. They were only reminders of a life I didn't want to remember.

Using a stick to poke through the remaining items, I tried to ignore the searing heat even when blisters formed on my feet and lower legs. Luckily, it didn't take long for me to find something I could use.

I bent down and used the bottom section of my nightgown to wrap up a small circular metal box. And even though the metal burned through my gown and to my hands, I maintained a tight grip. Pain was something I was used to.

Back in the forest, I removed the tree branch from over the necklace. The blood within it was back to looking frozen and still. I fell to my knees, letting my mother's jewelry box roll out of the nightgown and to the ground. The word "Sable" was elegantly etched into the circular lid.

The box, once a brilliant gold, now was a dark rust color with burned splotches. I opened the lid, knowing it would be empty. This box only ever contained one object: my mother's favorite ruby ring. She wore it more than any other piece of jewelry, and the box was only used to house the ring at night.

Carefully, I used a stick to lift the necklace from the ground. As I lifted it, the blood within the orb once again came to life. It thrashed inside the glass as if searching for a way out like a caged lion. I placed the necklace inside the jewelry box and closed the lid. With the necklace no longer in view, I let out a sigh of relief, but didn't relax too much. My task was not yet over.

I picked up the box and carried it to the long driveway leading to the destroyed mansion. The row of gnarled, angry-looking trees stood impervious to the earlier blaze. I walked past each one, eyeing them closely until I stopped in front of the third tree. It had a gaping knot in the center of the trunk as if a mouth forming the word "Oh!"

Using the same stick I'd used to transfer the necklace to the box, I dug at the base of the tree. I shoveled until the branch snapped, forcing me to use my hands. I dug as far as I could until the rocks became too big. After placing the jewelry box inside, I quickly buried it and made the top appear as if the ground had never been disturbed.

I stood up and inhaled deeply. With the necklace out of the way, I could finally concentrate on what to do next. There was no question that I would have to leave New York. Erik and Sable would come looking for me. My only hope was that they'd think I had died in the fire.

In the meantime, I needed help, and there was only one person whom I felt I could trust: Liane. I had to find a phone.

It took my about twenty minutes to find my way to the nearest neighbor. I wasn't worried about them recognizing me, as I'd never met them before, nor had my parents. According to Erik, our neighbors were below even a friendly nod. It wasn't that they were poor; in fact, quite the opposite. They had a huge stucco home and drove a Ferrari, but they were regular humans, which placed them well beneath the rank of the Segurs.

The housekeeper who answered the door didn't hesitate in letting me inside. One quick look over me—ash and soot covering my bottom half—and she asked, "You were in that fire, weren't you?"

Before I could answer, she told me her name was Lucy and that she was the one who had called the police the night before when she saw the fire on her way home. They had told her that because of all the recent fires in the cities, and because the fire was so far out in the country, no fire fighters would be coming. Instead they sent two police offers who, according to Lucy, simply watched the house burn down.

"They may as well have roasted marshmallows on that there fire," she said with obvious disgust. Then she asked me the one question I was hoping for: "Did everyone else get out okay?"

"It was only me and Eve, the Segurs only child," I said. I couldn't tell her I *was* Eve. I didn't look anything like myself anymore, and who knew if they'd ever seen me from the distance before my transformation. "I tried to get to her, but the fire spread so quickly! And then I was so overwhelmed by smoke that I passed out not far from the home."

"You poor thing. This is just like all them other fires in the city," Lucy said, biting at her lip. "It's scary, it really is. All these terrorist attacks. I'm thinking of moving with my children, maybe out west. There don't seem to be many fires there."

The inside of my chest collapsed. This is my fault. People are frightened because of what I have done.

Her brow furrowed and she clucked her tongue. "I wonder why terrorists would go after the Segurs."

I shrugged. "Do you mind if I use your phone? I need my friend to pick me up so I can go to the police. I'll let them call Eve's parents with the bad news."

"Of course, whatever you need." Lucy handed me her phone. "I'll be in the kitchen when you're finished. I'll make you some breakfast."

As soon as she was gone, I dialed Liane's number. She answered on the fifth ring.

"Liane?" I asked, but a giant lump in my throat prevented the word from coming out right.

"Eve? Is it really you? Where in the hell have you been? I've been calling and calling. One more day and would've stormed Boaz's castle. Why haven't you called? I've been so bored—"

"Something's happened, and I need your help," I blurted.

There was a brief silence on the other end. "Of course, anything. What's up?"

I was either too afraid or embarrassed to tell her everything so I didn't. "I don't think I mentioned this, but I moved home a couple of weeks ago."

"Oh no! Are you and Boaz having problems?"

"Not really," I lied. I didn't want the conversation to come anywhere near Boaz and the fact that he was dead. That conversation would have to wait until I was safely out of the state. "I just felt it was time to return home."

"Oh," Liane said. I heard the confusion in her voice. "Then what's wrong?"

"My parent's home burnt down last night. There's nothing left."

"That's horrible! How are your parents?"

"They weren't home."

"That's good, right?"

I paused. "Liane, I need you to promise you won't say a word to anyone of what I'm about to tell you."

"Of course. That's what sisters are for."

"I'm glad you said that." I tapped my fingers on the windowsill in front of me. "I need your help getting out of New York, and you can't tell a soul, not even Boaz."

"Why?"

"I need everyone to think I died in that fire."

"But *why*, Eve?"

"Please, Liane, just trust me. This is my chance to get away. They all must think I'm dead, even Boaz. He'll tell my parents otherwise."

"But I thought you loved him."

"Maybe. I just need to get away. Will you please help me?"

Liane sighed. "Sure. What do you need?"

"I need to borrow some money and clothes. And a ride to the nearest bus station or airport."

"Are you sure about this?"

"Absolutely."

"All right. I'll do it. Where are you now?"

"I'm at a neighbor's house, two miles east of my parent's home. Their address is 215 Birch Street just outside Chesterfield. It's a large white stucco home."

I could hear Liane scribbling in the background. "I'll be there as soon as I can. It will probably be a few hours."

"Thank you, Liane. You don't know how much this means to me."

"It's nothing. I'll see you soon. Be safe."

The receiver on the other end clicked. I waited a few minutes before returning to Lucy in the kitchen.

"I hope you're hungry," she said when I walked in. "And when you're finished, you can shower. I'll have clothes waiting for you when you get out."

I ate, showered, and dressed quickly. With each passing second, I mapped out my next moves. I would head to Chicago, a place my parents didn't like. I would get an apartment, a job, maybe as a waitress. It'd been my plan before Boaz came into my life.

Liane arrived early. After thanking Lucy for her hospitality and assuring her that I was going directly to the police, I hurried out to meet Liane before she could come into the house.

She jumped out of the car and threw her arms around me, embracing me tightly. After releasing me, she said, "I saw the home. It really was destroyed, wasn't it? Looks more like a bomb went off than a simple fire."

I averted my eyes. "Let's just get out of here."

"You got it," she said and returned to her seat behind the steering wheel.

"Is this new?" I asked when I closed the passenger door. The black-leathered seat felt like it had never been sat in before, and the inside of the Lexus was immaculate.

"It is. You like it?"

"It's amazing."

"It was a gift. So what's with your light hair?" Liane asked. "You look so different."

I ran my fingers through the long strands. "Thought I'd go all-

189

natural."

"It's … interesting," she said and then laughed.

Liane and I checked into a hotel just outside New York City near a bus station. During the drive over, Liane had kept the conversation light. She spoke of William and their latest adventure to Louisiana. Not surprisingly, this adventure *had* included a monkey. It panged me to hear of their fun and what I'd be missing. The only thing I wouldn't miss was the part where we were cruel to others.

"Do you ever have regrets?" I asked Liane once we had settled into the room.

Liane jumped on the bed and stretched out, a licorice rope between her lips. "Like what?"

I sat on the bed next to her. "We did some pretty horrible things to people."

"It's all in good fun. Besides, no one was really hurt. And since when did you care?"

I shook my head. "I just feel bad sometimes."

Liane sat up and wrapped her arms around her bent knees. "I admit, some of our pranks went too far, but that's never going to happen again, right?"

"What do you mean?"

"Well, you're leaving. Who knows if we'll ever see each other again?"

I hadn't thought about that. "You'll come visit me, won't you?"

Liane tilted her head and smiled. "I'm sure I will." She reached over and grabbed her purse off the nightstand. "Speaking of travel, here is your bus ticket to Chicago. It leaves at 5:30 a.m. Once you get there, take a cab to the Weston Hotel downtown. I've booked you a full month. I figure that should be enough time to get you on your feet, maybe find a sweet job pole dancing or something."

I laughed and playfully shoved her. "I don't know how I will ever repay you."

"I'll think of something. Now come on. Let's go have our last night out on the town."

I frowned.

"Not as witches," Liane said. "As sisters."

***

Before sunrise, I dressed quietly, careful not to disturb Liane who I knew was not a morning person. She'd also drunk quite a bit at dinner the night before and would probably have a massive headache if wakened too early. Instead, I wrote a short note, thanking her for everything and promising to call her as soon as I was settled.

I stepped outside into the crisp early morning air. I was about to begin a whole new life, and it would be entirely my own creation. This exhilarating thought made me walk faster toward the bus station. Other than an occasional dog barking, the streets were deserted and quiet. I stopped at an intersection and looked both ways before crossing. As I moved to take a step forward, someone grabbed me from behind. A cloth that smelled of chemicals and jasmine pressed against my nose and mouth. I struggled for a brief moment before the strong fumes overcame me.

Before I lost consciousness, a familiar voice said, "Where do you think you're going?"

25

My eyes fluttered open to a thick and heavy darkness. It was unbearably warm; great beads of sweat rolled down the sides of my face. I lay flat on my back against an unknown, hard surface, and when I raised my arms, they thumped short against something solid. My fingers groped the flat surface above me, and I winced in pain when a sliver slipped through my forefinger. Coarse wood boards ran the length of my body six inches above my face.

Mouth open, I sucked in the warm, stifling air. *Where am I?* I turned my head to the side and felt something brush against my cheek. I reached for it and rubbed it between my fingers. It felt like a plant. A memory stirred, and I inhaled deeply. The smell of jasmine was like a slap to my face. My breathing quickened as realization of where I was and what had happened came back to me.

I pushed up against the rough wood. Surprisingly, it took great effort, and I wondered how long I'd been trapped in what I now recognized as a crudely made casket. For my body to be this exhausted, I must've been trapped for several days, if not weeks. My heart raced, and my stomach felt hollow.

Using all the strength I could muster, I pounded my fists against the boards above me. At the same time, I bent my knees as far as they'd go and pushed upwards, but the boards didn't budge. "Erik! Sable! Please. Get me out of here!"

My cries punctured the darkness; the terror in my voice only made me cry harder. Over and over, I screamed until my throat burned.

Finally, I begged. "Mom."

The word hovered above me, trapped.

I thought back to the night's events before my parents took me. How did they even find me? The only person who knew where I was—

I stopped breathing—was Liane. Was she capable of betraying me like that? We were best friends, but the more I thought about it, the more I realized she would turn me over. I'm sure some kind of reward was involved. And me admitting remorse for our past actions probably repulsed her. She truly believed supernaturals were far superior to humans and would never feel sorry for them.

Fear turned to anger, and my body tingled, starting in my feet. Magic was coming. *No!* I closed my eyes tight and traveled to the one place that offered protection: Eden.

It had been well over a year since I'd visited; the exact same time I'd met Boaz. The place was more beautiful than I remembered. Clear, sea green water surrounded an island lush with trees and grass, golden sand at its edges. A mountain swept up the west side. On its backside was a steep cliff that I'd jumped from many times in the past, but that wasn't my goal today. I lowered myself onto the warm sand next to a purple flowering plant. Waves rolled to shore in a soothing patter, one after the other.

With my mind disconnected from my body, I could finally reason a way out of my current nightmare. My parents had taught me many things, but the only lesson worth remembering was that there was a solution to any problem. You just had to find one you could accept. I dug my toes farther into the wet sand, burying my feet.

What I thought unthinkable had finally happened. Erik had threatened to bury me alive my whole life as a form of punishment, but I always thought it was just that—a threat.

A wave to my left crashed to shore. In the distance, two dolphins danced upon the waters, jumping and diving. I had a vague recollection of speaking to them years ago. I smiled, the pain of my physical state completely gone. But I knew I had to return if I had any chance of surviving. And I did want to survive. I had to make things right and find Him, the one who finally set me free. Reluctantly, I left Eden but with a new, calm determination.

Back in the crudely made casket, I pulled the jasmine away from my head and shoved it toward my feet. My fingers traced the wood boards, carefully searching for any weaknesses. Eventually I found a slivered piece above my face that pulled off easily. I continued to pick at the wood, attempting to pull back its many layers. I flinched when my fingernail broke below the quick.

I told myself to breathe slowly, concentrate. I couldn't succumb to the darkness. I'd come so far in life, overcoming more obstacles than anyone in ten lifetimes. I wasn't about to give up now.

I tore off another piece of wood. Blood dripped from my fingertip and onto my cheek. I didn't stop to give my fingers the time they needed to heal.

I thought back to my time as Alarica. It felt like years ago, but in actuality, it couldn't have been more than a month ago, depending on how long I'd been lying unconscious in this grave. My parents and Boaz thought their dream was finally realized when I was transformed. All they had lived for, fought for, was realized the moment they put that damned necklace around me and gave life to Alarica. But not even they could imagine the horror she would bring, and in the end, they, too, ran in fear. Who knew how many more would've been destroyed if it had not been for Him, the vampire who showed me mercy when I deserved none. He even had the opportunity to kill me after I'd lost consciousness but didn't for some reason. What did surprise me, though, was the fact that he'd left the necklace. Something I'd have to ask him about when I find him.

Another wood chip peeled back. I switched to picking at the wood with my left hand, as the fingers on my right hand were raw and bleeding. I needed to give them a few minutes to heal.

I would find Him. I would get out of here and find Him.

I pried at the wood with my left hand, but it was almost as raw as my right, making it difficult to pick at the wood. Tears stung my eyes. I clenched my jaw tight and continued to work feverishly at the boards despite the pain.

I used my pinky—the only finger with feeling left in it, to touch the hole I had created in the board. It wasn't even half way through. I pushed on it as hard as I could and felt it flex under the pressure.

Magic could fix this so *easy*. But that's what my parents wanted me to choose: magic or trapped forever.

I choose neither.

I waited a few minutes then felt my fingers. They felt okay, nails had even grown back, and so I continued again, picking slowly at the wood. This time was much harder than the first. The wood in the center was more solid and didn't give away as easily. I worked as hard as I could until my fingers needed to rest. Little progress was made.

Time for a different approach. There was nothing in my pockets, but I did find the end of my zipper on my jacket. I wiggled it back and forth, twisted and pulled until the small metal tab popped off. The end of it would last much longer than my nails.

I started the process again. Hours seemed to pass, possibly even days. When I'd feel hopelessness and panic set in, which it seemed to do every so often, I would go to Eden. Time became irrelevant. That's how it is with the dead.

Sliver after sliver, the board eventually broke down. With my focus entirely on the task, I failed to notice a small piece of earth when it fell to my face–that is until a handful of dirt broke through. I covered my hands over the hole and turned my head to cough out the dirt that had partially fallen inside my mouth. Then, very carefully, I curled my fingers inside the earth and around the rough wood edges.

With all my might, I pulled the board down. It caved under the pressure like a battered melon, crushing my chest. I didn't have time to gasp for air before dirt began to fill my nose and mouth. I quickly dug my bare heels into the bottom of the casket and pushed up. My arms reached upwards, moving the dirt out of the way. The top part of my body soon became encased by moist earth, making it extremely difficult to move.

I focused on my legs—the only part of me that could still move as they were still partially beneath the unbroken section of the crudely made casket. I wiggled my feet under me, and with my knees bent, I propelled myself toward the surface and my freedom. My hope was that I was in a shallow grave.

My hands broke through to the cool surface above, but just barely. I tried to use my legs, but now they too were encased by the impacted earth. My hands, not far out enough to render any assistance, wiggled uselessly.

The earth's grip tightened around me like a boa constrictor. I tried to inhale any last remains of air, but dirt rushed into my throat. As my mind burst into dark reds and blacks of impending unconsciousness, I thought of Him. I relaxed my body and pictured the vampire in my mind. I would take him to Eden, I decided. He would fit nicely there.

I was almost to Eden when something took hold of my hand and lifted me out of the collapsed grave. Night air rushed at my face, and I tried to breathe it in but only choked further. A hand clasped my chin and tilted back my head. Cold fingers reached into my mouth and scooped out the majority of the chalky dirt. After several coughs, my lungs finally filled with air.

I struggled to sit up but collapsed to the ground, exhausted. A man's legs stepped away from me and toward a tree. He appeared to be leaning against it, but I couldn't be sure as I was too tired to move the matted hair out of my eyes.

I breathed quietly, trying to ascertain my surroundings with what little view I had. I appeared to be in a forest with thick vegetation all around. It must've been a full moon because the bright lunar light cast ghostlike shadows all around me. I wondered about the stranger who stood not far from me.

Breaking the silence, the man spoke in a heavy English accent. "That happened to me once."

26

"What?" I asked. The word hurt my raw throat.

"Being buried alive. It was a wretched experience."

When I said nothing, the stranger spoke again, "My name is Charlie, Alarica."

I winced at the sound of my former name. "That's not my name."

"Then would you be so kind to tell me what your name is?" he asked.

I hesitated, not sure if I should give him my real name. Whoever this was, there was a good chance my parents had sent him to watch over the grave, which meant he already knew my name. "Eve. There is no Alarica."

"How can I be sure?"

My brows furrowed. Wouldn't someone sent by my parents know that I didn't have the necklace anymore? They did put me in this grave, after all. But if we weren't related, how else could he have found me? I chose not to answer him, but instead asked my own question. "What day is it?"

The man's jacket scraped against the tree as he lowered himself to the ground. "Tuesday."

"No, the actual date," I said.

"April 15th. How long have you been in there?"

I swallowed hard, which made my throat hurt even more. That meant I'd been in that hole for almost two weeks. A wave of nausea washed over me. "How did you find me?"

"Your mother told me—sort of." He chuckled to himself.

"To save me or kill me?"

"Neither, actually," he said.

"Then why would she tell you where I'm at?

He hesitated. "She didn't verbally tell me."

"I don't understand."

Charlie clicked his tongue. "Basically, I read her mind. It took some time and some *special* convincing, but eventually her thoughts gave your location away. How did they capture you anyway?"

I lifted my hand and swept the hair away from my face, giving me a clear view of Charlie. Even though he was sitting down, I could tell he was tall by the way his crossed legs stretched across the ground. He looked to be in his mid-twenties and had curly brown hair that was long on top and short on the sides. Tight curls dropped below his eyebrows and into his almond shaped, green eyes. He watched me, his expression full of concern.

But appearances could be deceiving.

I knew men like Charlie. They were excellent manipulators. "If you can read minds," I said, "why don't you just read mine and leave me alone."

"I only use my abilities when I have no other choice. So far you have been most cooperative."

"So if I stop answering your questions, you're going to violate my privacy with your mind-reading skills?"

Charlie's expression turned cold. "I will do whatever necessary to be sure you will not hurt anyone ever again. It's not about me or you; it's about innocent lives—innocent people that *you* killed."

His rebuke stunned me. "I'm sorry, I shouldn't have said that. I'm just not used to people doing things other than for themselves."

Charlie's warm smile returned. "There is much for you to learn about people and the good they are capable of. I'm afraid your parents skipped this important life lesson."

I remained silent, too ashamed to speak again.

"Don't worry," he said as if sensing my thoughts. "It will take a long time, if not years, for you to learn to trust others. You can't undo a lifetime of abuse in one day. But the most important thing you must remember, Eve, is that you are no longer a victim. They have no more power over you unless you let them."

"And how do I know I can trust you?"

"Easy." He jumped to his feet and came toward me. I cowered, unsure what he was going to do next. He raised his unarmed hands. "Don't be scared. I just want you to touch my hand. I'm going to open my mind to you so you can see my true intensions, okay?"

I nodded.

Charlie lowered his right hand and held it toward me. It took effort, but I managed to raise my arm and touch the back of his hand. A sudden flash illuminated my mind and within that light there were thousands of pictures, layers upon layers of Charlie's memories: his first lost tooth, the Christmas were he got his first bike, his first kiss. The memories came so fast that I barely recognized most of them, but I did learn something. Charlie was one of the good guys. His whole life was filled with laughter, kindness, and love, so unlike my own.

Satisfied, I withdrew my hand and asked, "How do you know so many things about me?"

Charlie returned to his place against the tree. "Partly my psychic ability and the other part through our connections with different people. You'd be surprised what I'm able to find out about a person."

I bit the inside of my lip and averted my gaze. Moonlight broke through the tree branches and encased me in its light. I wasn't used to being in the light. If I were stronger, I would've slid into the shadows.

I moved my hand beneath my chest and pushed down on the ground, forcing my body upright. Charlie moved to help, but I raised my hand to stop him. I slowly maneuvered myself into a sitting position.

"Can I ask how you ended up in this predicament?" he asked, his gaze lowering to the collapsed grave.

"My parents captured me as I was running away. I thought they'd believe I was dead and not try to find me, but I was wrong." I paused at the sudden pain in my chest. Liane's betrayal was almost worse than being buried alive.

"Why would they think you were dead?"

"A fire burned my house down. I was hoping they'd think I was in it at the time, but they obviously didn't. They found me and gave me something that knocked me out. And when I came to, I was in there." I motioned my head to the hole next to me.

"What happened to Alarica?"

"A vampire destroyed her. He tore this necklace from my, I mean, Alarica's neck. It was controlling me."

Charlie frowned.

"What is it?" I asked.

"It's odd that a vampire, who doesn't work for us, would do something like that and then not kill you."

"Work for you?"

"I guess I should explain who I am and the company I work for." Charlie brought his knees to his chest. "There's so much to explain, I don't know where to begin." He sat for a minute and then continued, "Have you heard of the Deific?"

I said nothing.

"No, I guess you wouldn't have, considering who your parents are," he said.

But that couldn't be further from the truth. I had heard the word "Deific" before. It was the only word my parents had forbade me to use. When I was ten, I'd said it after overhearing the word used by a guest of my parents. I'd asked my mother what it meant, and instead of answering, she grabbed me with inhuman strength and dragged me to the cellar where I remained locked up in the dark for days with only dirty water from a broken pipe to sustain me.

When my parents finally released me, they lectured me for

hours on how that word was not to be used ever in their house, all the while a large feast of chicken and potatoes sat untouched behind them. I eagerly agreed to anything they said just to have one bite, but when they finished their lecture, they whipped me three times and gave me stale bread to eat instead. I never said the word "Deific" again.

"The Deific," Charlie began, but stopped and looked at me sitting awkwardly on the ground. My arms were shaking just trying to hold up my body. "Why don't we go somewhere more comfortable and then I'll tell you everything."

I shook my head. "I want to know now."

"If you insist, but I'm going to keep it brief. You obviously need food and a lot of rest." He straightened his legs again.

"The Deific is a secret organization created several hundred years ago. We have one purpose: to bring balance between good and evil. Whenever evil, regardless of what form it comes in, becomes too great, the Deific steps in. It doesn't matter if the evil is human, witch, monster, demon, or vampire, the Deific always right the balance by any means necessary. And that is why I am here. We discovered that a witch named Alarica was the cause all the recent fires, the ones that have killed a lot people. We'd never heard of a witch named Alarica so we were very concerned."

"Did you come here to kill me?" If he had tried in that moment, I don't think I would've stopped him. It was what I deserved, wasn't it?

"I came here to kill Alarica, but you just informed me that you are Eve. We've never had concerns for the daughter of Sable Whitmore and Erik Segur, though I must admit when you were born, we were worried." Charlie furrowed his brow. "By the way, how did you become Alarica?"

"It wasn't by choice. It was my parents and—Boaz," I could barely say his name.

His eyes grew big. "Say that again?"

In a louder voice, I said, "Boaz."

"I know this may be difficult for you, but I must know more about this Boaz." Charlie's tone was hard, yet he managed to keep his expression gentle, encouraging me with a small smile.

I breathed in deeply to relieve the pressure on my chest, and then said, "He was a vampire. My parents introduced him to me when I turned eighteen, almost a year ago." *Had it only been that long?*

Charlie leaned forward. "What does he look like?"

I groaned, his image still fresh in my mind. If only I could forget his face, but he refused to be stuffed into the confines of my mind with the rest of my past, leaving me with a constant reminder of who I was and what I'd done. "I can't. I'm sorry."

"Please, it's very important."

"He had long black hair and dark green eyes," I blurted.

"No offense, but you just described ninety percent of vampires."

My muscles tensed. "You don't know what you ask. You couldn't possibly ..." I forced myself to calm down. Boaz was gone, so what did it matter? Why was I getting so upset? I met Charlie's gaze and said, "He had a tattoo of a snake on his forearm."

Charlie reared back. "It can't be."

"Why?"

He was talking to himself, but too quietly for me to make out any of the words.

"What's wrong?"

Charlie stopped mumbling and looked up at me as if he was surprised to still see me there. He cleared his throat. "That's the thing, Eve. That vampire, Boaz ... he was already dead."

"What do you mean, he was already dead?" I pressed. "Because he's a vampire?"

"No," Charlie said. "We killed him once before. If what you are saying is true, he came back. Are you sure you have his description right?"

I swallowed around the tightness building in my throat. He'd been killed before, and didn't really die. What if he came back again?

"Eve?" Charlie said, waving his hand to catch my attention again. "I said, are you sure you described him right?"

I nodded, my hands trembling, unsure if I could even form words.

Charlie dropped his hand back to the side. "I've worried you. I'm sorry, but right now we need to focus on Alarica. You were telling me how she came to be. Please, go on."

I took a deep, shaky breath, and wrung my hands together. It was time to move on, and that meant getting everything out on the table. "My parents put a strong spell, more like a curse, on some old silver necklace with a glass orb gripped between what looked like spider legs."

I wondered briefly if I should've begun at the true beginning, the part where Boaz injected me with some kind of immortal serum, but the time didn't feel right.

Charlie balled his fists again, and I noticed something flash in his eyes, but when he didn't say anything, I continued, "The orb was filled with blood. Whatever they did to it changed me. The moment that thing was around me all I could feel was hate. I smelled it, breathed it, I could even taste it. I was filled with such rage that I couldn't help but destroy everything in my path. Physically, my body couldn't contain the power." My voice cracked.

"It wasn't you, though, not really," Charlie said. "True darkness has a way of transforming people into what it wants for itself. Your ability to choose was taken from you the moment that necklace went around your neck."

"But part of it was me. They were my feelings, my pain that Alarica used. If it wasn't for the vampire who'd stopped me, I would've hurt so many more people."

Charlie leaned forward. "I can't imagine what you've been through all these years, but you have a chance now at a new beginning, a new life."

"I don't see how's that possible. My parents will see that my grave has been destroyed, and know that I'm free."

"We'll take care of the grave, and as for your parents, they don't matter anymore."

"You're wrong about that. Erik will never give up. He will hunt me down until I'm dead."

Charlie pursed his lips together. "Right. Your father. There's something I should tell you." He clicked his tongue again.

"What is it?"

"Your father, well, he's dead."

27

"Dead?"

"By his own hand, I think," Charlie mumbled, rubbing the back of his neck. "It was strange. We captured your parents about a week ago and were questioning them when all of a sudden your father keeled over. His heart just stopped. Personally, I think he stopped it himself."

Erik was dead? A feeling sort of like being punched in the gut sucked the air from my lungs, and my head began to spin. I looked up to the circling trees above. Charlie said something else, but I didn't hear him over the ringing in my ears.

"Eve?"

"I need to get out of here," I said before I lost the ability to speak all together.

Charlie scrambled to his feet. "Hold on. I'll help."

He wrapped my arm around his shoulders and easily lifted me to a standing position. I leaned into him, trying hard to keep my feet beneath me, as he walked me through the dark forest.

I didn't know where he was taking me, nor did I care. Erik was dead. The man who had tortured me mercilessly, the man who was also my father. I should feel glad, but the feeling wasn't coming. In its place came a barrage of emotions too much for me to process.

When I stumbled over a log, Charlie's hand gripped my waist. "Just a little bit further," he said. "My car is just over that ridge."

It wasn't long before the forest gave way to a grass field with blades that came to my knees. The full moon provided plenty of light, but I tripped again. This time, Charlie didn't steady me. He scooped me up and carried me in his arms. Too exhausted to protest, my head fell against his chest, and my eyes closed. I didn't think about anything except for the steady movement of Charlie's footsteps, the swooshing of his steps through the tall grass, and the sound of his steady heartbeat. Before I knew it, I fell asleep.

I woke when Charlie set me down and opened a car door. The black metal of the vehicle—a sports car of some kind—was shiny and had sharp lines that curved up toward the front of the car and then smoothly curved back down into a V on the hood, meeting the lines on other side of the car. A six-inch, silver metal statue of an angel with wings perched on the front hood.

"Nice car," I mumbled, my eyes still half-closed. Charlie helped me into the leathered passenger seat, then rounded the car to hop in behind the steering wheel.

With a press of a button, he brought the engine to life. "Go back to sleep. We have about an hour's drive."

Charlie drove along a deserted road, passing several small towns and rural farmhouses until eventually there was nothing but trees. The area was not familiar, but the taller mountains in the distance told me we were going toward Canada.

He turned the car onto a bumpy dirt road that wound itself through an overgrown forest. It had probably been years since someone else had driven on this same path. I leaned my head against the window and, as I'd done my entire life, I didn't allow myself to feel anything. Hearing of Erik's death had brought many emotions to the surface, and they had almost overwhelmed me, but now, under the soft moonlight, I thought of nothing.

Charlie glanced sideways at me. "I'm sorry about your father."

"Don't be. It was a good thing."

"I had no idea he'd do something like that. Maybe I would've handled things differently."

"What of my mother? Where is she?"

"We have her. She won't be leaving anytime soon."

I breathed a sigh of relief. "So I really am free?"

Charlie took his eyes off the road to address me. "No. There are others who may not believe you are a dead, especially Boaz."

"Boaz won't be looking for me."

"How can you be sure?"

"He's dead. At least I think he is, but if he was able to come back from the grave once … "

"How?"

"I blew up his house with him in it."

"Did you actually see him die?" he asked.

I repressed a shiver. "No."

"Then we can't assume he's dead. I'll get a team together to search for him. But in the meantime, you need to stay hidden for a very long time."

"Why?"

"It wasn't just Boaz who would do you harm. Both sides of your family would love to get their hands on you."

I silently agreed, remembering the encounter with my Grandfather months ago. "So is that where we are going now? To hide me?"

"Yes."

After a moment of silence, I turned abruptly to Charlie. "What did Sable do when she saw Erik die?"

"She laughed. He died right next to her, and she laughed."

He pressed on the brake, slowing the car when the dirt road became more difficult to navigate. There were times when I thought the car wouldn't fit between two trees but somehow it managed to squeeze through. Finally, the forest opened to a wide clearing and in the middle was a small log cabin.

"Here we are," Charlie said, taking the keys out of the ignition. "It's not much but we did make some improvements." He opened his door and headed toward the cottage.

I stepped out of the car. "What is this place?"

"This is your new home," he answered without turning around.

"My new home?"

Charlie opened the door of the cottage and then looked back at me. "Where else would you go?"

"I was going to Chicago," I said, but suddenly realized how bad of an idea that was now. I couldn't use Liane's money or support, not after what she did to me.

"It's much safer if you stay here, at least for a while."

I nodded and followed Charlie inside the darkened home. Lights flipped on, pushing the darkness to the corners of the room.

The cabin was surprisingly modern with gray walls and black and white furniture. Teal-colored pillows and a matching ocean painting hanging on the wall balanced out the room. In a way, the painting reminded me of Eden, and I wondered if Charlie somehow knew about my private sanctuary.

From the hallway, Charlie called, "You'll have everything you need here. A woman named Nora will drop off groceries and whatever else you want every Saturday. Just make a list." He returned to the living room. "The rest of the home is in order. Bedroom and bath are at the end of the hall. There's even a small library."

"Why are you doing all this?" I asked.

Charlie opened a refrigerator in the kitchen and removed cheese and turkey. "Sandwich?"

I lowered myself into a chair at the counter. "Please."

"So why am I helping you, you ask?" he said as he removed a knife from a drawer. He proceeded to cut the turkey into thin slices before saying, "I sense a lot of anger and fear in you. It's created a darkness that's nearly overtaken your mind and heart, but there's this light …" He closed his eyes and tilted his head as if tuning in to a distant sound. "It's fighting against the darkness." He opened his eyes. "It's bright, but it needs time to grow."

I didn't realize my mouth was open until I closed it.

He continued. "I want to give you the safety and the time you need to become the person you were meant to be. That's why I want to help you. The Deific, however, they see you as viable force for good and want you on our side."

"I don't want to be on anyone's side," I said.

Charlie placed the turkey and a slice of cheese in between two slices of bread and handed it to me. "And that's all right. For now. But the time will come for you to choose sides. Battles come in many different forms, and we all must face one, if not many, at some point in our lives. And when that fight comes, we must choose a side."

I took a bite and thought about it, slowly chewing. After I swallowed, I opened my mouth to speak, but he interrupted me.

"Don't make a decision now. It's going to take time for you to heal and to discover who you are. Nothing else matters." He slid a glass of milk toward me. "You have a lot to think about and years to do it in."

"Years?"

"You'll be surprised how long it takes to overcome what you've been through. It won't be easy, but I think this place will help you heal. It's helped others."

While Charlie put away the food and wiped off the counter, I glanced around the small cabin, focusing lastly on the ocean painting. "How did you know to prepare all of this? I thought you came to kill me—I mean, Alarica."

"The Deific doesn't always trust my gift. I told them I'd find someone other than Alarica, but they still had me prepared to kill her just in case."

"I mean no disrespect, but how exactly were you planning on killing Alarica? She was pretty much invincible."

He smiled. "I didn't come alone." Charlie straightened. "You'll find more food in there, and there's clothing in the bedroom. After I leave, I suggest a hot bath and perhaps some fresh clothes."

I glanced down at my jeans and t-shirt. They were covered in so much dirt that I couldn't tell what color they were anymore.

"There's a phone in the library," he said and rounded the kitchen counter toward the front door. "Please only use it to call Nora or myself. Our numbers are in the desk."

"You're leaving?" I asked. My hands began to shake, and I quickly moved them behind my back. The thought of being alone right now suddenly terrified me.

Charlie's shoulders sagged. He turned and stared directly in my eyes. "Eve, you have suffered through horrible things no child should ever go through, but that time is over—no one will hurt you ever again. You were a victim once but no longer. Never think of yourself as a victim. If you do, then you are still empowering those who have harmed you. Go forward and choose to live your life, because if you're always looking in the past, then you'll never have a future."

"Will I see you again?" I asked.

"I hope so, but something tells me it won't be for a very long time. Do take care of yourself, and when you're ready, call me."

Without another word, he left, closing the door behind him.

28

The first several days at the cabin, I thought of nothing, afraid the smallest memory might overwhelm me. I repeated the most mundane tasks, keeping life as simple as possible: wake up, shower, eat, go for a walk, read, eat, read some more, walk some more, eat again. Every day I told myself that after a good night's sleep and a decent breakfast, I would leave in the morning. But the next day came and went. Soon the days turned into weeks and weeks into months until time stopped entirely. I didn't think of my parents, or Boaz and Charlie, or even the vampire with the sorrow-filled eyes. I had become like the large oak tree that grew next to the cabin: predictable, steady, and unaware to life beyond its branches.

Nora was my only visitor. She was an older, large woman with long brown hair that was always pulled back into a thick braid. Freckles sprinkled her ruddy complexion like cinnamon, and her bottom lip continually stuck out from a wad of tobacco. She wasn't the most eloquent speaker and often cursed for no reason. I had never been around anyone like her before, but I grew fond of her straightforwardness and her plaid shirts and tight jeans.

On the days Nora visited, she brought me all the food I could ever eat plus letters from Charlie. I never read them, though. Instead I placed them in a drawer for another day. And every few months, Nora would come with new clothing, but I often refused as I didn't want to accept anything I couldn't pay for. I already felt guilty for using the cabin and food. Somehow I'd pay them back. One day.

When Nora would come, very few words would pass between us. Our dialogue consisted of the weather, what food she'd bring, and other impersonal things. It wasn't that I didn't want to get to know her, but it was just easier for me to exist as a shadow, unknowing to the present and future, but most importantly to the past. Occasionally, I would catch Nora staring at me, but gratefully, she never asked any questions.

After what I assumed was a short time, but in actuality was many months, I found a crossbow and a several arrows in the small attic of the cabin. This gave me something new to do, so I spent a lot of my time in the forest, practicing at different targets until I became quite good. I could throw an apple into the air and shoot an arrow straight through its heart.

One early spring morning, I returned from target practice, the crossbow in hand and quiver on my back, to find Nora resting against the bumper of her beat-up pickup truck. When I approached, she spit on the ground.

"You've been practicing again," she said.

"Yup." I walked by her and onto the porch where I placed my bow. "You're here early. What's up?"

"I'm old, fat, and tired. That's what's up." Nora spit again. "And I'm tired of wasting my time."

"Excuse me?" I turned around, startled by her words, and for the first time in a long time, I really looked at her. Nora's head was sprinkled with gray hair, more so then the thick brown hair I remembered her having, and she seemed thinner. My eyes widened. "Has so much time passed?"

"It ran right over the top of me."

I took a few steps toward her. "I'm sorry I didn't notice sooner."

"About that. It's time you put your big girl panties on and get out into the world. No more hiding."

I smiled. "I know. I'll leave in the morning."

Nora laughed, but it turned into a sharp cough. When she finished, she wiped her mouth the back of her hand. "You've been saying that bull crap for seven years."

I gasped. "Seven years?"

"Seven long years for me, but you still don't look a day over nineteen."

I looked down. "I never explained—"

"And you don't have to. I've seen stranger things than a girl who doesn't age." Nora spit again. "I can't come up here no more. I've got family out west who's going to take care of me."

"What's wrong?"

"It doesn't matter. What matters is getting you out of this hellhole you've created for yourself. I kept thinking you'd grow tired here, but you've become too comfortable. Someone needs to kick your ass into action, and seeing how I'm the only one around, it might as well be me."

My legs grew weak, and I stumbled back until I collapsed into a chair on the porch.

Nora straightened and came slowly toward me as if approaching a skiddish animal. "I know this will be hard, but you have to listen to me. You are too valuable a person to simply exist in some remote part of the world. People out there need you, your gifts and your talents, but the only way you'll be of any use to anyone is if you learn to feel again. The good, the bad, the ugly, which I'm sure you've had your fair share of."

I shook my head vehemently. "I can't do that."

"Why the hell not?"

"I'm afraid of myself, of what I might do. All I know is hate and anger."

Nora straightened and rocked back on her heels. "There's only one thing that will destroy that. You have to forgive. Forgive all those who have caused you pain."

"That's impossible."

"Anyone tell you, you complain a lot? Nothing's impossible. You just take a forgiveness knife to your heart and cut out all that hate, otherwise you'll continue this empty existence forever."

My heart raced. "Why should I forgive them? They don't deserve it!"

Nora reached out and placed her surprisingly warm hand on my cheek. "It's not for them, dear. It's for you, because *you* deserve it."

"I don't know how to forgive." I wasn't even sure I knew how to feel anymore.

Nora squatted in front of me until she was at eye level. "Deal with the past, with all those who have hurt you. And as you remember, you'll find that with everything they did to you, you had a choice in how you responded, whether it was to run away or let yourself be filled with hate. They may have bound you physically, but they couldn't touch your mind. Think back. They never had any power over you. They still don't, if you don't let them. Once you realize this, you will be able to forgive because you know they can never hurt you again. And then, despite any obstacles, you will be free to experience happiness and love."

I scowled. "I wouldn't know what to do with love."

Nora smiled. "That doesn't matter. Love will know what to do with you." She straightened and removed an envelope from her back pocket. "Let this be your last letter, Eve. Remember your life. See that they had no power over you. Then forgive."

After dropping the letter into my lap, Nora touched the top of my head and then walked to her truck. The rumbling of the engine coming to life made me jump.

I didn't say anything, didn't feel anything as Nora disappeared into the trees, but I did ponder her words until I finally admitted I did want happiness, out there in the real world. And maybe if I could feel it, I could get over my self-loathing and finally do some good in the world to make up for all the horrible things I'd done.

I began with Charlie's letters. Tentatively at first, afraid to read about the world outside my little cabin, but as I read over his words I found myself starving for the next letter and then the next. I tore through them, reading for many days.

Charlie spoke about the Deific mostly, about each of his missions and how they were helping people. It was evident that he loved his job and believed in what he was doing. After some time, however, his words focused on one thing: *Moira,* a woman he'd met while at the library. She was an elementary school teacher and a sports enthusiast. Charlie shared with me their many adventures, even the ones that didn't go so well like the time they got stuck in the mountains and had to hike out. But he cherished every moment and all because of her, the woman he loved.

Eventually they married. I shed a tear of joy when he shared with me his wedding vows to Moira. He truly was happy, and in a way I envied him. Maybe one day I could be that happy too.

But after many more letters, something changed. He no longer spoke of Moira, and he lacked the passion he once held for his job. His letters were dark and spoke only of his hunt for evil in the world. This new side of Charlie worried me. Something horrible had happened to him, and my heart ached to help him.

I clutched the last letter to my heart. There's no way Charlie could've known it, but after reading his letters and realizing that he was probably telling me things he told no other, I felt closer to him than anyone else in my life. Charlie had unknowingly become my dearest friend.

It was time to change, to make things right.

When I looked around the old cabin, I realized it was more a prison than a home—a prison I had created. Since I was going to live an eternity anyway, I determined right then and there that it wasn't going to be in this stuffy cabin, and it wasn't going to be without joy. The thought of what I was about to do terrified me, but I knew no other way.

I waited for darkness to reclaim the sky before I set out into the woods. With the kind of emotions I was about to invoke, I needed to be as far from the cabin as possible for fear of any damage I might cause. My leg tripped over a log, and I almost fell.

Pick up your feet. Don't stop.

It took every ounce of strength I had to keep walking through the forest that smelled like dirt and wet leaves. My life was difficult enough to live the first time, but to deliberately relive it again made me physically ill.

I looked up, hoping to see the moon, which had always comforted me, but tonight it hid itself behind angry clouds. A bolt of lightning split the night sky in half, and a roar of thunder came right after, shaking the ground beneath my feet. I pushed forward as far as I could until I collapsed by a mossy stump. I leaned against it and wrapped my arms around my knees. It was time. Face my past so I could move on to my future.

I closed my eyes and remembered, starting with my earliest memories. One after another, they flashed before me: my father standing near my bed, dangling a venomous snake in his hand, my mother's "quiet" room for days on end, the beatings for refusing magic. I remembered it all.

The memories seemed to last for hours, and during the more painful ones, I sobbed uncontrollably while struggling to breathe. I was so consumed with the pain that I almost forgot to do as Nora asked: to remember how I responded to their abuse. I didn't have to think hard. My refuge had always been Eden. Whenever the pain became too unbearable, I'd disconnect my mind from my body and travel to my secret island where my parents had no power over me.

My memories and thoughts came to a grinding halt. *They had no power over me.* No matter what they did to me, they couldn't touch my Eden. Eden was my own, and only I could control it. It was like a switch had been turned on, and suddenly everything seemed brighter. My parents never had any real control over me. Nothing they did could change who I wanted to become. They were as insignificant as the spider that now crawled up my leg. I flicked it off into the darkness.

I took a deep breath. Cool air flowed freely into my lungs, and my chest felt lighter as if someone had cut several tight bands from around it. I didn't know if what I was experiencing was forgiveness or not, but I did know that I no longer cared about what my parents had done. This process was easier than I thought it would be. Maybe it was because my parents never pretended to be anything else. For as long as I could remember, they never claimed to love me. They made their intentions known to me at a very early age: we were not to have a normal parent/child relationship. This is where I had failed. I expected my parents to love me simply because I was their child, despite what they constantly told me. *What a fool I've been.* I almost smiled.

The dark clouds above the canopy of trees cracked, and the first drops of a spring rain fell through. It felt good on my skin and gave me added strength for what I needed to do next.

I could've stopped right then and refused to remember the rest, refused to forgive the rest. My parents weren't the only ones who had hurt me. It was Boaz and *his* friends, specifically Liane. My whole body filled with hate as I remembered. The rage came upon me in great waves, but I didn't try to stop it—I unleashed it.

29

The black magic, darker than night, raced from my fingers and toes, spreading across the landscape and up the trees as great finger-like appendages in search of its next victim. The cold blackness killed everything it touched. Budding flowers wilted to ash, wisps of grass turned brown and dead, and unsuspecting insects and animals rotted within seconds.

I remembered every moment, every second, with such clarity that I felt as if I were watching my life play out on a movie screen. My whole perspective changed as I saw Boaz slowly manipulate me into using magic. It was his gentle voice, his tender touch, and his eagerness to please me that caused the blinding shroud to come over my eyes. I chose to ignore his darkness that was always right there on the surface, waiting anxiously to come out.

I'd been so stupid to trust him. His true nature had been revealed on multiple occasions, but my desire to be loved and accepted made me ignore the obvious. I justified all his behavior and eventually my own, thereby becoming a slave to evil's master.

The weight of all my past actions crushed me, making it difficult to breathe. All the innocent lives destroyed because I had been a fool. I tormented myself with visions of their burned bodies and terrified cries. The heavy darkness, mixed with the sounds of their tortured souls, pressed upon me, stealing the last of my breath. They willed me to die as they anxiously waited to escort me to hell where I belonged. I wanted to answer their cries and give them what they wanted.

But that would be the easy way out.

It would be easy not to live, not to deal with the consequences of my actions. Hell wouldn't be much different from living in the cabin, alone, existing only in an empty shell. I was comfortable living like that. It was a coward's way of life, and I had embraced it.

I fought against the darkness, willing it away. I was not yet ready to let it claim me, not when I still had the chance to make it right. The weight upon my chest lifted slightly as hope grew in my heart, a small light to push back the darkness. The light reminded me of the vampire who had saved me from Alarica. I bit the inside of my cheek. If he hadn't stopped me...

I thought of Charlie and the Deific. If Charlie had found solace in the work he did there, then maybe I could too—if they would have me. And then I would locate the vampire, to tell him thank you. I pulled myself to my knees and took several deep breaths. Then, as fast as my body would permit, I returned to the cabin, stumbling along the way, but with each step, I became stronger and more determined.

When I reached the cabin, I hurried into the library and opened the small drawer inside the desk. Only one thing was in it— Charlie's card. I picked up the phone and dialed his number.

Please answer.

He didn't. Instead, after a few rings, a woman's voice said, "Thank you for calling First Choice Accounting. May I help you?"

First Choice Accounting?

"Hello?" the lady asked again.

"Um, may I speak with Charlie?"

"Charlie who?"

I closed my eyes, trying to remember if he'd ever told me his last name, but my mind drew a blank. Even his letters hadn't revealed his last name. "I'm sorry, but I don't know it. He works for the Deific. Do you know the name?"

The woman paused. "May I ask who is calling?"

"My name is Eve. Charlie asked me to call." *A lifetime ago.*

"One moment." I heard a series of clicking sounds in the background. After almost a full minute, she said, "Charlie isn't here right now, but we will have a car pick you up in two hours to bring you to him."

"Do you know where I am?" I asked.

"We do, Eve."

My heart skipped a beat when she said my name. "Where will I be going?"

"To our New York office. Charlie will be waiting for you here. The gentlemen's name that will be picking you up is—" I heard the clicking sound again— "Garret. Do you have any questions?"

"A million," I said, laughing weakly.

"Everything will be all right, I promise," she said. "Just wait there. Maybe pack some food for the trip. It's a long drive."

"Okay, thanks."

The woman said goodbye.

I hung up, my hands shaking.

After quickly packing what few belongings I owned, I dropped into a chair near the front window and waited. I was too nervous to do anything else but sit and imagine how my life was going to change. The image of the vampire with the sorrow-filled eyes came into focus. The sharp angles of his face, his dark hair and arched eyebrows.

Sooner than expected, headlights shined on the front of the house, bathing me in its glow. The horizon behind it burned a bright orange and pink, a sign of the rising sun. A tall, well-built man stepped out of the dark sedan in a blue suit and red tie. He was bald and sported a shiny metal stud in his eyebrow. Before he reached the front door, I stepped outside and closed the cabin door firmly behind me.

"Eve?" he asked, startled by my abruptness.

"That's me."

"I'm Garret. I'll be taking you to New York." He looked down at the small bag in my hands. "Do you have any other luggage?"

I shook my head.

"Let's hit the road then." Garret returned to the car.

I paused before following him. No turning back now. It was time to embrace my new life. Just before I ducked inside the back of the sedan, light from the rising sun warmed my face.

Garret didn't say a single word the entire trip, which took several hours, but I didn't mind. I'd been out of society for so long that I wasn't sure if I knew how to have a normal conversation anymore.

The closer we came to the city, the more clustered buildings and people became. Garret drove fast and aggressively along the roads, weaving in and out of traffic like a professional. That, combined with all the people and tall buildings and passing cars, made me nauseous. I closed my eyes tight, willing my stomach to settle.

I wished then, and several other times after, that I was back in the cabin at the top of the mountains away from it all. But then I would remind myself why I was doing this. This is how I could make it right, I told myself again. My personal comfort no longer mattered.

Glancing down at the smooth skin on my hand, I wondered when I'd tell Charlie about me being an immortal. What an awkward conversation. I'm not even sure what that meant really. I healed quickly like vampires and died like them too, but lacked any of their other abilities. What was I exactly?

Eventually, Garret pulled the car into an underground parking lot beneath a tall, dark brown building and pushed a button on the side of a metal stand. A tall gate opened wide and he drove inside.

"Are we here?" I asked.

Garret turned right between two rows of vehicles. "This is it. I'll drop you off at the elevator at the end. Go up to the fourth floor and ask for Charlie."

I clutched my bag tightly, my heart pounding. What if I've waited too long and I'm no longer wanted? Where will I go then? *So stupid.* I should've at least written Charlie back, even once.

Garret parked the car, but I didn't get out. "Something wrong?"

Anxiety swelled in my chest and my feet began to tingle. *Magic.*

I needed to calm down. Relax and breathe deeply.

"You all right?" Garrett asked, staring at me with a creased forehead.

I nodded then swallowed the lump in my throat before opening the door. The underground garage was cold and smelled like an old basement. I said goodbye to Garrett, then pressed the up button.

The elevator vibrated and moved upwards. No going back now. I took a deep breath as the doors opened to a well-lit reception area.

A woman with short curly blonde hair and glasses greeted me from behind a desk. "Good morning. May I help you?"

I quickly stepped out and said, "My name is Eve. I'm here to see Charlie."

"Nice to meet you, Eve. I'm Sarah," she said, smiling big. Sarah was younger, nineteen I guessed. There were fashion magazines scattered on her desk and three kinds of fingernail polish, each with lids open, directly in front of her.

"Good to meet you, too," I said, forcing a smile. My feet were still tingling.

Sarah stood and rounded her desk toward me. "I'll take you back. Follow me. By the way, I love your hair. Is that your natural color?"

"Yeah, and thanks," I said and followed her through a maze of white and black cubicles, each one filled with people sitting at built-in desks, headsets wrapped around their heads, and staring at computers. A few of them glanced at me, but for the most part, no one seemed to care. We turned a corner and stepped into a long hallway. At the end sat a dark-haired teenage boy who was hunched over, scribbling furiously with a fat red marker on something shiny and silver.

"How's it going, Derek?" Sarah asked.

The boy didn't look up. His hair was combed neatly to the side, and he barely seemed to fit in the chair he was sitting in; his legs lengthened way past the seat. When we came close, Derek stood and

225

took a hesitant step toward us, head still down, eyes staring at the shiny object in his hands. Suddenly, he thrust it toward me, revealing what he'd been working on.

My eyes lowered, and I opened my mouth to say thank you, but instead a scream tore through my lungs.

30

I screamed again and fell to the ground, crawling backwards away from the strange teenage boy. In his open palm was an exact replica of the silver necklace Boaz had given me.

Sarah stared at me with her mouth open, eyes wide.

"Get away from me," I cried, but the boy took several more steps toward me.

The door at the end of the hallway flew open and out stepped a man with brown curly hair. He moved quickly toward Derek and spun him around away from me. "Derek, let me see what you made."

With the necklace no longer in view, I relaxed a little, but my heart still raced.

Sarah kneeled beside me. "Are you okay?"

A few people from the cubicles had come rushing over. Sarah waved them away and said, "Nothing to see here. Get back to work!"

"What a beautiful necklace. May I hold it?" the brown-haired man asked Derek. The man's back was to me. He was several inches taller than me and broad shouldered.

Derek shook his head vehemently and again thrust the necklace toward me.

"Who is that?" I asked Sarah.

"Derek Asher, an autistic boy who works here. He's completely harmless, I swear."

I looked up, my gaze meeting that of the boys. His wide-set eyes were gray and full of innocence, something I had never seen in anyone else before. I stood up slowly and reached for the necklace. It was cool to the touch.

"Did you make this for me?" I asked, keeping my focus on Derek. The tin necklace felt like a thousand pounds in my hands.

Derek smiled but didn't answer. Instead, he walked by us, taking extra care not to touch me as he passed. I stared after him until he disappeared around the corner.

"I'm sorry about that, Eve," the man said. "I should've been more prepared."

That voice. I turned to him. His hair was shorter on top and there were lines in his face he didn't have before, but I recognized him. "Charlie?"

The corners of his mouth turned up slightly, and he nodded.

Surprising even myself, I threw myself to him and buried my head into his chest, tears blurring my vision. He stroked the back of my head tenderly and guided me into an office, shutting the door behind us.

After a minute, I calmed down and pulled away from him. "I'm sorry." I sniffed. "It's just so good to see you."

"It's about time. I was starting to doubt my abilities," he said, motioning me to sit down in a plush, high-backed blue chair. He sat across me, bringing his bent, right leg up to rest upon his left knee. Behind him was a mahogany desk; a vase of red roses and a neat stack of papers sat upon its top.

Although it had only been seven years, Charlie looked much different than I remembered. There were deep lines between his eyebrows and a two-inch scar on his right cheek. His eyes had changed the most. They were still green, but no longer sparkled with life. They reflected the pain I had read in his letters.

"How was the drive?" he asked.

"It was fine. I'm just glad that it's over and that I'm finally here. Sorry it took me so long."

"You came exactly when you were supposed to."

I cleared my throat. "Yeah, well, thanks again for taking care of me for so long. And for the letters. They meant a lot to me."

He chuckled uncomfortably and shifted his position on the

chair. "I wasn't sure you were reading them. Honestly, they meant a lot to me too. Writing them was cheap therapy."

It was my turn to squirm. "I didn't read them until a couple of weeks ago, but I wish I would've. I might've come back much sooner."

"You took the time you needed."

I shook my head. "I owe you so much."

"You don't owe me anything. The work you're going to do will more than make up for any debt you've incurred."

I immediately tensed, not because I didn't trust him, but because I was afraid of using magic. "What kind of work?"

"Let's get the formalities over with, and then we can talk about your future." Charlie reached for the nearby desk and removed a thick manila envelope from off its top. He reached inside and removed several papers. "As your parent's only child, upon their death, you inherited everything." He handed me a single sheet.

"My mother?" I asked.

"She died four years ago. There was an earthquake, and the facility she was being held in collapsed, killing everyone inside. It was a terrible disaster."

Both my parents were dead.

"You've inherited everything," Charlie said. "We transferred the funds to a Swiss bank account under an alias. I hope you don't mind, but we didn't want to give anyone the ability to track you. If you'd just sign this paper, then everything will be transferred to your new name: Eve Andrews."

"But don't people think I died?"

He shook his head. "Only missing. Your body was never found in the fire. After your mother passed, we filed paperwork showing you were alive, and then created the new identity. It was all done in secret. There's not a chance anyone will find out who you really are."

I glanced down at the paper. The dollar amount was staggering. "This is all mine?"

Charlie nodded.

"What will I ever do with this much money?"

"Whatever you want."

I set the paper in my lap.

"What made you finally come?" Charlie asked.

"Besides Nora threatening to beat me up? The desire to make things right. I've done some horrible things and wasted a lot of time doing nothing about it."

"It wasn't you."

"But it was me, specifically my stupidity that caused it all. I let my hunger for black magic consume me, and I'm still not sure I've rid myself of it. "

"Time will fix that, or I should say what you choose to do with your time. We'll help you, too."

I tightened my jaw. "How?"

"By teaching you to use your abilities correctly."

"What?" I asked, my heart racing again.

"We'll teach you to use them for good," he clarified.

"I've heard that before. I'm not using magic again. I think there's been a mistake." I stood nearly knocking my chair backwards.

"Eve, that's not what I meant. Please, sit back down, let me explain."

I hesitated, searching his eyes. I knew this man. In his letters, he had admitted to being afraid of the dark for years and learning to overcome this fear. He'd spoke of having children with Moira. He told me his weaknesses and insecurities. This was a man I could trust; his eyes spoke the truth. I returned to my seat.

"Because of the experiences you've had in life," Charlie began, "you've only been taught to fear and to hate. Do you think only negative emotions give you power?"

I glanced down, my gaze finding my worn brown loafers.

"There are other emotions you can use that aren't dark," he

continued. "Emotions that don't fill you with the anger you despise. You can feel hope, love, peace—all the feelings that are good in this world. These emotions are far more powerful than what you're used to feeling, and they will give you the ability to use your gift in ways you never thought possible."

"But will it change me?"

He smiled big, finally reminding of the man I first met in those woods so long ago. "Of course, but for the better. Love has a funny way of growing inside you to the point where you're no longer aware of yourself, and you become consumed with the desire to help others."

"I don't think it's possible for me to feel anything good," I whispered.

"Nonsense. We'll help you find love even in something as small as a flower." He glanced at the roses sitting on the desk.

"Does anyone else here know about me or other supernaturals like vampires and demons?" I asked.

Charlie's expression grew serious. "It is for you to tell who you want about yourself, and as for the real monsters of the world, well, we can't tell just anyone. A few of us know the truth, but most people have to be eased into such things. Their sanity depends upon it."

"What of the boy? How did he know about the necklace?"

"Derek?" Charlie clasped his hands together, pointer fingers up, and placed them under his chin in a thoughtful expression. "He has the ability to see the past and future and expresses it through art. We found him in an orphanage in England when he was nine and adopted him."

I frowned. "The Deific adopted a boy?"

"No, no, of course not. It was Henry who adopted him."

"Who's Henry?"

"He is the founder of the Deific. He recognized Derek's abilities right away and thought he'd be better off here. Derek lives upstairs in an apartment, and then works here after school doing odd jobs."

"So Henry lives upstairs, too?"

Charlie cleared his throat. "No, Derek lives with a nanny, but Henry visits him often."

"Why would he adopt a boy and then not take care of him?"

"It's complicated. You'll see soon enough. Henry is anxious to meet you when you're ready."

I was curious to meet the man who could start such an organization. I stopped suddenly and sat up straight. "Something's not right, Charlie. You said Henry started the Deific, correct?"

"Yes."

"But that's impossible. You told me the Deific has been around for hundreds of years. If he's the founder then he must be extremely old." I shook my head, trying to understand. "He would be too old unless—" My head snapped up, and I stared at Charlie in disbelief.

He was shaking his head. "You weren't supposed to find out like this. He wanted to be the one to tell you."

A vampire. "How is it possible that a vampire could start something that does good in the world?"

"How is it *im*possible? Didn't you say that a vampire once helped you?"

I hesitated, thinking of the vampire with the sorrow-filled eyes. He had helped me and not just by saving me from Alarica. Somehow he transferred light into me when we had touched, and it spotlighted all of the terrible things I'd done. I'm not sure I would've questioned Boaz had I not met the vampire in the park.

"We are all free to choose," Charlie said.

I opened my mouth to speak, but he up his hand and stood. "You can ask Henry your questions when you meet him. He's much better at explaining all of this than I am. Until then, you can stay in an apartment upstairs until you find your own place to live. Sarah will show you the way."

I followed him to the door. "And what do I do with myself in the meantime?"

"Tomorrow Sarah will have you meet with one of our specialists to help you better understand your gift. It's important that you learn to use magic the right way."

"I will do this, but I want one thing in return."

"Name it," he said, his hand resting high on the door jam.

"I want your help finding someone."

"Who?"

I took a deep breath, and on my exhale said, "The vampire who saved me from Alarica."

31

When Charlie didn't say anything, I asked it again. "Please. I need to find this vampire."

"Why is he so important to you?"

"I'm not sure, but I felt something with him, a connection somehow. I know that sounds weird, but for some reason, I feel it's important that I find him."

"Then we will help. I'll speak to Henry about giving you access to our private database."

I thanked him and gave him another hug. Sarah was waiting outside to escort me upstairs.

"So, what do you think?" she asked, after walking me through the three-bedroom apartment. "It's not super chic, and could use some major updating, starting with getting rid of this tan carpet, but at least it's clean. That's more than you can say for a lot of other apartments in the city."

"I think it's perfect," I said, trying to hide my enthusiasm. It was almost twice the size of the cabin with a living room, office, and a large kitchen. "And it's so warm." The one thing the cabin hadn't been.

Sarah scrunched her nose. "It's actually freezing in here. The thermostat hasn't been turned up in like forever."

"Compared to what I'm used to, this is warm. I think I'm going to like it here."

***

I woke early the next morning feeling better than I had in a long time. I looked forward to being around others and learning more about the Deific and myself. In the closet, I found a note from Charlie that read: "I hope these clothes fit and are to your liking. Sarah picked them out."

235

I smiled. Charlie hadn't lost his touch when it came to knowing what I needed.

I dressed quickly in black slacks and a long sleeve white blouse. I pulled my hair back into a loose ponytail, applied a little makeup, and called it good. Downstairs, the Deific hummed with production. It was 8:30 am.

"Good morning, Eve. Did you sleep well?" Sarah asked. Her eyes twinkled and she leaned forward, resting her elbows on the desk.

"I did, thanks. And thank you for the clothes. They're great."

"Are you sure? Cause we could go shopping together and you could pick out something more your style."

"No, really, the clothes are perfect, but I would like to go out and see the city sometime. Maybe you could show me around?"

"Absolutely. We'll have a girl's night out."

"That will be nice. Is Charlie in yet?"

"Yup. Office number 452. Same room you were in yesterday. You remember how to get there?"

"I think so. Thanks."

I made my way through the cubicles, having to turn around a few times, until I finally found Charlie's office.

"Come in," he said when I neared the doorway. He closed the laptop in front of him and leaned back in the chair behind his desk. The lines between his eyebrows were etched deeper than yesterday, and his mouth was pulled tight. "How are you today?"

"Better than you by the looks of it. You okay?"

"Nothing you need to worry about. Today I want you focusing solely on your training with Dr. Skinner."

"Who's that?"

"One of the most remarkable men you'll ever meet. He has an insight on life that will change a person, if they're open to it."

***

I opened the door to Dr. Skinner's office. A balding, heavy-set man greeted me. "You must be Eve."

He stood and walked around his desk to shake my hand. He was barely taller than me, with brown hair that was tousled on top of his head in curly waves. When I took hold of his palm, I glanced into his steady brown eyes and felt at ease.

"It's nice to meet you," I said.

"Oh, no, the pleasure is all mine. Have a seat."

I eased myself into a chair and looked around. Except for a giant framed photo hanging on the wall behind his desk and a vase of roses, the room was void of personal belongings. The picture was a black and white photo of a young girl whose eyes seemed too narrow for her face. She had dark hair pulled into thick pigtails and was smiling cheerfully. But the smile didn't come from her small upturned lips—it was in her eyes.

"I know you just got here yesterday, but have you had a chance to visit with Charlie much? I know you two are close." He lowered himself back into his seat.

My gaze dropped to the floor. "It feels strange to say that we are close when we've only seen each other a couple of times, yet I still consider him my closest friend."

"Letters will do that. They can be extremely personal."

"You know about the letters?" I asked.

"I was the one who suggested he write to you. I figured it would be a good outlet for him, while also giving you a way to still connect to this world." He leaned back, his expression thoughtful. "I hope you know he expects nothing from you. Charlie spoke of you often while you were away, wondering how you were doing. He really cares about you."

I remained still in guilty silence. Couldn't I have at least written a stupid letter?

"He was happy when he heard you were returning, but I don't think he was very surprised."

I looked up. "What do you mean?"

"A couple of days ago, he told me an old friend was coming to visit. I wasn't sure what he meant, but I knew better than to question him. Sure enough, you showed up. Charlie's ability is as sure as the rising sun. I never doubt it."

I nodded in agreement.

"Do you want anything to drink?" he asked.

"No, thank you, but I would like to begin. I was hoping to visit with Charlie more. Something was bothering him when I saw him earlier, and I want to see if I can help."

Dr. Skinner nodded slowly. "The last several years have been rough for Charlie. I just hope one day he can let the past go so he can live life again."

I swallowed hard. "What happened to him?"

"That's his story to tell, which I'm sure he'll share with you when he's ready." Dr. Skinner opened a drawer and removed a gray folder. "I've looked over your file, and I must say, you've led a very difficult life."

My lips tightened. "It's in the past. Can we talk about something else?"

He observed me carefully, then said, "I understand you are different from most witches in the sense that it is your emotions that give you the ability to use magic, correct?"

"I wouldn't say all of my emotions. Mainly it's just pride, hate, anger, and fear."

"Why just those?"

I shrugged. "I'm not sure. It's just what my parents taught me."

He leaned forward, elbows on top of his desk. "Have you ever felt love?"

Boaz. My insides twisted, and I tightened my fists. "I don't think so, not real love anyway."

"Have you ever felt happy?"

"I thought I was happy once, but it wasn't true happiness like what I read about in Charlie's letters."

"How about peace?"

I thought for a moment. "I don't think so. I've felt indifferent, but I don't think that's the same thing."

"It's not. Have you ever felt compassion?"

The vampire with the sorrow-filled eyes immediately came to mind, and I nodded. "That's what originally kept me from wanting to be like my parents, and it's what ultimately saved me when I went to far."

"That's good. We'll build on that later. How about beauty? Have you ever felt beauty before?"

I shrugged. "I've seen beautiful things."

"But have you felt it?"

"Is that possible?"

"For you, yes, but for most normal humans, they can only appreciate and love beauty." He reached over to the vase and withdrew a long stemmed rose. "Look at this rose and tell me what you see."

I eyed it carefully. It was a red rose in full bloom with a sweet smelling aroma. "It's beautiful, but it looks like every other rose I've ever seen."

"Look closer."

I focused harder, this time noticing the many lines that ran in an intricate pattern across its velvet skin.

"Keep looking," I heard his voice say in an eager tone.

I took a deep breath, inhaling its fragrance. The air swirled around the rose in a circular pattern, and I froze, unsure if I'd imagined the strange movement. I stared harder, going deeper beyond the layers, until I barely noticed the room fading away around me.

It was the delicate veins of the rose traveling to an unknown destination that held my attention. Then, as if they had been doing it the whole time, the lines were physically moving, following some predestined path. The visible ambrosial aroma twirled again in a rhythmic pattern, round and round, as if it were dancing to an unheard symphony.

I tilted my head ever so slightly, attempting to hear the enchanting music that seemed to be making the rose come to life. The sound was a faint whisper like the gentle humming of busy bee on a warm summer day. I remained still. The patterns continued to move until I could no longer distinguish one line from another.

The entire rose stirred in a constant fluid motion, yet I could still see each individual petal. The gentle humming soon separated into a thousand voices of a great chorus, but they were soft and reverent as if they sang in humble praise to something beyond my comprehension. The harmonious song combined with the swaying aroma, which had wrapped itself around me in a tender embrace, brought tears to my eyes.

"Eve?" a distant voice asked.

The room came into focus, and I wiped my eyes. "What was that?"

Dr. Skinner smiled and said, "That was beauty in its purest form. As you just witnessed, beauty is an action. It will continue to create the grandeur of this rose until its life span ends. But just like everything else in this world, beauty has an opposite—ugliness. It, too, is an action and creates its object to be loathsome and dark, with intentions to serve its own selfish desires. In a similar manner, these two opposites also affect humans."

He took the rose from me and turned it over in his hand. "A rose has no choice but to be beautiful, but a human has been given the ability to choose whether to be ugly or beautiful. Their actions make them so. I'm not talking about physical appearance. I'm speaking about the kind of beauty that brings joy or the ugliness that wishes to harm.

"Everything has its opposite: love to hate, joy to sorrow, happy to sad. Each of these emotions will change a human, sometimes temporarily, but other times the change is permanent. However, you are different. These emotions not only change the inside of you, but give you the ability to use your powers. The more powerful the emotion, the more powerful the magic.

"Your whole life you've been taught that magic could only be used through negative emotions. You were told this because your parents knew the only way to obtain their selfish pursuit of power was to have you feel hate. You would not desire power if you felt love. The desire for power cannot exist in the light of purity and truth. It belongs with its dark brothers: envy, anger, jealousy. Your parents understood this very well and were very careful to ensure that light stayed out of your life. But I want to stress to you that the positive emotions of love, peace, compassion, and joy are just as powerful as their counterparts and when these emotions are turned outward, you'll be able to use magic in ways you never thought possible.

"To truly change, a person must first start with their inner self. They must learn to forgive themselves of their own inadequacies and realize their own nothingness before they can ever truly become great."

"I have to realize that I am nothing in order to help others?" I asked.

He smiled kindly. "Of course not. What I mean by one's nothingness is when a person recognizes their many faults and their inability to rid themselves of those faults, then they become humble. They strip themselves of all pride. When this happens, a person stops thinking about themselves all together and their thoughts and concerns turn to others. In this manner, they lose themselves. This is when true power comes. But this is a long way off. We must first teach you to seek out beauty and experience joy so that you can use your powers properly."

"Is it addictive?"

He chuckled. "It's unquenchable. Love continually grows. It starts first with self, but then includes family, friends, neighbors, until nothing is wanted more than to save the entire world. So yes, it can be addictive, but in a remarkable way."

"Will you teach me?"

He shook his head. "I wish I was great enough to teach you how to love, but I am highly inadequate. Only pure innocence can teach you what you need to know." He removed a sheet of paper from the gray folder and handed it to me. "I've arranged for you to work at a nearby school called "The Academy" starting tomorrow. The students there will teach you more about happiness and unconditional love than I ever can."

Written on the paper were an address and a description of the school. "Are you sure about this? I've never been around children before."

He leaned back in his seat. "They will love you. These children don't know how to do anything else. You'll see."

32

I found Charlie just before lunch. He was in the exact position I'd left him in earlier that morning, but this time papers were scattered all over his desk. He didn't seem to be focused on any one particular.

"Is everything okay?" I asked.

"It's as good as it's going to get," he answered, his eyes downcast. "How did it go with Dr. Skinner?"

"It went well. I'm working at the Academy tomorrow morning with some special children that are going to help me." I stepped into the room and closed the door behind me. "Look, I know you barely know me, but I feel like I know you really well. Something bad happened that's changed you, and I'd like to help. It's the least I could do."

He raised his eyes, meeting my gaze. "I will be the only one to take care of this problem."

"And what is the problem exactly?"

"A man. I've been searching for him for several years."

"Can't you use your ability to find him?"

His eyes narrowed, and his voice chilled. "Don't you think I've tried? It's all I do every day, every night. I think of him, picture him in my mind, feel my hatred for him, and yet, he still escaped me, but two days ago he was spotted. In this city."

I lowered into a chair, my legs weak by his confession. This was not the Charlie I remembered. "Who is he?"

"Someone who should've died a long time ago. He took something very precious from me, and I won't rest until he ceases to exist." He shook his head. "I shouldn't be telling you any of this. You're not ready."

"But I am—"

243

The door flew open. A young man was panting heavily like he'd just run up several flights of stairs. "They've got a hit, Charlie. They're leaving now."

Charlie stood up, knocking his chair backwards. "Without telling me?"

"I told them to wait for you, but they wouldn't." The young man saw me for the first time and frowned. "Who's this?"

Charlie rounded his desk. "We have to go. Now, Lance. Get my gear ready."

"Yes, Sir." Lance ducked out the door.

Charlie hurried after him, but I stood and grabbed his arm. "I want to help."

He shrugged it off. "Not now."

I wanted to say more, but he was already down the hall, walking quickly away from me. I blinked. Then blinked again. For years, I'd been holed up in my own prison, doing nothing to atone for the many sins I'd committed against others. Now finally I have a chance. I may not be ready, but I couldn't just sit on the sidelines anymore. Too much of my life already had been spent doing *nothing*.

Without any further hesitation, I hurried after Charlie, but when I reached Sarah's desk, I couldn't find him anywhere. "Where did Charlie go?"

"One sec." Sarah lowered a cell phone from her ear. "Um, he didn't really say, but I bet it was the second floor."

I turned to my right and pushed open a stairwell door. Just as I did so, a door closing echoed below me. He was close.

I bounded down the stairs, but stopped when I reached the door to the second floor to peer through an elongated window. Just on the other side was a large, gym-like room, the floor covered in blue mats. Hanging punching bags and all kinds of weight lifting equipment were on the left. On the right, at least a dozen people were pulling on black vests and grabbing weapons from off of the wall. Their movements were hurried, almost panicked as they prepared for what looked like some kind of police raid.

But these people weren't police or any kind of military. They worked for the Deific, restoring balance to any one group or person who might be a threat to mankind. That's what Charlie had said, anyway, all those years ago.

Near the front of the pack, Charlie was in a heated debate with a tall and broad shouldered man with red hair. I quickly slipped inside.

"You should've told me!" Charlie yelled.

The man with red hair shook his head. "We need them alive. I can't trust that you will have the restraint to make that happen."

"Don't worry about me," Charlie said and shoved past him to exit through a glass door.

While the rest of them continued to dress, I took my place among them as if I was meant to be there. I removed a black full-body suit from off of the wall and pushed my feet through the leg holes. The leather-like material was thick yet felt incredibly light. I wondered what we might be encountering to need something like this. Maybe I was in way over my head.

"Who are you?" asked a woman with dark skin. She was standing a few feet away, her feet shoulder width apart.

I pulled the sleeve over my arm and zipped up the front. "Charlie asked me to join."

"Are you from the Seattle office?"

I nodded and held out my hand. "Name's, Eve."

"I'm Kelley." She shook my hand.

"So what are we up against?" I asked her.

"Vampires. A whole nest of them living right under our noses." She motioned me to follow her. "Is there a weapon you prefer?"

I looked them over, knowing exactly what I wanted. I skipped over the guns, knives, and daggers, stopping only when I found a crossbow near the bottom of the wall. I picked it up. "This will work nicely."

"Good choice for vamps. Wooden arrows are over there on the shelf." She nodded toward a few rows of black shelves a good head taller than me. "Personally, I've never liked them. I prefer the Colt 45-70 Peacemaker. No matter what kind of bullets, it always brings the peace." She smiled and patted the side of her hips where two handguns were holstered.

While I found the arrows, Kelley explained to a few of the others who I was. None of them questioned my presence. Maybe people came from the Seattle office often? Still, it confused me how they could be so trusting.

The glass door opened, and the redheaded man Charlie had been speaking to earlier stuck in his head. "Let's move!"

I finished placing the rest of the wooden arrows into the quiver on my hip and followed the others out, keeping my head down in case Charlie saw me. Our footsteps echoed as we descended all three flights of stairs. My heart pounded, and I could barely catch my breath. It wasn't the fear of danger I was about to put myself in, but more the fear of using magic. I hadn't used it in years and didn't want to, but what if I had to use my abilities to save my life? I gripped the bow tighter, hoping that time wouldn't come.

Outside, three black SUV's were parked on the curb, their engines idling. Charlie was sitting in the passenger seat of the first one, staring straight ahead. When told, I climbed into the backseat of the last vehicle with two men. As soon as the doors closed, the driver—a woman—pressed on the gas. Kelley was sitting in the front passenger seat.

Even though the car was full, no one said a word. The air was heavy, and I could practically taste the nervous energy on my tongue. The weight of the crossbow helped calm my nerves. Had I not learned how to use it, I may not have come.

We had only been driving for ten minutes, when the car came

to a stop in a run-down part of the city. Many of the small homes looked abandoned with their windows boarded up and grass as high as my knees. I was glad it was daytime.

"Everyone out," Kelley said. "Cut through a couple of back yards to your right until you reach a home with olive green siding. When you get the go-ahead, swarm the place like its frat house on homecoming night. And remember, we're trying to take at least one of them alive."

Kelley jumped from the SUV, followed by the others. I was the last one out. Charlie was already scampering across the backyard of the vacant home in front me. I was pretty sure he would be upset if he knew I was here, but he'd said once that he wanted me to choose which side to fight on. This was me doing just that.

I waded through tall grass then ducked through a broken fence like everyone else. The house we were descending upon looked worse than the neighborhood. Overgrown trees and shrubs had grown all around the warped structure, breaking even the back porch and a few of the windows. Little daylight touched the partially collapsed roof. Vampires must love it here. From what Boaz had told me, most vampires didn't live a life of luxury like him. They chose to exist in the shadows, hidden from both mankind and other supernaturals where they felt it was safer. But Boaz never feared others. I know now it was because he could use magic where other vamps couldn't.

Kelley signaled with her hand for us to stop. I froze, partially blocked behind a shed. Charlie turned to me just then, but I quickly lowered my face and waited several seconds before I looked up again. Charlie was facing the house, seemingly unaware of my presence. I exhaled the breath I'd been holding.

"Get ready," Kelley whispered.

I unhooked an arrow from the quiver on my hip and loaded it into the crossbow, careful to keep my finger off the trigger. A few men closer to the home pulled down what looked like binoculars over their eyes. My guess was they were night vision goggles.

A moment later, Charlie motioned for these men to go into the house first. They carefully stepped around the broken steps and onto the porch where one of them attempted to open the back door, but it was closed tight. Had I wanted to use magic, I could've easily opened it, but fear clenched my heart at the very thought.

Charlie made a motion with his hand I didn't understand. The lead man near the door shoved his shoulder into the door, knocking it down and making me jump. Kelley gave me a funny look, but I ignored her and tried to calm my racing pulse.

As soon as the men with the night goggles had gone inside, Charlie went in after them, indicating with a small nod that the rest of us should follow. When it was my turn to go inside, I hesitated for the briefest of moments when faced with the darkness within the home. Maybe I should've waited. Without my magic, I was only as good as the aim of my arrow, which wouldn't be that great without light.

Kelley nudged me forward, so I stepped inside. The air was unusually cold, but then I heard the gentle hum of an air conditioner coming from somewhere within. Behind me, Kelley turned on a flashlight. Its beam lit up small sections of the room. There was a yellow couch covered in dust and crumpled up potato chip wrappers. A TV had fallen over on its side onto what I thought was brown carpet, but other parts of the floor were more gray in color. To my left was a narrow kitchen. I turned on the small light attached to the top of my crossbow, illuminating the space. Dishes were piled high in the sink. By the looks of them, they hadn't been used in years. Vampires had no need of them.

A series of popping sounds made the other three in the room with me freeze. It wasn't like a gun going off, but more like someone cracking their knuckles … only louder. I couldn't see Charlie or the others as they had already moved farther into the home. Kelley was standing to my side, shining her light into a hallway. I raised my bow in that direction, my finger hovering over the trigger.

In a split second, everything changed. Kelley reacted much quicker than I did. She spun away just as someone, *or something*, attacked her. I wasn't as lucky spotting the lightning-fast, inhuman movement, so when it slammed into me I flew back into the wall. I didn't mean to cry out, but it had been so long since I had experienced any kind of physical pain that I couldn't hold back the surprise.

I gritted my teeth and slid up the wall, back into a standing position, readjusting my bow to face forward. My small beam of light caught flashes of movement: an elbow to a cheek, a knee to a stomach, a splatter of blood across the wall. A gun went off. Kelley's peacekeeper.

Do something!

I waited a few seconds for the pain in my back to heal, then raised my bow at eyelevel and tried to focus on something, but everyone was moving too fast. Screams were coming from below, probably in a basement.

Just then, my bow was knocked from my hands. At the same time, a fist that felt more like a rock smashed into the side of my head. I collapsed to the ground, my vision swimming within a dark pool that was more red than black. Someone cold and heavy was pressing down on me, clawing his or her way toward my neck. I tried to fight it, pushing and shoving, but I was no match for the vampire.

I smelled its breath, a mixture of basement mold and rusted iron pipes, before I felt its tongue lap at my forehead just above my right eye. But then the vampire's body stiffened. He lifted up off me as if it wanted to get a better look at my face. The light from my crossbow caught the male vampire's expression. It wasn't hunger like I expected, but fear.

"What are you?" he asked, his milky-blue eyes wide.

I reached for the crossbow, but before I could grab it, the vampire was scurrying away from me and out the back door. One of the Deific's men bolted after him.

"Help me," a voice grunted.

I picked up the crossbow, rolled onto my stomach, and pointed it toward the hallway. Kelley was just inside, trying to fight off a vampire who had her pinned to the ground. My vision was still blurry, but I fired anyway, aiming just above Kelley. The arrow pierced the vampire in his shoulder. The blow wasn't enough to kill him, but it did give Kelley enough time to grab her gun and restore peace. His body burst into ashes and sprayed through the air. Kelley ran past the cloud, disappearing into the hallway and leaving me alone in the room.

I pulled myself into a sitting position, my back against the wall. Not far from me, the light from my crossbow shined on a body in a black jump suit lying on the floor face down in a growing puddle of blood. I instantly thought of Harriet, and my heart sunk into my gut. This was all my fault.

I attempted to move to help the woman, hoping she was still alive, but my vision continued to blur until the whole world went black.

33

"Wake up! Open your eyes!"

I heard the distorted voice, but I couldn't open my eyes.

"How bad is the wound?" the same voice asked.

There was a pause, then, from someone else, "What wound? There's nothing here. Maybe it was someone else's blood?"

"I don't think so," the first voice said. This time I recognized it. *Charlie.* He touched my head. "Perhaps you're right. Go ahead and go to the car. I'll try to revive her."

There was movement near my face, then a whisper. "Eve, I know you can hear me. I sense it. Open your eyes."

I focused hard on my eyelids until they fluttered open. Charlie's face hovered just over mine. There was a scratch on his cheek and blood near his hairline.

"Are you okay?" he asked.

I scooted away from him, remembering the woman who had been laying near me face down in blood. She wasn't there now. My back pressed against the wall of the dirty, rundown home. No one else was around, but there were voices outside.

"The woman?" I asked.

Charlie glanced to the same spot on the floor I was staring at. "She'll be okay. She's getting stitches now." His head swiveled back to me. "What are you doing here?"

My gaze slowly met his. "I came to help."

"And you passing out, was that you helping?"

"I didn't mean to."

Charlie stood and held his hand out to me. "Like I said before, you're not ready for any of this. Finish your training with Dr. Skinner and the children. "

I accepted his hand and let him pull me to my feet. "But I need to do something, like now. I need to feel that I'm finally making things right."

"You dying an early death isn't going to help that," he said.

I opened my mouth to tell him that I couldn't die, not easily anyway, but a figure appeared in the doorway.

"We're ready," said one of the men who'd been wearing the night goggles earlier.

"Good. We'll be right there."

When he was gone, I asked, "Did you find who you were looking for?"

Charlie shook his head. "There were only five vamps here, and we dusted all but one. It's my understanding that this last one had contact with you right before he bolted. And he said something to you?"

I shivered, remembering how the vampire had licked my forehead. "He asked me what I was."

He frowned and headed toward the front door. "As in, he sensed you are a witch? I didn't think that was possible."

I should've said something then about being an immortal, but Charlie was already out the door, seeming to ponder the vampire's interaction with me. Had he known the truth about me, he probably would've guessed that there must be something in my blood, something the vampire tasted, that made him fear me. I needed to figure out what that was and soon.

***

The next morning, I arrived to work with the children early. The Academy was smaller than I expected and looked more like an office building than a school. Inside, there was no reception area, but rather a great room surrounded by several classrooms with glass windows. The huge, circular room consisted of brightly colored boxes, a big plastic jungle gym, and all kinds of toys. Some of the classrooms were filled with desks, where others were full of large foam shapes and various sizes of balls.

A short Spanish woman in one of the smaller rooms was arranging desks into a semi-circle. She had auburn hair cut into a bob that fell to her pointy chin. Her nose was just as sharp, but her gentle brown eyes softened the rest of her well-defined features. She bounced and swayed around the room, dancing to a whistled tune I didn't recognize.

I really hoped I wasn't wasting my time. I should be back at the Deific, learning to fight, but if Charlie trusted Dr. Skinner's methods, then I would do as he asked, at least for a week. After that, I was going to do something a little more proactive. I was still embarrassed for the way I'd handled myself yesterday with the vampires.

I took a deep breath, then tapped the window and waved at the whistling woman.

The woman poked her head out and said in a Spanish accent, "Can I help you?"

"Yes, my name is Eve. Dr. Skinner sent me here to work as a teachers-aide for the next few weeks."

The woman yelped and threw her arms around me. "That's right! I completely forgot. I'm so glad you're here. You are going to have so much fun. Are you excited?"

I tried to keep still, but the woman was incredibly strong for her small frame.

"I am excited," I said once I caught my breath.

The woman finally stepped away. "You have no idea how much of a difference it is to have another pair of hands. I'm Mamita."

"Nice to meet you," I said.

"It's wonderful to meet you, too. The kids will be arriving in the next fifteen minutes so let me show you around before they come."

After Mamita had given me a tour of the place, which wasn't much more than I'd already seen, she set me in a chair by the front door where I could watch the children as they arrived. Ten minutes later, a boy who looked to be about eight years old walked in. His straight hair was cut short and combed neatly to the side. He had a difficult time walking, one leg shuffled awkwardly over the other, and many times I thought he would trip, but he managed to stay upright. After hugging who appeared to be his mother, he headed straight for a small TV in the back of the great room, but not without casting me a sideways glance. He wouldn't look directly at me, but his hand came up just a little, and he waved briefly. I waved back, but I couldn't be sure he noticed.

After him came a steady stream of many more students. Each child had some kind of a physical problem, and each one was unique. One boy came in with the aid of his driver and promptly laid down directly in the middle of the floor and fell asleep until a teacher woke him up minutes later. Another heavy-set girl eagerly entered through the door, opening it with such force that it banged against the wall behind it. She moved toward the TV that was playing a Disney movie and asked the teacher to turn on the captions. Meanwhile, a younger girl with long blonde hair spotted me instantly. She sat on the floor at my side, mouth gaping open. I said hello, but she didn't respond. She merely smiled.

The day went by quickly. I observed doctors and therapists who came in and out at various times throughout the day to work with specific students. They were all patient and kind with the children who at times seemed rude and abrupt. It didn't take long for me to realize this was because most of the children had a difficult time understanding the teachers and, at the same time, make themselves be understood.

Every child had their own special ability: some could write beautiful poetry, others were math whizzes, several could draw amazing pictures, and one older girl shocked me with her ability to play the piano.

At first, I didn't know what to think of the children. I asked myself, *Why? Why were all these children born with such challenges and trials?* But the children didn't seem to be bothered by their handicaps. They all seemed happy and content with what they'd been given.

After just a week, it dawned on me that the children were meant to teach others around them the real meaning of love and compassion. The children had no sin, no guile, no secrets, and no second agendas. They were pure-in-heart and spirit, and they reached out silently, hoping others would see past their outward disabilities to their beauty within. Their love was unconditional and held no boundaries.

The children changed my whole outlook on life and, for the first time, I felt what I could only describe as joy. I was excited to see the children each day and share in their happiness when they accomplished even the smallest task. But when the children went on outings, I was hurt by how many people looked right past them, failing to notice what they were trying to teach the world. Their adult hearts were closed to things they felt they couldn't understand. It made me sad to see how they were all missing what I now considered to be the most beautiful things on earth.

When I wasn't at the Academy, I was with Sarah. She introduced me to her friends and took me all over the city. She even invited me to go work in the soup kitchen serving the homeless every Sunday morning. My relationship with her was very different from how it had been with Liane, and after some time, I was able to recognize it as a true friendship.

After a few short weeks of working at the Academy and hanging out with Sarah, I experienced another first: I went to sleep with a smile on my face and dreamt—not of darkness or monsters, not even of myself.

I was standing a few inches above a dark and murky water. The pungency of seawater and rotten fish stung my nose. The sliver moon shined just enough for me to see a wood dock protruding out into what appeared to be a lake, but because of a thick mist, I couldn't see any structures beyond.

A lone figure, tall and erect, stood motionless at the end of the dock. I squinted, trying to see who it was. My heart stopped beating when I realized it was the vampire who'd saved me from Alarica. He held completely still, as if a guardian statue built to protect land from the monsters of the sea, but every once in a while, his body shifted, betraying his identity.

He wore loose fitting jeans and a dark jacket that hung just below his waist. His short dark brown hair was less than a quarter of an inch past his scalp, and his hooded eyes were drawn tightly together. Whatever held his attention appeared to be causing him pain.

I moved toward him, wanting to get a closer look. Suddenly, his eyes shifted in my direction. I stiffened and sucked in air. His eyes scanned the area, but passed over me. I was invisible to him.

He jerked his head to the left as if he'd heard a sound. He glanced back in my direction one last time before he turned around and disappeared into the fog.

I woke and sat up in bed, heart racing, as the early morning sun spilled into my room. Inexplicably, I was certain of one thing: Whatever had just happened, it wasn't a dream.

34

After working at the school, I stopped by Charlie's office. Dark circles slung under his eyes, but he managed a smile and said, "Hey, you. It's been awhile."

"I've been busy at the Academy." I slid into the nearest chair. "How have you been? You look tired."

"Nothing I can't handle. Have you met Skinner's daughter yet?"

"His daughter? Does she work at the Academy?"

He shook his head. "She's a student, a fourteen-year-old girl named Madeline."

"Maddie? I had no idea."

"The picture in his office is of Maddie when she was four," he said.

I tilted my head back, surprised. "Maddie is the most talented piano player I've ever heard. I'm surprised Dr. Skinner didn't mention her."

"It was Maddie who made him the man he is today. Before she was born, he was a Psychiatrist in a ritzy mental hospital that only cared about patients as long as they came with a high referral fee. Maddie changed her father's outlook on life; whether it was a gift she gave him or whether it just happened, he became a new person."

"There is something special about her," I agreed. "Hey, are you available tonight? I want to talk to you about something."

He blinked a couple of times, practically staring right through me, before saying, "Sure. Let's do it over dinner. I'll come get you when I'm off."

"That will be nice."

Charlie opened his mouth as if to say something more, but seemed to think better of it. He returned his attention to the computer on his desk. "I'll see you tonight then."

***

For dinner, Charlie took me to a pizza parlor. At first I thought it was an odd choice, but a few minutes in, I was grateful for the family atmosphere of children's voices and clanking dishes. It made what I wanted to talk to Charlie about seem less serious.

Charlie guided me to a table in the back corner, opposite the small arcade. He didn't ask me right away why I needed to talk to him. Instead, he told me about his childhood with his only sister. While we ate, I laughed with him as he described his many adventures, including the time he was grounded for months when he'd painted the living room walls a florescent green while his mother had been out. This was the first time since I'd returned that Charlie reminded me of the man I'd met in the forest—happy and full of life.

"So tell me about the children at the Academy," he said. "I'm curious to hear your experience."

I told him everything about the special kids, how they made me feel, and how I felt I was growing in ways I still didn't understand. Charlie listened carefully and seemed to be pleased with my progress. Eventually, though, the conversation died down, and I began to squirm in my seat.

"Maybe this would be easier if you just spit it out?" Charlie asked, seeming to sense my anxiety.

I smiled and on an exhale said, "I had a dream last night, but it wasn't really a dream. It was three-dimensional, like I was really there. I could actually feel a spray of water and smell the sea."

"What was the dream about?"

I explained the strange scene and the vampire on the dock. Charlie leaned back, brows furrowed.

"I was really there, Charlie."

"Did it feel like the future?"

I shook my head. "I don't think so. It felt like it was happening that very moment."

"I've never heard of psychic abilities showing the present. It's always the future or the past."

"But why *him*? Why am I seeing *him*?"

"That's a question only you can answer. There's obviously a connection between you two, but you must be careful that it is a good one. Even evil can attract."

I remembered Boaz, but gratefully I felt none of those negative emotions with the nameless vampire. "Have you spoken to Henry about giving me access to the records you told me about?"

"I have. Henry is very sensitive about who sees the Deific's database, but I have reassured him. You should have it this week." His gaze moved to the pile of torn napkins in front of me. "You think you can lighten up on the napkins?"

I looked down, stunned at how unaware I was of my hands. "Right. Bad habit." I moved the pile to the side to join our half-eaten pizza.

Charlie stood suddenly. "I need to get back. There's something I have to do."

"Does this have anything to do with the vampire that escaped the house we raided?" I asked, standing to join him.

"Could be." He took my elbow and guided me toward the front door. "I have to make a few calls first to confirm, but I sense that he's in the north part of the city, in a club I've actually been to."

"Did you just sense that?" I asked, trying hard to keep up with his fast pace.

He averted his eyes, his cheeks reddening. "I've been mentally searching for him for a long time, but all of a sudden he just appeared on my psychic radar."

"Do you think that's deliberate?"

"Possibly." He opened the front door.

A cold wind lifted my hair when I stepped into the night. I

wrapped my jacket tighter around me. "Can I help?"

"I'll let you know what I find out." He opened the passenger door of his SUV for me. After I slid in, he said, before closing the door, "When you go to sleep tonight, I want you to think of him—the vampire. If it is a connection thing, you may see him again."

***

I was sitting on hard dirt. A few sparse trees stood tall around me, their limbs sagging and leafless. A strong breeze that smelled of fish and salt water cut through my thin pajamas, and I hugged myself tightly, trying to keep warm. I gritted my teeth.

Where am I?

From what I could see, it looked like a park. Not far away, swings creaked in a breeze beside a long slide. Large dirt patches littered the grass. It wasn't a well-maintained park, which meant I was probably on the wrong side of town. But what town? The same thick fog surrounded the area, blocking my view to anything beyond it.

For some reason, my attention was drawn to the thickest tree in the park—a large maple tree. That's when I saw *Him*. He was standing as still as the tree he stood behind, his gaze staring into the fog. For several minutes he remained in this state. I didn't think he was even breathing.

Just then, a tall man stepped out of the mist, wearing a bulky coat that looked much too big for his skinny frame. He walked quickly with his head down, hands stuffed into his pockets. He passed the tall maple completely unaware of the vampire hiding behind it until it was too late. The man retrieved a handgun from his coat pocket, but in a move I almost missed, the vampire looped his left arm around the man's right arm and jerked up, snapping the man's arm at the elbow. The man opened his mouth to scream, but before any sound erupted, the vampire sunk his teeth into the man's neck, seeming to paralyze him with fear. Seconds later, he fell face-first to the ground—dead.

I sucked in a shaky breath, my eyes wide and full of horror.

How could I be drawn to *this?*

The vampire stared down at his kill before he collapsed onto all fours, startling me. His hands clawed at the hard dirt exposing the whites of his knuckles, and his back arched up as if he was an intense amount of pain. Even his breathing became erratic—short and quick sips of air.

I stood and walked behind his hunched body, wanting desperately to understand what was happening. But after just a minute, his breathing relaxed, and he let go of the earth to reach over and unzip the man's coat where he retrieved a concealed package wrapped tightly in a brown paper bag. The vampire gathered it up with one hand, stood, and with the other hand, grabbed the man by the back of his coat and dragged him off until he disappeared altogether into the fog.

I tried to follow him, but the moment I stepped into the haze, I awoke in my room back in New York City just as the alarm went off.

35

The following day, the children at The Academy were let out early for parent/teacher conferences. With time to kill, I headed to the Deific.

"You're off early?" Sarah asked me when the elevator doors opened. She closed a book. "I'm so bored. Maybe I can get off early, and we can go to a movie or something."

I strolled over to her desk and spotted Charlie through the glass window of the conference room. He was kneeling on top of a long table scooting papers and photos all around. "Possibly. What's up with him?"

"He's been like that all morning. I wish he'd find a hobby or something." Her eyes went big and she grabbed my arm suddenly. "I met a guy last night! I almost called you, but it was midnight."

"Where?"

"At my apartment. This is totally cliché, but we were doing laundry together. He's new and gorgeous. I got his number and—"

There was a knock on the conference room window. Charlie was motioning me inside.

"Let's finish this conversation later," I said to Sarah. "I want to hear more about this mystery guy."

I walked away and opened the conference room door.

"You must've gotten out early," he said. "Good." He turned his attention back to a series of photographs spread out across the long table.

"What is all this?" I picked up the nearest photo. It was of a couple dancing in what looked like a bar.

"The club I told you about last night. I had one of our guys take a bunch of pictures of everyone in the club. You recognize this vamp?" He held up a profile picture of a man sitting at a table with

263

short hair.

I examined it carefully. "I think so. It was pretty dark in the house, but I think that's the one who attacked me."

"That's what I thought."

"So why all the other photos?" I asked.

"Just seeing if I recognize anyone else."

"The man who took something from you," I stated. "One day do you think you might be more specific?"

He gathered the pictures up. "One day. Your laptop is over there."

I followed his gaze. A black case rested upon a small table.

"Be sure this is what you want," he said.

His words gave me pause. I wasn't sure what I wanted from the strange vampire, but there was one thing I did know—I wanted to know more. "I'm sure."

The briefcase felt heavy in my arms as I carried it up to my apartment. Inside my room, I carefully unzipped the black bag and removed the laptop. On a yellow sticky note attached to its top, Charlie had scribbled the username and password and then given explicit instructions to tear the note up when I was finished.

After a few deep breaths, my hands hovering just above the silver metal of the computer, I opened the laptop and entered in the codes. Immediately, a database of some kind appeared. The first entry was a man named Alvin. It showed a photo of him, gave a brief history off to the right, and declared his threat level—his was high. It was no one I knew. I hit the next button.

I continued to press next many more times, flashing through pictures of men and women I'd never seen before. Occasionally, I would stop to read their history. They were vampires, witches, psychics, demons, diablos (I was surprised to discover that they actually existed), and even some creatures I'd never heard of before.

I stopped abruptly. The image of Boaz flashed on the screen. It was a black and white photo taken in 1863. On the right side his history read:

Name: Boaz

Age: Unknown

Status: Possibly dead (see history)

Current location: Unknown

Priority: Extremely High

History: Boaz was made known to the Deific in 1863. Agent Matthew Thomas found him in Pennsylvania working as an advisor to General Lee during the Civil War. After careful observation, the Deific determined his actions dangerous to society. Agent Thomas and Agent Smith were sent to restrain him. Both Agents and Boaz came up missing shortly after. All attempts to locate them have failed. Boaz reappeared in 2012 when he made contact with Eve Segur (daughter of Erik and Sable Segur—see file). Eve claims Boaz is dead but death not witnessed. Agents unable to find proof of life or death.

I looked away, frustrated by the rush of feelings toward Boaz. It wasn't revulsion like I expected to feel when seeing his face again. Instead, I felt a longing for the incredible power that we had experienced together. It frightened me to think I still had a desire for dark magic.

I quickly changed the picture before I allowed my thoughts to linger on him any longer. I hit next through many more pictures, even coming across my parents files whose status both read 'deceased'. My own record contained a picture that looked as if it had been taken at the airport, although I hadn't been aware of it at the time. There was a brief account of my history along with a short mention of my time with Boaz. I was glad to see my threat-level was nonexistent.

Several more images flashed—supernatural beings that roamed the earth in secret. There were so many! Only occasionally would I see one whose file indicated that they were not a threat. A couple of them I recognized as employees of The Deific. I clicked next.

All of a sudden, I came face to face with Him. I glanced to the right of his picture, anxious to put a name with his face: "Lucien."

The sound of his name felt right upon my lips as if there could be no other. The photo was taken ten years ago in Seattle, his last known location. He stood in a crowd of people, staring up. His face was easy to pick out among all the others whose faces emanated worries and frustrations, hope and joy. But his expression was blank, void of any emotion, except for his eyes. They were full of pain.

An immediate longing washed over me, and I yearned to be near him, to remove him from the crowd of people who took no notice of his suffering.

I was surprised by my feelings toward him. I barely knew him, and yet here I was, unable to tear my eyes away from his face. I searched his features, wondering again if it were possible that I'd somehow met him when I was younger. A friend of my parents, perhaps?

After several minutes, I finally glanced down to read his history but was disappointed to find there was none. Under priority it said, "Use caution." I connected the laptop to a printer on my desk and printed his picture, studying it for a few more minutes before I got ready for bed.

Instead of going through my usual nighttime routine, I went straight to bed, anxious to see if I could visit Lucien in my dreams again. It took me awhile to fall asleep, but eventually my eyes closed, his image engraved on my mind.

I "awoke" in his world, recognizing it immediately. It was night again, yet blacker than the night before—thick clouds overhead blocked the moon's light. I was standing on wood planks and water sloshed nearby, but the same fog blocked my view to anything around me. I pursed my lips, wondering if the haze was real or part of the dream. Maybe it was time I used a little magic. I closed my eyes and concentrated, thinking not of dark things, but of all the good that had recently come into my life. With little effort, I willed the fog away. When I opened my eyes, the mist had cleared, giving me a clear view of the surroundings.

I was at a marina. Boats bordered the dock, swaying gently to the rise and fall of the water. Occasionally one of them would rock hard enough to ring a bell. An old boardwalk followed the outline of the water, and on the other side, cramped shops with chipped wood and faded paint reflected a dying part of what was once probably a bustling area. In the distance, lit up skyscrapers protruded sharply into the sky.

Not far from me, a lone figure sat on a bench. *Lucien.* I approached him slowly. He was leaning forward, elbows resting on his knees, chin in hands. He stared out over the water, unmoving. Cautiously, I sat next to him. He was completely unaware of my presence. I didn't dare touch him for fear of disrupting whatever magic was making this possible. Instead, I relaxed, enjoying the peace I felt simply by being near him. I only wished he could feel it, too, but he seemed to be beyond feeling.

I remained with him for several hours, as still and quiet as he, but when I felt the sun in New York tug on my senses, I fought it. I did not want to wake up. It felt right to be with him.

But then I remembered I was due at the Academy.

I turned to Lucien one last time and lifted my hand to his face. When my fingers grazed his skin, his head snapped in my direction just as I disappeared. I sat up, my eyes opened wide, and glanced down at my hand. It was tingling where I'd touched him.

36

Before school started, I stopped in the Deific to return the laptop to Charlie, but he wasn't in his office.

"Sarah, do you know where Charlie is?" I asked at her desk.

She placed her hand over the telephone's mouthpiece. "He's training on the second floor."

"Great, thanks. Oh and by the way, I love your shoes."

She smiled and wiggled her pink high heels that were sticking out from beneath her desk, then returned her attention to the telephone in her hand. Sarah didn't know the Deific's whole truth. Like everyone else in the building, she thought they only sought out individuals on the FBI's most wanted list or any other people who threatened mankind. She probably would die if she knew how often they were actually hunting monsters. Sometimes I was tempted to tell her, but her life was so normal. I didn't want to cast a shadow on that.

Downstairs, there were only a handful of people scattered throughout the gym-like room, all of them in the middle of a full workout. Charlie was on a blue mat in the corner, sparring with a man I recognized from one of the cubicles upstairs. Charlie glanced over at me and waved. He said something to his partner and then jogged over.

"How's it going?" he asked, wiping sweat from his brow with a small towel.

"Good. I didn't mean to interrupt. I just wanted to give this back to you." I handed him the briefcase.

"Set it over there." He motioned to the wall nearby. "We can discuss it later, but first I want to know if you've ever learned to fight."

"Like punching and kicking?"

He smiled and nodded.

I swallowed. "Without using magic?"

"Especially without using magic."

"Not once."

"I think it's time you learned. In our line of work, one needs to hone all of their skills. We could practice before work."

"Really? I'd like that." I'd always wanted to learn to fight. My gaze drifted to the weapons on the wall, specifically the crossbow.

Charlie noticed. "Kelley told me you're pretty good with the crossbow. You must've found my old one in the attic of the cabin."

"That was yours?"

"My father gave it to me when I turned sixteen." Charlie stretched his hands high and twisted his torso. "I'm going to be sore tomorrow. Let's start training when I get back in a week or so."

"Are you going on vacation?"

"I wish. It's work related. We discovered the vampire at the bar has been making a bunch of phone calls to someone in Ireland. I'm going to check it out with a few others." He glanced over my shoulder. "Here's our team leaders now. I don't think you've met them."

I turned around. Walking toward us was a tall, well-built man with long blond, almost white hair and hazel eyes. Next to him moved a slightly shorter African American woman with a high forehead and long dark hair. She was extremely beautiful, but the closer they walked, the more I realized something was wrong. I took a step back and then another, my heartbeat racing. These two were not regular humans; they were vampires.

I was about to warn Charlie when I stumbled backwards over a weight bench.

As I fell, the vampires' eyes widened, and they glanced at each other. Charlie and the male vampire reached to help me up, but I accepted only Charlie's hand. The female watched it all with a small smile, arms crossed at her chest.

"Are you okay, Eve?" Charlie asked.

"She recognizes us for what we are," the male vampire said.

"Don't worry, miss. We won't hurt you."

I quickly recovered and stood up. "I'm fine. I was just startled is all."

"I guess I should've warned you first," Charlie said, laughing awkwardly. "Eve, this is Michael and Alana, our team leaders. They're our best undercover agents. Alana and Michael, this is Eve. She recently joined us about a month ago."

"Nice to meet you," Michael said. "We didn't mean to scare you."

"I wasn't scared. Just surprised to see vampires in a place like this."

"Judgmental much?" Alana asked, her voice smooth yet condescending.

"Be kind to Eve," Charlie said. "She hasn't had good experiences with vampires in the past."

"And we haven't had good experiences with witches. That's what you are, right?" Alana asked.

"Enough," Charlie said. "We're all here for the same reason. Let's not forget that."

"You're right," Michael said. "We will do our best."

Alana huffed loudly. "This has been fun, but we need to leave in a few hours."

"Right," Charlie said. "I better get ready. I have to take care of a few things before I go."

"Wait," I said. "I need to talk to you about what I found."

Charlie began to walk backward toward the door. "Bring the laptop up. I'll have some time in about an hour."

As soon as Charlie disappeared, Michael said, "I'm sorry we got off on the wrong foot, but you must know we won't hurt you or anyone here."

"How did you come to know of the Deific?" I asked—or rather, more like demanded.

"Henry invited me, and I said yes."

"Why?"

He looked past me. "I was a good person when I was a human, thanks to a great family who taught me strong morals and a respect for life. When I was turned into a vampire over a hundred years ago, I hated myself. I didn't know how to control the insatiable hunger, but I didn't want to hurt humans, either. I became a raving lunatic, shouting things on the streets, behaving irrationally. My mind fought my body and it caused me to go mad. Luckily, Henry found me and helped me through it. I owe him my life."

"And what about you?" I asked Alana.

"I'm here for him." She motioned her head toward Michael.

"Your turn, Eve. How do you know about the Deific?" he asked.

"Like you, I was found. By Charlie, though. He helped me."

"But why you?" Alana asked.

I touched my light hair, thinking how different I probably looked from my former self. They may not know me, but every supernatural I had ever encountered had at least had heard of my parents. "I am the daughter of Erik and Sable Segur."

They looked at each other and appeared to be communicating silently.

Alana turned to me. "We heard she died."

I smiled, arms outstretched. "Standing right here."

"That explains a lot," Michael said. "But you are the last person I thought would ever come here."

"You hung around a rough crowd," Alana said.

"A lot has changed. I've changed."

"Then welcome to the Deific," Michael said. "You will be a useful ally."

"I hope you're ready," Alana said in a mocking tone.

"Ready for what?"

"Ready to fight the evil you once so lovingly embraced."

Michael turned abruptly to Alana. "Have you so easily forgotten your own sinister past?"

Alana glared.

"It's fine," I said. "She's right. I need to be ready, and I'm working hard to make sure my past stays where it belongs."

"Just like the rest of us, right, Alana?" he asked.

Alana forced a smile. "Of course."

***

I didn't stick around to chat with Alana and Michael. Their motives seemed innocent enough, but I still couldn't accept that vampires would choose a life inside the Deific trying to stop evil. Ignore it, sure, but actually try to stop it? Accepting Henry as both a vampire and the founder of the Deific was hard enough, but …

I shook my head and leaned against the elevator.

What was wrong with me? Lucien had stopped me from using my abilities against others not once, but twice. Clearly vampires could be good. My head ached at all these new thoughts. Along with my world, my whole mindset was changing. Lines were no longer clear but blurred. How would I know whom to trust?

I waited in my apartment until an hour had passed. When I returned, Charlie was in his office on a telephone call. He motioned me inside and indicated that I should sit down. I sat in my usual chair and placed the black briefcase on my lap.

Charlie said goodbye to whomever he was speaking with then hung up the phone. "So tell me about what you found."

I withdrew the photocopy of Lucien from my pocket and unfolded it. "This is him," I said, handing it over. "The vampire who saved me. The one I visit in my dreams."

"You said visit?" Charlie asked and took the photo from me.

"A few times now. I go to sleep and wake where he is."

He studied the photo and frowned. "How strange that it would be him out of all others."

"Why?"

He looked up. "Out of all the supernatural beings in our world, he's remained a mystery. We've sent in multiple people, even vampires, to try and find something about him, but he refuses to speak with anyone. We watched him for a long time to determine if he was a threat, but he did very little. It's as if he's stuck in a private bubble unaware of the rest of the world."

"So he's not dangerous?"

"Not in the sense you mean. We have no record of him deliberately harming others, but he has fought every single person we sent in, one he almost killed. It's as if he will not allow himself to be freed from whatever inner torment he's putting himself through."

I considered this. "Do you think that's why I'm drawn to him?"

Charlie shrugged. "Could be. Maybe you've had similar life experiences."

"It's more than that. I feel at peace when I'm with him. It's almost as if—" I tried to find the words, tried to understand. He was like my Eden. His presence was as calming and soothing as the warm sandy beaches and the gentle rolling waves.

When I didn't finish the sentence, Charlie asked, "Didn't you say you felt a connection with Boaz, too?"

I flinched at the sound of his name. "Yes, but it was the complete opposite. That connection was a violent one obsessed only with power. With him, I was in a constant state of hate and anger. I craved the power as if it were a drug."

"Interesting. Everything has its opposite including people. Maybe you found Boaz's."

"Charlie," I began, nervous to reveal the real motive behind my visit. "I was wondering if you could use your gift, maybe find out something about him?"

He shook his head. "Don't you think I've tried? We want to

know about him as much as you do. We've had many psychics try to read him, but somehow he has blocked us."

"So if you can't see anything about him, what about me? Could you try to see my future? See what would happen if I try to meet him?"

Charlie looked doubtful. "A person should not know their future. I only use my gift if absolutely necessary."

"Isn't this necessary? You want to find out something about him, and I know I'm going to meet him eventually. I don't want to know all of my future, just a year or so ahead and just my future with Lucien, if there is to be one."

Charlie's lips twisted, and he looked away.

"Please, Charlie. We'll both get what we want."

He narrowed his eyes and sighed. "Very well. Give me your hands."

I placed my palms in Charlie's. He held them and looked into my eyes before he closed his own tightly. The deep wrinkles in his forehead gathered together in concentration, and soon his eyes began to move back and forth behind his eyelids.

Several minutes passed. His expression changed many times from anger to sadness and even an occasional smile broke on his face. Finally, he dropped my hands and opened his eyes, which were glistening with tears. I waited patiently for him to speak. He leaned back in his chair.

After a moment, he spoke. "Four years ago I married the most amazing woman I had ever met."

"Moira," I said.

He nodded. "She was my match in every way, and I was never happier than when I was with her. But together we experienced more pain and sorrow than any couple should have to endure. A lot of lives were ruined because of our union. I used to wonder if it was worth it." He looked up at me. "But I never wonder now. It was worth it, and I would do it all over again if given the chance."

"Then you think I should see him?" I said, hopeful.

"That's not what I'm saying at all. The pain and misery I just witnessed was ten times greater than anything I had to endure. If you meet Lucien, he will try to kill you, and he will break your heart. The path this choice will put you on will nearly destroy you and those close to you. Lives will be lost."

My heart sank, and I lowered my gaze.

"But," Charlie said, taking my hands again, "the love between you two is remarkable. It's pure, kind, and unselfish. I've never seen anything like it. You will experience happiness with him that will make you extremely powerful. Together you will do a lot of good and save a lot of lives."

"So what do I do?"

"Only you can decide that."

I sighed. "I was hoping this would be easy."

Charlie smiled. "It's not meant to be easy. True happiness and pure, unselfish love is only meant for those who are willing to sacrifice all that they have for it. You will taste bitterness before you taste joy."

37

Charlie had been gone for ten days. I'd been looking forward to his return ever since he told me he would teach me how to fight. It was exciting to think I could use something other than magic to defend myself, and I was glad when Dr. Skinner had agreed.

"It's important you know how to fight," he told me a few days ago. "Magic should only be used as a last resort."

I looked forward to my meetings with Dr. Skinner. During our last few, I'd begun to use my abilities again, starting with small things like moving objects. He taught me how to use my experiences at the Academy to call upon my abilities. It was hard to choose just one as I had so many.

The process of using this new kind of magic worked just like he said it would. Instead of beginning in my toes, however, the power was first felt in my chest; a warming sensation that spread to the rest of my body. The room became brighter, images sharper, smells sweeter—the exact opposite of dark magic. What I was experiencing, Dr. Skinner had explained, was the magic of beauty.

It was during this time I decided to tell him about Lucien and what Charlie had told me about my future. He was concerned, but not so much for me. His concern was for Lucien.

"I don't care who or what you are," he said. "One should not live like that. Based on the feelings you have when you're around him, I'd say you were meant for each other."

My heart leapt unexpectedly.

"But that doesn't mean you should be together," he added quickly. "Lucien can only be saved if he chooses to be. Just because you feel a connection doesn't mean he will too. You must proceed with caution. That means no more visiting him in whatever dream-like trance you're putting yourself in."

I began to protest, but Dr. Skinner raised his hand. "At least until you make a decision. You need to choose freely without any distractions."

I agreed, but that was three days ago and now, as I sat on the gray couch in my apartment, flipping through mindless TV channels, I thought of Lucien and wondered what he was doing.

I'd gone back to see Lucien a few times while Charlie was gone. Lucien never did much. He was always looking into the distance, but I was never sure at what. And during all this time, he'd only fed twice, and each time he seemed to know his victim.

On my last visit, I'd followed him while he dragged a dead body to an alleyway where he opened a rusted manhole and dropped the body inside. Afterwards, he'd leaned against a brick wall of a warehouse doubled over in pain. His suffering had been difficult to watch.

I glanced down at the time on my cell phone. Almost ten o'clock. Charlie was returning today, but he wouldn't be back at the Deific until noon. I had enough time.

Sleep came easily. I materialized in a dark, run-down bar that reeked of grease and beer. A few people sat separate from each other, heads down while they held theirs drinks protectively. No one spoke, each of them too wrapped up in their own problems to care about anyone else's.

I couldn't see Lucien anywhere, but knew he had to be close. When the door to the bar opened, letting in a blast of cold air, I stepped through it before it closed. The sun's morning light was just beginning to touch the sky, pushing back much of night's darkness. I loved this time of day. It was a reminder that no matter how bleak my work seemed, dawn would always come.

Ignoring the people around me, I stood on a sidewalk in front of a long row of buildings. Across a street that was just beginning to get crowded with morning commuters was a children's hospital. I looked around, eventually spotting Lucien not far from its entrance. I moved to be near him, the feeling of peace and serenity growing with each step, but was momentarily distracted by a mother and small boy walking out of the hospital. The boy was shouting and fighting against his mother who held him tightly, but her soothing words did nothing to calm him. He must've kicked her hard, because suddenly she dropped him, and he bolted into the street and in front of an oncoming car. An instant before the car smashed into the boy, Lucien appeared, shoving him out of the way. Instead, the car crashed into Lucien, and he flipped up and over the hood, his body shattering the windshield.

The mother rushed to her son, who was crying even louder now, while I bolted for Lucien. I rounded the car to the driver's side, but when I got there, Lucien was gone. The driver opened his door, and he, too, glanced around for the man he knew he had hit.

I looked up and down the streets. There were several alleys— one in particular drew my attention. It was about one block up and partially concealed by a shipping truck. I jogged over to it.

As I suspected, I found Lucien sitting on a wooden crate with his jacket off. His torn sleeve was pulled up around his bicep and very carefully he was removing shards of glass from his bloodied arm. His wounds healed almost immediately.

I stood in front of him, wishing he knew that I was there and had witnessed what he'd done.

One last large piece of glass protruded from his forearm. He moved to take it out, but his hand stopped and hesitated above it. Instead of removing it, he suddenly slammed his fist on top forcing it deeper into his arm. He threw his head back in pain, but did not cry out. His eyebrows tightened and his jaw muscles bulged.

I stared in horror. I had no idea his self-torture went as far as this. My gaze lowered to the embedded glass in his arm, and I concentrated hard. Using my feelings toward him to invoke magic, I imagined the shard of glass sliding out of his arm. Lucien jumped when he felt it begin to move. I concentrated harder. The glass broke free from his flesh, and I mentally tossed it to the ground.

Lucien glanced around, his expression a mixture of anger and surprise. I was glad. I wanted him to know that someone was watching over him. Hopefully this would make him think twice before he decided to hurt himself again.

It was my turn to be surprised when Lucien, his voice full of hatred, growled, "Leave. Me. Alone."

"Lucien?" I asked as if he could hear me.

"Leave me now, or I swear I will find you and rip your heart out!"

Frightened by his sudden hostility, I obeyed.

38

"How was your trip?" I asked Charlie, who seemed surprised to see me waiting for him in his office. After I'd woken from being with Lucien, his office was the only place I wanted to go. Maybe it was where I felt safest.

Charlie dropped his suitcase and removed a black leather jacket. "It was horribly successful."

"What's that mean?"

He dropped into his chair as if he was exhausted. "Bad things are happening, Eve."

"Is this at all connected to the vampire you are searching for?"

"It reeks of him, but I can't be sure yet. This is the most frustrated I've ever been. The one time I really need my gift, it fails me."

Gently, as if my next words might hurt him, I asked, "What did this vampire do?"

Charlie sunk farther into his chair, if that was possible. Even the color drained from his face. I almost told him to forget it, but then he spoke.

"He killed Moira on our second year anniversary. Left her like a present in our bedroom, my anniversary gift tied to her lifeless hand. You see he was paying me back for a raid on his *house*. We killed six of his newbie vamps, but only after they refused to listen to reason."

My throat felt like it was in my stomach. "I'm so sorry," I managed to whisper.

"So am I." He breathed a few times, the air thick with his sorrow. Finally he said, "You were waiting for me. Did you need something?"

"I just wanted to see how you were." The words seemed hollow in the heavy room.

281

He laughed miserably. "Well, now you know." He closed his eyes like he'd bitten his tongue and then opened them. "I'm sorry. I don't talk about my wife's death. Ever. But I think about it every second of the day. I'll be in a better mood later. Do you want to meet up later tonight to begin your training?"

"Only if you're up for it," I said.

"I will be."

I stood and walked to the door. "I'll see you then ... and Charlie, if you ever need anything, please let me know."

I left, my heart aching. What was the point of using my abilities for good if I couldn't help those closest to me? Somehow, I had to find a way to sense exactly what people needed to make them feel happy and at peace. I'd never heard of such a spell, but if magic could destroy faraway places, surely it could do this? I vowed to find a way.

***

I didn't visit Lucien again. My last encounter made me realize how difficult it was going to be to try and release him from his self-made prison. Before I returned to him, I wanted to ensure I was stronger both mentally and emotionally. Because of this, I worked harder than ever with Dr. Skinner, forcing myself to do things I didn't think possible. Even he seemed surprised by my progress.

"You don't need to push yourself so hard, Eve. All of this will come in time."

But I didn't have time. Every night, a growing uneasiness gnawed and chewed at my gut, making me physically ill. Something terrible was going to happen to Lucien, and in his current condition, I was afraid he would welcome it.

I used this urgency to train harder with Charlie. He was shocked by how quickly I'd picked up on marital arts, but not as surprised as I was. It came naturally to me as if it was what my magic wanted. It wasn't long before I was able to predict Charlie's moves and block his attacks with ease.

"So, tell me again. You've never had any lessons?" Charlie asked after getting thrown over my shoulder. I helped him up.

"Nothing formal. I used to imagine I could fight when I was younger."

"And I used to imagine that I was a dinosaur, but you don't see that happening. What's your secret?"

I laughed. "Have you ever thought that maybe I'm not that great and you just really stink?"

"Believe me, I've considered that."

In the corner of the room, I spotted Derek. I'd come to love the teenage boy who followed me around from a distance. I'd often catch him watching me with a look of wonderment on his face. This look always made me feel special somehow.

"One second," I said to Charlie.

Charlie collapsed to the ground. "Take all the time you need."

"Don't get too comfortable," I called behind me as I jogged over to Derek. I was careful not to touch him when I sat on the floor next to him. "How's it going, D?"

Derek rocked back and forth. Normally I would leave him alone, giving him the space he required, but there was anxiousness in his eyes.

"What is it, Derek?" I asked.

Instead of speaking, he reached inside a backpack sitting on his other side and removed a shoebox. One of the sides had been cut off, and inside he had created a miniature replica of the Deific office upstairs. I recognized it immediately because of the roses shaped out of crumpled red paper upon all the desks. On the floor of the box, little human figures made out of tin foil were lying down; red marker dotted many of them in the exact location of their hearts. Glued high on the cardboard wall were two men. Over their faces Derek had scribbled a black marker. Directly below them, I saw myself. I was made out of tin with long yellow yarn for hair, and all around me he'd glued thin strips of yellow ribbon like sunrays spreading out.

"What's that?" Charlie said behind me.

I jumped. "I'm not sure. Derek just handed it to me."

Charlie crouched down to get a better look. His body tensed. "Something's wrong. Do you feel it?"

I did feel something but was it was the art project that disturbed me, or something else?

Charlie stood suddenly. "I have to go. I'll see you upstairs."

"Do you want some help?" I called after him.

He didn't answer but raised his hand and waved before he darted out the door.

I turned back toward Derek. "I wish you could tell me what this means. It's beautiful. I can even tell which one I am." I reached to touch the top of his head but stopped, remembering his dislike for touching. "Do you want to come upstairs?"

He shook his head vehemently.

"All right. You don't have to," I said, startled by his reaction.

Upstairs, Sarah stopped me. "So are you coming tonight? I want you to meet Jesse."

"Um, probably," I said. "One sec." I walked quickly to Charlie's office, where I found him speaking urgently into the phone.

"Check it again," he yelled and slammed the receiver down and looked up at me. "We need to get everybody out of here."

"What's going on?"

"I don't know how it's going to happen, but we're going to be attacked."

"When?"

"Soon. I can't tell for sure, but I feel it. My skin is crawling; it's horrible. We need to get everybody out *now*."

"Has security noticed anything strange?"

"They said everything's fine," Charlie said as he walked out of his office.

I followed. "Do you know who's going to attack us?"

He stopped and faced me. "That's the strange thing. Whoever it is, they feel—" he chewed his lip before continuing. "—wrong. Could be vampires, witches, I don't know. The signal is all messed up."

I didn't like the word *wrong*. "I'll help get everybody out."

Thumping loudly against the wall with his fist, Charlie announced to the office that they were going to have a practice fire drill. Annoyed sighs and moans filled the air.

"But it's almost five o'clock!" someone said.

"Can I get coffee while we're out?" asked Sarah.

"Sure, whatever. Let's just get going. I'm timing you." People stood but no one took it seriously. Charlie jogged up and down the aisles trying to hurry them along. "You're being timed people. Move it!"

Without warning, the lights overhead turned off. Only a little streetlight found its way through the slated blinds, but it wasn't enough to help us maneuver about the many cubicles.

"Sarah!" Charlie called.

"Yes?" she said, her voice still casual.

"Call security."

I heard the phone being picked up.

"That's strange," Sarah said. "The phone is dead."

"Eve!" Charlie called, the panic in his voice unmistakable.

"I'm over here," I said next to Sarah.

"Get everyone into my office and lock the door behind you, do you understand?"

I called out, "Whoever's still left in here, follow the sounds of my voice if you can't see me."

Several people, unknown to me in the darkness, found their way over. I told them to follow the length of the wall until they reached Charlie's office. Meanwhile, I heard Charlie hurrying around the office opening all the blinds, but the dim, orange streetlights barely reached us.

I tapped Sarah's shoulder. She had yet to move from her desk as she was on her cell phone talking about the current excitement with a friend. The light from the phone lit up her thrilled face.

"Get off the phone, Sarah," I said.

She lifted a finger to signal 'in a minute'. I snatched the phone from her hand and tossed it into the wall. As soon as it hit, there was a loud explosion near the floor's break room.

"What the hell was that?" Sarah asked.

The silhouette of Charlie's body slid skillfully over a desk toward me. "Get down!" he yelled and pulled Sarah's desk on its side and jerked her to the floor next to me. He withdrew two revolvers from within his jacket. A few people who hadn't quite made it to Charlie's office began to run. Sarah scrambled after them.

"Go with her, Eve," Charlie said.

"I'm not leaving you. I can help."

"It's too soon. You'll get yourself killed."

"I won't," I said, wishing I had just told him already about being an immortal. "I'll be—"

A shrill cry pierced the air behind us, from a direction we weren't expecting. I turned around, my heart almost beating from my chest. A dark figure of a man was gripping a woman by her neck with one hand high in the air, her legs dangling beneath her.

"Let the killing begin," he said, and he tossed the woman across the room.

39

Charlie fired his gun, drilling one bullet after another into the looming figure's chest. The man's body jerked, but he kept moving forward with frightening determination. That's when I knew. He wasn't a man. He was a vampire.

A sound snapped. Charlie swung his gun around and fired at another vampire. Again the bullets did nothing but slow him down. Charlie stood up and darted across the room, attempting to draw the intruders away from Sarah and me, but only one took the bait.

I gritted my teeth. Two very different kinds of magic inside me fought for control. There was the rush of anger and fear, but also something new—a fierce desire to protect those I cared about. I was afraid to let the new feeling take over, worried it might not be strong enough, but when I saw the nearest vampire pick up Sarah by the hair, I had no doubt which magic would be more powerful. The love for my friend was far stronger.

Mentally, I took hold of a chair and pushed it toward the vampire. It knocked his legs out from under him, and he dropped a still-screaming Sarah. I rushed to her and half-dragged her into Charlie's office with the others. A few men stood ready to charge out and help fight, but I pushed them back.

"Stay here and get everyone out the fire escape." I closed the door and turned back around to focus on Sarah's attacker, but he was gone.

On the other side of the room, Charlie was trying to get out from beneath another vampire. I lifted a paperweight from a desk, and using a combination of strength and magic, threw it at the longhaired vampire. The paperweight hit him directly in the temple, and he fell off Charlie, stunned.

Charlie scrambled toward me. Blood from a deep cut above his eye dripped down his face. He took me by the arm and pulled me toward his office. "You're getting out of here. Now."

From above, hiding in a corner, the vampire who had attacked Sarah dropped down. He lunged for me, but Charlie pushed me out of the way and kicked at the vampire, making the vampire stumble back several feet. Charlie quickly removed two wooden daggers from each of his sleeves.

"You came to the wrong office," he said and swiped at the vampire in a circular motion. He missed but was already swiping with his other hand, so when the vampire moved, Charlie was able to catch the vampire's shoulder.

The vampire growled, showing the razor sharp fangs that filled his mouth, and rushed Charlie. Judging by Charlie's wide-eyed expression, he was faster than Charlie expected. The vampire slammed into Charlie, sending his body flying into a wall behind him, which buckled under the pressure.

I jumped to my feet and thought of the moves Charlie had taught me. I punched my fist hard into the vampire's throat, causing him to stumble to the ground gasping for air, a habit he had no need for. I moved to help Charlie, but already the vampire was back on his feet and coming for me again. He swung his fist quick and hard, easily connecting it with my face. I fell backwards directly into the arms of the other vampire who I'd hit with the paperweight. He wrapped his arms around me.

"You're going to pay for that one, beautiful," he said in my ear.

Charlie struggled to get up.

"Eve," he mumbled. The other vampire kicked him hard in the face, and Charlie fell over unconscious.

I grabbed the arm of the longhaired vampire holding me and bent over quickly, flipping him to the floor. I needed powerful magic and fast. I thought of the children at the Academy, of Charlie, and of

288

Lucien. This filled me with a burning power hotter than I thought I could stand. In one fluid motion of my finger, I sent both vampires flying through the air. Their bodies smashed high against the wall where they remained frozen, arms outstretched. My head burst into a million colors of pain, but I maintained their position.

"Say cheese," the longhaired vampire said.

I looked up just as a bright flash filled the room. Over by the window, the dark outline of a man or vampire—I couldn't be sure from this far away—had taken my picture. Before I could react, he jumped through the window, breaking the glass as he went. Both vampires laughed.

I responded by raising all the pencils from the desks. They came together and rushed at the two vampires, but I stopped them inches before their hearts. They weren't laughing any more.

"Settle down there, missy. We were just having some fun," Longhair said.

"Right. Harmless fun," the other said. "So let us down, and we'll get out of here."

"Who sent you?" I asked.

Silence.

"I will ask one more time. Who sent you?"

They glanced at each other but remained silent. I didn't hesitate. Mentally, I shoved one of the floating groups of pencils directly into the heart of the longhaired vampire. His body wilted and caved within itself until there was nothing left but dust.

I fell to my knees, the pressure in my head reaching a whole new level, but I still managed to maintain my grip on the last vampire. Through my clenched teeth, I said, "Tell me who sent you or you'll end up just like your friend."

"The Dark Prince," he said, his bottom lip quivering like a puppy.

"The Dark Prince? I need a real name." I let the pencils hover closer.

"I don't know! Really, I don't!"

"Why was my picture taken?" I asked, pressing my hand to my aching head.

"For the Dark Prince. He told us to keep our eyes out for a powerful witch."

The pain in my head spread to my body, and I wondered how much more I could take. The vampire slipped a few inches.

"Having some difficulties?" he asked, his voice dropping a tone.

I dropped to one knee, and that's when I felt it—a hand gently touching my shoulder.

"It is enough," a kind voice said, though I couldn't be sure if I'd heard the words or if they had been placed inside my head.

My gaze turned upward. I stared into the face of another vampire but knew there was nothing to fear. His commanding presence personified one who abhorred darkness and cherished truth and light. I felt his power, greater than anything I'd ever encountered, but it didn't frighten me. I found comfort in it.

Henry, the founder of the Deific.

He nodded and smiled as if he'd read my mind. Maybe he had.

I let go of my mental grip on the vampire, but Henry, his arm out stretched, kept the vampire pressed against the wall. A second later, the pencils shot forward, piercing his heart.

I stared at him, my mouth open. He could use magic. The only other vampire I knew who could do that was Boaz, but he had to steal it from me to do so. It wasn't this way with Henry, though. So how was he able to do it? I shook the thought from my head. I had to help the others first.

I ignored my aching body and moved to attend to Charlie, but Henry stopped me.

"He's fine and will wake soon," Henry said.

"What about the others?"

"They made it safely outside. The police will be here any minute, and I don't want you answering any questions in your condition." Henry walked to the back of the office. He didn't have to ask me to follow—I did so instinctively.

Inside the office's break room, he opened a cupboard and reached to the very top. He must have pressed a button, because all of a sudden the cupboards swung open, revealing a room the size of a closet. Once inside, I realized it was an elevator. Henry pushed the button going "up".

I glanced sideways at him. He was staring at the doors with a blank expression, and yet I felt as if the whole space was brimming with all kinds of emotions. Henry had wavy light brown hair, and his golden eyes matched the color of his tanned skin. He was dressed surprisingly well in a dark suit and a floor length overcoat. His full lips parted when he said, "We're here."

The doors opened into a library and what I thought was the top floor. Henry walked over to a hutch and withdrew a blanket and pillow. He carried them to a leather sofa in the middle of the room. "You'll have to stay here for tonight and probably part of tomorrow. The police will be busy for a while."

I immediately sat down, the pain in my head making it difficult to stand. "How did you know to come?"

"Just a feeling. I would've come sooner, but our other offices were hit with much heavier casualties. I helped them first because I knew you were here."

"But we've never met," I said.

"Not officially."

"The Dark Prince," I said suddenly. "The vampires called whoever was in charge of this attack 'The Dark Prince'."

"I know. I questioned one of them in our London office."

"How long ago was that?"

He looked down at his silver watch. "Twenty minutes."

He was using magic to travel, much like I thought Boaz had.

"Oh, and the one who got away took my picture," I added.

For the first time, the calm in his demeanor cracked, and he frowned. "Were you able to find out why?"

I shook my head.

"That is disturbing. I'll get someone to look into it as soon as possible. How are you feeling?'

"My head hurts."

"It's like that in the beginning."

"I never felt that when I used magic before. It was the opposite. If I didn't let the evil out—" I stopped, embarrassed. I didn't know how much he knew about me.

"Withholding evil's power can be very painful," he said as if he understood.

"But why do I have pain? The magic I'm using is good."

"Because the good is you—a part of you anyway. When you let it go, your body responds physically. Whereas when one is evil, the evil only wants to escape and spread like a virus." He narrowed his eyes in concern. "You need to get some rest."

"Wait! I want to ask you something." I wasn't sure how long it would be until I would have the chance to speak with him again.

"Then ask."

"I don't understand how—"

"A vampire can be good? Use magic?"

"Both."

"I can use magic because I was like you before I was turned. A witch. And I am good because I choose to be, Eve. There are certain eternal truths about our universe that can never be altered. Free agency is one of these. Every living creature has the ability to choose good or evil, life or death."

"Then why are vampires evil? Most of them," I corrected.

"It's the power, the blood lust. It's very difficult to overcome.

Once a vampire crosses a certain line, like taking a life without provocation, it's almost impossible for them to rid themselves of the evil."

"How many good vampires are there?"

"Only a handful. Very few choose to live our way."

"What of Lucien? Do you know him?"

Henry looked past me. "I've watched Lucien for a long time, hoping. But he seems to be stuck."

"What happened to him?"

"He changed history."

"What do you mean?"

His gaze returned to mine. "It is not my tale to tell."

"Then do you know why I'm drawn to him?"

"It's the ancient power within you both."

"I've felt it before with someone else, but it was an evil feeling."

"Boaz," he said, surprising me. "All of your lives are connected, including Lucien's to Boaz's and even to mine."

"How is that possible?"

Henry's jaw tightened. "There is a long history between all of our families. I wish I could say more, but there's too many unknowns right now. One day I will tell you everything."

This revelation surprised me, and I leaned back into the cushions.

"I find it interesting that the good in you is drawn to Lucien," he said. "It gives me hope."

"Why?"

"If the good in you is drawn to him, then that means there is still good in him, too. The problem is he doesn't know it."

"How can I make him see it?"

"I don't know if you can." He stopped and tilted his head slightly as if listening to something far away. "I need to go. You've come a long way. I'm proud of you." He pointed to a refrigerator behind me. "There's food in there if you need it."

I glanced at it briefly, but when I turned back, Henry was gone.

40

It was a long night. What Henry had said about all our lives being connected had kept me awake, so I rose early to search the many books on the shelves, trying to bide the time before I could go downstairs. Most of them were history books, all dedicated to the dark creatures of the world.

I turned down the third aisle of bookshelves and scanned the titles. I stopped when I recognized a symbol that had been burned onto the outer spine of a brown book. It was a picture of the same fighting lions at my grandfather's house. I removed it from the shelf.

It was a faded leather book, loosely bound; several of the pages were no longer connected. Carved on the front was the Whitmore family crest. Unfortunately, most of the words inside had faded, but from what I could decipher, the book had been a Whitmore journal handed down for generations. The Segurs were mentioned many times, and the passages I could read were always negative. It was true what Boaz had told me: the Whitmores had hated the Segurs.

Only two other names were mentioned: the Bradys and the Archers. None of these names were familiar, and since I was unable to read the full text, I couldn't determine their connection to my family.

Boaz's name was mentioned just once. In dark ink, on the last page of the book, a heading read "In Service to Boaz". Beneath this, several names followed, most of which had been crossed out. The final entry was on January 12, 1889. This must've been the time when the Deific came in possession of the book. I closed it and placed it back on the shelf.

By five o'clock the next day, I could wait no longer. I returned to the elevator and, after listening carefully through the wall, slipped into the empty break room. I stuck my head into the office and looked around.

Desks had been pushed back into their rightful positions and the cubicle walls stood upright, only a few missing. The smell of roses was stronger than usual, but not strong enough to cover the smell of smoke from the explosion. A cold breeze swept through the office stirring up several loose papers. The wall the vampires had blasted through must be covered poorly, if at all.

Only a handful of people were working. No doubt Charlie had offered everyone the day off. Those who were working were somber and lifeless. One man, I remembered his name as John, leaned against the wall, staring at nothing as if he was sleeping with his eyes open.

I moved into the room and made my way through the maze of cubicles to Sarah's desk. She was organizing a file cabinet with her back to me. Every now and then, she would reach up and wipe a tear away with a tissue.

"Sarah?" I asked.

She jumped, turned around, and gasped. Her arms flew around me, nearly knocking me over. "You're here! We thought they took you!"

I shook my head and released her. "I'm fine. How is everyone else?"

Sarah didn't get a chance to answer. Charlie appeared before me with a bandage above his eye and a dark bruise on his forehead that spread into his hairline. By his expression, I couldn't tell if he was angry or happy. His face twisted into so many emotions in such a short amount of time that I couldn't help but give him a weak smile. He didn't say a word. Instead, he grabbed me by the arm and pulled me into his office.

"Where have you been?" he asked as soon as the door closed.

"I've been hiding upstairs in some library."

He paused, thinking. "How did you know of that place? The last thing I remember is one of those men holding you. Better question, how did you get away?"

I smiled. "Magic. It just came to me, and you and Dr. Skinner were right. It didn't frighten me, didn't change me. Other than leaving me with a pretty good headache, it was amazing."

Charlie dropped into his chair, a great sigh leaving his chest. "Thank goodness. I've been so worried."

"I'm sorry. Henry showed up and thought it best if I avoided the police. He took me to the private library through the break room. Cool hideout, by the way. So does anyone have any theories on why those men attacked us?"

Charlie rubbed his temples. "Not a clue. All the Deific offices were broken into, but only one item was taken, and it just happened to be from our office."

"What was it?"

"The briefcase you gave back to me yesterday."

"What would they want with that?" I asked and began to pace back and forth. It didn't really give them any relevant information they should care about. Almost everyone in the database shared their same interests and desires.

Charlie lowered his hands. "It seems to me that if bad guys are trying to find other bad guys, then they are either trying to knock someone off, or they want to get everyone together for some bad guy convention. I'm guessing it's the latter."

"I think you're right," I agreed. "There's something else. Before Henry came, I had a chance to question the vampires. One of them said 'The Dark Prince' was behind this."

The color immediately drained from Charlie's face, and his mouth opened.

"Do you know him?" He didn't respond, and that's when I knew. "He's the one who killed your wife, isn't he?"

"I should've known," he whispered. "It's all been leading up to this."

"So what do we do?"

Charlie straightened. "We fight."

41

The next several days, Charlie worked overtime. Many calls were made to the other Deific offices, and several agents were sent undercover, including Alana and Michael, who seemed to be more upset than anyone.

Before they left, Michael pulled me aside. "Henry told me that one of them took your picture."

I nodded.

"When did he take your picture? Was it before or after you used magic?"

"After."

His brow wrinkled. "Someone thinks they've found you. Watch your back, Eve."

His words sent a cold chill up my spine. There were only a couple of people who might try to find me: Boaz, if he somehow survived, and any relatives. The thought of coming face to face with either of them rocked my frame.

After Michael left, I went into Charlie's office. Papers were scattered all over his desk; several of them had spilled onto the floor. Charlie's head was lowered and rested in his hands. I thought he was asleep until he suddenly jerked upright and stared at me as if he'd never seen me before. Dark circles hung beneath his eyes and his brown hair was wildly out of control.

"Okay, Charlie. This is getting ridiculous!" I said. "Go home!"

"How can I? The man who murdered Moira is out there, and now he's come back for more blood. I have to stop him, but—" He picked up several papers and tossed them off his desk. "—I can't find him!"

"Maybe you're too close to the situation." I sat in the chair across from his desk and slouched down. "Take a break and come back and look at everything with a new perspective. When's the last time you ate?"

His shoulders slumped forward. "Maybe you're right."

"Of course I'm right. Let's go get something to eat and then you are going to go to bed. If you won't leave the Deific, then at least crash at my place for a few hours."

He sighed and rubbed his eyes. "There's a truck stop diner just outside the city. It's private and they have the best eggs benedict."

"Eggs it is," I said, pushing my way back out of the chair. Charlie was looking at paperwork again by the time I reached the door. I practically had to drag him away.

***

It was especially dark outside as we drove away from the city and its light. Only the glow of the full moon shined, casting an eerie quality along a thin layer of frost blanketing the cold ground. Spring would come sooner than expected thanks to an unusually mild winter.

There were few cars on the road this time of the night. Charlie hadn't said much, and I left him alone to his thoughts. It was strange to have him so quiet, but I didn't try to bring him out of his somber mood. Tonight, no matter what, I was going to tell him the truth about me. Now how to start the conversation …

Charlie stiffened and sat up straight. "Not now," he moaned.

"What is it?"

He glanced in his rear view mirror. I turned around to follow his gaze. Behind us, a car's headlights shined brightly in the distance.

"I've got that same feeling I had when the Deific was attacked."

"But where? I don't see anyone." The car behind us had turned off, leaving us alone on the road.

Charlie glanced at my waist. "Put your seatbelt on."

Knowing I was immortal, a seatbelt never seemed important, but I obeyed anyway. I pulled over the shoulder strap, but my hand slipped off. I stretched it out in front of me. "Um, Charlie, your seatbelt—" The gray seatbelt strap was jagged on one end as if it had been torn.

Charlie's hands tightened further on the steering wheel. "Get in the back."

I began to crawl in back of the vehicle but stopped. "The back ones are ripped, too."

Ignoring the road stretching out in front of us, Charlie turned to me. "It's you they're after, isn't it?"

It seemed an eternity that I stared into his eyes, when in reality it was only a fraction of a second before something big and hard smashed into the side of Charlie's Toyota. It had come from a side street traveling at a fantastic speed. Our car flipped several times, and I rolled with it until I was finally thrown from the passenger window.

My body landed in the weeds on the shoulder of the road, and something cold pierced my chest on the right side of my sternum. I cried out in horrific pain, clawing at whatever had stabbed me.

The car stopped rolling several feet from me in a twisted heap of broken metal and glass. The still night held its breath, and so I did, too. I wasn't sure who could be around, and I didn't want to give my location away. The ground was wet, and it soaked through my sweater and to my skin. But the icy coldness was secondary to my pain. I lifted my head. There was some sort of a stake sticking out from my chest.

Charlie's moan from within the car broke through the silence. The night gasped for air in a voice of a thousand different sounds: a horn honked in the distance, a dog barked, crickets chirped, and a loud engine revved. The truck that had hit us slowly crept forward; one of its headlights was broken. The remaining good light shined on the upside-down Toyota.

Charlie was cursing as he struggled to get out of the car. After kicking the door open from the inside, he crawled out. His clothes were torn and his head bloody.

"Eve!" he called.

"Here," I whispered loudly, hoping those in the car wouldn't hear me.

Charlie limped toward me, dragging one foot behind the other. The truck slowly turned, following his movements. The one good headlight turned Charlie into a dark shadow.

He knelt next to me, and his expression turned to horror when he saw my condition. I could only imagine what I must look like. Many of my wounds had already healed, but I could still feel sticky blood covering my body. Charlie inspected the stake in my chest, the one wound that wouldn't heal until he removed it.

"What is this?" I asked, clawing at it again.

"I think you've been stabbed by a roadside memorial cross," he said, his voice cracking.

Whether from shock or because it really was funny, I began to laugh.

"How can you be laughing?" Charlie said. "You should be dead!"

He tore the bottom of his shirt and held it tightly against what he thought was another wound on my head.

The truck behind us inched forward, reminding me of our dangerous predicament. "Charlie, you have to listen to me. I need you to drag my body into the woods."

"No way! I'm not moving you. You could bleed to death!"

"But they're watching us. Pull me into the woods—now!"

For the first time, he remembered the truck and was surprised to see it still there. He stood up and shouted, "What do you want?"

Its engine revved.

"Get me out of here," I whispered again. I didn't want whoever was in the truck to see me heal.

This time, Charlie didn't argue. He took my arms and pulled me into the woods, away from the threatening truck. An unexpected ravine made Charlie stumble, but he managed to keep me on my back even though I practically slid to the bottom. The light from the truck remained above us, spreading along the tops of the tree branches.

"Get this thing out," I said once we were safely into the forest. I stood up and used my own hands to try and pull the cross out.

Charlie looked dumb struck. "How can you be standing?"

"I still have legs. Please, help me!"

"If I pull that out, you'll bleed to death."

"Trust me, I won't. We have to get out of here before they follow us on foot, and I don't want to run with a stake in my chest." I continued to struggle with the splintered wood.

"This is insane! You were just thrown from a car and stabbed in the chest, but you act like you've only stubbed your toe."

The sound of a truck door opening made my heart pound. I grabbed Charlie by the shoulders and in an urgent voice said, "If we don't get out of here now, we're both dead. Do you understand? Now rip this thing out of me!"

Charlie grabbed the cross with both hands and pulled while I pushed away from it. Finally it broke free. Blood poured from the open wound, and I cried out and fell to the ground.

"I told you it was a bad idea," he said and helped me up.

Two figures stepped into the beam of the headlights. A deep, raspy voice called down. "Leave the girl, and you might just live."

Charlie pressed his torn shirt to my wound.

"You leave your girl, and I'll leave mine," he shouted back.

The figures turned to each other. The shorter of the two jumped down the gully at an impossible length.

By this time, my wound had healed, and I no longer felt any pain.

"Let's go," I said, grabbing Charlie's hand. As I turned to run, Charlie bent down and picked up the bloody wood cross. We didn't make it far before the two vampires appeared before us, blocking our escape.

Charlie stepped in front of me before either of the vampires could speak, holding up the cross like a weapon. Something must've happened to his shoulder in the accident, because he flinched at the movement.

"What do you want with us?" he asked. "We don't want to fight—"

Charlie's words were cut short by the vampire's meaty hand, which had closed around his throat. Charlie's eyes widened when the vampire easily lifted him off of the ground.

I reacted quickly, grabbing the cross from Charlie's hand and driving it into the vampire's heart. His shocked expression lasted only a moment before he crumbled lifeless to the ground. Charlie dropped to his feet gasping.

The second vampire lunged for me, but I was ready, my powers having grown even before the car rolled. I raised my hand palm-up in the direction of a tree not far from us and closed my fingers. Its roots let go of their hold on the earth, and when I jerked my hand in a downward motion, the tree crashed upon the charging vampire, barely missing Charlie. The tree limbs pierced through the vampire but just missed his heart.

"Let's go!" Charlie said, grabbing my hand to run.

We raced up the gully toward the idling truck. I hopped behind the driver's seat and jammed the clutch into reverse. The truck was clawing its tread into the road before Charlie could close the door.

"I think we're okay," Charlie said after we'd driven a few miles. "We're not being followed."

I glanced into the rearview mirror. Only darkness reflected back.

"Do you want to tell me what happened back there?" Charlie asked. "How you're acting like you weren't just thrown from a car?"

"I'm a fast healer."

"You might have blood that clots fast but not that fast. Are you using magic?"

Lights from a gas station appeared over a small rise in the road. I pulled into its parking lot and drove behind it. When I stopped the car, I turned to Charlie. "I am a fast healer," I repeated. "Look." I pulled down the top of my blood soaked shirt just below the clavicle where the stake had pierced me. "See? There's nothing there."

He touched it lightly with his fingers. "How is this possible?"

"I don't know how else to tell you other than to just come right out and say it, so here it goes: I'm immortal."

"But how?"

I faced forward out the frosted window. "Boaz."

"He bit you? But wouldn't that make you a vampire?"

"I wasn't bitten. I was injected with his venom, but it had been altered. I received only the immortal part of it, not his power or blood lust."

"Why would Boaz do that?"

"It's a long story," I said and wrapped my arms close to my chest. Even though the heater was on in the truck, I couldn't get warm.

"I think it's time I heard it," Charlie said.

"I do, too." I took a deep breath and began my story at the beginning, speaking first of my powerful and abusive parents, the pact they'd made with Boaz, the way I'd naively and foolishly fallen for Boaz, how he turned me, and finally I ended on the necklace and how Lucien had saved me.

When I was finished, Charlie stared at me with his mouth open. "And I thought my life was difficult."

"I'm sorry I didn't tell you sooner. The timing never felt right."

"Timing is everything," he agreed. "But that still brings us back to why vampires, and quite possibly The Dark Prince, are after you. What's the connection?"

I shook my head, a sudden panic swelling in my chest. "You don't think Boaz is actually alive and calling himself The Dark Prince, do you?"

Charlie laughed. "I've met the vamp that calls himself that ridiculous name. It's not Boaz."

"Then maybe someone else from my past is working with him. It could be my grandfather, my aunt, or—" I swallowed hard, still unable to stomach her betrayal. "My former best friend, Liane. She is the one who told my parents where I was before they captured me and put me in that coffin."

Charlie leaned back into his seat, seeming to ponder my words. "I'll have some people look into all of them. It's important we find this connection before anything else bad happens."

I agreed, not liking at all the sick feeling spreading in my gut.

42

The next day, Charlie left town. Michael had called and insisted he come to Ireland as soon as possible. Charlie didn't tell me what for, but by his expression, I knew it was bad. He wasn't sure how long he would be gone for, but he assured me he would have men look into the people from my past. He also assigned two Deific guards to follow me around. Just in case.

Because of this new threat toward me, I pushed my abilities as far as I could, which helped me develop a new gift that not even Dr. Skinner could explain. With certain people whom I came in contact with, I would only have to look at them, and instantly I knew their feelings, thoughts, and intentions. They always seemed to be individuals who were going through a difficult time in their life. It was as if their souls screamed for relief and somehow I was able to tune into their cries. Sometimes I wondered if my magic grew this way because it's what I wanted. Now, maybe, I could be more of a help to both Lucien and Charlie.

This new ability was exhausting at first, but with the help of Dr. Skinner, I learned to magnify it, giving me the ability to call upon it at will. I was especially excited to use this gift to help the children at the Academy who couldn't communicate, but to my surprise, it was useless. They had no worldly sorrows or heavy burdens despite their obvious physical afflictions.

Unfortunately, the people outside the school were not like the special children. They did have heartache, and I couldn't find enough hours in the day to help them all. I spent what time I could walking the streets, searching for those whom I might help, much to the dismay of my two bodyguards who kept a mild interest in what I was doing.

It was during this time I decided to return to Lucien. Feeling other's pain and burdens weighed me down, and I desperately needed the peace and comfort his presence gave me, but this time I stayed at a distance, afraid I might upset him again.

Lucien led a simple, predictable life. Most of his days were spent by the marina. Something about the water seemed to soothe him. When he was away from the sea, he appeared more tense and agitated. He fed very little, but when he did, it was as if he had researched his victims first and knew exactly where they would be. Because I spent only small moments with him, I was never able to find out how he chose his victims. The only thing they all had in common was some kind of bag or briefcase that he always disposed of with their body.

There was no joy in Lucien's life. Even feeding seemed to cause him pain, yet he didn't stop. I longed to remove his suffering, wanting desperately to help him feel the same peace he gave me. As the days passed, I found it harder and harder to stay away. It was only a matter of time before I knew I'd have to move to Seattle. I worried how I was going to tell Charlie, who had become my closest friend.

Charlie was gone for a full ten days. He'd called once while he was away, telling me that his men found nothing out of the ordinary with my grandfather, who had fallen ill almost a year ago. Anne still lived with him and apparently she rarely left the house. As for Liane, two years ago she disappeared, and it was like she didn't exist anymore. I wasn't sure how worried I should be about this. Liane may have ratted me out to my parents, but I don't think she would actually cause me physical harm. But then again, dark magic is extremely alluring. Who knew what she was really capable of?

When Charlie did return, he knocked on my door at almost two in the morning.

"Don't you sleep?" he asked when I opened the door. His right cheek was scabbed over, and his eye was circled with shades of purple and blue.

I opened the door wide to let him in. "What happened to you?"

"You can't go anywhere with Michael and not expect a fight." He moved into the living room and dropped onto my couch. "Am I disturbing you?"

I joined him on the sofa. "Not at all. Did you just get back?"

"An hour ago. I wasn't going to bother you, but I had a feeling you were awake."

"Do you want something to eat?"

"No. I won't be staying long. I just wanted to tell you what I discovered."

I waited quietly for him to continue.

"It's as I feared. The Dark Prince is recruiting on a large scale, but not just recruiting. He's creating new vampires at an alarming rate. We took care of one of their cells in London, but there were at least three others." He took a breath. "We're asking everyone at all the Deific offices around the world to spare all their fighters."

"I'll help," I said without hesitating. "Whatever you need."

"If we weren't desperate, I'd say no. It's still so soon for you."

I was about to say more when there was another knock at the door. Charlie jumped to his feet. "Are you expecting anyone?"

My pulse raced. "No."

Charlie's pinched face relaxed and he smiled. "It's Henry."

"How do you know?" I asked.

Charlie walked to the door and opened it. Henry stood in the doorway, his expression serious.

"I apologize for the late hour," he said, looking first at Charlie, "but I knew you were here talking to Eve about what you learned in Ireland, and I'd like to be in on the conversation."

Charlie motioned him inside. "I don't know how you do it. I'm the psychic one, yet you always seem to know what's going on."

"You look a bit beat up," Henry said to Charlie. "Had you waited, I could've helped."

"We did just fine," Charlie said, closing the door behind Henry.

"Besides, I know you have your hands full with the other Deific offices."

"What's going on with them?" I asked, shifting my position to be more upright on the couch. It was strange having Henry in my home. Not in a bad way, but his presence was so powerful and commanding that I felt my house should be cleaner or more formal. *Something.*

"You can relax, Eve," Henry said. He lowered himself into a chair opposite of me so we were at eye level. That helped. A little.

"A few of the Deific offices that were attacked a couple of weeks ago had high casualties," he continued. "Their morale is low, and it's been difficult not only finding replacements, but getting the current ones to stay. Out of all the Deific offices that were attacked, yours had the least casualties. It was also back up quickly and running smoothly."

I glanced at Charlie wondering where Henry was going with all of this.

"The real reason I've come is," Henry said, looking at Charlie. "I want you to do what you've done here, but in our Seattle office."

My head jerked toward Henry. This was my opportunity. I could feel it. Henry glanced over at me as if he sensed my excitement, but he didn't say anything.

"I want you to heal that office, Charlie. They need you."

Charlie was shaking his head. "I can't leave. Not now. There's way too much happening. I need to be in the field."

"Don't worry about that," Henry said. "I'll take care of it."

"But I'm no healer. I can barely manage myself."

"You do a fine job, and I don't mean a healer in the literal sense. Your energy and leadership will give life to those still working."

Charlie narrowed his eyes. "You could've asked this over the phone, and when it wasn't the middle of the night. Why are you really here?"

Henry leaned back in his chair, looking thoughtful. His gaze slowly turned to me. "I want Eve to go, too."

I inhaled a quick intake of breath.

"Not only will she be able to use her new ability to help those who are suffering, but she'll also be able to find someone she's been looking for."

Charlie snorted. "The vampire, Lucien? Is he really worth both Eve and I leaving New York? That seems like a waste of time, when we should really be out helping Alana and Michael."

"Lucien *is* important. He is more valuable than anyone knows, and the Deific needs him. This just cements why I need you two in Seattle. Eve is the only person who can bring him in, but I need you, Charlie, to make sure she's safe doing it. There's a war coming, and without Lucien, we don't stand a chance."

43

The move to Seattle was harder than I thought it would be. Mostly because I had to say goodbye to Sarah and the children at the Academy. I promised to come and visit, and Sarah promised to come visit me. It was just temporary, she'd said. I wasn't so sure.

Both Charlie and I had little to move so the transition went quick. What did take a while, however, was finding a home of my own. Charlie tried to convince me to stay in the same apartments as him, but I felt strongly that I needed to be on my own. Eventually, I found a two-story home in a nice neighborhood within two miles of the Deific office.

The office itself was a miniature replica of the New York office. Standing three stories high, it was tucked between two much taller buildings. There was nothing architecturally pleasing about it. It was such a plain square building that one could easily walk right by it without ever noticing it.

The employees were as Henry described: broken and full of despair on behalf of their friends and coworkers whose lives had been lost. Charlie was wonderful with them. His humor and gentle nature did as Henry expected. Within two weeks, the mood had lightened dramatically.

Finding Lucien proved harder than I anticipated. I recognized a few landmarks from my dreams, but whenever I visited them, he was never there. I was anxious to find him as Henry's words had frightened me, and I didn't want to waste any more time. Charlie hadn't been much help. He'd been so focused with helping the people in the office that he hadn't brought up Lucien's name, but I couldn't do this alone anymore.

"Charlie," I said in his office after a staff meeting, "I need some help."

He looked up from an open folder in his hands. "This is a first. How may I be of service?"

"It's time we found Lucien. I've tried finding him myself using landmarks from my dreams, but it hasn't helped. I was wondering if you would use your ability."

Charlie pushed the folder away and sighed. "I know it seems like I have forgotten the task Henry gave us, but I haven't. Lucien has been on my mind a lot."

"Then why haven't you said anything?"

He averted his eyes. "I don't think it's time yet. I have a bad feeling about Lucien. He's nowhere near ready, and I don't want you risking your life."

"But you heard what Henry said! The Deific needs him. You know that for every second we waste, The Dark Prince only grows stronger. I thought you wanted to finish him!"

Charlie jumped to his feet and pointed his finger at me. "Do you think I like being here, especially knowing my friends are out there fighting? I should be out there with them, destroying the bastard who killed my wife! Instead I've been sent here to find a vampire who could possibly kill you. Forgive me if I'm a little hesitant!"

I was too stunned to respond right away. I'd never considered how hard this might be for him. "I don't know what to say. I'm sorry."

Charlie dropped back into the chair and inhaled deeply. "No, I'm sorry. There's so much going on up here—" He tapped his head. "—that sometimes I snap. I shouldn't speak to you like that. And you're right. We do need to find Lucien, but we must proceed with caution, do you understand?"

I nodded.

"Do you still have that picture of him?"

I reached into my back pocket and removed a folded piece of paper. Charlie took it and smoothed it out. "Come see me after work. I should have something then. Oh, and would you meet with a couple of employees? I'm not sure how to help them."

"Of course," I said. "And Charlie?" His gaze met mine. "Thank you."

During the next couple of hours, I spoke with two women. They had been close friends with a couple of the deceased, and they couldn't understand why their friend had to die. They believed in the Deific and what it stood for, but thought it should've been better protected or at least have been given a warning about the attack. My senses told me that these women weren't necessarily looking for changes. They simply needed to talk about what happened, and maybe through that they could understand better what happened.

"How about we start a support group?" I offered. "We could meet every Wednesday night to discuss what happened, how we can prevent it in the future, and more importantly talk about the ones we miss."

"That's a wonderful idea!" Susanne, the older woman, said. "I'll post an announcement today."

A few hours later, I returned to Charlie. He looked agitated and shook his head at me before I had the chance to speak. He stood up and pulled his coat on. "I'm sorry, but it's too soon. Lucien is too dangerous."

"What do you mean?"

"The more I looked at his picture, the more I felt how dangerous he is. He's done something horrible, and I don't want you to have anything to do with him. Not yet."

"I don't care what he's done in the past," I said.

"You should."

In a softer voice, I said, "Charlie, I've seen him do good things. There is hope for him. Besides, you've seen our future. You know what he's capable of!"

"That's in the future. He needs more time."

I steeled my voice and stared Charlie straight in the eyes. "I need to know where he is now, but I promise to keep a distance until I know it's safe."

Charlie huffed and pursed his lips together. "Fine. Come with me. I think I know where he is, or at least the general vicinity."

Thirty minutes later, Charlie parked at the same marina where I'd seen Lucien before. He got out of the car and tucked his hands into the pockets of his leather jacket. A sharp wind twisted his curly hair. He attempted to smooth it back, but it was futile. He turned and gave me a forced smile.

I watched him walk away, grateful for our friendship. In another lifetime, I might've actually liked him more than a friend. He was strong, loyal, kind—my lingering gaze stopped when I found the dock where I first saw Lucien standing. My heart stopped beating. *Lucien.* My longing to be with him made my heart ache and my body go numb. But I felt something else tug at my senses, a new feeling. It was an urgency of some kind. Something was wrong.

The car door opened and Charlie jumped in, bringing with him a strong gust of wind. "That wind cuts through you sharper than my Uncle Jack chews through a thanksgiving turkey."

"Did you sense anything?"

He turned to me. "Did you know my uncle actually sharpens his dentures before thanksgiving?"

"Charlie, please,"

He let out a long, drawn out sigh. "He's not here."

"I could've told you that," I said.

"It wasn't a complete waste. I sense that Valium Vampire will be here in a couple of hours."

"Who?"

"Forget it. Let's get something to eat and then we'll come back." He started the car and drove from the parking lot.

"Do you feel anything else?" I asked.

He frowned. "Like what?"

"Like something's about to happen. And it involves Lucien."

"I don't. What are you picking up?" Charlie asked.

I shrugged and looked out the window. "Maybe it's nothing."

A couple of blocks away, Charlie and I sat in a small cafe next to a wide window. The light spilled in and reflected off a freshly wiped table. Charlie did most of the talking, speaking mostly of the Deific employees. I tried to follow along, but I couldn't get Lucien out of my mind.

"Eve?"

I looked at him. "Hmm?"

"I was asking you what you think we should do for Don."

Don was the night janitor at the Deific. He recently went through a divorce. "I'll go talk to him and see if I can figure out what would be best," I said.

All of a sudden, Charlie tensed and grabbed my hand on the table. "Valium!"

"What?"

"In a few seconds, Valium, I mean Lucien, will pass by this window."

I stopped breathing and slowly looked outside. Even though I could still hear the bustling sounds of the restaurant, time slowed as if it, too, was holding its breath as much as I was.

On the sidewalk in front of me, Lucien stepped into view. I wasn't sure it was him at first because he was dressed completely different. He wore a black suit jacket that was unbuttoned, and beneath it, he wore a black vest over a red shirt. His hooded blue eyes looked angry as he stared ahead, unaware of everyone and everything around him. He walked with purpose and with a confidence I rarely saw in anyone. I wished time would stop so I could capture his image, but even as I thought it, he passed by.

Go after him! My body jerked into action and moved toward

the door. Outside on the sidewalk, I followed his every movement—walking away from me.

A hard thump on my shoulder sped up time. Two men walked by, one of who had purposely bumped into me. When he was a few feet away, the man who had nudged me turned around and stared. It wasn't his red spiked hair or his many tattoos of crossed bones all over his body that frightened me—it was his smile. It spread across his face the way oil coats the sea.

"Vampires," I heard Charlie hiss behind me. He pulled me back into the restaurant. "You didn't tell me he had friends."

"He doesn't. They're following him. We'll have to warn him when we see him at the marina. Let's go."

Ten minutes later, we were back in the same parking spot overlooking the marina. I checked my watch every few seconds. Charlie tapped on the steering wheel to unheard music.

"Something feels different," he said.

"What do you mean?" I asked.

"I don't think he's going to show."

"Why? You said earlier he'd be here."

"Well that's before I saw the other vampires. It changes things."

"What's the point of being psychic if everything can change?" I didn't like the sound of my voice, but with every passing second, my anxiety grew.

"Look, I never said the gift was perfect. I only said I was."

I ignored his attempt at a joke and got out of the car. I glanced at my watch again. He should be here by now. Charlie exited the vehicle on the other side.

"I'll go walk around, see if I can pick anything up," he said.

I turned the other way and walked down the pier.

When we met up again several minutes later, Charlie said, "I've got nothing. It's like he disappeared or something."

I sighed. There was only one way I could find him now.

"Could you take me home?"

"We could look some more if you'd like, drive around, see if I pick up anything."

I shook my head. "I think I'm going to go home and see if I can locate him in my dreams."

"You didn't tell me you were still doing that. I'm not sure how safe that is."

"I appreciate the concern, but I'll be okay. Would you mind taking me home? And please stay close to your phone. I may need you in the middle of night."

"I get that a lot."

I smiled. "I don't doubt it."

He blushed. "Oh, come on. It's been years since a woman has looked at me like that. I got extremely lucky finding my wife, some might even call it magic." He winked.

I laughed. It was good to see Charlie more relaxed. Maybe Henry sending Charlie here wasn't really for the other people, but more for himself. I liked this side of him a lot.

Too many hours later, when I was back at my home, sleep finally came, and I was transported to Lucien. The sight of him made me sick. He was alone inside a narrow room with concrete floors; above him, a florescent light flickered sporadically. Glass was shattered across the floor along with shards of wood from a nearby broken table. There had been a struggle, and Lucien obviously had lost. His body hung upright in the center of the room, unconscious, with his hands tied together, hanging high above his head.

At first glance I thought he was still wearing the red shirt from earlier, but as I drew closer, I saw that his arms had been slit from shoulder to wrist, bathing his body in blood.

44

I frantically looked around for a way to help Lucian, my legs weak even in this dream-like state. Lying in the corner was his crumpled up jacket. Unable to physically touch anything, I mentally used magic to make the jacket rise into the air. I ripped it in two and then wrapped the halves around each arm to slow the bleeding. I then focused on the ropes tied around his wrists, but they were tied too tight. *I need to physically be here.* I gritted my teeth and moaned in frustration. Where was I?

The only door to the room was closed, and when I tried to open it with my mind, I discovered it was locked. And I was not mentally strong enough to force it open. Surveying the room, I found it to be some kind of shed encased with concrete. I crossed the room to the broken table lying on top of scattered papers and searched for anything that might help.

And then I found it—letterhead that read: Oakridge Storage Units. I willed myself back home and woke up. While I dressed, I telephoned Charlie.

He answered after the seventh ring. "I found him, Charlie."

He yawned. "Found who?"

"Lucien, and he's hurt."

"But he's alive, right?"

"Barely." I threw on my shoes.

"He's a vampire, so if we just wait until morning, then he'll have healed himself. Can you call me back in a few hours?"

"No! There's something wrong with the way he's been hurt. He's not healing."

There was several seconds of silence. Finally, Charlie said, "Fine. I'll pick you up in ten minutes."

I hung up the phone and went outside to wait for him.

***

Following directions on my cell phone, I guided Charlie to the storage units. Once he parked, I jumped out of his car and climbed the gate that blocked the entrance into the units.

"Which one is he in?" Charlie asked after he removed a messenger bag from behind the driver's seat. He skillfully scaled the fence and landed next to me on the other side, the strap of the bag across this chest.

"I'm not sure. Can you find out?"

I followed him as he briskly walked up and down the long gravel driveways between the cinderblock storage units. When he reached the end of the second aisle, he stopped in front of a black door. "In here!"

He made an attempt to throw his shoulder into the heavy door, but I stopped him. "Allow me."

I focused my gaze on the lock built into the bulky door. It took little effort for me to break it open.

"My power pales compared to yours," Charlie mumbled.

I rushed inside and worked quickly to untie Lucien's hands. I tried to catch him as he fell, but his weight was too much for me, and he collapsed to the concrete floor.

"Nice catch," Charlie said.

I scowled. "Maybe you should help me."

Charlie bent down and inspected Lucien's wounds. "Those are some nasty cuts. He must've been cut by a Saranton knife."

"What's that?"

Charlie poked at Lucien's eye as if seeing if he was really unconscious. "It's a magical knife created for the sole purpose of paralyzing a vampire. It won't kill him, but if those wounds don't heal, then he'll never wake up."

"How can I fix it?"

"Fight magic with magic," he said.

"What does that mean?"

"Use the power within you. It will take a lot of concentration. Think of all the good in your life and your feelings for those who are important to you. If you have enough, then you will be able to heal him."

"What if I can't?"

"Then he dies." Charlie must've noticed my shocked expression because he quickly added, after clearing his throat, "I don't know that for sure. Look, I have complete faith in you. You can do this."

I knelt beside Lucien and gently touched the top of his head. I imagined our first meeting together very differently.

After I removed Lucien's torn, blood-soaked jacket from around his arms, I stared at the wound, trying to figure out what to do next. A lot of the bleeding had stopped, but the deep gash remained open. I touched the beginning of the cut at his wrist and gently rubbed my thumb over the raw skin.

It felt different to be this close to Lucien physically. In my dreams, his presence was calming, but physically touching him, made every nerve in my body come to life. I could hear a soft humming in the air much like the sound I heard when I felt the beauty of the rose. My eyes moved to his face, and I resisted the urge to caress it as I was keenly aware that Charlie was leaning over me, breathing loudly.

"Nothing's happening," Charlie said.

"Give me a minute."

I looked at the wound and imagined the skin regenerating. Nothing happened.

"Come on, Lucien," I whispered.

I focused harder and still nothing. Then I remembered Charlie's instructions. I thought of the last several months at the Deific. *Had it been that long?* During this time, the world had finally become a beautiful place. I'd made a best friend in Sarah, and I loved being around the children. They, more than anyone else, had taught me how to love and be happy with life. I thought of Charlie and the Deific, and all the great work they were doing and the many lives they had saved. And finally, I thought of Lucien. I wanted him to see and feel beauty as I did. I wanted him to let go of whatever it was that caused him pain. But most of all, I wanted him to see *me*.

My emotions swelled and my whole body tingled, starting in my heart. The feeling spread throughout my limbs and finally down to my thumb that was touching his wound. His skin began to heal.

Charlie gasped. "Amazing!"

The entire process took less than ten minutes. I wished it had been longer.

"When do you think he'll wake up?" Charlie asked.

"It could be anytime. We shouldn't leave him here in case those vampires come back. Let's take him outside."

Charlie bent over and lifted Lucien up over his shoulder. "We can take him to my place."

"Absolutely not! He'll probably kill you," I said as I walked behind the storage units.

Charlie stopped moving. "So why am I trying to save him?"

"Let's put him over here." I pointed to a stack of wood.

"Gladly." Charlie dropped him on the ground hard.

"Careful," I cried. I positioned Lucien in a more comfortable position.

"I don't get why we are doing this. Even you admit he's dangerous."

"He won't be. We just need to give him some time." I stood and looked down at him. "I wish we had a blood pack or something. He's going to need it when he wakes up."

"I have some," Charlie said.

I turned to him. "Why do you have blood?"

"You should always have blood with you when working with

vampires. For negotiating purposes."

"To negotiate for what?"

"My life, for starters." He swung the messenger back over his shoulder and reached inside.

When he handed me two bags of blood, I placed them in Lucien's lap.

"He'll be fine," Charlie said. He tugged at my arm. "Let's go. I can still get some sleep if we go now."

Reluctantly, I followed him to the car.

On the drive back, Charlie shifted in his seat. And then again, huffing as he did so.

"What's the problem?" I asked.

He glanced at me sideways. "It's Lucien. I have a horrible feeling that this is happening too soon."

"He may be dangerous, but that's only because he knows no other way."

"And how do you plan on showing him another way if he won't let anyone near him?" he asked.

"I'm working on it."

***

Much to my dismay, sleep eluded me. I couldn't get Lucien out of my mind, so as soon as it was light, I took a cab back to the storage units. I walked behind them only to discover that Lucien was gone. The blood bags had been thrown against the side of a building and with his finger, he had traced the words: *Leave me alone.* My heart sank. How was I going to get through to him?

I arrived at the office before anyone else. Surprisingly, Henry was waiting for me in my office, sitting on a chair in the corner. "I understand you met Lucien?"

I smiled and set down the donuts and napkins I'd brought in for the staff. "I don't know how you do it, but it's a little creepy all the things you know before you've been told. Yes, I met Lucien. He'd been attacked by two men and left for dead in a warehouse, but Charlie and I saved him in time."

"Was he aware of what you did?"

I sat down behind my desk and grabbed one of the napkins, my fingers fidgeting with the white paper. "Not until after he woke up. We left some blood bags for him, but he destroyed them. I don't know what to do, Henry. I don't think he'll let anyone into his world."

"Then you need to upset his world," he said, his eyes boring into mine.

I tore the napkin in two. "How can I do that if I can't even get near him?"

"Eve, you've been watching him for a long time. What have you learned?"

I frowned, trying to think. No one ever approached Lucien, and when he did encounter someone, it was always deliberate and ended badly for the other person. Until now. "He chooses to be alone."

"You're right. So if you can't go to him, make him come to you." His voice, always calm, had a hint of playfulness to it.

I wasn't sure how I could do that, but it made sense. Henry leaned over and stopped my hands from continuing to shred the napkin. "You need to want this with every fiber of your being. It will be difficult and frightening at first, but if you really commit, you will get through to him."

I tossed the napkin away and sighed. "You're right. I've been afraid, but I do want this. I know there is good in him." I nodded. "I'll do it. I'll find a way to make him come to me."

***

The moment I committed to Lucien, I felt something new grow inside me like a determined spring chick anxious to shed its cramped shell. I let it all go—including my doubts and fears for the future. My experiences up to this point, whether good or bad, had made me who I was today. If I could, would I change any of it? A month, or even a week ago, I would've said yes. I always thought that if I could go back to my younger self, I would tell her to run away because she wasn't strong enough for the storm brewing in her future. But now I know that storm was crucial to my development. I needed those moments as much as a caterpillar needs a cocoon.

I am ready.

No more doubts.

No more fears.

I knew who I was, and I deserved to be happy. Finally, I believed this.

I left work early to prepare myself for what was to come. I vowed to become something beautiful in Lucien's life no matter the cost. His soul was as valuable as mine. When the clock turned midnight, I had only to think of Lucien to be near him. My ability no longer required me to be asleep.

I found him standing between two warehouses down by the marina. He was gazing into the stormy night sky; the occasional crack of lightening reflected in his blue eyes. I couldn't read his stony expression, but at least he looked well, which meant he had fed.

Lucien didn't feel my approach. I circled him until we came face to face.

"Lucien," I whispered.

His eyes closed as if feeling a gentle breeze.

I leaned forward on the tips of my toes and gently brushed my lips against his.

"I'm coming for you."

About the Author

Rachel was born and raised in Idaho, a place secretly known for its supernatural creatures. When she's not in her writing lair, she's partying with her husband and four children. Her love for storytelling began as a child when the moon first possessed the night. For when the lights went out, her imagination painted a whole new world. And what a scary world it was …

Visit Rachel McClellan's website at www.RachelMcClellan.com to read her other many novels, including the exciting sequel to The Devil's Fool, The Devil's Angel, book two in the Devil Series!

The Devil's Angel

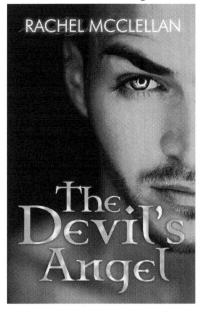

28839814R00187

Made in the USA
Middletown, DE
28 January 2016